By Fire Possessed

Doña Gracia Nasi

Sandra Toro

By Fire Possessed

Doña Gracia Nasi

Gaon Books

Gaon Books
P.O. Box 23924
Santa Fe, NM 87502
www.gaonbooks.com

Library of Congress Cataloging-in-Publication Data
Toro, Sandra.
By Fire Possessed: Doña Gracia Nasi / Sandra Toro.
p. cm.
Includes bibliographical references.

ISBN 978-1-935604-06-8 Cloth
978-1-935604-17-4 Pb
978-1-935604-18-1 ebook
1. Nasi, Gracia, ca. 1510-1569--Fiction. 2. Jewish women--Portugal--History--16th century--Fiction. 3. Jews--Persecutions--Portugal--History--16th century--Fiction. 4. Jews--Europe--History--16th century--Fiction. 5. Jewish women--Turkey--History--16th century--Fiction. 6. Marranos--History--16th century--Fiction. 7. Sephardim--History--16th century--Fiction. 8. Political fiction. I. Title.

PS3620.O5877B9 2010
813'.6--dc22

2010017547

Manufactured in the United States of America.
The paper used in this publication is acid free and meets all ANSI (American National Standard for Information Sciences) standards for archival quality paper.
British Cataloguing-in-Publication data for this book is available from the British Library.

Cover Design by Gloria Abella Ballen

To Jose Angel, My Love,
And "The Wind Beneath My Wings"

And

To Penny Adamo, Best Friend,
Cheerleader, And Confidante

Acknowledgements

Dr. Alfred Baer sent me a clipping from *The Jerusalem Post* in 1990 along with a note, which suggested that I consider Doña Gracia Nasi as a heroine for my next novel. I rushed to the Library of Congress' Judaica section and began researching Gracia and the Spanish Inquisition. Immediately, I was hooked. We'd all read much about the Holocaust but next to nothing about the Inquisition. Yet, as noted historian Benjamin Netanyahu wrote in *The Origins of the Inquisition in Fifteenth Century Spain,* the seeds of the Holocaust were sown by the Inquisition.

The seminal work of British historian Cecil Roth—his many volumes not only on the life of Gracia and her nephew, Joseph Nasi who became the Duke of Naxos, but on the Inquisition in Italy and Spain, and the lives of many notables of the Renaissance era—enabled the writing of this novel. During the early years of the twentieth century he translated documents, articles and books, and himself created a body of work that provided the starting point for my imagination. In writing this novel I have changed nothing that is historically known. Where history is silent, my novelistic imagination has taken flight.

After researching for several months, I contacted my editor in New York City; she was totally disinterested in a historical novel about this fabulous independent woman who was an amazing entrepreneur and political genius.

Other opportunities claimed my attention, but I stored my research in a huge box, certain that some day I would get back to writing about this inspirational woman and horrendous time in the history of the Jewish people.

With the encouragement of my husband Jose and dear friend, Penny Adamo, I opened the research box in July of 2006 and wrote the first complete draft of *By Fire Possessed.* Penny introduced me to her literary friends in Mobile, Alabama, who agreed to be my first readers. Thanks to these friends: Arthur and Venetia Prince, Diane and Henry Schwarzberg, and Henry's mother, Agnes Tennenbaum who is a survivor of Auschwitz. Thanks also to Joyce and Gerard Toubiana, Jean and Roland Fry, and Penny's husband, Joe Adamo. Rabbi Steven Silberman of Ahavas Chesed

Synagogue and President of the Congregation, Ruth Lichtenfeld added their words of encouragement.

We relocated to Albuquerque, New Mexico in March of 2008, carrying the manuscript and box of research in the trunk of our car—I didn't trust it to the movers! Shortly after arriving in New Mexico, I not only learned a great deal about how the long arm of the Holy Office of the Inquisition reached all the way into Northern New Mexico, but I discovered that hundreds of families who trace their ancestors back to the 16th Century in what was then New Spain, are descendants of conversos. Indeed, the name Mendes is common here in New Mexico.

Shortly after settling in, thanks to good friend Eileen Stanton, I was invited to join a long-standing critique group of published writers. Their helpful editing, questions about Jewish practices, and moral support have brought me to this day, the final manuscript. Heartfelt thanks to Eileen Stanton, Paula Paul, Madge Harrah, Donn Byrnes, Pat Sutton, Kelly Williams, Penny Durant and Walt Williamson.

It is my fervent hope that my children, grandchildren and great-grandchildren, and yours too, will read and cherish this book. We who are fortunate enough to have been born in the United States take freedom of religion and freedom of the press for granted. Gracia Nasi's life proves that we must be ever vigilant!

Dr. Ron Duncan Hart and Gloria Abella, the publishers of Gaon Books, have thrilled me with their enthusiasm for *By Fire Possessed.* They are a joy to work with, and I thank them with my whole heart.

Finally, to my first reader and ardent supporter, to my computer guru, to the man who is "the wind beneath my wings," Jose Angel Toro, my beloved husband—words will never be able to express my gratitude to you.

Sandra Toro
October 1, 2009
Albuquerque, New Mexico

By Fire Possessed

Doña Gracia Nasi

Chapter One

Bloody Sunday
Lisbon, Portugal
1497

"I can't believe you're doing this!" Francisco Mendes stomped into the parlor, and flung his cloak onto a bench. Red-faced, he confronted his father. "We trudged across Spain in blazing heat, fighting off bandits and Dominican thugs, and for what? So you can force us to go with you to the king's chapel to be baptized!" No sooner were the words out of his mouth, than he regretted them.

As if reeling from a physical blow, his father's ashen face shrunk even deeper into his body. Puffy bags under his eyes testified to sleepless nights. Mottled flesh quivered beneath his chin. Dr. Benjamin Mendes, a tall man who prided himself on robust health, had become old, frail and vulnerable, seemingly overnight.

How could this tower of strength, who each morning of his life wrapped his arms with tefillin and prayed to the God of Moses, this medical giant who tended the crowned heads of Spain and Portugal, betray his deeply held beliefs, his very identity, and succumb to the king's threats?

Dr. Mendes raised his head and with pleading eyes responded in a measured voice. "I cannot force you to do anything, Francisco. You are an adult; you make your own decisions. But I must decide for your brother—I will not permit him to become a slave to some Christian farmer. And I must protect your mother, she's already suffered enough."

Francisco avoided his mother's swollen red eyes; he couldn't bear to see her pain. He paced to the parlor window, drew the drapery aside and looked out at the raucous crowd assembled outside his parents' home. Four soldiers on horseback, armed with swords and lances, controlled the crowd and prepared the way for the king's men who would escort the Mendes family to the castle for the conversion ceremony.

Francisco turned back to his father and, in a softer voice, implored him: "Can't you see how he's using you? Making you an example to our people! It's obscene."

His mother approached him. She placed a restraining hand on his arm. "Francisco, please, you must try to understand. Your father is only doing what he has to do to save our lives. You are our foremost Talmudic scholar, the religious leader of our people. You must never forget that the first commandment of Moses is to Choose Life."

He looked down at her; his once-beautiful mother's face bore a horrible scar over her right eye, the result of a rock thrown by a priest as they walked across the Spanish plain.

Today, in preparation for their visit to St. George Palace, she was dressed in somber navy silk. His father's black velvet frock coat appeared several sizes too large. Young Diogo, looking like the perfect little gentleman, sported a forest green version of his father's best doublet with fine white leggings.

He freed himself from his mother's hand and sat down beside his father on the oaken bench. He patted his father's hand and said, "I understand, I do understand. You do what you must do."

A week earlier King Manuel's soldiers had posted announcements all over town, even in Francisco's warehouse: "All children of Jewish parents between the ages of four and fourteen must be presented this Friday, March 19, the year of our Lord 1497, at the Cathedral for baptism." That March 19 was the first day of Passover, one of the most sacred holidays remembering their freedom from repression in Egypt, was a cruel signal to Jewish families that they were not free.

Five years earlier King Ferdinand and Queen Isabella had expelled more than one hundred thousand Jews from Spain. King Manuel had welcomed more than twenty thousand, and he had permitted the six hundred most affluent, best-educated families to live in Lisbon. As was their tradition, these six hundred families lived in close proximity to one another, in modest town houses that took up several blocks near the waterfront warehouse area.

For five years they had lived quietly in the *Juderias*. Unmolested, they practiced their religion, educated their children, and pursued their professional lives. With the king's announcement, chaos and anguish swept through their small community. Day after day, night after night, mothers and fathers argued, wept, consulted with their neighbors and prayed for a miracle.

Francisco spent the week agonizing over his family's plight. As the personal physician to the king, Dr. Mendes was the most powerful member of the Jewish community. He'd begged his father to defy the king on this matter.

Dr. Mendes attempted to explain the king's predicament. "He's basically a good man, and he has no animus against the Jews. His vision for Portugal—and his own legacy as king—is to see the Iberian Peninsula united under one ruler, and he believes that ruler will be his heir, the issue of his marriage to the Infanta. Believe me, Francisco, she is even more fanatical on the subject of Jews than her mother, Queen Isabella.

"King Manuel told me in confidence that Isabella is under the spell of her confessor Torquemada. Years ago he made her take a vow that should she become queen, she would devote herself to getting rid of the Jews. Her daughter has proclaimed she will not step foot into Portugal until Manuel banishes all Jews from the country."

"So," Francisco had answered, "once again politics wins out and the Jews pay the price."

"Once the marriage contract was signed," Dr. Mendes explained, "Manuel realized what a mistake it would be to lose the brains, talents, craftsmanship and money our people provide to his kingdom. He regrets he made the promise. His solution is to 'save our souls with baptism' and keep us in his kingdom.

"The king has promised me there will be no Inquisition in Portugal. He told me personally he values our people; he wants us to thrive in Portugal. He told me that he doesn't care what we do in the privacy of our homes, as long as we attend Mass, baptize our children and get married in the Church."

"In other words, lead a life of total hypocrisy! A life of lies."

After a week of tense discussion, Dr. Mendes had summoned Francisco for a final meeting before acceding to the king's demands. He made one final plea for understanding. "Francisco, he has great hopes for you especially. He wants you to build a huge trading company. If our family converts today, he will pass a law forbidding disciplinary actions against conversos for twenty years."

"What if he dies?" Francisco asked. "Who knows who the new king might be? We'd be at the mercy of the Infanta!"

The door burst open and Francisco's best friend, Dr. Daniel Nasi, deathly pale and sweating, yelled, "It's started! They're rounding up the children and attacking adults!"

Horses' hooves clattered against the cobblestones, soldier's shouts shattered the silence. A woman screamed, men shouted, more horses galloped down the street.

Francisco looked from his father back to Nasi, then took his mother in his arms and kissed and hugged her. He hugged Diogo, saying, "Take care of mom and dad." He turned back to his father, bent and kissed his forehead. "Do what you have to do, I understand."

He followed Daniel out to the street, mounted his horse, and they raced together toward Jew Street.

Armed soldiers on horseback, holding children in their arms, galloped toward the church. Two soldiers on foot, brandishing swords and daggers, forced open the door of a small house. "Open up you Jews, we've come for you!" one of the men yelled as he succeeded in pushing the door open. Francisco and Daniel stopped their horses and watched as soldiers tore screaming children from their mother's arms and tossed them into mule-driven wagons. Deeply angered, the two men dismounted.

A peasant shouted, "All Jews must convert or die!"

The masses understood that all Jews had to convert, and they were dragging men, women, and children into the churches to forcibly baptize them. Many who resisted were killed. As the two men watched, a Jew was stabbed, close enough that Daniel could catch him in his arms. He commandeered a wagon from one of the farmers and rushed the dying man to his hospital.

The soldiers proceeded down Jew Street, barging in each home and grabbing the children. Francisco followed on foot, leading his mount behind him. When the soldiers burst into the home of David Benveniste, a distant cousin of Francisco's who had fled from Spain with the Mendes family, David courageously greeted them, holding his small son tightly in his arms. His wife and daughters were nowhere to be seen. Perhaps, Francisco thought, they had fled to the home of their relatives in the country.

"You will not take this child," David yelled at the soldiers.

"We're harvesting children today," the tall burly guard answered, tearing the boy from his father's arms and racing back outside to throw the child in the hay cart.

David pulled a dagger from his belt and chased after the soldier, screaming curses at him even as onlookers shrunk back from the terrifying scene. From behind David, the second soldier swung his sword, neatly severing David's head from his body. The head fell to the cobblestones, wobbled down the street a few inches, then stopped, face up, eyes open, blood spilling out of the neck.

For Francisco it was as if the world had stopped spinning in its orbit.

He had seen the gore of a bullfight, the pierce of the joust, the bloody results of fist and knife fights; he had never witnessed a man beheaded.

Instinctively he knelt down and picked up the severed, now-bloodied head. He crushed it to his chest as one might hold an infant to shield it from harm. He shouted, "Stand clear!" at the crowd of onlookers, some of whom were cheering. Without a pause, he marched toward the Benveniste home, kicked the door shut behind him as he entered the house, and carried his cousin's head upstairs to the bedroom. Placing it on the pillow, he pulled a sheet up and wrapped it tightly around what was left of the neck.

Then, unable to contain his emotions for a moment longer, he lurched toward the night pail, kneeled and vomited, again and again, until only green bile remained in his throat. He poured cool water from a pitcher over his hands, splashed it on his face, spit out the remaining sour bile into the pail. He dampened a white linen cloth with the cool water and crawled back to the bed. He stared for a long moment at David's face. Dark red blood matted his chestnut-colored beard, crimson spots freckled his cheeks and nose. Tenderly, Francisco wiped away the blood then with clean fingers he closed the eyelids.

He soothed dark curls back under David's skullcap, leaving his high forehead bare. As tears fogged his eyes, he recited the Hebrew prayer for the dead.

"Yitgadal veyitkadash shemei..."

"On the morrow, David, we will lay you to rest in sacred ground. Rest peacefully now." He kissed his cheek, then raised the sheet and covered David's head.

He ran downstairs and out the door, intent on saving David's body and burying it with his head.

The king's men had moved down the street. He could see them in the distance gathering more small children and throwing them into the hay cart.

With vicious efficiency, soldiers had already stolen David's body, the evidence of their slaughter. Where the body had lain, russet colored stains dried atop dark gray cobblestones. Francisco's horse had disappeared, and in the rush of human confusion around him, he started walking almost in a daze toward the Cathedral.

Adding horror on top of horror, at the Cathedral the king's officers had announced that the baptized children would not be returned to their parents. They would be kept and given to Christian families who would raise them according to the Christian faith.

Held back by lines of armed guards, inconsolable parents stood dazed in the street unable to understand that they would never see their children again. Guards on horseback patrolled the lines with swords drawn. Dozens of priests sprinkled holy water and recited the Latin prayers over the heads of the children. Acolytes recorded their names and ages and the names of their parents.

Francisco was shocked at the scenes of cruelty and grief before him, and in that moment he saw parents shrunken and bent coming out of the Cathedral. In a perturbed grief and shock he walked back to the Juderia with them. In groups of five or six men and women were gathered outside their homes, weeping, cursing, questioning their God and their king. Francisco could find no words to console them, no spiritual insight from the Torah.

"How could a merciful God, the God of Abraham and Isaac, permit this to happen?" one distraught father asked him.

At moments like this, he regretted his scholarship, his earnestness in the study of Talmud. He had never meant to be a rabbi, a teacher, a religious leader. His ambition was to be a successful merchant. But the preeminence of his father as personal physician to King Ferdinand and Queen Isabella, and now to King Manuel, and his own reputation as a bright star of Talmudic learning had cast him in the unwelcome roll of rabbi to his people, teacher and interpreter of the Law of Moses.

First, they'd asked him to teach their young sons, prepare them for Bar Mitzvah. Next, he'd been asked to officiate at weddings and ritual circumcisions, which was a joy. Only recently had the community begun to rely on him to find the appropriate words to bury their dead, and arbitrate their legal disputes. Truly, as his father had told the king, Francisco had unwittingly become the Chief of the Jews in Lisbon

That night he lay in his bed unable to sleep. When he closed his eyes, visions of children being thrown in hay wagons, of a father killing his daughter rather than let her be baptized, flashed across his brain.

If the church and the king wanted the Jews to publicly be Catholics—adopt baptism, confession at Easter, and marriage in the church—but would permit them to continue to observe their customs, rituals, and deeply held ethical beliefs in the privacy of their homes, we could probably live with that, he told himself. We can teach our children to live with that level of hypocrisy. But the authorities demand more than that: they want to destroy, to eradicate our People. In the five short years since Ferdinand and Isabella had banished those who would not convert, they had instituted the Inquisition to punish those who continued to practice Judaism in the privacy of their homes. They had begun to burn conversos at the stake, and all it took was for a servant to tell church authorities that a family did not eat pork and shellfish, that they changed their bed linens and bathed before Shabbat.

Ironic, he thought, that bathing on a weekly basis was a sure sign you were Jewish. And washing your hands before meals was even more damming evidence. Yet his father, and other eminent medical men in Europe, had come to the conclusion that it was because Jews practiced the ritual washing of hands before eating, that they escaped so many contagious diseases that ravaged the peasantry.

And we are hated because we study and understand finances and history and philosophy! For two thousand years we have taught our girls and boys to read and write, first in Hebrew and secondly, in the language of their homeland. We are the most literate and learned people on earth. It is our tradition, our custom, our very way of life that is at stake. They want to take our very identity from us.

He remembered the defeated appearance of his father that afternoon. He punched his pillow in anger, turned over in bed and vowed he'd get those children back if it took all his money, his cunning, even his life.

****

Two days later, Daniel arrived to the Mendes house. Exhausted and famished, he ate a quick meal and sat down with Francisco in the parlor for a brandy.

"Seventeen reported deaths, several hundred wounded, and 1,817 children were baptized and have been sent to live with Catholic farmers," he reported. "These are the figures reported to King Manuel this morning, and they track the numbers I've seen at the hospital."

"I'm surprised the numbers aren't greater," Francisco responded, "I believe I would have chosen death rather than let my children be kidnapped and turned into slaves. I'm thankful I didn't have to make that choice." He sipped his brandy. "Our people are in mourning. There's nothing I can say to help them, give them solace. We must find a way to influence the king."

"I will begin my campaign with the king tomorrow morning," Daniel said. I believe he will listen to us now. I will try to get him to agree to meet with you. We must get those children back, regardless of whether they are to be considered Christians or Jews. We must bring them home to their parents."

Chapter Two

At Sword Point

King Manuel did not agree to meet with Francisco. He was too busy negotiating the issues of his marriage with the Infanta and felt that even meeting with Francisco would undermine his negotiations with the Spanish crown.

Seven months later, on a sun-drenched autumn afternoon, Daniel Nasi arrived unexpectedly at Francisco's store with dreadful news. "The Infanta is not satisfied that the children have been forcibly converted. She is concerned about the twenty thousand Jews left in Portugal who have not converted. She had demanded that Manuel expel them."

Francisco sat at his desk in his small office in the back of the store. He slammed down a brass lion, picked up his dagger and began to pace. "More bloodshed! More mass graves!"

"The deadline for expulsion is fourteen days from today," Daniel added. "Manuel has already sent soldiers out to round up Jews in the smaller towns. The first I heard of it was today."

"They'll be arriving soon. Where will he put them?" Francisco asked.

"There's talk of using the old *Os Estâos* palace normally used for diplomatic receptions. It's damp and dirty, but it's a fortress, easy to guard."

Later that same day, as Daniel and Francisco were finishing a meal of chicken and rice, a soldier burst into the house. At this affront Daniel pointed out that he was the king's assistant physician.

The taller guard sneered, "That's right Doctor. We know who you are. You and Don Francisco Mendes are at the top of the king's list. He wants you to set the example for your fellow Jews and be first to convert."

Leaving them no time to finish their meal or gather warm clothing, a contingent of six armed guards marched Francisco and Daniel down the cobblestone streets and herded them into the courtyard of *Os Estâos* palace. Behind them more and more of their Jewish friends were being pushed into the courtyard. Dominican friars harangued the crowd from every side, shouting that they had to convert or die in the fires of hell.

Thousands of Jews were being herded like animals into dank, dark rooms that quickly became deadly. There was neither food nor water nor latrines. Priests toured the palace, preaching non-stop to prisoners. "Accept Christ, and we will give you sustenance. You will be free to resume your lives. You will lose nothing. Simply accept Christ! If you do not accept

Christ, you will be expelled from this country." Apostate Jews joined the Dominicans, trying to persuade people to convert.

A riot broke out on the third morning when several men tried to overtake one of the guards. Seven men were slaughtered—beheaded, as a lesson to the other prisoners. Francisco and Daniel gathered a minyan, ten men, and said Kaddish for the dead, then assisted the guards in removing them from the palace. Shortly after noon, families who still had small children began to line up on the ground floor, asking for baptism. The parents could no longer bear to hear their children cry for food and water.

On the fourth morning, Daniel Nasi announced to Francisco, "This is insanity. I'm getting out of here."

Mournfully, Francisco hugged his closest friend since childhood. "Go see my parents, Daniel. It would be a blessing."

"Yes."

He joined the line of families waiting for baptism.

The Dominican friars continued their march through the palace.

A guard brought Francisco a letter, written in Hebrew in the hand of Diogo on the fifth morning. "Our father has suffered a stroke. He cannot walk or talk, but we can communicate with him by asking him questions that he answers by squeezing our hands. Mother cries all day when she is not with him. Please, Francisco, convert and come home. We need you. I wait for you every day outside the palace with our wagon. Look for me."

Francisco allowed himself the luxury of tears as he folded Diogo's letter and placed it inside his doublet. He looked at the line of Jews waiting for baptism, moving toward freedom. He felt pangs of envy, wishing his conscience would allow him the same decision. He was their rabbi; he must set the example and tell them to choose life. But he couldn't bring himself to do it. Not yet.

Later in the afternoon he awoke with a start when a rat began nibbling on his foot. A few feet away, another fat rat feasted on a pile of feces. He stood and walked toward the aisle where soldiers were pulling men to their feet.

"Mendes, we need you. We've got dead bodies to remove."

He joined his fellow able-bodied Jews as they carried seventeen bodies to mule-driven wagons just outside the palace doors. The men mumbled prayers for the dead as they carried them to the wagons. "Where will you take them?" one man asked.

"Outside the city. The king's ordered a huge hole, we'll burn them, then cover with lime."

Jewish martyrs, Francisco thought, *without even the dignity of a gravestone!*

Daniel arrived early the next morning, bringing with him a large jug of water, some fruit and an egg and potato *torta* "from the king's own kitchen." Francisco drank half the jug of water, wolfed down the food, and drank more water. While he ate, Daniel briefed him on his father's condition. "He will not live much longer, Francisco, and he yearns to make peace with you." Francisco nodded his understanding.

Daniel guided him to a small alcove where they could have a private conversation though an armed guard watched their every move.

"I spent two hours with the king yesterday. He hates what is going on here, never imagined it would result in these deaths. He is not an evil man, Francisco! The *Infanta* has convinced him that by forcing us to convert, they are saving our souls. She and her mother are adamant about this. Isabella responds to two people, Torquemada and the pope."

Francisco's face grew red with fury. "I will not submit to the moral authority of that pope, who in spite of his vow of celibacy, has dozens of mistresses and illegitimate bastards, and who, everyone knows, is sleeping with his own daughter!"

"I grant you, the pope is pure evil. Torquemada is pure evil. But King Manuel is a good man, a good man who is horribly conflicted by what he feels he is forced to do."

Francisco pounded his fists against the stonewalls of the castle. "I will think on what you say, Daniel. I haven't been able to convince myself to get in that line yet. But for my father..."

"He needs to see you at least once more before he dies. Diogo and your mother need you too."

During the rest of that day warring voices reverberated in his head. His mother's voice telling him "*the first law of Moses is Choose Life. Francisco, you have an obligation to lead our people, to tell them to choose life.*"

And his grandfather's voice, teaching him Hebrew for his Bar Mitzvah, "*You will be sorely tempted to convert to Christianity as you make your way in the world. Don't succumb to that temptation!*"

* * * * * * * * * * * * * * * * * * *

Francisco was awakened from a fitful slumber the following morning by a splash of water on his face and the smell of incense that momentarily overpowered the smell of vomit and feces. He looked up to see a priest, resplendent in black and blood red satin, waving a silver salver over his head and reciting the rites of baptism in Latin.

Two guards pulled him to his feet and with a dagger held firmly at his throat guided him to the hall of registry. He was marched to the front of the room, seated in a straight-backed chair, and with the point of a sword digging into the back of his neck, he was ordered to sign his name and the date.

His mother's voice told him, "*Choose Life! Come home.*"

Hot tears filled his eyes. Unwilled, he watched his hand reach for the quill. He watched, mesmerized as his hand signed his name. He could barely read his own handwriting through the flood of tears.

His father's voice, "*You must lead our people. The King knows that you are the Chief of the Jews. You must set the example.*"

He thought, "*Outside there will be water, food, a bath, and clean clothes.*" He signed the date with a flourish, stood, and marched toward the door leading out of the palace with as much dignity as he could summon.

When the day set for the Expulsion came and went, the remaining prisoners were informed that by their failure to leave the country by the appointed day, they had forfeited their freedom and were now slaves in the service of the king. In panic, a few more finally agreed to convert to gain their freedom. For those who still refused to accept baptism, holy water was sprinkled on them and they were declared to be Christians.

A few days later, King Manuel sent a letter to the kings of Spain proclaiming, "There are no more Jews left in Portugal."

****

Without knowing that fate awaiting those still in the fortress, Francisco walked out into the cold, drenching rain, pouring rain, welcome rain. His body, encrusted with lice, craved wetness, water. His soul craved cleanliness, purifying. His lungs sucked in great gulps of fresh air. His legs almost buckled under him, he was light-headed with grief and with joy. Suddenly, he was on the ground, too weak to get back up. A stranger reached down and lifted him up. He walked another block.

"Francisco, Francisco, I'm here. Come over here!"

Diogo stood by a small wagon attached to an old mule. Francisco made it across the street, Diogo steadied him as he climbed into the wagon and collapsed on the hay. Diogo handed him a bottle of milk and an apple-filled pastry his mother had made. Francisco ate the pastries while the rain poured over his hair, face, and filthy hands.

"Father?" he asked, when he caught his breath.

"He seems better this morning. He's waiting for you."

Chapter Three

The House Of Mendes

Ten months after the forced conversion Francisco Mendes was astonished to receive a messenger from King Manuel instructing him to present himself at the court for an audience the following evening. Previously the court had conducted its business with the Mendes trading house through emissaries. "Would Sr. Mendes please send his finest rugs he has recently received from Persia?" "Has Sr. Mendes any sheets from Holland?" "Have you received a shipment of the new vermilion hose yet?"

Though Francisco had nothing but contempt for the king and his court, he nonetheless relished the opportunity to sell merchandise to the royals. Word had spread among the wealthy professional and merchant families, and they, too, came to his trading house for the latest in luxurious items from the Far East and Europe.

The following evening, shortly after seven, Francisco, dressed in his finest black velvet doublet and lace shirt, presented himself at the royal palace. He'd heard his father speak of its magnificence, but that hadn't quite prepared him for the reality. After passing through a huge courtyard surrounded with battlements, he was ushered through the massive marble and mirrored entrance halls, past numerous sumptuously uniformed guards. At last, he was led into the private royal chamber.

King Manuel, at twenty-nine, was only six years older than Francisco. He was standing with his back to Francisco, looking out a window. Once more Francisco wondered at his strangely misshapen body: his arms were so long that his hands dangled beneath his knees. The king turned immediately and offered his hand to Francisco. As was expected, with a sick feeling in his stomach, Francisco knelt and kissed the offered hand. Now he understood the full meaning of the popular proverb, "Many kiss the hand they would gladly see cut off."

"Glad to finally meet you, Mendes." He indicated a chair with a nod, and sat down himself opposite the chair he'd indicated to Francisco. "I've been hearing about you for several years now from your father. And others too." He poured two glasses of wine in what appeared to Francisco to be Venetian goblets, then handed one to his guest. "I understand you are also a connoisseur of wine, so I've asked for a fine bottle to be sent up from my cellar. Allow me to toast our future relationship, Mendes. I propose that you and I do business together."

Francisco had been watching the king closely for clues. He was not a tall man, with dark wavy, almost stiff hair just like his own, an olive complexion, dark almond shaped eyes, a bit stocky. He was known to be an expert at fencing and hunting, a good horseman. Clean-shaven at the moment, sometimes he sported a mustache. He quickly appraised the king's clothes. Just as Daniel had indicated, he wore the finest velvet doublet garnished with gold *passementerie*, obviously from France. The lace ruffle at his throat was probably from Venice, and the silk appeared to be from India. His tailors had done a superb job, but his hose were not of the finest quality. Francisco had better hose in his warehouse.

"Your Majesty, I would be pleased to do business with the royal house. How may I be of service?" What a marvelous actor I am, Francisco thought, not even a quaver in my voice. My mother would be proud!

"Let me tell you my dream. I want Portugal to be the leading commercial nation in the world. Wealthier than England, France, Flanders and Spain. Do you understand me?"

Francisco nodded.

"I've sent Vasco de Gama, with four ships, to develop a trade route which will enable us to bring the finest of everything from every port, no matter how distant, here to Lisbon. We will be a gathering port, bringing in cloths from Egypt, India, Japan and selling it to France, Venice, Constantinople. Not just clothing stuffs but furniture, tableware, swords, furs, and fine gems. Pearls and rubies and sapphires from the Orient. Do you follow me?"

Francisco found himself mesmerized by Manuel's hot glittery eyes, his rabid enthusiasm for his dream. It felt seductive and at the same time thrilling beyond his own wildest dreams.

"My king, we share the same dream." Francisco leaned forward and reached out but caught himself before he touched Manuel. "What would you have me do?"

"I have commissioned the building of half a dozen large cargo ships. I will send them to all the ports of the world to gather the finest goods and bring them back to Lisbon. Then I want you to buy the goods from me and sell them to merchants from all over the world. They will have to come here to Lisbon to buy these silks and gems and priceless glass. Understand?"

"So they will buy from me and take back to Europe..." Francisco drifted off into a sort of reverie trying to figure out the exact logistics. The king swallowed the last of his wine and refilled his glass.

"We need not only a splendid fleet of ships and navigational skills—both of which we will possess in abundance—but we will need agents skilled at negotiation and diplomacy, shrewd, and at the same time fluent in languages and finance. That's where you Jews—ah, *conversos*—come in." The king momentarily blanched, clearly embarrassed at his slip of the tongue. "You understand me, Mendes?"

"Eventually you may wish to build ships of your own," the king added, watching eagerly as Francisco processed the idea.

Francisco responded, "We will need to develop a way of exchanging money, perhaps letters of credit. With the seas full of pirates, it wouldn't make sense to carry gold..."

Manuel interrupted impatiently. "Your father tells me you're a genius when it comes to money. You figure it out. Come back to me with a plan."

The two men talked through two bottles of wine for nearly two hours, each feeding off the other's enthusiasm and excitement. Finally, the king signified he had a dinner engagement. The conversation would have to end. Francisco asked the question he'd wanted to ask all through the conversation. "Exactly how much, Your Majesty, would you expect in profits?"

"I would expect to receive one quarter of your profits."

Francisco felt his eyebrows shoot up in surprise. That was a bit steep.

Quickly, the king added, "And I will take a five-percent tax on pepper and other spices. Don't forget, dear fellow, I shall be giving the House of Mendes—that's what I think you should call yourself—the monopoly on the spice trade. And that includes all the pepper in the world. You can set the price, and I hope you'll set it very dear." The king stood and walked toward Francisco's chair. "Now tell me, what is in that package which you clearly meant to give me hours ago. My curiosity has finally gotten the best of me."

Embarrassed, Francisco reached down and picked up the gift he had meant to present to the king on arrival. Daniel had told him he dared not arrive empty handed; Manuel expected an important gift on this visit and on all future visits. Such was the price of royal favor.

"Your Majesty, this is a rare *object d'art* from Constantinople." The king had already sat back down with the heavy gift in his lap. He uncovered it. Francisco continued to tell him about it. "This horse was carved from a very rare large piece of a gemstone called *lapis lazuli.* It is mined deep in the mountains of a part of the Ottoman Empire by people called Afghanis, and the carving was done, if my sources are correct, in Egypt. I hope you enjoy it, sir."

King Manuel beamed with pleasure. "Ah, Mendes, this is very special. You know how I love horses! Very fine, indeed! You have excellent taste, exactly as your father told me. Which reminds me, I want you to find the finest pearls in all the Orient for my Isabella. And I understand in France the men wear gold rings with large diamonds. See if you can find me a very large, perfect diamond. I want a ring of that kind for myself. And, Mendes, be a good fellow and always think of me first when you get a new shipment in. Feel free to come, bring things yourself, anytime." The king rose again, carefully setting the lapis horse on his desk.

Francisco, following his lead, rose and walked toward the door.

"Think on what we've discussed, but discuss it with no one else. We need to get our plans together and agree on them. And we must be fast. Before Borgia gets the same idea. I wouldn't put it past him," the king said.

Francisco nodded his head, realizing the king was referring to Pope Alexander VI.

"My men will give you a tour of the gardens, and be sure to take a good look at the view. It's the best in all of Portugal," Manuel added with a flourish. Again, Francisco nodded his head. "I'll send for you next week," were the king's final words.

Rather quickly, his mind spinning with snippets of ideas, Francisco found himself being led through the formal, perfectly symmetrically aligned gardens in which Manuel took such pride. The half-moon cast a silver glow over the deep green hedges. A horrible screech, almost like a person being tortured, suddenly came out of nowhere. And then another. Francisco's guide smiled knowingly and pointed toward an area beyond the hedge of tall boxwood. Francisco picked up his pace, and the two men rushed toward the tortuous sounds. There, nestling near a molten silver-blue lake were dozens of the whitest birds Francisco had ever seen.

"Ah," he murmured, "these are the famous white peacocks! How many?" he asked, remembering his mother's enthusiastic description after her last visit to court. "Beautiful to look at, hideous to hear!"

"More than one hundred," was his guide's response.

Francisco turned and wandered back to the courtyard, trying to concentrate on the scene but constantly returning to his conversation with the king. He forced himself to listen to what his guide was saying. This high hill had once been a fortress of the Moors. Now the soft yellow battlements, while offering the protection of a fortress, enclosed a gracious palace, splendid gardens, a lake, and provided a panoramic view of Lisbon, the Tagus River with its docks and warehouses and quays and, from another vantage point, the hills of Sintra beyond.

"This is where," his guide said, "the King and Queen sit to watch the bullfights. They don't even have to leave the castle grounds." Yes indeed, Francisco thought, the king is not only protected in his domain, but from this vantage point he can see much of what goes on in the city below.

Francisco thanked his guide and left the castle behind and walked down the steep, winding cobblestone streets into the Baixa, the heart of the trading district. The half-moon gave a tenuous light for his walk home, and it was suitable for his thoughts.

I must develop a large cadre of agents, men who are loyal to me above all others, men I can trust totally. *Conversos*, Jews like myself, he thought, as he dodged to his left just in time to miss the contents of a chamber pot being emptied from a third story window.

Two lurking cats struck at one another with a hissing sound then scampered away in opposite directions. As he passed three young boys huddled on the street corner playing dice in the light of a flickering candle, he thought to himself, "Boys need to be educated from childhood in languages, diplomacy, finance. If I could recruit them when they are ten or twelve, educate them, hire the tutors myself, the best minds from our people..."

A woman who frequently visited his shop smiled shyly from an open door. She was holding a baby girl bedecked in handmade lace. He nodded to her, thinking of the hundreds of Jewish parents who'd been robbed of their children by this king he was forging a business alliance with...that miserable, no good...ah, but it will do me no good to be bitter. I must find a way to influence the man to do good instead of evil to my people.

He heard the song of two birds from cages on a wrought iron balcony dripping with flowers, only one floor above the street.

I will never trust that man, he told himself. No matter how much business we do together, no matter how many gifts I take him. I will not allow myself to trust him.

But I will use the relationship for all it's worth. I will make money, big money, for my family, for myself, for my people. I will bring as many "family" as possible into the business. We Jews will make ourselves indispensable to Manuel, to the royal court.

He nodded at a merchant who was locking his doors on the *Rua da Aurea*, Gold Street. I wonder, he thought as he continued on his way through the Baixa toward the *Juderia*, if it would make sense to also get to know the pope. How does one do that? I must think on it...

His mind reeled with the new vistas opened by the conversation with Manuel. Lisbon as a gathering port from which to sell to the world! A brilliant concept, made to order for the House of Mendes.

"House of Mendes" he said aloud. It sounded good, perfect. A banking house, a trading house. Even perhaps, a fleet of ships as Manuel had suggested. He could imagine the cargoes: Brabant laces, coarse cloth from Bruges and Ghent, Castilian woolens, glazed tiles, well-tempered swords and daggers, tapestries, Venetian mirrors and glass. Where had he heard about a silk quilt embroidered in gold threads? And silver cabinets, fur coats of marten and weasel. Woods gilded in gold and sienna.

He passed his warehouse, and walked along the docks for a long while, watching as the moon hid behind a passing cloud. Yes, he would become a business partner with the king. With this king and any other royal house which wanted to do business with the House of Mendes.

But of one thing he would be sure. He—and his people, the Jews—would benefit just as much as the royals.

Two weeks later Francisco was again summoned to the king's presence, this time their meeting was set for early in the afternoon. Francisco had long since decided on the next gift he would offer the king, and as he entered the private chambers and kissed the king's hand, he immediately offered the large package to Manuel.

"Ah, what have we here?" Manuel exclaimed greedily as he tore off the wrapping. "A chess set! Ivory, how splendid! Your father must have told you how much I love the game."

Francisco smiled, thinking of his father's advice. "There's no better way to cement the relationship. He loves to play the game, but he must win. Don't ever make the mistake of beating him."

Manuel held up the large black queen. "Ebony?"

"No, Excellency, it is black jade. Very rare."

"We must play, right now! I'll order some sherry..."

For more than four hours the two men played chess. Three times Francisco nearly beat the king but each time contrived, after giving him a difficult game, to let the king win. The king was in great spirits when Queen Isabella's chambermaid sent word that the queen insisted on seeing Manuel. "I must go," he apologized, "but you must come back tomorrow. We'll continue. And we must talk about business. I've had such fun but even a king must work! Come back tomorrow, Mendes, and I might even let you win a match."

The next afternoon Francisco's only gift to the king was his presence. After they completed the match begun the previous day, Manuel told Francisco that the queen was unwell, and neither his father nor Dr. Nasi were able to relieve the horrible pain in her head. "So, we must talk business as I will surely be summoned to her bedside soon. What do you think about my plans to make Lisbon the greatest port in the world?"

"I've thought of little else, Excellency. We must educate a cadre of agents who we can send to all the great cities of the world to buy for us and to establish offices with the other royal families."

"Precisely. We must be able to trust them; they must follow exact orders. They must also be able to place themselves in the right spots to get secret information. A sort of spy system," he added, chuckling at his cleverness.

"Excellency, before we go any further, there's something on my mind I feel I must bring to your attention."

"Of course, Mendes. Speak your mind. We must be frank with one another. What is it?"

"As a result of your edict in March of 1497, nearly sixteen months ago, hundreds of Jewish children were taken from their parents and baptized."

"Yes?" The king's manner had abruptly changed, he was angry.

"Now all my people have been converted to Catholicism, but only a handful of the children have been restored to their natural parents. Now that their parents are Catholics, couldn't you see it in your heart to decree that all the children be returned?"

The king walked toward the window and looked down at his gardens. Francisco heard the distant screech of a peacock.

"I know you want your people, all your subjects, to admire and respect you, to revere you and gladly do your bidding..."

The king turned and studied Francisco's face.

"I'm sure my people will be of great assistance to the crown in carrying out your plan to make Portugal the wealthiest country in the world," Francisco continued.

"Your people have the finest minds when it comes to commerce and finance..." the king said in a flat voice, his eyes boring into Francisco's.

"They will never be content, able to concentrate on the task at hand, as long as they are worried about their children. If you restore their children to them, you can count on their loyalty and devotion to your cause." Francisco had made his case. He stopped speaking and stared back at the king, his very silence insisted on a response.

Manuel turned back to the window and appeared to be watching something in the far distance. Francisco sat perfectly still, feeling the beat of his heart in his throat.

"We would like to have a baby, but Isabella hasn't conceived yet." He seemed to be talking to himself, so Francisco did not respond. "Now, she is ill..." His voice trailed off.

The king turned, walked back to his customary chair and sat down. "By now these old Catholic families have become attached to the babies..."

"On the contrary, Excellency, in most cases the children are being trained and used as servants. A great waste. These children should be properly educated as they are traditionally tutored in our homes. Then, they would grow up to be of service to Your Majesty's dreams."

The king's face relaxed into a small smile. "You have a way with words, Mendes. You'll do well negotiating with my competitors." He stood and walked to his desk and stroked the back of the lapis lazuli horse Francisco had given him. "I think of you all the time, Mendes, every time I look at this horse. A beautiful thing...I'll think on your request. I'll pray on it. I'll summon you when I've made my decision."

Manuel walked toward Francisco, extending his hand. "My guards will show you out."

Three weeks passed without a word from the palace. Meanwhile, Francisco learned from Daniel Nasi that Isabella had recovered for several days, only to be back in bed with a terrible headache. "I fear for the worst," Daniel reported to Francisco, "there's something strange in her eyes."

Then, without warning, a messenger appeared at the shop to tell Francisco the king wanted him immediately; he shouldn't even bother with a trip to the barber first. Francisco walked with the messenger back up the hill to St. George's castle.

"Glad you could come on such short notice, Mendes," Manuel began. "Isabella's feeling fine today, and I need a bit of relaxation." He pointed toward the chessboard and the two men sat down. Two games later, they broke for lunch and as Manuel poured a glass of sherry for Francisco, he reached for a document, which he handed to Francisco. "This will please you..."

To his astonishment, Francisco read the edict which announced by order of his majesty the king, Manuel I of Portugal, all children of Conversos, formerly Jews, were to be returned to their natural parents within one month, under threat of "severest punishment."

"Thank you, Excellency, my people will be so pleased."

"Perhaps," the king said with a wry smile, "your people will pray for the health of the queen."

Chapter Four

The Massacre Of 1506

The king's wife, the Infanta Isabella, died a few months later, leaving no heir to the throne. King Manuel, ever anxious to unite all of Iberia under his dominion, quickly married Isabella's younger sister Maria who pleased him by promptly becoming pregnant and producing a son who would, at a surprisingly young age, become the new ruler of Portugal. Meanwhile, the bad news for the "New Christians" was that Maria, following her parents' instructions, constantly harangued Manuel to institute an Inquisition in Portugal similar to the one the infamous Torquemada was conducting in Spain.

To the great delight of the Nasi and Mendes families as well as the other forcibly converted Jewish families, King Manuel valued the contribution they were making to Portugal's place in world affairs more than he valued the "purity" of their Catholic beliefs. True to his word, he did not investigate their religious practices in the privacy of their homes as long as they maintained outward manifestations of being Christian.

The king, with the help of the Jewish merchants, had created the finest fleet of ships in the world; Portugal had become in a few short years the undisputed ruler of the seas. Additionally, he embarked on a massive building program that would make his name immortal with the phrase "Emanueline architecture." Great churches and convents, palaces and fortresses such as the one at Belem, became world-renowned memorials to the golden age when King Manuel reigned supreme.

When his personal physician, Dr. Benjamin Mendes, died suddenly of a stroke in 1501, the king named Dr. Daniel Nasi as his new physician and subsequently, as a wedding gift, decreed that Daniel be head of the All Saint's Hospital and medical school.

One of Dr. Mendes last actions before his death was to play matchmaker for his young protégé. He arranged for Daniel to marry Rachel Levi, the daughter of his colleague, the former physician to the Duke of Albuquerque who, like Mendes, had walked across Spain to Portugal in 1492.

After a splendid solemn High Mass performed by the Papal Nuncio in the great Cathedral in Lisbon, the king himself attended Daniel's wedding reception that was held at Francisco Mendes' magnificent new house. Now that all Jews had become Catholic, they were no longer confined to the Juderias; consequently, Francisco had bought two city blocks and built homes for himself and his co-religionists.

His new house on the *Rua da Procenia* was the talk of the *Converso* community and even had elicited some comment at court. It was east of the quay, south of the *Alfama* district, within walking distance of his three new warehouses. Desirous of a certain symmetry and simplicity in the architecture, he had built an entire square block of new homes and was selling them to the merchant class of *Conversos*. Though he didn't admit to it, he would sell these homes and the ones he intended to build on the second block exclusively to his own people. He had his reasons, but only he knew what they were.

As the brilliant afternoon light waned and dusk descended on the afternoon of the wedding reception, Francisco settled down for serious conversation at a small table at the far end of the courtyard with his younger brother, Diogo, and Miguel Hidalgo, a distant cousin from Castile.

"Tell me about Spain," Francisco said, thinking of the horrors perpetrated against *Conversos* during Torquemada's reign as Grand Inquisitor. "Now that Torquemada is dead, have things eased up a bit for our people?"

"Not at all," responded Miguel, whose family had converted to Catholicism a generation earlier. "At the *auto da fé* in Toledo last February over one hundred conversos were burned. But things are even worse in Cordoba. There Diego Rodrigues Lucero has begun an unbelievable reign of terror. He burns anyone he can find who has a drop of Jewish blood."

"In reality," Francisco said, "I know that after he burns them, he confiscates their property and wealth. What the Jews don't seem to realize is that the Church is after their wealth, their property, and could care less about their souls. It's all a sham."

"And that could happen here too," Diogo exclaimed excitedly. "The Jewish merchants have become wealthy, and they control much of the action on Gold and Silver Streets. Just wait, when the Catholics get envious enough, we'll have an Inquisition here too." Diogo was handsome with perfectly straight hair that looked like black silk, and his flashing brown eyes were always filled with mischief, belying his substantial brainpower.

Francisco regarded his sixteen-year old brother with awe. He always did have a way of getting straight to the point, and he would make an excellent negotiator someday, if he could learn to control his temper.

"Just last month," Miguel continued, "that monster Lucero burned alive one- hundred-seven persons. Do you know what their crime was? Nothing!" he said before Francisco could respond. "Nothing except listening to some crazy street preacher!"

"What do you hear from your spies in Rome? What's the Borgia pope up to these days?" Francisco asked with a smirk on his face.

"Unbelievable! He recently had a huge party, all the best families in Rome in attendance. The entrance hall was filled with human statuary, young men and women, completely naked, their bodies painted in gold paint, all in various erotic poses. After dinner, the guests were treated to a sex show. Hired actors and actresses performed unspeakable sexual acts for all to witness."

****

Five years later Diogo's prophetic words about the uncertainty of their existence became reality. On April 19, 1506, as Francisco, Diogo, and their mother were finishing breakfast, they heard a loud, frantic pounding on the front door. Francisco brushed his disheveled hair off his forehead, felt in his robe to see if he had his dagger, then answered the door. It was one of the men who worked in his Baixa warehouse, red in the face, panting, with blood running out of his nostrils.

"Señor Mendes, you must come. The Christians are on a rampage. They've butchered one of our men, and they're taking him to the Rocio to burn his body. Those Dominican friars are leading a pack of angry people..."

Francisco grabbed the man and pulled him into the vestibule, then locked the door. "Come in, Lopez, and catch your breath."

Diogo and Deborah, who had followed Francisco into the vestibule, guided Hernando Lopez into the kitchen, seated him, and Deborah began ministering to his bloody nose. Meanwhile, Francisco went through the house dismissing all the servants, telling them to go directly to their homes and to stay inside until he sent further word to them.

"Now," Francisco said as he returned to the kitchen, "tell me exactly what happened."

"We were at Mass in the Jesus Chapel of the church of Saint Domingo, listening to the Dominicans preach as you instructed."

"Yes, go on."

"Father Orfeo was preaching about the Jews, about the need to wipe out heresy, about how the Jews are the cause of the pestilence, the bad crops!"

"Stupid priests!" Diogo yelled, hitting the table.

"Go on, Lopez," Francisco demanded, silencing his younger brother.

"The sun was streaming through the window, hitting the crucifix just so, and several of the people in front of us started whispering that it was a miracle. Pedro laughed at them, and pointed out that the reason the crucifix was so lit up was because the sun was hitting it directly. Two men in front of us grabbed Pedro, pulled him out of the Church, and stabbed him. Before I could do anything, the whole crowd was down on me too. Father Orfeo began shouting 'kill the heretics, kill the Jews,' and they grabbed me and all the other New Christians and marched us toward the Rocio, threatening to burn us alive. Like in Spain. I managed to stab the low-life holding me and broke away. You've got to do something to stop them, Senor Mendes."

"I told you this was going to happen," Diogo said bitterly to Francisco.

"You must speak to the king," Deborah counseled her son.

"He's away. In Aviz. It will take a day to get a message to him. Damn! Of all the times for him to be gone! I told him those Dominicans were going to pull the house down on him. Damn!"

All three men stood. "Diogo, you go to all our shops and warehouses. Close them, send the people home and order them to stay put at home. After you close down the three new warehouses, go to the Baixa warehouse and wait there for me. If the riots spread beyond the Rocio area, you can offer safety to the Conversos in the Baixa warehouse.

"Lopez, you go with Diogo and do whatever he tells you to. I'm going to get Rachel Nasi and her baby and bring them here so I know they are safe."

Diogo nodded at Francisco, already aware of his brother's plans for the safety of the women and children. They had been expecting something like this to happen for several weeks. On Passover Eve, Father Orfeo had taken two policemen and burst in on a large Converso family celebrating the Passover feast in the privacy of their home. They had been imprisoned, but King Manuel had seen to their release only two days later. Ever since then the Dominicans had been working the populace into a frenzy, excoriating the Jews, calling them heretics, and urging the people to take the matter into their own hands, since the king seemed to be ignoring the whole situation.

Consequently, Francisco had carefully planned for the worst, knowing the House of Mendes would be a prime target for agitated peasants. He had removed all the precious stones and gold from his shops, office and warehouses and put them in secret vaults inside a specially constructed wine cask in the subterranean passage beneath his house.

Now, as he prepared to go get Dr. Daniel Nasi's wife and three year old son, Samuel, he armed himself with a dagger and sword.

On hearing the frightening news from Francisco, Daniel insisted he must go down to the *Rua da Juderia* and get his mother-in-law Aviva and her sister-in-law Miriam and bring them to the safety of Francisco's home. While Francisco took Rachel and Samuel back to his home and ushered them down into his wine cellar, Daniel, armed and with four of the king's guards to protect him, went for Aviva and Miriam Levy.

He could scarcely believe his eyes when he rounded the *Rua de S. Pedro* that led into the Jewish quarters. Two Dominican friars were leading a mob through the street with an uplifted crucifix, crying "Heresy. Kill the Marranos." Hundreds of peasants had been joined by German, Dutch and French sailors.

Women and children were being pulled out of their homes and beheaded on the spot. He felt himself get dizzy when he watched a baby thrown out of an upper story window, impaled on a spear, then set afire. If this was happening in full view on the streets, what was going on inside the houses?

With fierce determination and the assistance of his guards, he guided his horse through the angry mob, finally reaching his mother-in-law's home, dreading what he might find inside.

He was too late.

The beautiful Aviva had obviously put up a struggle, to no avail. Her clothes had been torn off, she'd been raped, perhaps repeatedly, her throat slit and her breasts cut from her body. Miriam fared no better. Her head was severed from her body, her abdomen slit from the navel to the groin.

Daniel, used to blood, could not stop the bile from rising in his throat. He closed his eyes, vomited, staggered toward the awful scene on the floor. He sat a moment beside Aviva's body, weeping for himself as witness to this unbelievable carnage, for Aviva, for all his fellow Jews.

He was brought back to reality by a sound. Something, human or animal, was in the room. His grip tightened on his dagger and he stopped breathing and listened, hoping for a repeat of what had sounded like a whimper, or perhaps a muffled sob.

Again, he heard it. A human sound, an uncontrollable sob. Coming from under the bed.

Dagger in hand, he crawled toward the bed and peered under. A small child huddled back against the wall, trembling in fear.

"I won't hurt you, little one. I'm a doctor. Come out, come out," he coaxed to no avail.

When his quiet voice failed to reassure the child, he moved the bed away from the wall and picked up the frightened bundle of human flesh. A girl, perhaps six years old, her clothes torn away from her body, bleeding profusely from between her legs.

His teary eyes cleared and his medical instincts took over. He grabbed a piece of cloth and wrapped it like a diaper around the child's genital area, then wrapped her in a blanket and made his way out of the house through a back entrance which led him to an alley. He would take her to the hospital where she and lots of others would need his emergency assistance.

The massacre continued through the Jewish quarter until every home had been destroyed and every person thought to possess an ounce of Jewish blood was killed. Many of the bodies were left lying where they fell, but dozens of them were scooped up by the delirious peasants and carried back to the Rocio Square where they were added to the bonfire that had been consuming human flesh for hours.

Shortly after noon Francisco called together two of the thirteen-year-old boys who were students in his special school. (All those over fifteen had been armed and sent to work with Diogo.) He dirtied their faces, hands and clothes with water and clay and gave them instructions to go down to the Baixa area, specifically the *Rua Aurea* and the *Rua Augusta* where the mob was looting, murdering, and burning the shops of the *Converso* merchants, and, mingling with the mob, the boys should suggest repeatedly that they go down to the Mendes warehouse and loot it.

The boys appeared astonished at his instructions. Francisco smiled and said, "I have a surprise! Just do as I say. Then come to the small door on the north side and we will protect you."

Within half an hour the mob stormed the street side doors of the warehouse. By this time Francisco had his men ready. They waited in hiding, as the mob clamored into the warehouse and helped themselves, with much hilarity and glee, to the cloth and spices and leather goods. When the last of them entered the warehouse, the iron doors were shut with all of Francisco's men outside. For that afternoon at least, Francisco succeeded where Lisbon's mounted police had failed. Finally, the Old Christian mob was under control and the New Christians were standing well armed, outside of the warehouse.

Chapter Five

Restitution

Four days later Francisco sent to the All Saint's Hospital for Daniel, who had not returned from the hospital since he carried the wounded six-year-old girl there. Francisco sent for Daniel because he received word that King Manuel was on his way to the Mendes home for a meeting with Francisco regarding the prisoners in the Mendes warehouse.

Francisco had not shaved or bathed since the outbreak of hostilities, nor had he managed more than a few hours of sleep. He let the women and Samuel come up from hiding, but sent them upstairs to stay until some disposition was made of the prisoners in the warehouse. He was tired, angry, and in no mood to be polite to any man, much less this king who had forced the Jews to convert to Catholicism.

The king arrived with an unusually reduced entourage of only four men.

Francisco ushered him into the living room without the usual ceremonial greetings, nor did he offer him a glass of sherry, as he would have done under other circumstances. Daniel, looking equally unkempt, waited by the window that looked out onto the courtyard. He nodded to the king.

"I've come," the king began, clearly unnerved by the unspoken hostility in Francisco and Daniel's faces, "to offer my personal condolences. I'm shocked, scandalized by what has happened. I never imagined..."

"I'm told you've taken Father Orfeo and his Aragonese friend into custody..." Francisco interrupted.

"Yes. I have them in the castle dungeon. And about thirty others who are reputed to have been the leaders of the mob."

Daniel, bleary eyed, walked toward the king's chair. "What kind of punishment does Your Majesty deem appropriate?"

"Death. For sure."

"More than two thousand of our people were mutilated, beheaded, their limbs severed from their bodies. Our women were repeatedly raped, then murdered and burned. Our babies were impaled on spears, then burned..."

"Yes, I know. I know. Nothing ever so dreadful...in my kingdom...I can't believe it..." The king thumbed his right hand in his left nervously.

"Garroted and burned," Daniel said with a voice of steel that Francisco had never heard before. "All of them. They must be treated as they have treated us..."

The king gasped, then turned ashen. "You're not referring to the prisoners in the warehouse. You can't possibly mean..."

"No," Francisco said, "Daniel is talking about the ones you have in the castle dungeon. Those responsible for causing the massacre, the Dominicans and the rabble-rousers. They must be garroted and burned."

"I agree," the king said emphatically. "I agree completely. And I'm going to fine all the inhabitants of Lisbon one-fifth of their property and use the money to make restitution to you and all the merchants whose shops were looted. And we'll build new homes for all those whose homes were destroyed."

"How will you make restitution for the lives, for the dead mothers and wives, for the murdered children?"

The king stared at his good friend and personal doctor, Daniel Nasi. "You aren't yourself. I can understand it after what you've been through, but..."

"More than four thousand people are critically wounded. More than two thousand already dead. More will join them. We have torn up every sheet we own to make bandages. As I stand here before you, more than four thousand of your subjects are burning up with raging fevers."

"I've organized a burial detail," Francisco said, standing up and walking toward the window. "We've buried four-hundred-forty-three bodies. The others were burned by the mob. The longest day I live, I will never recover from what I've experienced in the last few days. Neither will any of our people, Your Majesty."

"I don't know what to say. I can't bring dead people back to life. I can't tell people not to hate Jews. I can't control what the Church preaches." Manuel threw up his hands and looked helplessly from Francisco to Daniel.

"My brother, Diogo, only twenty-one, a brilliant future ahead of him, lies upstairs with a raging fever from a spear wound."

The king looked frantically at Daniel. "Why don't you take him to the hospital? He should be there."

"Your Majesty, I have over four-thousand patients in a hospital meant to care for two-hundred. He's better off here where his mother can nurse him."

"Ah, Francisco, we must decide what to do with your prisoners. That is our most urgent decision right now."

Francisco sat down and looked squarely at the king. "What would you suggest?"

"They've been held for four days and nights without food and water, more than seven hundred people, I'm told. This must end. It's inhumane treatment. I won't have it."

Daniel, with no inflection in his voice replied, "Francisco and I were held, along with twenty-thousand others, for more than four days without food and water to force us to convert to Catholicism. I seem to recall that you were the person who ordered that inhumane imprisonment."

The king ignored Daniel. "Francisco, I've come here, to you, to discuss this reasonably. I could have summoned you to the palace, but I thought the decent thing to do was to come to you. Now, try to be reasonable so we can put this behind us and get on with our plans for Portugal. What is your price?"

"My price? Hhmm. Very sensible. I like the way you put it."

"Well?" Manuel tapped his knee nervously.

"You can't expect, after this trauma, for those Conversos who are still alive to feel safe here. Many of them will want to leave Portugal. But you passed a law in 1497 forbidding them to leave. You'll have to change that."

"Consider it done."

"They won't just want to leave; they'll want to sell their homes for a decent price and take their possessions with them."

"I will issue an edict permitting anyone who desires to leave the country. The New Christians will be permitted to buy bills of exchange for money or merchandise, they will be permitted to sell their land and homes, and they can leave or come and go without royal consent. I will let them trade on land and sea and export money or merchandise, as long as it is exported on Portuguese ships."

Daniel took a seat and listened carefully, then asked, "What about punitive measures against relapsed Catholics? Or as the people call us, *Marranos*. Swine. Many people feel this is the beginning of a Portuguese Inquisition."

"Never. Never during my life. I will pass a law protecting New Christians. I will make common law applicable to your people, and I will assure you there will be no inquiry into any New Christian's religious practices for the next twenty years. Now Francisco, what more can you ask?"

"How soon can you get all these laws on the books?"

"I give you my word, Francisco. When have I ever betrayed my word to you? I only regret I wasn't here when this began. I would have put a quick stop to it."

"You will personally see to the punishment of the men in your dungeon?" Daniel asked, reminding the king of his promise.

"Immediately."

"And financial restitution will be made to those Conversos who lost homes, businesses, their families, husbands and fathers?"

"Yes. All the citizens of Lisbon will pay for these atrocities. I promise you."

Francisco stood. "Then we will go release the prisoners in the warehouse. Right now."

****

Four years later in 1510 while the Bishop performed the baptismal rites for Daniel and Rachel's baby daughter, Beatriz da Luna, Francisco let his mind wander over the past years. An uneasy peace had settled in after the horror of the massacre of the New Christians. The king had met Francisco's demands, former Jews were allowed to leave Portugal and take their money with them, and thousands of families had fled to Constantinople, Antwerp, and even to a primitive place in the New World called Brazil.

Francisco decided to remain in Lisbon, always keeping his options open. King Manuel had been extremely careful in his relationship with the *converso* population after the massacre. He welcomed them into his court and his daily life, always urging them to take more risks in their business expansion plans. Whenever Daniel went to him for more money for the medical school, he granted it. Whenever Francisco took an idea to him, he pursued it with enormous enthusiasm.

And yet his former plan to assimilate the Jews into the population at large failed completely. Prejudice against people of Jewish blood was rampant, fed by the continued preaching of the Dominicans. The peasants needed to blame someone for their hard lives, and the Dominicans pointed the finger at the *conversos*, accusing them of secret heresy and stealing their money.

Nevertheless, the House of Mendes was thriving. They now owned four large caravels which roamed the sea-lanes, their capitan's searching for new ports where they could buy and sell goods, make contacts, exchange money and passengers. Yes, life was good, Francisco thought, as the baptism concluded and the Nasi family and their guests filed out of the great Cathedral. *But we must always be on guard. At any moment, catastrophe could strike again.*

Hours later, after a large christening party, Daniel and the Mendes brothers came into Rachel's bedchamber for a quiet visit.

Rachel greeted the men with warm hugs, and the four settled down before the fireplace. Daniel filled their sherry glasses and they talked of the intimate confidences of family.

"We're making plans for Diogo to open a branch of our business in Antwerp," Francisco announced, fingering his new mustache, his eyes twinkling with excitement.

"Business must be thriving!" Rachel said.

"Yes. We can't hire people fast enough. The young men in my school don't seem to grow up quickly enough to keep up with the demand, but I will hire only our people."

Diogo added, "We can't seem to build ships fast enough either."

"I'm happy for you both," Rachel said. She patted her husband's arm affectionately, "but neither of you are married! I'm sure Daniel recommends it highly."

Daniel smiled. "I do, Rachel, but these two men are married to their business. They'd make horrible husbands."

"No doubt," Francisco agreed with Daniel. "On the other hand, if you have any ladies you'd like to recommend..."

"Unfortunately," Rachel answered, "most of the young girls from *converso* families are betrothed before they reach ten. You must look for a young widow, Francisco."

Francisco patted his younger brother on the back. "This young fellow is the one who should get married. Before he gets in trouble."

"Yes," Rachel scolded Diogo, "you must make it your first order of business to find a bride in Antwerp, Diogo, for the sake of the family name. Someone must carry on the family line. We must replenish our people."

Diogo smiled a wicked smile. "I'd like nothing better, my dear cousin. Too bad your little princess isn't fourteen or fifteen. We could make a match right here!"

"Diogo's problem," Francisco said in a chiding tone, "is that he has too many women in love with him. He can't make up his mind. Not that they're always the right sort, mind you."

At that moment Samuel and his small white terrier burst into the bedroom. "Mother, look what Diogo brought me! My very own telescope!"

Eight-year-old Samuel climbed on the sofa next to his mother but objected as boys his age are want to do, when she tried to put her arm around him. He wanted to be a man in the eyes of these men he idolized.

"Too bad you've plans for Samuel to be a doctor," Francisco said, eyeing the small boy. "We could use more family in the business. I'd like to open a branch in Venice and one in Constantinople, too."

"My, my," Daniel joined in, "you really are ambitious."

"Someday. It's our dream," Diogo said in a hopeful voice. "We'll be the most important international trading bank in all of Europe. That's our goal."

"In order to grow and expand," Francisco added, "we're got to build more ships, train our own crews, have our own trusted agents in every port in the world. Men we can trust totally. And the way it looks, we can use every relative we can find—and trust."

"Speaking of trust," Daniel said quietly, addressing his remarks to Rachel, "I've asked Francisco to take on the task of a naming ceremony for our little one."

"Ah, yes." A warm glow filled Rachel's eyes. "Her Hebrew name will be Chana, and we will call her Gracia, even though her Catholic name is Beatriz."

Francisco spoke, his voice newly solemn. "I will see to it this week. What a pity we cannot celebrate that as we have celebrated this charade today."

No one spoke, each of them silent with his or her own memories.

Finally, daring to break the silence, Daniel asked Francisco, "How goes it? Have you heard of any suspicions? The last thing you need in your life is an informer."

Francisco answered. "So far, so good. It's hard to say no to good people, but we must limit participation in our secret services to closest family and friends. It's a terrible risk, an awful responsibility to know we could bring another catastrophe down on our heads."

With large eyes that seemed to take in everything, Samuel looked from Francisco, to Diogo, to his father. "Don't you ever wish we weren't God's chosen people?"

Everyone was thoughtful as Francisco reached over and ruffled the boy's dark hair. "That's the kind of thing I could count on Diogo to say when he was young. You already know how to ask questions, young man!"

The following Saturday morning, with only ten men in attendance in the subterranean synagogue beneath Francisco's home, Rabbi Francisco Mendes added the name *Chana bat Rahel* to the roll of God's chosen people in Lisbon.

Chapter Six

A Husband For Beatriz
Lisbon—1524

"Father, I've decided I'm going to be a courtesan. You can stop worrying about who you are going to marry me off to," Beatriz announced, as she finished playing his favorite music on her harp.

Momentarily startled, Daniel Nasi looked up from his book ready to reprimand his fourteen-year-old, always rambunctious daughter. He saw the grin break out on her face, then become a full-fledged smile.

He beckoned with his hand. "Come, sit beside me and tell me what you know of courtesans."

"Hhmm...wouldn't you like to know! Does King John have lots of lovers? C'mon, Father, you're the Royal Physician, you must know." Beatriz sat next to her father, and he put his arm around her shoulders.

"If I did know, I wouldn't tell you. Besides, your brother Sam is the king's doctor now, not me. John prefers a doctor his own age, easier to argue with and to ignore if he chooses.

"Father, you didn't answer my question. Does John have lots of lovers?"

He shook his head. "I've retired from all those court intrigues, and my only obligation is to my medical students. Tell me what you know about courtesans. I should have known better than to let you go to school with a bunch of boys..."

"That's the one thing you've done right, Father. Letting me go to Francisco's school."

"So, I've only done one thing right?"

"What I meant was, that's the best decision you've made. I love my school! Besides, I didn't learn about courtesans from boys. I learned it from our study of history and diplomacy. Professor Guedes emphasizes that in order to deal with any royal court, it's necessary to know all about the women who share the bed of the king or the pope or the cardinal."

"I agree with your professor."

Beatriz continued, "Courtesans have lots of influence on what is or is not done. I would love to be the secret influence behind a king, but being from a *converso* family, I'm obviously not going to be invited to marry a king."

"Thank God for that!" Daniel put his book down on the lamp table and looked at her. "Beatriz, you're just trying to get me riled up. No more about courtesans!" He paused for a moment before continuing, "You've turned down all the eligible men in Lisbon. Your mother is giving me fits.

She claims all the young women she knows are betrothed by the time they are ten. You are fourteen."

He paused, then stood and walked toward the library window, looked out, and then looked back at Beatriz. "And it's clear that you are not only precocious but fully developed physically at a very young age. Your mother is right. You should be betrothed."

"Ugh! Why does every conversation end up like this?"

"Do you have any recruits, Beatriz, any eligible candidates you'd like me to meet?"

"I've told you Father, the boys at school are silly, dumb, immature. You'll only consider a *Converso,* so that leaves out ninety percent of the men in Lisbon."

He nodded his head in agreement.

"Give me my dowry, it's enough for me to live on forever, and I won't have to be subservient to any man. I hate the very idea of marriage."

Daniel Nasi looked at his eldest daughter, his favorite child if the truth were known, the person the sun rose and set on as far as he was concerned. In truth, he agreed with her. He didn't know a young man he considered her equal, either in brilliance or in beauty. He too had been dreading the day when circumstances would dictate that she become betrothed.

"It would be a tragic waste of beauty if you didn't marry, my dear. Besides, think of the children you'll produce. They'll have your blood; they'll be little replicas of you. No, my dear, your mother's right. You must marry and soon."

"Why soon?"

"Aside from your rapidly advancing age, times are very uncertain for *conversos* since King Manuel's death. We can't predict what John will do. He's only a boy, twenty-three years old, and even his own father told me he was an imbecile."

"Samuel says he's stupid, but he warned me not to repeat it."

Daniel nodded, "But he's a fanatic where religion is concerned, and he's flirting with the idea of bringing the Inquisition to Portugal. He wants the additional power. And I suppose he also wants the property he would confiscate from the Jews. You can be sure greed is always the major motivating factor. So...your mother and I would be much relieved to know that some very exceptional man was pledged to take care of you. After all, we won't live forever."

"Father, give me my dowry, and I'll go live in Antwerp or Constantinople. I'll ask Francisco to give me a job as one of his agents. After all, I lead every class in school. I speak seven languages, I can out-argue, out-negotiate any one in his organization."

"You know Francisco doesn't hire women as agents. The only reason we let you go to his school was because you were so advanced...well, it made sense at the time. I didn't dream you'd get your hopes up."

"I've a better idea, Father. It just hit me! I'll marry Diogo. He's handsome, he's smart, he's one of the richest men in the world."

"And he's the world's greatest rake! No, my dear, I'd rather see you married to Francisco. Even though he's nearly my age. He's the more stable of the two men."

"Hhmm..."

Daniel could almost see the wheels turning in Beatriz' mind. Francisco had been like a second father to her all these years. The affection they felt for one another was palpable whenever they were in the same room.

"He's my favorite person in the whole world," Beatriz said, her voice dreamy and warm, "next to you and Mother, of course. Why hasn't he ever married?"

"I don't know. I've never asked him. I guess the right woman has never come along. And he's dedicated to his business."

"Maybe I'll ask him to marry me, see what his reaction is," Beatriz said as she sat down in front of the harp and played a rippling chord.

"Don't be ridiculous, child," Daniel answered, opening his book again.

"You must be very excited, going to your first ball at court," Francisco said to Beatriz as they walked out of his home and headed down the street toward her home. It was their daily ritual now, for the past two years that she wait in his library each afternoon after classes until he came from his office. Then, after a glass of sherry and a recounting of the day's major events, he would walk her home, as she was not permitted on the sidewalks of Lisbon unless escorted by her maid or a member of her family. Francisco, as her father's oldest and dearest friend, was considered family.

"Oh yes, I'm excited. My dress is splendid, thanks to you. Mother and I argued over the style, but I won, and it's quite..." her eyes danced devilishly, "grown-up, I guess you'd think. Sort of Italian. Father's worried. He thinks King John will be very taken with me."

Francisco smiled at his protégé. This was his favorite activity, walking her home. She was so full of spirit, optimism, and expectations for the future. Ah, the enthusiasm of youth! To be her age and know what he knew of life…

"Do you think the king will ask me to dance?"

Why did that question cause a stab of pain in his chest? If he didn't know better, he would think she was flirting with him. Or baiting him. But that was nonsense. "Yes, I imagine if he's not totally inebriated by the time he sees you, he'll have the good sense to ask you to dance. That's the purpose of this ball, for the king to meet some more of the young people in his realm."

"I'm going to be sure Samuel introduces me. I've been practicing my curtsy."

"You amaze me, Beatriz. This is a side of you I'd not been aware of." Francisco was surprised at the scolding sound of his voice; he hadn't meant it to come out that harshly.

"You imagine I'm not fascinated by the court like everyone else? Why?"

"No…I guess I haven't seen this flirtatious side of your personality before."

Francisco took her elbow to assist her across the cobblestone street. "Strange, I've never noticed your ebullient personality," he said, in a self-deluding exercise of futility that was not convincing even to him.

Beatriz stopped walking and turned to face him on the sidewalk. Eyes flashing angrily, she asked, "Tell me, Francisco, have you noticed that I'm a woman? Or do you still think of me as a little child?"

Francisco felt heat creep up into his face. She was staring at him with seductively mocking, slightly smiling, but determined eyes.

"I am a woman now, Francisco, and my parents are desperate to find me a husband. How do you feel about that?" she demanded.

"I suppose…you're sixteen now. I guess if a suitable candidate could be found…" They began walking toward her home again.

"You know all the important, suitable, wealthy, intelligent men in the world. Surely you must know someone…"

"Your father tells me you turn everyone down…"

"What about Diogo? He's not married…"

"Not a good idea. He's not…"

"I think I'll become King John's mistress. I know he can't marry me because of my Jewish blood..."

"You'd find him stupid. He can't even master Latin..."

"Why not you, Francisco? Don't you find me attractive?"

She had stopped again, and was tugging on his arm, forcing him to look squarely at her.

"Any man who isn't blind would find you attractive, my dear Beatriz, but I..."

"I'm waiting. Don't tell me you're too old. Lots of men marry women thirty or forty years younger."

"If you would stop interrupting me, I was going to tell you that I lead a very dangerous life. I do lots of things that, if known, could get me burned at the stake or imprisoned for life. Your parents want you to marry someone who can provide you safety, and I can't. This whole discussion is ridiculous..."

"It's ridiculous because you don't love me, you don't find me attractive."

They had arrived at the front of Beatriz' home. It was Friday night, he wouldn't see her the next day unless...they had to finish the conversation now. "Let's walk a bit more," he said, taking her elbow and guiding her up the walkway.

"I have never once, not for a second, thought of the possibility of marrying you. You're like a daughter to me, even though we are only very distant cousins. Believe me, Beatriz, I couldn't love you more if you were my own flesh and blood."

"Then I am not brilliant enough to suit you, right Francisco?" she asked in a harsh voice.

He nodded. "One of the most brilliant persons I've ever known, certainly, by far, the most accomplished woman."

As he tried to calm her down, Francisco felt overwhelmed with conflicting emotions, even sudden unbidden lurid thoughts of desire. The image of this gorgeous young virgin, naked, on his bed, her luxurious dark hair spread over his silk sheets...beautiful Beatriz sitting across from him in his formal dining room...Beatriz in his arms, dancing...Beatriz walking with him on the quay in the lustrous moonlight...

"Father warned me that the whole idea was ridiculous. I guess I've made a fool of myself," she said as she turned back toward her home.

Francisco shook himself from his reverie to concentrate on her words. "You've discussed me with your father?"

"Of course. Several years ago, I thought he might have mentioned it."

"No. And you can be sure the idea never occurred to me."

"Well, I guess I'll have to test my charms tomorrow at the ball. See if there are any eligible husbands there. I trust you'll be watching." She opened the front door and paused to look back at him, seductively.

Francisco couldn't help himself, without thinking he blurted out, "You'll save me a dance, won't you?"

"I thought you'd never ask!"

For a ball at the Royal Court Francisco ordered up his most splendid carriage. Constructed of gilded wood and upholstered in burgundy velvet, it was drawn by a team of perfectly matched roans with glistening silver studded halters. He arrived, as planned, promptly at eight to pick up the Nasi family.

Greeted by Daniel who was dressed in black velvet festooned in gold lace, the men joined Rachel in the library for a before-ball glass of spiced wine. Regardless of their feelings for this particular king, Francisco too felt especially stimulated by the prospects of an evening at the royal court, and recognized the same feelings in Rachel and Daniel.

Rachel was exuberant at the prospect of introducing Beatriz, a most unconventional daughter, to the highest society of Lisbon. She had shunned the usual pursuits of daughters of wealthy families, needlework and gossip, in favor of traditionally masculine pursuits, fencing, horsemanship, languages, physics, and astronomy. Her sense of her own talents and achievements had made her imperial, dominant, demanding. Rachel feared they would never find a suitable husband, yet she felt enormous pride in Beatriz' sense of herself, her formidable ego and self-esteem.

"And where is the lovely flower?" Francisco asked, drumming his hand impatiently on the back of a chair.

"She's surprising us all, wouldn't even let her mother help her dress," Daniel answered, hearing at that moment the swish of taffeta skirts. "Maybe that's her now!"

Beatriz waltzed around the corner and into the room. An audible gasp, like a strong summer breeze, swept through the room. Her black hair had been combed and secured on top of her head with tiny tendrils escaping in front of her ears and at the nape of her neck. Her mother's long gold earrings fell from her ears. The long sleeves of the royal blue silk velvet gown covered only an inch of shoulder, then curved low revealing smooth white cleavage. Twisted gold braid caught the velvet immediately beneath her breasts, and wound around her tiny waist, then the sumptuous velvet flowed over her rounded hips and cascaded onto the floor.

Beatriz smiled at her father and mother, pirouetted for them, then walked directly to Francisco and handed him a matching velvet cape. He felt breathless, dazzled.

"Did I put your gift of fabric to good use, Francisco?" she asked lightly, taking advantage of his astonishment.

"You look quite...breathtaking!" He accepted the cape and held it for her.

"Perhaps you should take up dress design," Daniel said with pride in his voice. "Your mother tells me you insisted on this design. It becomes you."

"See, Mother, I told you the men would love this gown."

Rachel smiled indulgently at her daughter. "I only question the propriety of an unmarried woman wearing a design like this."

"Yes," Francisco agreed, "I understand what you mean. She will drive the young men mad tonight."

"Precisely." Beatriz smiled at them. "That's the plan. Shall we go?"

Francisco's gilded chariot carried them into a massive courtyard surrounded by battlements. Liveried grooms held the team of roans while they alighted in front of the huge double doors of St. George's Castle. As Beatriz stepped down into Francisco's strong arms electric currents traveled up her spine, making her scalp tingle. He held her a moment too long, kissed her forehead and released her. Taking her left elbow in his massive hand, he guided her into the castle's marble and mirrored entrance hall, past a dozen sumptuously uniformed guards.

Her brother Samuel and his wife, Judith, who had recently delivered their second son, baby Samuel, joined them in the long line waiting to be presented to King John. The guests moved slowly down the long Persian carpeted-hallway, past minstrels, clowns, outrageously costumed dwarfs and strolling musicians who created an atmosphere of gaiety and celebration.

As they entered the Presentation Room, Francisco announced their names to the Master of Ceremonies who, in turn, presented them to King

John III. The king remained seated on his bejeweled gold and burgundy throne, merely nodded his head as each name was announced.

To Beatriz he seemed tiny, a pimply teen-aged boy sporting an attempt at a goatee. His stringy, greasy dirty-blond hair fell to his shoulders. His body was encased in a full length scarlet velvet cloak lined in ermine with a matching scarlet and ermine hat from which a tall white plume fluttered.

Rudely ignoring her parents and Francisco, the king stared, mesmerized, at Beatriz, his lust-filled eyes roamed freely over her body. "Samuel, you told me your sister is brilliant, but you never told me she is beautiful. Stunning. I'm enchanted."

He motioned to one of his pages, and said in a voice everyone could hear, "I want Señorita Beatriz at my table! See to it."

From the Presentation Room they were ushered up wide marble steps and into an immense ballroom filled with rectangular banquet tables which faced the king's table which sat on a raised platform at the far end of the room. Two colossal stone fireplaces flanked the king's table. Flickering torches and wall sconces blazing with hundreds of candles illuminated the room.

"This room is magnificent!" Beatriz gushed, holding onto Francisco's arm. "Those gold taffeta draperies are the most splendid I've ever seen."

"Yes. I imported the silk from Venice more than ten years ago. The fringe was made to order in a little shop in Florence."

Beatriz' eyes traveled upwards to the frescoed ceiling. Francisco watched her face light up in amazement and appreciation. He told her, "It took four men three years to paint that ceiling, exactly to Manuel's specifications. It's probably the finest work of art in all of Lisbon."

"It's too bad more people can't see it, only those of us who get invited to the castle"

"And it's totally wasted on John. He cares not a wit for art, I'm told."

When they arrived at the table reserved for them, in the front row facing the king, a randy-looking young page informed Beatriz that she was to follow him. She looked helplessly at her parents, at Francisco and her brother.

Her father, stern-voiced and ashen-faced, anger flashing in his eyes, nodded to her. "You must go."

Francisco, with a scowl of disapproval, stepped between the page and Beatriz. "Señorita Beatriz begs the king's indulgence, she would prefer to remain with her family."

The king's majordomo Dominic, an overbearing tall muscular man, intervened.

"Señor Mendes, His Majesty has commanded me to seat the Señorita on his right. It is a singular honor, you should be proud." He turned to Beatriz. "Follow me, Señorita, you must not keep the king waiting.

Mastering the trepidation and fear in the pit of her stomach, Beatriz stood to her full height, cautioned herself to display only self-confidence. Her goal, after all, was to make Francisco jealous, to force him to recognize her as a woman. What better way than to dazzle the king with all of Lisbon looking on.

She followed Dominic to the raised dais, smiling vivaciously at the opulently-dressed young courtiers as they stood to introduce themselves. After she was seated next to the throne-chair and her goblet was filled with wine, six trumpeters signaled the entrance of the king. The audience rose as one to their feet and strained their necks to get the best possible look at their young monarch.

Dressed in a royal purple velvet toga sashed in emerald green satin, wearing a jeweled gold crown, the king made his way slowly from the back of the room to his throne chair. When he reached Beatriz, he held out his hand for her to kiss his ring, then he, in turn, kissed the back of her hand.

"Your beauty overwhelms me, Señorita. Why haven't I met you before?"

"I am only now old enough to attend a ball, Your Majesty," she answered, overcome by the putrid smell that emanated from his body. Does he never bathe? She recognized an overdose of musk of civet intended to cover his rancid body odor.

"Your father and my father have been friends and business partners since before I was born, I can't understand why you and I have not been introduced before this evening," he said, as Dominic served him fish stew in a silver bowl.

While she followed his conversation, Beatriz noticed that all the other guests were served with fine white and gold porcelain, but the king ate only from silver or gold vessels. He drank ale, not wine, from a diamond and ruby encrusted gold chalice, telling her, "Francisco Mendes had this chalice made for me in Antwerp, and though it's meant to hold wine, I much prefer ale."

Beatriz tasted the fish stew tentatively, trying to avoid the shellfish which was strictly forbidden by her real religion. King John, taking note of her lack of enthusiasm for the stew, said, "Does the soup not meet your approval?"

"It's very good," she lied, and with a demure smile added, "Forgive me, Majesty, but I'm suffering from nerves, sitting here with you. I'm sure you understand."

Following the first course, the waiters brought in huge silver platters of roasted piglet, wild pheasants, quail, and goat. To Beatriz' astonishment, the king eschewed the fork beside his plate, and picked up a big piece of pig meat with his fingers and ate it, letting the fat drip down onto his velvet tunic.

"They eat with forks like we do," her father had told her earlier in the day, and indeed, most of the young people at the king's table were using their forks. But not John!

Beatriz realized the king was watching her every move. She had refused the pork but asked for pheasant and quail. "You do not eat pork?" he asked, and she realized he was testing her. Was she still a Jew?

"Oh yes, I love pork," she answered. "But I rarely have a chance to try pheasant and quail, and I can only eat a bit or this dress will no longer fit!"

"A beautiful dress it is, I like it very much." he said, gazing lustfully at her bosom.

When he turned his attention to the young woman on his left, Beatriz looked out into the audience at Francisco. Their eyes met and held, she recognized his pride in her and his apprehension. As compared to John, Francisco appeared so distinguished, his thick wavy dark hair sprinkled with gray, his impeccably tailored doublet frosted with lace, his high cheekbones and perfectly groomed beard. She longed to run to him, to run away from this smelly, ill-mannered oaf. But she had no choice.

Chapter Seven

Consequences

The ball was Saturday night. On Monday afternoon King John created something of a scandal by arriving unannounced at Francisco's home, requesting an audience with one of the students in Francisco's special school. He wished to see Beatriz, the young woman who had enchanted him Saturday evening. He had danced seven dances with her before her parents whisked her away home, but he'd been unable to get her out of his mind all day Sunday. After inquiries, his staff had tracked her down. He would see her alone, without her parents and half of Lisbon watching.

Now, as he waited impatiently in Francisco's living room, one manservant ran upstairs to the school to fetch Beatriz while another jumped on his horse and flew downtown in the direction of Francisco's Baixa warehouse.

After much nervous conferring, Beatriz arrived in the living room accompanied by Professor Guedes. She curtsied and kissed the king's hand. He asked her to sit a moment and asked Professor Guedes to wait outside the door.

Beatriz, dressed in the demure white linen blouse of a student and a long navy skirt, her hair falling down around her shoulders, looked like a different woman, younger and innocent.

"You didn't tell me about your studies," the king said, after seating himself across from her. "I had to track you down through your brother. Myself, I've never had a mind for languages. Never even mastered Latin."

"But so many books are in Latin! How do you read them?" she asked, delighted there was a subject she could engage him in.

"I try not to read. If I need to know something, I ask one of my ministers to tell me. Saves time."

"You don't read for enjoyment?" Beatriz noticed again that his face was covered with ugly pimples, and his complexion seemed oily.

"No In fact, it's the last thing on earth I would find enjoyable."

"What do you like to do?" His fingernails were also dirty, she noticed, as she took a bite of a small cake the servants had provided, along with sherry.

"Hunting, fencing, racing my horse."

"Do you play chess?" she asked, hoping for something they could do which would prolong the visit until Francisco arrived. She'd been assured that he was on his way.

"Yes. My father taught me, His favorite chess set was one given to him by Señor Mendes, ivory and black jade."

And that story is part of our family lore, Beatriz thought as she rose and moved toward the chess set in the back of the room. "Would you care to play a game?" she asked, smiling her most beguiling smile and remembering Francisco's stories: you never beat a king, but you've got to give him a good run for his money.

King John joined her at the chess set, and she was two moves away from having him in check, he was a terrible player, when Francisco rescued her.

"Your Majesty, how good to see you."

Beatriz watched as Francisco kissed the young king's hand.

"The ball was splendid, very gay indeed! Now, what can I do for you today?"

The king sputtered, a bit embarrassed, and then said very bluntly, "I've come to call on Señorita Nasi. I'd hoped to have a bit of privacy with her, if you don't mind."

"I see. Perhaps if you would permit me, I'll notify her father you are here."

"No, damn it, that's quite unnecessary. We don't need to involve her parents."

"But, Your Majesty, surely a person of your deep religious sensibilities understands."

"Mendes, loosen up. I'm not going to run off with the lady this afternoon..."

"But, Sir, the very least I must insist on, as I am responsible for her well-being and her reputation while she is at my school, is that a female chaperon be present. I'll send for one of my maids."

"Mendes, please calm down!"

"Beatriz," Francisco said, taking a new tack, "What are your feelings in this? Are you comfortable here, alone with the king?"

"No, Señor Mendes," she answered formally, "That's why I asked that you be present. I'm astonished, a bit overwhelmed, as you can imagine...a visit from the king..." Beatriz, in a magnificent bit of theater that Francisco recognized as such, wiped her forehead with a hanky, and said, "I really can't finish this chess game, Your Highness. I'm much too overwhelmed."

The three of them settled stiffly into chairs. Francisco insisted on refilling the king's glass with sherry then poured one for himself. A heavy, awkward silence descended. Finally, the king, who was visibly agitated, turned to Francisco. "You're not going to leave us alone then?"

"No, Your Highness, with all due respect, I do not consider it appropriate for a young man to be alone with a young woman of good reputation he is not betrothed to, even if the young man is a king. Not in my house. Not with a young woman whose reputation I'm responsible for."

"What do I have to do? Invite her to the court?"

"That would be more appropriate. He parents would make arrangements for her to be chaperoned. Surely you understand that."

The king stood then turned to Beatriz. "Very well. I will be in touch with your father."

After the king and his retinue left, Francisco called for a brandy. Beatriz rushed to the window and was watching the last of his retinue disappear, then she turned and looked at Francisco who was staring at her. She ran toward him and rocked back and forth in his arms, laughing, as he had never seen her laugh before. When she could finally stop, she said, "Imagine! The king is smitten with me! That dirty slimy smelly little toad wants me! Me! We can't even carry on a decent conversation!"

Francisco sat her down in a chair, and without taking his eyes from hers, in a deathly serious voice said, "I think you've bitten off a huge chunk of trouble. This is not a game, Beatriz. You cannot play with the king's feelings and not get burned."

For a long moment Beatriz said not a word, simply smiled slyly at Francisco. "What about your feelings?"

Francisco gulped his brandy. "My feelings?"

"I'll bet you didn't think the king would respond this way, did you?"

"Anybody with eyes could see what he felt when he was dancing with you Saturday night. I didn't think he'd pursue it though, didn't realize he was so arrogant and irresponsible."

"Since we're all Catholics now, does that make me fair game for him? A marriage possibility?"

"Persons of Jewish blood are not permitted to hold public office. I don't know if his council would interpret being the wife of the king as a public office, but the populace would be up in arms. You know as well as I do, Beatriz, that the peasantry, and the Dominicans, are waiting for a chance to erupt again, a new massacre of the Jews. Never would he marry you, not if he values his life."

"Well, that's good. I'll not consider marrying him either."

"Then what is this all about?"

"That's for me to know and you to try to figure out, my dear Francisco." Beatriz kissed him on the forehead as she buzzed out of the room and swept back up the steps, taking Professor Guedes with her.

That evening, after a thorough briefing by Francisco, Beatriz' parents called her into the library for a conference. Everything about their voices, as well as their agitated expressions indicated this was a major crisis, something which must be resolved immediately.

"How am I to respond when he summons you to the castle tomorrow? We can't refuse him; we've got to let you go. Do you have any idea what you've gotten us all into?" her father demanded as she sat down.

"If he summons me, mother will accompany me. That's perfectly legitimate. He's made such a show of being religious; he'll have to live with his own trap. He cannot require my presence without a chaperone."

Her father seemed old and frail, something she'd never noticed before. "What you don't seem to understand is that the king can require anything he wishes, and get it!"

"Father, all I did was go to a ball, dance with the king, try to be charming as I was with every man there, and I've done nothing, absolutely nothing to encourage his advances. You're blaming me unfairly. I can't stand him, I think he's a squirrel."

"But," her mother chimed in, "if he invites you to the castle you've got to go and be charming again. And that will lead to more and more trouble."

"There is a solution," Beatriz said calmly, hopefully.

"What?" both parents asked.

"Announce my betrothal."

"That's a perfect solution, except you've chased or shamed away all prospects," her father stated.

A slow smile crept across Beatriz' face. "There is a man I would very much like to marry. I've loved him forever. He's one of the few people in this world whose company I always find stimulating. He's a decent, God-fearing Jew, a very religious Jew, in fact. And he's the wealthiest man I know. He would be a wonderful husband for me."

Beatriz watched her parents process this information. Her mother was completely mystified, but in her father's eyes she saw a gradual understanding.

"I'm not sure he thinks of me in the way a man thinks of a woman he wants to bed. But that's only because he remembers me as a small child. I'm working on that part of our relationship."

Even as she said the words, Beatriz saw in her mind's eye the look on Francisco's face as he'd watched her dancing with the king. A mosaic of conflicting emotions: pride and fear, desire and jealousy, love and anger. No mistaking it, last Saturday night he'd felt the pangs of love for the woman she'd become.

"Francisco!" her mother gasped. "My God!"

Tears had formed in her father's eyes. Beatriz looked at him, wondering at his tears.

"I love that man," he said, his voice quavering, "and not for a minute could I bear to see you hurt him. He's too fine a man."

Emotion constricted her own throat, and she felt her eyes get watery. "Father, what makes you imagine I would hurt him? I've told you, I love him more than any other man I've ever met. And as you said once, think of the brilliant children we would produce! If any man could keep me safe, it's Francisco, with all his resources."

"I've never understood why Francisco never married," Rachel said, shaking her head in wonderment. "He's so much older..."

Daniel silenced Rachel with a gesture. "He's not that old, he's a virile man. That's not a problem."

"The only problem," Beatriz said through her tears, "is that he doesn't think of me as a possible wife to him."

"Don't be too sure about that. He was mighty upset this afternoon, furious with King John. I know a good deal about human emotions, and I was watching a jealous man. I must say, Beatriz, you've convinced me. I'll sound him out." Daniel smiled softly at his beloved daughter. She knew precisely what she wanted and would eventually have it all. "Meanwhile, you go ahead and work your magic on him. You've got my blessings."

Beatriz laughed ironically. "He's the only man in the world who could care less about my dowry, that's not even a consideration."

For two days there was no word from the king. Two afternoons in a row Francisco walked Beatriz home, their conversations stilted and distant. Finally, as they neared her door on Wednesday afternoon, to his great relief, she invited him in for a glass of sherry.

It seemed to him that in the space of five days his whole world had turned upside down. He had become obsessed with thoughts of Beatriz.

Images of her assailed his waking and sleeping dreams. Her laughing voice echoed in his mind. The vision of her dressed in blue velvet accentuating her womanliness followed him through his warehouses and counting houses. And the thought of her in the arms of that pimply, ignorant, randy kid nauseated him.

He had never imagined himself in love with any woman, never craved the presence of any one woman in his life. He had arrogantly prided himself on not needing a spouse, a lifelong partner. And he'd rationalized his situation by convincing himself that given his dangerous life as a rabbi for his people, he was doing all potential wives a favor by not involving them in his intrigues, his flirtation with danger.

Since Beatriz had walked into the library dressed in that blue velvet dress he'd been forced to accept her as a voluptuous, desirable woman. Now, as she sat opposite him demurely dressed in her school attire, he could not stop the throbbing in his groin. He could not see her, think of her name, smell her perfume without a physical reaction. Always proud of his self-control, she had defeated that control by her simple presence.

"Francisco," she said, her voice quiet, cautious, "I love you."

He played her voice, her words over and over again. Surely it was a mirage, a dream.

"When I was a little girl you used to promise me that when I grew up I could marry any man I wanted to. Do you remember promising me that?"

It has to be a dream.

"And I used to tell you that you would be the man I would want to marry. You always laughed."

He sipped his sherry. Then, as if watching a man who looked like him, who sounded like him, he stood and walked to her and pulled her gently out of her chair. She looked up at him, wistfully, almost sadly. Then she reached for his head and pulled it down to hers. She kissed him hard on the lips.

February 10, 1528

Dear Diogo,

Since Daniel and Rachel announced that Beatriz was betrothed to me, John began to deal with the House of Mendes as if it is his arch enemy. He's sent a small troop of guards to stand watch over our warehouses, as if we're going to try to smuggle something of his out of the country.

Meanwhile, because the crown has designated the New Christians as the tax collectors, we are the object of envy, scorn and fanaticism. I live in constant dread that the forces surrounding John will soon convince him to bring the Inquisition to Portugal. He is already seeking ways to abandon his father's policy of not investigating the New Christians and their religious practices.

As to your last letter, your idea about the stones is quite correct. I will begin now to ship larger and larger amounts to you. I'm so glad everything is going so well for our business in Antwerp. I suspect the day is not far distant when we will all be joining you, as a matter of life or death. Pray for us,

Shalom, Francisco

****

Late on a Friday afternoon, an hour before the Jewish Sabbath would begin, the Nasi family and the Mendes family secretly gathered in the synagogue beneath Francisco's home. Diogo had returned from Antwerp for the occasion and had agreed, after his brother's coaxing and coaching, to assist in the Jewish marriage of Francisco and Beatriz.

The *ketubah* was prepared following Spanish Jewish custom, defining the financial, emotional, and personal obligations of Francisco, as the husband, to Beatriz. It was his contract to her for life. He signed the *ketubah* with Diogo and Daniel also signing as witnesses.

They would be married publicly the next day at the great cathedral, in a splendid ceremony befitting two of the most illustrious families of Lisbon. But in their heart of hearts, that ceremony would be a sham. This ceremony, the one taking place under the *chuppah* was their real wedding, their dedication to live a life together according to the Law of Moses.

Beatriz had chosen to wear her mother's wedding gown, a confection of finest silk moiré garnished with Burano lace and embroidered with tiny seed pearls. Francisco was dressed in a splendid black velvet doublet with heavy lace ruffles.

Following tradition, they stood under the *chuppah* flanked by Beatriz' parents and Francisco's mother, Deborah. Standing immediately behind the couple were Beatriz' sister, Brianda, and her brother Samuel with his wife, Judith.

Solemnly, Diogo read the *ketubah*, Francisco's vows to Beatriz, and at the end gave it to her for save keeping. Francisco kissed her amidst cheers and tearful eyes. Then, they went back through the dark tunnel, back up to Francisco's hidden library door, and into the dining room where a magnificent Sabbath dinner awaited them.

As they passed through the library, Beatriz squeezed Francisco's hand. "I can't believe it. We're really married. Finally."

"Finally and forever," he murmured as he kissed her hand and marveled once again that this gorgeous woman loved him. He smiled inwardly, thinking of Diogo's comment the evening before. "Who would believe that sassy, smart-mouthed kid would become such a magnificent woman? And that she would fall for an old man like you!" Perhaps, he mused, Diogo felt a bit of jealousy when he saw Beatriz for the first time in more than seven years. She was the kind of woman who dazzled every man, who stopped conversation when she entered a room. She walked in an aura of resplendent beauty, a kind of beauty which radiated from within, magnified geometrically by the fine clothing she designed herself to accentuate her God-given loveliness. A cherished, carefully-nurtured child, some might even have said spoiled, she had grown into a woman who captivated everyone with the combined forces of her beauty, her intellect, and her obvious goodness.

"How lucky I feel this moment," he whispered in her ear as he seated her to his right at the long dining table then signaled to the butler to pour the wine.

Throughout the dinner Francisco raised his glass to toast Rachel and Daniel who had produced his beautiful bride, his brother Diogo for coming all the way from Antwerp, and his new in-laws, Samuel who was currently the doctor to King John, and Beatriz' younger sister, Brianda. Always close, the families were again, as they had been over the centuries, united by marriage.

Finally, after desert had been served, he announced that he had never been so "perfectly happy in his entire life as he was at that moment," but Diogo promptly brought down the house with laughter when he said, "Wait an hour. I'll bet an hour from now you'll be feeling even better." It was, of course, no secret that the bridal couple would consummate their marriage that evening, not waiting for the blessings of the hated Catholic Church.

****

Francisco discussed the latest news about King John as he rode with Beatriz through the street leading to his fourth warehouse. She rode beside him, preferring the exercise of riding to playing the prominent "lady" in a carriage. "John's fanatical hatred for our people will eventually become an inquisition, even if it isn't called that."

"Is there anything we can do to stop it, or at least buy time?" she asked.

"Yes," Francisco answered grimly, halting his horse at the rear door of the warehouse. "We can begin, slowly and under cover, to move our people elsewhere in the world. And we can prepare an escape plan for our own family. And we can continue to bribe the pope."

"We are bribing the pope then. I suspected as much."

"Smart lady, Beatriz. But the less you know about that, the better."

"We, you and I, seem to be prime targets of John's malevolence."

"Yes," he answered, assisting her off her horse. "And if we don't actually commit any crimes, break any of his rules, he'll probably find a way to invent an infraction to charge us with."

Beatriz followed her husband into the warehouse, into his private office where she knew he kept the most precious jewels in a hidden vault. Their project for this morning was to prepare a shipment, which would leave that afternoon on one of their ships destined for Diogo in Antwerp, with a stop first in England. Francisco had agreed to loan the English crown a large sum of money. It was being transferred to London in this shipment.

She sat at the desk, which was now her base of operations, and began going over the bill of lading with meticulous care. This was the part of Francisco's business she enjoyed the most. As she opened the ledger book, she reminded herself once again how lucky she was that he shared so much with her, that he had never expected her to be happy supervising a household. Now, if only she would become pregnant, she could give him the ultimate gift, a child to continue in his footsteps.

June 10, 1531
Dear Diogo,

In answer to your last letter, Beatriz has tragically suffered another miscarriage. This makes three, and with each passing year our doubts grow stronger that we will ever have a child. You can imagine how unhappy this makes her, she blames herself, and I blame myself. I tend to think my age has something to do with it. Who knows? Perhaps it is simply God's will. Nevertheless, that is our major sadness. Otherwise, personally, we love each other more with each passing day. She is truly the shining star in my firmament.

As to the political situation, it's getting more out of hand every day. And yet I cannot bring myself to uproot my entire family, all my employees whose welfare I must be concerned with, and flee in the middle of the night. I don't even care about the wealth we would leave behind, as you have plenty there to support all of us, but the idea of uprooting all these families...Yet, it might come to that eventually.

My informants tell me that a few months ago John sent his ambassador to Rome with instructions to request permission to establish a formal Inquisition in Portugal, based on the Spanish model. Only John wants complete control over all of it; he wants to name the Grand Inquisitor, and make all the rules.

We have countered by sending Diogo Pires, a professing Jew who luckily has the ear of the pope and the College of Cardinals, a substantial sum of money with which to "convince" the pope and cardinals what folly an Inquisition in Portugal would be. Pires suspects, however, that Cardinal Pucci might also be taking money from John III, and if so, Pucci might be swayed finally by who put the most money into his greedy pockets.

Only Beatriz knows how much I've contributed to this effort; it is my main "charity!"

When I think of the grandeur that was Portugal during the reign of Manuel, I feel like weeping. We were the greatest country in the world then, only a few years ago. Now we are in severe decline, overloaded with public debt, taxes, unable to educate our children or provide for their health. I sometimes wonder if John III realizes what he would lose if all the Jews were simply to leave; the leaders of industry, men devoted to the cultivation of science, skilled artisans, and most importantly enormous sums of money would leave the country.

The guarantees Manuel gave us for individual security and material immunity and safety from religious persecution, expire in 1534. I don't have any illusions that John III will renew them; rather, I think by then he will have succeeded in Rome, and we will have an official Inquisition here in Portugal.

I am most truly sorry to give you all this dreadful news, Diogo, but more and more I need to move our business interests into your capable hands in Antwerp. It seems to me that it is the only sensible thing to do.

Now about you: when are you going to tell me you've found yourself a Beatriz? Nothing would make me happier than to know you are experiencing the happy family life that has come to me so late in life. God love you and bless you, my dear brother.

Shalom, Francisco

Chapter Eight

The Vatican Vacillates
Lisbon—June 14, 1532

"We have nothing to look forward to here but death! That's what this all comes down to," Francisco shouted as he paced back and forth at the foot of Beatriz' bed, waving the papers he had torn from the front of his warehouse that afternoon. "I can't believe John can double-cross us like this, after all the guarantees his father made! He's a madman."

Beatriz propped herself up a bit more on her linen pillows, took a deep breath, trying to calm the deep pit of fear which was rising in her stomach, making her once more nauseous. "Surely, with money in the proper hands, Francisco, you can get us out of here..."

"It may be too late. We're already being watched by the king's spies." He saw the look on her face and regretted mentioning the spies. It would only frighten her and that wasn't good for her in her condition.

"We should have left last December when you first heard about the pope's treacherous decision."

"I couldn't leave then, leave all my employees, men who I've known since they were children in my school..."

"Thank God you've gotten most of them out."

"Yes," he said, sitting down on the bed beside her and taking her hand. "Fifty-four families. At least I've saved those lives."

"I'm afraid," she said. He could see that she was trembling; her hand was icy. "The king must be suspicious of all those warehouses you've closed."

"He has six guards posted around the clock at the last one," he said, deciding it was best not to hide anything from her. She was clever enough to find out for herself, far too clever for her own good. "I can't see trying to escape with you pregnant."

She was silent for a long time.

"What exactly does the new law say?" she asked finally, reaching for the papers in his hands.

As she read, he stood and paced again, explaining each provision.

"Basically, it prohibits anyone with any Hebrew blood to leave the country for any reason. Anyone who tries to escape will be killed and all his worldly goods be confiscated by the government."

"Sounds to me like John has us specifically in mind."

"Yes, and we must be careful not to endanger our employees. Any captain or master of ships that carries Hebrews out of Portugal will be condemned to death. Any New Christian who sends money or property out of the country is subject to banishment and confiscation of all remaining property."

He stopped pacing long enough to look at her. Her face was ghastly white. Her lips were trembling. She whispered, "We endanger ourselves with every move we make, every word we speak, even in the privacy of our homes. Darling, I'm terrified, and I'm angry!"

He bent over and kissed her forehead, "I want you to be angry, angry and strong!"

He paced back to the window and continued. "The law sets up a whole court system to deal with New Christians who are caught following the old Jewish ways." It was as if he was venting his anger at some unseen agent of the king and he wanted Beatriz to understand his anger at the king.

"Portugal has become a prison for us," she said, her voice scarcely above a whisper.

"Sooner or later John will fabricate some reason to have us arrested and tried before the Grand Inquisitor!"

Tears streamed down Beatriz' face. "Oh, Francisco, what shall we do?"

Francisco sat on the bed beside her and patted the swelling of her abdomen, then kissed her eyelids. "You and I, we could be so happy, so perfectly happy," he said softly.

Beatriz caressed his hand with hers. He knew she was worried about the baby, just as he was. It was the first time she had passed the two month mark, if she didn't miscarry for one more month the chances were good that she might actually produce the child they longed for. Ever since she realized she was pregnant she had stayed in bed for most of the day, trying to prevent another miscarriage. Now he'd given her this terrible news, this news they had known was coming, yet hoped somehow would be annulled.

"I want you to promise me something," Francisco said, standing and pacing again. "I want you to promise me you will never remarry if I'm killed, or burned at the stake, or whatever..." He turned and looked at her, his eyes watering. "I know you are a normal young woman, you enjoy the pleasures of the bed. And I wouldn't for a minute deny that to you. But don't remarry. Take lovers instead."

He saw the shock on her face but silenced her before she could speak. "Hear me out. If you marry, the control of the House of Mendes will fall into the hands of your new husband. If you simply take lovers, you'll always control your own wealth. In wealth there is power. Never forget that. Never surrender that power to any other person."

"I can't believe you, a rabbi of your people, could advise something like that!" She sounded both stunned and angry.

"Don't forget, we Jews are above all, a practical people. Survival is what's at issue here. And for you to survive in the cold hard world out there, you're going to need all the wealth and power you can accumulate. Don't ever surrender that to anyone, not even a member of your family. I say this, Beatriz, because I care more than anything else, what happens to you. You are the dearest treasure of my life. I must find a way to save you from the fire that's about to consume this country."

"No, darling, you must find a way to save us all. Us, our baby, our parents, my brother Samuel and his family, and my sister, Brianda."

Francisco made an ugly face. "Above all, don't trust that mindless sister of yours. She hates you, mark my words. I've seen the way she looks at you."

"Don't be silly, Francisco. She's my little sister, she's simply jealous of all I have. She wants a man like you. How can you even imagine she hates me? That's ridiculous."

"Don't ever forget, I warned you about her."

"What are you going to do next?" Beatriz asked, handing the papers back to him.

"I'm slowly going to get the rest of my employees out of Lisbon, then somehow, I'm going to get our family out. Meanwhile, we've got people in Rome who are trying to persuade the Pope to rescind the Bull. Diogo, himself, may go pay a visit to His Holiness, if we can set up an audience. The key, we all know, is money. The Vatican always needs more money, of that you can be sure."

****

June 17, 1534
Dear Diogo,

It's late at night as I take pen in hand to tell you the latest from Rome. But first, in answer to your letter, every day little baby Reyna looks more like her beautiful mother and shows every sign of being equally intelligent. She brings great joy to our life, though some days

I wonder at the wisdom of increasing the numbers of our people. To what end? Only more persecution, only more uncertainty.

Pope Clement VII is genuinely compassionate when it comes to the plight of the Jews of Portugal. I know he's written John ordering him to obey the provisions of the Bull of April 7, and he's also asked the king to annul the law forbidding us to leave the country. The king has responded by implying that the pope has received enormous bribes from the Jews, (which, of course, is true).

I think for the time being it's wise to keep most of our money and jewels in Antwerp with you. If I need anything, I'll let you know. Meanwhile, dare I say it..."Keep the faith!" Beatriz and little Reyna send you their love.

With affection and respect, Francisco

****

"Four months of relative peace of mind, and now this!" Daniel shouted as he waved a copy of the order Francisco had received by courier from his agent, Duarte da Paz, in Rome.

"You're the doctor," Francisco responded. "Do you think the pope was poisoned, as Duarte suggests?"

"Impossible to tell without having examined him, but face it, Francisco, the pope was younger than you are. Only fifty-six. Bad stomach pains for three months, now he's dead." Daniel sat down across from Francisco. "I suspect some sort of slow acting poison was being fed to him on a daily basis. But who's to know for certain?"

Francisco continued stacking manuscripts and tying them in bundles. The two old friends were secluded in his fourth floor library. "And, as Duarte says, thirty-six devils in red hats have elected a seventy-year-old man, a model of celibacy, mind you, a man with two bastard children and four grandchildren, and made him Pope Paul III."

"Do we know how he feels about the Jews?" Daniel asked.

"No. But we have reason to believe he'll listen to the recommendation of Clement VII and 'protect this miserable people'. Surely he's cognizant of the gifts we've made to the Holy See."

"What does your intuition tell you?"

Francisco sat down behind his oak desk and sighed, rubbed his eyes, then folded his hands in front of his face. After thinking for a few moments, he looked at Daniel with weary, sad eyes. "I'm so sick of all this bribery business. All we Jews want is to live, quietly, peacefully with our neighbors. Someplace in the world where we can be safe and sleep soundly at night. We must move our families to Antwerp..."

"I was afraid you'd say that."

"I'm old and tired, too old to pull up roots and leave, but I've got to think of Beatriz and Reyna."

"And I'm concerned for my children and grandchildren too."

"Charles V may decided to side with King John, and conveniently forget that the House of Mendes loaned him one-hundred-thousand *cruzados* only a year ago. No head of state has the influence Charles has on the Holy See. It's only a matter of time before Paul III will suspend the Bull of April 7 that stopped the Inquisition."

Daniel sadly nodded his agreement.

Francisco tied a bundle of manuscripts into a package, then continued, "That's why I'm sending my books and manuscripts to Antwerp, and I've told Beatriz to pack her fine linens and china. Little by little, we'll ship the things we value to Diogo. We're going to have to flee for our lives, but we might as well take as much with us as we can."

****

Beatriz rushed up the three flights of stairs, holding tightly to the wax-sealed envelope their courier had brought from dockside. She recognized the seal of Duarte da Paz. But even as she knocked softly on Francisco's study, she felt her heart pounding in her temples. She so hoped for something positive, some bit of good news to cheer her ailing husband. He'd been suffering so much lately: pounding chest and jaw pain in the middle of the night, insomnia, weight loss, and he was always out of breath. Lately his clothes had begun to appear big on him, she'd called the tailor to come refit his favorite tunics and doublets. She worried about his health, just as she fretted over his elderly mother Deborah's health. Both of them were distraught over what was happening to the Jews in the outlying provinces of Portugal.

Almost daily they received news of new arrests and tortures, new sentences of life imprisonment and confiscation of property of the New Christians. And the pope seemed reluctant to enforce what he claimed was his position on persecution of the Hebrew people.

She heard her husband's weak voice call out, "Come in." Taking a deep breath, she opened the door and carried the sealed envelope to him. He was lying on the upholstered bench she had moved into his study, reading one of his favorite passages from the Torah. His complexion grew grayer, or was that only her imagination, as he recognized the seal on the letter.

She handed him a paper knife from his desk while he shifted into a sitting position. He invited her to sit next to him, to share the contents of this latest communication.

"After all, my darling, I've been trying to teach you everything I've stored in my brain through all these years of living. I must share this travail too, because it's only a question of time before you will have to take the responsibility and make the decisions."

"Don't speak that way, Francisco, I beg you."

"My darling," he patted her arm, then put his arm around her shoulders, "when you inherit the House of Mendes you will become the world's wealthiest and most powerful widow. That kind of power can either corrupt you or turn you into one of the world's great heroines. I prefer the latter. So I must share with you everything I know, everything I suspect. I must, unfortunately teach you to be devious for you to survive." He unfolded the thick letter and began to read aloud:

"Duarte writes on August 15, 1535, ten days ago." Francisco scanned the first page, and then handed the letter to Beatriz. "You read it aloud, that way we can both know what he's saying I must lie back down again, my chest hurts..."

Beatriz pulled a chair close to his bench, and then proceeded to read.

My dear Francisco,

At long last I have made substantial progress that I hope will be permanent, or at least as permanent as anything can be in this world of political intrigues.

Pope Paul III is now thoroughly persuaded of the corruption of King John. He also understands that John is a genuine fanatic, unlike, for example, Henry VIII who merely wants to satisfy his appetite for a new wife every now and then.

Nevertheless, the actions of the English king have clouded the pope's dealing with the Portuguese king. Paul lives in fear that John might proclaim a Church of Portugal in the same way Henry has confiscated all the Catholic property in England and proclaim that he is the head of both the church and state.

What we are witnessing is a grand battle between the power of the Holy Roman Catholic Church and the power of the state, every state in Europe that has any Catholic population at all.

The pope has offered King John these options: first, the cessation of confiscations of property from the New Christians and an end to the trials for heresy. If the king rejects this, then the pope will grant him an Inquisition, with the caveat that all those accused have the right to appeal to the nuncio (whom the pope himself will appoint) and to leave Portugal and come to Rome to argue their cases. Finally, the pope offered a third option. He recommended to John that he grant a general and absolute pardon of all converts, whether at-large or prisoners, and give them one year to freely leave Portugal, taking their possessions and wealth with them. After that year has passed, the king will be free to establish the Inquisition on whatever terms he desires.

The pope now believes that the initial conversion by violent force in 1497 was a travesty, that no New Christian or his descendants should be held to that forced conversion. Pope Paul III believes that Jews should be free to resume the public practice of their religion. However, he's willing to concede that if King John wants to remove them from his kingdom, he should give them the term of one year to leave, and then begin his Inquisition.

My information is that the king has rejected all three options, and is still arguing for an Inquisition on his terms. So the debate continues, ad nauseam. My guess is that the next ploy will be to get Charles V to bring his irresistible influence to bear on Pope Paul III.

The pope's position on the New Christians being permitted to leave Portugal is the one issue I don't think he will ever waver on, no matter what. At the moment, the matter is at an impasse. This can continue indefinitely, unless the king decides to break with the Vatican completely and do what Henry VIII has done. Meanwhile, he's been threatened with excommunication by the pope if he continues to arrest and torture the New Christians. Things are definitely stalemated.

My best wishes to your lovely wife and daughter. I saw Diogo three weeks ago in Antwerp, and he is the picture of robust health and well-being. He, too, is contributing to our cause magnificently.

Sincerely, Duarte la Paz

"Surely this is good news, isn't it, Francisco?" Beatriz asked as she folded the letter and placed it on Francisco's desk.

Francisco smiled weakly, and took Beatriz hand in his own. She was alarmed at how sweaty his palm was. She reached for his forehead, but it was cool to her touch.

Francisco answered, "I'm beginning to think of Pope Paul as a splendid, rational and pragmatic leader. He's a strong voice on our behalf at the Vatican. I only hope he sticks to his principles against pressure from John and possibly Charles."

Though they were momentarily relieved of severe anxiety, Beatriz continued to wake each morning with a deep pit of fear in her stomach, even as she continued to help Francisco pack their most cherished belongings. They dared not let the servants suspect their plans, so they packed in the evening after the servants had retired or gone to their own homes. After the clock chimed eleven at night, two stevedores knocked on the fake doors in their first-floor library, were escorted to the fourth floor library, and from there removed the packages, barrels and crates and carried them to the warehouse and from there to waiting ships, bound for Antwerp.

****

Conscious of the fact that he was known to be exceptionally close to Pope Paul III, Beatriz and Francisco personally greeted the Bishop of Sinigaglia with a great show of deference at the front door of their home. Though they'd met him many times socially and watched him preside at marriages and christening of Portugal's most elite citizens, they had never before been requested to receive him privately in their home. They knew he was leaving for Rome in two days, and this meeting could only have to do with the pope's rumored indecision on revoking his Bull of October 12, 1535, which effectively nullified the Inquisition in Portugal.

He was a tall man, Beatriz thought again as she ushered him into her drawing room, overweight and with the ruddy complexion and blood-streaked eyes of a man who overindulged in spirits. After they had exchanged pleasantries and accepted the obligatory glass of sherry from the butler, Francisco told the Bishop that his wife Beatriz, "who is also my business partner these days," would remain and participate in their conversation. Beatriz understood that in addition to being his partner, she was also serving as a witness to whatever dirty business the bishop intended to transact with her husband.

The bishop cleared his throat, indicating that the small talk was finished. "Your people," he began, "promised in writing certain payments in exchange for the Bull of October, for no Inquisition. I've come to you to collect, Francisco, since you are chief of the Hebrews."

Beatriz watched the color rise in her husband's face. "Exactly who made these promises in writing?"

"Your attorney in Rome, Duarte de Paz."

"How much did he promise?"

"Thirty-thousand escudos."

Francisco rose from his chair, his face now burning with anger. "That's obscene!" he shouted at the Bishop, causing the old man to blanche as if physically hit. "There is no way the Hebrews in Lisbon could raise that kind of money. And I find it reprehensible that you have the nerve to come here, you an ordained man of God, requiring us to pay money to the pope for the right merely to continue to exist. We've met every requirement, we've converted, we follow the rules of the Catholic Church, we receive the sacraments. Now you are extorting these utterly outrageous sums of money."

Beatriz could barely keep a straight face as she watched Francisco perform, posturing about the sum of money, which, considering what they had already invested, was a relatively small amount.

"Francisco," Beatriz interrupted, "perhaps the Holy See would accept a smaller payment with the promise of more money in the future."

The bishop smiled gratefully at Beatriz.

"Nonsense. There will be no end to this kind of extortion. They will keep us on tenterhooks for the next hundred years."

"It is not difficult," the bishop interjected in a sarcastic tone of voice, "to imagine the populace getting out of control again like they did in 1506..."

Francisco wheeled on the bishop, nearly striking out. "Is that a threat?"

"No, no my good man. Calm down. I'm merely repeating some of the things my parish priests report to me. There's a lot of anger against the Jews out there in the countryside. It's not impossible that things could get out of hand again."

"Indeed. Especially if the Dominicans and Franciscans continue preaching their hate-filled sermons. Why don't you do your job and discipline your preachers?"

"We try to, my dear man. But it's difficult to keep the populace under control when they see the Hebrew people possessing all the money and business and so on..."

Wearily, Francisco sat down again. "So, how much money will it take to keep the pope true to his own conscience, to keep him from buckling under to Charles V?"

"The sum mentioned to me was thirty-thousand escudos."

"Preposterous! Out of the question." Slowly, reluctantly, Francisco reached inside his tunic and pulled out an envelope.

The bishop's eyes were riveted to the envelope, a look of cold greed shining through.

Beatriz knew exactly how much money was in the envelope; she had counted it out for Francisco that morning, taken it from their special hiding place in the caverns that had been dug deep under their house.

Slowly, Francisco handed the envelope to the bishop. "This is a down-payment, my own money, five thousand escudos for Pope Paul III. He can expect a similar amount a year from now if he keeps his word and does not nullify the Bull of October 12."

"Will you put that in writing?"

"No, but you have my word. And I'm known as a man of my word. And you have my wife Beatriz as witness. That's all the guarantee you need. I'm sure the pope will understand. To have something in writing is as dangerous for him as it is for us."

"Ah! Perhaps you are correct. I shall give this to the pope and we shall see what he decides. In the meantime, I wish you and your family the best."

After they had closed the door on the bishop, Francisco laughed aloud with both anger and sarcasm in his voice. "Did you notice how quickly he wanted to leave once he got that packet of money in his hands? The dirty bastard, they're all greedy venal men, hardly what I'd call princes of the Church. Remember that, my darling, Beatriz. Remember that in your future dealings with Rome."

Chapter Nine

Death Comes To Dinner
April, 1536

"I feel dreadful that I'm going to miss Father's birthday dinner, but at least he'll have you there, his oldest, truest friend." Beatriz' voice was harsh, and she coughed each time she spoke. Her entire body was feverish and she felt miserable. She watched him button the last button on his shirt.

Brianda had the same symptoms so their father, Dr. Daniel Nasi, had forbidden them to come out in the cold, even for his birthday dinner. Instead, her brother Samuel had brought his two sons, also afflicted with the malady, which their father called the grippe, to the Mendes residence so that they might entertain one another when they felt well enough to be out of bed.

Samuel's oldest son, Joseph, now sixteen, especially enjoyed the company of his Aunt Beatriz because she was deadly competition at the chess board. And none of his own peers could beat him.

While those who were well in the two families would celebrate Daniel's birthday a block away at the Nasi home, those who were sick would congregate at the Mendes home to feast on chicken soup and dumplings and Beatriz' cook's mouth-watering apple tart. "Heaven knows we could all use some cheer these days," Francisco said, combing his sparse white hair in place. "What with Samuel having been fired by the king and Daniel relieved of his duties at the hospital..."

"Why is the king suddenly angry with my family? Do you have any clue?" Beatriz asked, as she took her handkerchief out of her sleeve to wipe her nose again.

Francisco sat down beside her on the bed. He reached over and felt her forehead. "Still a bit feverish."

"You're avoiding my question, darling. That's not like you."

"My guess," he began, "only a hunch, mind you, is that he's somehow gotten wind of the five-thousand *escudos* I gave the bishop a couple of months ago. The king's got more spies at the Vatican than we do. Sooner or later he's sure to find out."

"So he's getting back at you by hurting my father and brother?"

"He's always been aware of our close friendship, ever since his father attended your parent's wedding reception. Everyone knows how close we are."

"An envelope full of escudos could have come from anyone. Now, I understand why you refused to put anything in writing like the bishop wanted. That would have been hard evidence."

"Exactly. Nonetheless, I'm expecting personal retribution from John. He'll find a way to get to us..."

Beatriz reached for her husband's face and pulled him toward her. "I love you so. I admire you so..."

Francisco looked weary and elderly, she thought, as she watched him stand up, straighten his clothing, and walk toward the fireplace with a slight limp. She knew that his bones and muscles never ceased to ache, and he tried hard not to complain.

"I'll be glad when the weather warms up a bit. Your pains don't bother you as much in the summer," she said, thinking she might have good news for him as summer approached, something to take his mind off the constant threats from the king and the pope.

He stoked the fire slowly then turned back to her. "It's time for me to go. I'll give your parents your love; meanwhile you keep our little one well. So far, luckily, she's escaped the grippe."

"It certainly seems that way," Beatriz answered, sitting up in bed and reaching for a heavy dressing gown. "In fact, I'll go check with her nanny and see what the little princess is up to this afternoon. She's probably reading, as usual. Have you ever heard of a child reading this young?"

"She's a genius, like her mother. Haven't you figured that out yet?"

"Let me walk with you down to the door, I'm really feeling quite a bit better now."

"No, darling, go look in on little Reyna. That's more important. Save your strength. I'll be back in a few hours. I'll try not to wake you."

"Oh, do wake me! I want to hear all about my father's party."

Beatriz watched as her husband limped toward the staircase, and then she turned toward the nursery. She had a nagging, hurting feeling in the back of her throat, a dreadful emotion about to bubble up, a return of the constant fear they lived with night and day. "God protect him," she whispered as she entered little Reyna's nursery.

****

Francisco felt mellow and happy as he watched and listened to his extended family at the table. He had decreed early in the evening that there would be no discussion of problems, only memories of happy times as they celebrated Daniel's long and healthy life. The three women were dressed in their finest new gowns made from fabrics he'd imported from Venice. His elderly mother Deborah wore black silk moiré edged in white Venetian lace. Rachel Nasi, nearly sixty, had chosen blue the color of a robin's egg and enhanced it with creamy lace collar and cuffs. Judith, the young wife of the young doctor Samuel, recently fired by the king, wore peach silk embellished with matching peach-colored lace.

Not to be outdone by the women, the elder doctor Nasi, Daniel, chose a navy velvet doublet while his son, the young doctor Nasi, wore forest green. They were an impressive lot, Francisco thought. All of them exuded confidence, affluence, education and refinement. *The best Lisbon has to offer,* he told himself as he placed his silver fork and knife on top of the cream and gold dinner plate.

Alfonso and Julius, substitute waiters who'd arrived that morning with news that Ernesto, the Nasi's long-time butler, was suffering from the grippe, immediately removed the dinner plates and silver. While they were in the room, the family conversation either stopped completely, or reverted to discussion of the weather and the newest stock in Francisco's warehouse. Through decades of servants' betrayals, Jews learned to speak very carefully when servants were in the room.

Moments later Alfonso arrived carrying a large silver tray with six spectacular hand-blown Murano goblets, each a different color, filled with deep red wine, a gift from Francisco's wine cellar. As the waiter walked around the table, giving each guest a goblet of wine, the women oohed and aahed over the magnificent goblets.

"I sent eighty to King John this week, and kept a dozen for myself and Beatriz, and decided that Daniel and Rachel should also have a dozen, as a birthday gift. I hope you enjoy them in good health," he added as he took the first sip of the wine.

It was a deep red port with overtones of berries and plums, he decided. But he was disappointed with the aftertaste; it was a bit too acidic.

He launched into the obligatory toasts: first, to the king. Then to the Pope, and finally to the Holy Roman Emperor. These toasts he proclaimed largely for the benefit of the servants who would report far and wide on the patriotism and religious zeal of the Mendes and Nasi families. After each name, everyone dutifully sipped, their faces filled with sarcasm and sneers.

Now for the real toasts. "To you, my dear mother, who guided us across the plains of Spain to this country where we have prospered beyond our wildest imaginations. We love you." Everyone enthusiastically cheered and sipped on their wine.

"To my oldest and closest friend, my boyhood nemesis, the only one who could ever beat me at chess...our two families go back to the thirteenth century when your illustrious ancestor Joseph Nasi de Ecija, a famous Jewish courtier and financier in the Castilian Court of Alfonso XI, loaned money to King Alfonso as well as Christian merchants. He was called "the richest man in the world," at that time. And if my instincts are correct, your beloved eldest grandson will follow in his footsteps. Diogo tells me that he has never seen such a quick mind for finances as that of your sixteen-year-old, Joseph. Who, by the way, is a great favorite of mine. To you, Daniel, a happy birthday. You should be a very happy and satisfied man this evening. I only hope that Beatriz and I are blessed with a son soon."

Francisco stopped, sipped his wine, and, assured that none of the servants could hear him, he added, "Regardless of her condition, the winds of early May look promising for shipping, we must be ready to..."

Deborah began choking which turned to vomiting. Daniel, seeing her face become blue, rushed to her aid and tried to loosen the tight ruffle around her throat. Rachel went to her side, but no sooner had she reached her than she began choking herself. She sat down on the floor, vomited a bloody mess over her blue gown, then began to clutch her stomach and wail in pain. Judith and Samuel ran over to assist Daniel, but within seconds both Judith and Daniel began to vomit blood and cry out in pain.

Francisco unsheathed his dagger and strode toward the kitchen. "We've been poisoned!" he bellowed, as he swung open the door to the pantry. *Why didn't I object to those two strangers serving us?* He chided himself as he walked through the pantry, now empty, and outdoors to the kitchen.

Three women lay bound and gagged, stabbed with multiple wounds, on the earthen floor of the kitchen. Their blood flowed over the ground. Francisco knelt beside each one and felt for a pulse. They were dead.

He stood, wiped his hand on his doublet, and walked back into the house through the pantry. As he stood in the doorway and looked at the carnage, his dagger still in his hand, he thought, *now I know where I've seen that man before. Alfonso...one of the king's men...*

He clutched his abdomen as fierce cramps doubled him over at the waist. His throat erupted. Blood and food and wine flooded the floor. He collapsed onto the floor, his face on the fine Persian carpet. His last thoughts were of his Gracia. *She is strong, she will prevail.*

****

Homero rolled over, clutched the pillow, and awoke. It took him a moment to realize where he was, on the bed in the guest bedroom at the Nasi home. The house was silent. Had he slept through dinner? Where was Don Francisco? Had he already left for home?

He stood up, straightened his clothes, smoothed his hair, and quietly walked down the back stairs into the pantry. He castigated himself on the way down, he should have never left the dinner to those two new waiters. What did they know about his families? Well, at least the two serving girls knew the preferences of his mistress.

The first thing he saw was the body of Don Francisco, half in the pantry and half in the dining room. His dagger laid where he had fallen, in a pool of vomit and blood, blood streamed from his nose, his mouth, his ears.

Homero stood transfixed in shock, unable for a long minute to comprehend what he was looking at. A mass murder. Dr. and Mrs. Samuel Nasi, Dr. and Mrs. Daniel Nasi, Don Francisco's mother, all dead, all lying in vomit and blood, their eyes open in shock and horror.

How will I ever tell Señora Beatriz?

He stifled the thought of fleeing; he struggled with his own queasiness. He wanted to run, oh, so badly he wanted to run.

****

It seemed Beatriz had just fallen asleep when she heard sharp knocking on her door. "Señora, Señora, you must come quickly!" She recognized the voice of Homero, their butler, who doubled as a driver when her husband took a carriage.

"What is it?" she called, fear clutching her stomach, her immediate thought was that Francisco must be ill.

As she grabbed for a dressing gown, her door burst open and Homero ran in following by two sobbing servants. Homero's cloak was bloody.

"They're all..."

"Calm down," she ordered in a stern voice, fastening her gown. "What's happened?"

"Murdered! Everyone's been assassinated." Homero reached for her arm and began to guide her toward the door. "Everyone."

She stopped dead still and forced him to look at her. "Now, Homero, take a deep breath. There. Now, tell me exactly what happened."

Dear God, she thought, needing to steady herself *help me be strong. Help me stand up to whatever endangers my family.*

"Your father and mother, your brother and his wife, Don Francisco, his mother...all assassinated...at the table."

She felt stunned, as if she'd been struck a blow.

"How? Were they stabbed? Where were you? Where were all the other servants?"

"Come. You must come with me, back to the house. See for yourself. Everyone is dead."

"Who murdered them?"

"I...I don't know, Señora. The scene in the kitchen..." Homero broke into sobs.

Beatriz knew she had to keep her wits about her. That's what Francisco would want. She guided him toward a bench and made him sit down. She turned to one of the sobbing women servants.

"Anna, go awaken Joseph and ask him to dress and meet me immediately. We must go to my parents' home. Hurry now!"

Beatriz rushed to her dressing room and quickly threw on heavy clothing, then returned to a sobbing Homero.

"...everyone in the kitchen was stabbed. Many times."

"And the people at the table in the dining room?"

"No, they were not stabbed. They are all collapsed on the floor. I don't know..."

Beatriz turned to the remaining maid servant. "Go quickly, and bring all the bed linens from the closet. You, Homero, go get two carriages ready. We will bring the bodies back here."

"Should I go for the police?"

"No. Not until I see for myself what has happened." She slipped a dagger under her cloak, thinking that all her training in fencing while she was a student in Francisco's school might be needed. "We'll take all the servants, leave my sister here with the children."

Nothing Homero had told her prepared her or Joseph for the scene they found at the Nasi home. Her father, Daniel Nasi was crumpled in a heap on the floor next to Deborah's chair. Her mother had obviously rushed to Deborah's aid also, but collapsed herself. Daniel's eyes were still open, his hands at his throat, blood was running out of his eyes and mouth.

Beatriz knelt beside her parents, closed her father's eyelids, then kissed each of them gently. Memories flooded her. Playing the harp for him, his face full of pride and concern as he watched her dance with King John. His glowing approval of her choice of Francisco.

Gently, with great tenderness she closed her mother's eyes. Always her model of beauty and elegance and dignity, she had fashioned herself after her mother. With tears streaming down her face, Beatriz instructed the servants to cover her parents with the linens she brought from her house and carry their corpses to the waiting carriages.

Finally, with a pain in her chest nearly unbearable, she turned to her husband Francisco. She bent over him, nearly lying on top of him and kissed his cheeks, his eyelids, his forehead. His gray beard was matted with drying blood and vomit, his body stank of feces. *I love you, my darling. I will clean you, I will prepare you for burial. I will save our children, our family. I promise you on all that we hold sacred.*

"I must etch this scene on my brain and never forget it," Beatriz said aloud, speaking to herself. She kissed her husband again and held him close, sobbed aloud, then motioned for Homero to take his body away.

Joseph, stifling his own vomit at the scene, tended to his parents Samuel and Judith. "What happened?" Joseph shouted to her, "What killed them?"

Beatriz, concentrating on her own thoughts could barely hear Joseph's screaming. "Father, I will kill the bastards who did this, I will destroy them if it's the only thing I do in my lifetime!" Over and over he said it, aloud and to himself.

Beatriz stood and looked at the table. Dessert had only been served, not yet eaten. Goblets of wine were half-filled; they'd reached that point in the meal where they'd begun toasting one another. Suddenly, everyone had collapsed.

Beatriz reached for the goblet at her husband's place. "I would guess," she answered Joseph in a firm voice, "if this wine is tested it will be found to contain some very strong form of poison." She then poured all the remaining port into one large water glass, taking it with her as evidence.

When all the bodies had been carried out of the dining room, she pulled her dagger out of her cloak, and, with her nephew at her side; they entered the pantry and went out to the kitchen. She thought that one of the servants must have done the poisoning.

But, the scene in the kitchen was just as bad. All three women had been stabbed to death, two from her own household.

It became clear that an intruder had administered the poison and killed the entire staff.

Beatriz turned to Homero. "After you take my family home, come back and bring these bodies home also. We'll prepare them for burial."

Through the long night Beatriz and Joseph and her remaining servants lovingly bathed the dead bodies and wrapped them in clean white shrouds. After Francisco's body was washed and the prayers were said, Beatriz asked to be left alone. She sat beside him, lovingly kissed his lips, his cheeks, his forehead and his closed eyes. She gathered his hand in hers and with tears streaming down her face, she spoke to him. "Francisco, my darling, I have loved you more than life itself. Our love created a beautiful daughter, Reyna, whom I will protect and cherish with all my might, with every ounce of my being. You've left us so much: values and courage, education and wisdom, religious beliefs we will never surrender. I promise you on all we both hold sacred that I will fight for Our People every day that God gives me life. Joseph and Samuel and Reyna and I will dedicate our lives to the House of Mendes and all it stands for. My love, look down on us and give us courage." At that moment she felt his strength pass through his hand into her being, she felt herself suffused with energy and physical strength.

Slowly she stood to her feet, gathered all her strength and wrapped her beloved in his white linen burial shroud.

When that sad task was finished, Beatriz allowed herself the luxury of more tears as she told the horrible tragedy to Brianda, then to twelve-year-old Samuel, her brother's youngest son. Little Reyna was too young to understand death or murder, but she realized something dreadful had happened when her nanny repeatedly shushed her and carried her away from her weeping mother.

Later the next morning the plain pine caskets Beatriz sent for arrived, and as word spread throughout the city of Lisbon, friends, relatives and employees of the House of Mendes began to arrive to offer assistance and condolences.

"We will bury them this afternoon," Beatriz announced to the stunned visitors, "in the ground we own in Belem. We will have our own private burial grounds."

Having commandeered the entire staff of the warehouse as gravediggers, Beatriz led the long line of carriages taking the bodies of her family to the outskirts of Lisbon. She led the prayers at the mass burial, and she was the one who shoveled the first bit of dirt into each grave, followed by her nephews Joseph and Samuel, and finally Brianda. Only when each casket was fully covered with earth, did Beatriz leave the newly consecrated cemetery.

Back at home, late in the evening, she received the police inspector and told him of the gruesome events of the past twenty-four hours. He promised a vigorous investigation, promised to prosecute whoever the villain was that perpetrated these brutal murders. "You need look no further than St. George's Castle," Beatriz answered stoically. The villain who masterminded these murders is even now gloating over his victory over the House of Mendes. But we shall see who has the last laugh!"

The inspector gave a helpless shrug. He would have liked to find justice for the grieving widow, but if she was right... If the king's men were involved, well, there was no use...

When the inspector and all the mourners finally left, after one in the morning, more than twenty-four hours since Beatriz last slept, she retired to her bedroom and unlaced her corset. It was then she discovered she was bleeding; it was then she felt the beginning of abdominal cramps.

Tears burned in her eyes as she felt the hot blood dribble down her legs. This too she would lose, this baby she'd so hoped would be a welcome surprise for Francisco.

Chapter Ten

Escape
Lisbon, Portugal—April, 1536

Beatriz closed the door of the guest bedroom where her sister Brianda had been staying for the past two months. Then, carrying a small lantern for light, she made her way down to the servants' quarters off the kitchen. Her housekeeper, cook, two maids and the coachman were sitting in their common room, sipping tea, playing dominoes, and gossiping. She could see that they were startled by her knock, but they quickly rose to their feet to greet her.

"I'm sorry to disturb you." She stopped, reminding herself to make her eyes teary and her voice wobbly, reminding herself that her story wasn't so preposterous; the Plague has infected all of Portugal. "I have terrible news. Brianda is ill."

The news was greeted with gasps and cries of "No, no!"

Teresa, the housekeeper, pulled her handkerchief out of her bosom to wipe away the tears that were forming in her eyes.

Deliberately, Beatriz paused, looking from face to face, letting the news sink in. She thought again of her enemies, King John, and Pope Paul. They were stalemated on the question of establishing an Inquisition in Portugal. It was only a question of time, perhaps days.

Then she began her carefully prepared speech. "My beloved late husband and my late brother of Blessed Memory taught me much about medicine, about taking care of people with..." Again, she paused for dramatic effect, not wanting to say the dreaded word. God forgive me for these lies, she thought, then continued. "They told me I must protect you as well as my family, so I've prepared these." From the pocket in her voluminous skirt she pulled small bags of gold coins and began distributing them. "I want you to go to your families, stay at least ten days, until the danger is over. This will tide you over." And then some, she thought, thinking of the generous stipend she was giving each of them.

She turned to the coachman, handing him a small sign prepared in her own handwriting: "Warning: Do not enter, plague in this house!"

"Homero, attach this to the front door before you leave."

"Are you sure you don't want me to stay and help you nurse Señorita Brianda, Señora?" Teresa asked, wiping away tears.

"No, no. Absolutely not. Joseph and Samuel will help me. You must leave tonight. Don't wait until tomorrow. Go to Mass, light some candles, and pray for Brianda's health. And for my nephews and daughter. Get ready now, hurry, start packing."

Abruptly she turned, afraid that if she watched their stricken faces any longer she would not be able to carry out her plan. These humble people had been so loyal to her family through so much adversity; it was almost cruel to deceive them in this way. But their own lives depended on her lies. She reminded herself that she must retire upstairs to the privacy of her bedroom immediately. She had much to do.

Within minutes after she heard the last of the servants leave, after she heard Homero nail the sign to the door, Beatriz gathered her two nephews, Joseph, who was sixteen and twelve-year-old Samuel, and her sister, Brianda, into her bedroom. They had all, as planned, changed clothes. Beatriz and her sister were dressed in the dark brown baggy pants of deck hands, their long hair hidden beneath tight skull hats, long wool scarves tied around their necks.

Beatriz glanced at herself in the mirror, and saw that the weight she'd lost since the murder of her husband caused her to look like an emaciated, overworked, anemic deckhand, perhaps suffering from rickets. The only problem was her face. The porcelain complexion that she'd inherited from her mother, and was normally so proud of, displayed none of the weather beaten signs of an experienced sailor. She hoped that under the cover of darkness, she'd be able to pass as a man.

Brianda, on the other hand, had the dark olive complexion and dark freckles of their father Daniel, but the ample bosom of their mother Rachel. She had bound her breasts tightly in order to pass as a man. Still, she had to wear a loose shirt, and bind her dark frizzy hair tightly in the skull cap.

Joseph and Samuel were dressed in the ragged clothes of street urchins, their faces smudged with dirt.

"Reyna?" Brianda asked, not seeing Beatriz' two-year-old daughter.

Beatriz pointed to an open trunk. "I hated to give her a sleeping potion, but Francisco prepared me, told me that was the way I'd have to take her." The tiny dark-haired child, who Francisco had proudly boasted was the perfect miniature of Beatriz, was sleeping soundly on top of a fluffy down quilt inside the large trunk.

"It's time now," Beatriz said calmly, looking around the bedroom that she shared for eight glorious years with her beloved Francisco. An awful chill swept through her, the visceral effect of the nearly devastating fear which was her constant companion for months, but she forced herself to continue. "Joseph, the men are waiting in the wine cellar. Please go call them."

Joseph, tall and athletic, turned and ran out the door.

Beatriz forced her tone to become firm and commanding. They would get strength from her example. "Brianda, you and I will carry this trunk." She closed the top of the trunk holding the sleeping child. "Samuel, you are entrusted with that big bag. Can you manage it?"

"Yes, Aunt Beatriz, it's not too heavy," he said, hoisting the large carpet bag over his shoulder like a trained stevedore.

Beatriz tried to sound as strong as Francisco when he held his weekly staff meetings. "Now, for the next hour it's imperative that we each remember the role we're playing. Our lives depend on it."

Moments later Joseph burst back into the bedroom followed by four strong men from the crew of the *Doña Gracia.* Beatriz directed them to a small room next to Brianda's where each man found a large trunk. They hoisted the trunks on their backs, and with Joseph leading the way, the stevedores next in line, then Samuel, then Brianda and Beatriz carrying the trunk with small Reyna, they went back down the stairs, through the hall to the library, through a secret door leading to steps that took them underground. Beatriz closed and locked the secret door in the library. Even though she knew she'd never come back to this treasured home, to Lisbon, there was no point in giving their family secrets away.

When they reached the area called the wine cellar, a wide hall with dirt for a floor, and mammoth wine caskets as tall as two men lining both sides, Joseph deftly inserted a key in a spot on one of the wine barrels, gave a huge tug and an entire half of the wine casket opened to reveal a dark tunnel. Their own personal "family catacombs."

Joseph picked up a lantern and summoned the group to follow him into the darkness. They trudged slowly, filled with fear, for what seemed like at least ten city blocks, before they arrived in what appeared to be another wine cellar.

"Good! You're here!" Captain Lope greeted them. He was the bright young navigator of whom Francisco Mendes had been so proud. Though the Mendes family owned a fleet of fifteen ships, Francisco's favorite ship was the *Doña Gracia* and the navigator in whom he had greatest confidence was Captain Lope. "Now, listen carefully. We must get you to cross from the front of the warehouse to the dock, board the ship and go into your cabin and stay there, quietly, until we're well into international waters. The crew must not suspect anything unusual is going on. Understand?"

Beatriz watched, pride momentarily overcoming fear as her young nephews listened intently. They would have to grow to adulthood fast now, she realized. No more time for child's play.

She stretched backwards to relieve the ache in her back that had been getting worse during the long walk, grateful for the moment to let the trunk with little Reyna rest at her feet. Captain Lope, seeing her stretch, understood and reached for the trunk. Quickly, Beatriz intervened. "No, Captain, this is a very special trunk. It must be carried carefully. My sister will help me."

Lope, understanding instantly, answered, "No, you and I will carry it together, at least as far as the warehouse entrance."

It was only minutes; it seemed an eternity. The walk from the front of the warehouse to the ship, and then to the private Captain's quarters was the most terrifying experience in Beatriz' twenty-six years. The king's men patrolled the docks, guarding against just such a departure as they were now making. If they were caught trying to leave the country, and worse, taking valuables with them, not only would they be tortured and murdered, but every sailor, every stevedore, every deck hand would be slaughtered.

Safe at last inside the captain's private quarters, the door locked, Brianda and Beatriz took off their hats and let their long curls cascade down their shoulders. They opened the lid to the trunk so little Reyna would have plenty of fresh air. Beatriz insisted that Joseph and Samuel at least wash the dirt off their faces, even if they didn't want to change into their own clothes.

The tiny cabin was crowded with their five trunks and carpet bags; a space meant for one man would be their home for however many days it took them to reach England. Then, and only then, would they be safe from the murderous intention of John, King of Portugal.

"Aunt Beatriz," Samuel asked as he finished wiping his wet face, "Uncle Francisco told me that he named this ship after the most beautiful woman in the world. Who is Doña Gracia?"

Beatriz smiled as tears filled her eyes. That sounded like something her husband would have said. He was the dearest man who ever lived. "Some day when you are old and gray, actually before then I hope, I'll tell you who Doña Gracia is."

What seemed like hours later Captain Lope knocked on their door to inform them that they were now safe, in international waters, beyond the reach of King John.

Beatriz gathered her sister and her nephews close beside her, above the trunk holding the sleeping child. "Come, my family," she said, realizing again that this was all that was left of what had once been one of the most illustrious families in all of Europe. And now their well-being was in her hands, her hands alone. "Come, we must thank our God." And singing words aloud which she had only whispered before, Beatriz led her family: "*Shema Yisrael, adonay eloheynu, adonay echad.* Hear oh Israel, the Lord our God, the Lord is One."

On that night a twenty-six-year-old widow altered the history of a nation. The world's largest privately-owned fleet of merchant ships would never again dock in Portuguese ports. Portugal would never again be the Mistress of the Seas.

Chapter Eleven

London

With Captain Lope's assistance, Beatriz and her small family settled in London in a fully staffed and tastefully decorated brownstone townhouse in the Charing Cross neighborhood, a couple of blocks from the magnificent mansion of Charles and Katherine Brandon, the Duke and Duchess of Suffolk. Charles and Diogo Mendes had become close friends and business associates in 1515 when Diogo first traveled to Antwerp and opened that branch of the House of Mendes.

Shortly after settling in Antwerp, Diogo had traveled to London to initiate business with the royal court. Diogo had told Beatriz that he met Charles on that first trip, and they instantly recognized one another as being soul-brothers, both delighting in the same pursuits: money, power, athletics, gaming and women.

Diogo had introduced Joseph to the Duke, his then-wife Mary Tudor, the sister of King Henry VIII, and his young son Henry Brandon, Earl of Lincoln, when Joseph went with Diogo to London in the summer of 1531.

During the escape from Lisbon to London, Joseph told Beatriz everything he remembered about the Brandons. Mary Tudor Brandon was the widow of the elderly King Louis XII of France, a marriage that Henry VIII had arranged for political purposes much against Mary's wishes. The French king died a few months after the wedding. Henry sent Charles to France to bring Mary and her dowry and jewels back to England, but in an unheard of act of defiance, Charles and Mary secretly married. Mary had been in love with Charles since she was a young teen-age girl watching him in the tilt yard where he was uncrowned champion of all jousting tournaments in the land.

A furious king banished Charles from the court, and sent the couple back to Suffolk, as he had made Charles the Duke of Suffolk years earlier. During their sojourn in the country they produced three healthy children and nurtured their love. Meanwhile, Henry plotted war against France, believing that in order to be remembered by history as a great king, he had to be a great warrior king. When all was in readiness, he sent for the Duke of Suffolk and his household was once again welcomed at Whitehall, Westminster, and Hampton Court.

Unhappily, Mary Tudor, only thirty-five years old, died after a long illness, a sort of wasting disease of weeks and weeks of horrible vomiting and diarrhea. She died in June of 1533. To further distress the Duke, his only son, young Henry, an heir to the throne, died of the same disease the next March.

Joseph told his Aunt Beatriz, "We enjoyed many chess games as well as one afternoon of hunting in the forests near Hampton Court during my visit to England in 1531. When I heard the news of his death from Diogo, it seemed unbelievable that such a healthy and strong boy, a potential future king, could be destroyed by a disease."

Beatriz arrived in London during what was a horrible year for the monarchy. In January, the king had fallen from his steed during a jousting match, hit his head and damaged the veins in his legs. The king remained unconscious for more than two hours, though that fact was kept from his subjects. Meanwhile, England was in an uproar because Henry had declared himself head of the Church of England, had confiscated the monasteries, churches and convents, and proclaimed them the property of the Crown.

In February he discovered that his wife, Anne, was having adulterous affairs with several of his courtiers, supposedly including her own brother. She was tried for treason and found guilty. She was beheaded the week Beatriz arrived. The Duke of Suffolk had been commanded by King Henry to attend the trial and the beheading.

Though Charles had never approved of Henry's divorce from Katherine of Aragon, and Mary Tudor had begged Henry not to marry Anne and had refused to attend her coronation, Charles Brandon hated the business of the trial and beheading, and when Beatriz first met with him, he was clearly exhausted emotionally and physically from the whole nasty business.

The day after they arrived, Joseph presented himself at Brandon's mansion and left a letter describing the massacre of his family, their escape from Lisbon, and their plans to eventually go to Antwerp. Joseph was counting on Brandon's business arrangements with Diogo, especially the outstanding loan of 100,000 ducats to Henry, to help Beatriz and himself be introduced to the Tudor court. Within twenty-four hours, Joseph received an answer by messenger inviting them to tea that same afternoon.

As Beatriz preceded Joseph into the large drawing room of the Brandon mansion, he couldn't help but notice her imperial bearing. Though her posture was always perfect, on this afternoon she seemed to grow several inches in height and grandeur.

They had only been seated a moment when Charles and his seventeen-year old bride, Katherine Willoughby, entered the grand room. As protocol demanded, Charles greeted Beatriz first. "Ah, Señora Mendes, we are so distressed to hear of these terrible happenings in Lisbon. Please accept our condolences for the loss of your loved ones." The tall, distinguished, silver-haired Duke held her offered hand with both of his then released her to Katherine.

Katherine, tall, slim, and blond-haired took Beatriz hand and pressed her cheek against Beatriz cheek. "*Bienvenidos a la corte inglesa y a nuestro hogar!*"

Beatriz, surprised to realize that Charles' bride was Spanish, answered, "*Es un alto honor y verdadero placer encontrarnos aqui!*"

Katherine then switched from Castilian to English. "Whatever we can do to help you and your family, Charles and I are most anxious to try to relieve your suffering."

They greeted Joseph enthusiastically, Charles commenting on his great growth in five years, as he was now taller than either himself or King Henry at six-foot-three-inches. "You'll make a fine jousting partner. We'll have to get you over to the tilt yard and fitted up in armor!" he enthused.

After they were seated again, the butler served tea to the ladies and brandy to Joseph and the Duke. Beatriz presented a large beautifully decorated box to Katherine, filled with individual jars of spices: nutmeg, cloves, cinnamon, four kinds of peppercorns, saffron, vanilla beans, coffee and cocoa beans, plus a large grinder for all the spices.

After a few more pleasantries, Charles said, "*Señora,* you must consider making London your base of operations. We are prepared to become your business partner and establish a relationship similar to that enjoyed by your late husband and King Manuel."

This kind of open door was exactly what Beatriz was aiming for. "My husband's partner, Diogo Mendes, and I have been thinking along those lines also, Your Eminence. We are prepared to enlarge our offices and permanent staff here in London immediately."

"Wonderful. And will you be making your home here?"

"We haven't made that decision yet, but my thinking is that we will go on to Antwerp where Diogo has his fine school. My nephew Samuel, who is now only twelve, needs to complete his schooling, and Joseph is to enroll at the University of Louvain near Brussels."

Charles nodded his understanding. "I spoke about you with His Majesty this morning and he asked me to convey to you his deep sorrow over your tragedy, and to implore you to come to Court and meet with him to discuss how we might assist you. He loves to design ships, and he envies your huge fleet, in addition to your maps. He also asked me to speak with you about your supply of fine gems, as he is anxious to gift his bride Jane with appropriate jewels before their wedding."

Joseph watched Beatriz' face light up, knowing that she had brought from Lisbon the most valuable gems the House of Mendes had ever owned. She responded, "I will speak with Jose Diaz tomorrow and we will select the finest gems and take them to His Majesty for his selection."

"Good, I will arrange it. And," he winked at his wife, "perhaps we will find something special for Katherine to wear to the wedding and coronation festivities."

They spent another hour discussing the textile trade, the new books which were being printed all over Europe, Martin Luther's demands, and the special pleasures of King Henry's Hampton Court. By the time they said their farewells, Katherine had invited Beatriz to bring little Reyna for a visit with her toddler, Henry, nearly the same age.

That evening Beatriz didn't miss a beat. She sat at the table writing Diogo a lengthy letter, listing all the different projects she had in mind: a contract for thousands of uniforms for the king's soldiers to be made with Mendes textiles in Salonika. Jewels for all Henry's courtiers. A huge wholesale and retail spice trade in England. Sales and shipment of fine Murano glass and French porcelain to Henry's many palaces. "And more ships for our fleet, Henry wants us to increase our fleet so he can perhaps 'lease' them when he wages war against France! There is no limit to the kind of profits we can make if we enlarge our operations here in England. And I like these people, when they are not beheading their wives!"

After she had sealed the letter to Diogo, Joseph said, "Now, tell me *Tita*, what's your impression of the man?" Joseph adored Charles, and wanted to become closer and closer to him even though he recognized Charles for the charming rascal he was.

Beatriz answered Joseph, "He covets great wealth. He has political power by virtue of his closeness to the Crown. His precipitous marriage to Katherine demonstrates his determination to have whatever woman he wants, and he's even more determined if they are possessed of wealth. Once he sets his sights on a woman, nothing stops him, not the Church or the king or the fear of alienating his own children. Of his appetites, his lust for wealth trumps his carnal desires, but perhaps that's also due to his age. He's not a young man any longer."

"Wow! You've got him pegged exactly right!"

"If we play our cards right," Beatriz continued, "we can use him very effectively to get what we want here in England. And I intend to do exactly that!"

What Beatriz didn't say that evening, but what Joseph believed she intuitively understood, was that their timely arrival in London filled a vacuum in Charles' life. It suited them both for him to take Joseph under his wing. He had lost a father and Charles had recently lost a son Joseph's age. Since his marriage to Katherine, he had been experiencing a bit of coldness from his best friend and mentor, King Henry. Bringing the business acumen and the financial resources of the House of Mendes into the inner circles of the Court would enrich the coffers of the king and his favorite duke. Brandon needed the House of Mendes more than they needed him.

A few minutes before noon the following day a messenger arrived at Beatriz' house with a note from Charles telling them to bring the jewels to Whitehall for a meeting with the king at five in the afternoon. Beatriz sent Joseph to the Mendes office to alert Jose Diaz and ask him to select the finest jewels he had in his care. Meanwhile, she retired to her bedroom and sorted out the jewels she'd brought from Lisbon. By the time Joseph returned to the house to dress for the meeting, she had prepared three black velvet cases with strands of large pearls, large cut and polished sapphires, rubies, emeralds and diamonds.

Beatriz dressed herself in a dove gray lightweight wool dress with a modest neckline, long sleeves, and a slim skirt. Around her neck she wore a two-strand pearl necklace with a large cabochon ruby clasp, which centered on her throat. She wore chandelier earrings of small cabochon rubies and diamonds and a large square cut ruby ring on her right hand. When Joseph first saw her so attired, he was a bit stunned as Beatriz rarely wore such elaborate jewelry, and certainly never in the day time. Of course, he told himself, this is special, an introduction to the King of England. She would know what was appropriate. He said nothing, other than to tell her she looked "splendidly regal and beautiful."

At precisely four the Duke of Suffolk called for them in his gilded coach. They rode through London streets, vaguely aware of the curious stares of the populace, trying to concentrate on all that Charles was telling them. "You will notice the King limps, the result of a jousting accident last January. His legs still give him trouble, and there doesn't seem to be much the doctor can do to relieve the pain."

They rode past the royal guardsmen dressed in red livery, their swords gleaming in the late afternoon sunlight. The palms of Joseph's hands and the bottoms of his feet tingled in anticipation. Finally, they arrived at the entrance to Whitehall. Joseph jumped out of the carriage first and held out his hand to Beatrice. With great agility, in spite of her high-heeled shoes, she came down the steps into his arms. Her face was flushed with excitement; the importance of this meeting was not lost on her.

They were immediately ushered into a room with a long table and high-backed throne-like wooden chairs. Jose Diaz who had been waiting for them, rose to greet the Duke and Beatriz. A waiter brought in crystal wine glasses and a decanter of claret along with some small pastries filled with various seasoned meats.

Presently, at a signal from the butler, following Charles example, they all rose. King Henry VIII strode into the room with great assurance, he was not limping, and walked immediately to Beatriz, taking her slim hand in his two plump hands, with a genuinely loving and tender smile, and a gentle voice, he said, "My dear, dear *Señora* Mendes, my heart goes out to you. We are so dreadfully sorry to hear about these horrors taking place in Lisbon. Ever since your brother-in-law Diogo began to come to court, we've wanted to meet your husband Francisco. We are so sorry..." And to Joseph's astonishment, he wrapped her in a great bear-like hug.

The King then turned to Joseph, and with a sort of salute he said, "Young man, we're going to get you outfitted in armor and see to it that you become our next jousting champion. I've a big bay gelding who needs the exercise, and I'm told you're good with horses!" Joseph nodded his assent, speechless in the king's presence.

The King then greeted Jose Diaz and seated himself, a signal that Beatriz was to begin the business of showing him jewels. Beatriz placed three black velvet boxes on the table. Diaz brought another two. Beatriz opened the first box and placed it in front of the King.

"Your Highness, these are our finest, most flawless diamonds. We have many more in our safe, smaller and cut and polished in different shapes. Would you tell us what you believe Lady Jane would like?"

He glanced at the diamonds then looked intently at Beatriz. "The necklace you have on…something like that perhaps, only with sapphires instead of rubies…"

On cue, Beatriz reached up to her throat and unfastened the ruby clasp and spread the two strands of pearls out in front of the King. She opened a second box and removed two strands with the largest pearls and placed them on a black velvet pillow in front of him. She asked Diaz, "Did you bring the fourteen carat sapphire from India?"

Diaz opened one of his boxes and took out a large rectangular deep blue stone. Beatriz draped the strands of pearls in a circle in front of the King and placed the large sapphire in the center front. "Your Highness, we would surround this sapphire with small diamonds to set it off; it would be a magnificent necklace for your queen."

A huge, warm smile broke out on his face. "Yes, yes that's exactly what I want. And for earrings?"

Beatriz reached up to her left ear and extracted her chandelier earring, placing it in front of the King. "This drop of rubies can be separated from the stud which fastens it to the ear lobe, and thus the stud can be worn alone during the daytime." She separated the ruby stud from the drop then put the ear ring back together. "We make this drop in several different styles." She opened the third box and demonstrated three different kinds of drops. Meanwhile, Diaz brought out two perfectly matched two carat sapphires that he recommended for the studs.

The King picked up a drop with graduated strands of diamonds. "This is what I like, and I want you to alternate diamonds and sapphires in the drop. Now, for a ring?"

Diaz opened the second box again and produced a very large sapphire, faceted, polished and shaped like a heart. "Your Highness, we would recommend surrounding this heart with fine small diamonds and mounting it in such a way that it stands up on the finger, like this." He produced a ring with a three pronged mounting which seemed to enlarge the stone.

"Perfect!" He smiled warmly at Beatriz. "You do good work, milady. And when can we have these pieces ready to present to the queen. I am planning a great event for June 7th and I would like Queen Jane to wear these jewels at that event."

Without even consulting Diaz, Beatriz immediately announced, "We will have these jewels back to you for your inspection in seven days."

"Excellent." The King stood, and they all stood in respect. He addressed Beatriz. "I've told Brandon about my ideas for working with the House of Mendes. I've got all this coronation business to contend with during the next month, but Brandon will be at your service. We very much want to enlarge the activities of your company here in England."

"Thank you, Your Majesty, you do us great honor."

After he swept out of the room, the waiter refilled their glasses with wine, and the Duke asked them to show him jewels for his Katherine.

Beatriz didn't realize the full import that afternoon, selling a few jewels to the king, but this was the beginning of a very prosperous and long term relationship with the English Court.

That Saturday morning Joseph received a note from Charles: "Dress for riding and meet me at my house at noon today." He was thrilled and scared at the same time. Would he be able to live up to Charles' expectations? How heavy would all that armor be? They had promised him one of the king's most spirited horses. Would he be able to handle him? This was known to be a very expensive and dangerous sport and Beatriz would never have agreed to it except for the fact that it promised continued entrée to the Court.

"The king is addicted to jousting," Charles told him on the ride to the palace. "He's much too old and should have given it up long ago, as I did."

Charles told him much about his jousting career and how it had cemented his friendship with the king. "The worst day of my life was the day his face was left naked, his visor not put down. My lance struck him, and he fell to the ground. His visor was filled with pieces of the splintered wood from my lance, I sat terrified and paralyzed, afraid I had either killed the King or damaged his eyesight. It was March of 1524, and though he blamed me not, I told him that day I would never joust against him again. And I did not. After that accident, the King got back up on his steed and ran six more courses in order to prove to his subjects that he'd not been injured. That's the kind of man he is!"

Joseph summoned all his courage and athletic skill and mounted King Henry's great bay gelding, dressed in a suit of armor that Charles Brandon had worn when he was young and trim. Up and down the tilt yard he guided the horse, overwhelmed by the great weight of the armor. How did they even move their arms in this turtle-like cage, much less knock their rival off their horse? It took him days of practice, agonizing muscle pain, and dehydration from all the sweating, but he was determined not to let these two great princes down. They believed in him, King Henry even came to the stables to watch him perform several times that summer, and he would live up to their expectations.

When, in January, Beatriz left for Antwerp, Brandon gave Joseph his suit of armor as a parting gift. He wore it many times during his university years and later after he'd become friends with Maximilian, nephew of the Holy Roman Emperor. They spent more hours in the tilt yard than in the university classroom. That time was not wasted. Oh no, not wasted at all!

The following Monday Beatriz met with Brandon to discuss enlarging the textile business in England. She asked Brandon to help her find at least three large buildings in commercial districts where the wealthy shopped. "I will create a huge emporium with bolts of fabric, velvets, silks, brocades, wool, linen and common homespun in all the colors of the rainbow, as well as trimmings: thread, ribbons, buttons, fringe, tassels, feathers, and fur. We'll lease out small spaces to dressmakers, seamstresses, tailors and milliners so the customers can choose the fabric then immediately contract to have it made up into garments. And we will also have a very discrete small jewelry shop on the premises where our own Mendes designers can entice customers to invest in fine gems."

In the weeks following this conversation with Brandon, his men located three suitable buildings. The first was on King Street near the Covent Garden Market where many of the richest families shopped. The second was on lower Thames Street near the Billingsgate Market, and the third was on Charles Street not far from Berkley Square. By October Beatriz had bought all three buildings, installed managers, hired women and men knowledgeable in fabrics and fashion design, and begun to entice seamstresses and tailors to rent space. And she began to receive very large shipments from Diogo of fine fabrics from all over Europe and Turkey. The employees of the House of Mendes numbered only twelve when she arrived in London; by the time she left in January, the House of Mendes had more than one hundred men and women working for them, primarily in the textile business.

Beatriz' next undertaking was to establish small spice shops either adjacent to or in the major food markets in the city. She designed new packaging for the spices, and offered several new spice grinders as well.

In spite of the fact that Charles Brandon attempted to seduce Beatriz, she managed to fend him off diplomatically while at the same time continuing to develop a close relationship with his young bride. "She will outlive him, and it is the Duchess of Suffolk who will keep the doors open in the Tudor Court for the House of Mendes," Beatriz counseled Joseph.

Her friendship with Katherine Brandon also enabled them to keep abreast of the latest in Court gossip. King Henry had decided, after he caused her to be beheaded, that Anne Boleyn was a "witch" and had poisoned Queen Katherine, his sister Mary Tudor, Charles Brandon's third wife, as well as Brandon's eldest son Henry. Rumor had it that she had also attempted to poison Princess Mary, and indeed Mary had the same sickness that killed Mary Tudor Brandon, but she recovered. These deaths were attributed to Anne because all the symptoms were the same, a slow wasting disease which could be caused by poison administered over a period of months by a servant in Anne's pay. In addition, all of these persons were in the line of succession to the throne if Henry failed to produce a suitable male heir, thus threatening her daughter Princess Elizabeth's claim to the throne.

Beatriz decided to remain in England until after the Christmas festivities, as they were reputed to be something really grand in the court of Henry VIII. She communicated her wishes to Diogo, and he agreed that it would be sensible to travel to Antwerp after the first of the New Year; he would send Captain Lope and the *Doña Gracia* to gather up the household and "bring you home."

Beatriz was pleased that she would arrive in Antwerp with several major accomplishments. She had cemented the business partnership between the House of Mendes and the Tudor Court. She carried with her a huge contract to manufacture uniforms for the King's guards and army. She increased the potential for textile sales in England, as well as for spices and fine gems. She arrived in Antwerp not simply as the widow of Diogo's brother and heir to his portion of the House of Mendes, but as a full partner in all the business activities of the House.

Chapter Twelve

Arrival In Antwerp

Beatriz and Brianda da Luna watched from the stateroom window as the *Doña Gracia*, accompanied by a convoy of forty-two Spanish and Portuguese ships, all owned by either the House of Mendes or Diogo's close business associates, the Fuggers of Augsburg, slowly made its way into the port of Antwerp. From the window they could make out the spires of three churches, one of which had to be the great Catholic Cathedral Diogo had told them about. The port was bustling with ships and people. Captain Lope had told them that on some days as many as five hundred ships were loading and off-loading cargo in this, the busiest port, a city of nearly twenty thousand inhabitants, in northwest Europe's greatest trading center.

To fulfill Francisco's plans for her future, and to guarantee even before she arrived in Antwerp that Diogo would recognize her as a trustworthy and competent business partner, she put her enormous grief on hold and rigidly disciplined herself and her sister and nephews to project an image of hardness and calmness.

Following the custom of the day, she dressed from head to toe in mourning clothes. Her lightweight black wool broadcloth gown was unadorned by lace or jewels; her long black hair pulled back into a snug chignon at the nape of her neck. A black lace Spanish mantilla covered her head and face; a small black velvet bag attached to the belt of her dress.

Brianda, at twenty-one, an unmarried woman, was entitled to wear white or grey while in mourning. She was gowned in softest dove grey, wearing no jewelry or mantilla, and her brown curls lay softly on her shoulders.

A soft knock, then the door opened and Don Diogo stepped in. Hesitantly he walked toward Beatriz, lifted the veil from her face, took her face in his hands and kissed each cheek softly. "Gracia, oh Gracia..." Then, he gathered her slim body to his in a hearty bear hug. As they hugged one another, sobs broke from their throats and they hugged even tighter. Finally, Beatriz pulled back and looked at this man who was world-renowned as the Spice King of Europe. She had not seen him in four years, and he was, if anything, more handsome than she remembered. Tall, with silken black hair beginning to show streaks of grey, he was muscular and trim, and possessed of gorgeous twinkling velvet brown eyes, which were now brimming with tears. Only nine years younger than Francisco, he appeared to be twenty years younger.

He turned to Brianda and repeated the kisses and hugs then he shook the hands of Beatriz's nephews, Joseph and Samuel. Finally, he turned his attention to little Reyna, picked her up and carried her in his arms as they made their way off the *Doña Gracia.*

Francisco had told Beatriz that Diogo's Antwerp operation prospered beyond their greatest dreams, and had become ten times the size of their Lisbon operation. Consequently, Diogo lived in great splendor, "like a true Prince!" As she walked down the gangplank and onto the cobblestone street of the old port, she was astonished to see the most magnificent large carriage, gilded in gold leaf, with deep green velvet upholstery and curtains, attended by two coachmen wearing cerulean blue Mendes livery. The carriage was pulled by two perfectly matched white Arabian steeds, outfitted with bridles enhanced by silver fittings. Following the lead carriage were two additional carriages, much less opulent, all with the seal of the House of Mendes enameled onto their doors.

The coachmen assisted the women up the stairs of the coach and directed them where to sit. When the entire party was inside the carriage, Diogo climbed up and seated himself directly behind the coachmen so he could speak to them through a small glass window.

"I am in awe!" Beatriz said, unable to contain her surprise at the ostentatiousness of Diogo's carriage.

"Beautiful, isn't it. There are only two like it, the other one was made for the Holy Roman Emperor, Charles V."

The carriage took them onto a beautiful tree lined boulevard, the Kipdorp. After a few blocks, Diogo opened the small window and spoke to the coachman. "Drive us all the way around the block, then back to the gates." He gestured to his left, calling their attention to a massive brick, stone and marble five-story mansion. Tall gas lights alternated with pear trees all along the sidewalk in front of the mansion. White shutters and ornate flower boxes overflowing with ivy enhanced the architecture. "This is my home," he said with great pride, as they passed by wrought iron and brass gates and an arch that was three stories high. He pointed to the next mansion, a slightly smaller version of the first one. "That is your home, Beatriz."

She gasped as she looked out the window at the adjacent mansion, which was nearly a mirror image of his. As they turned the corner, he continued: "This is the school of the House of Mendes. We educate nearly two hundred young men between the ages of twelve and twenty-four. We teach a full curriculum: six languages, mathematics, geography, cartography, astronomy, navigation, warfare, naval history, accounting, classical Greek and Roman history and literature. And we've recently added international relations, diplomacy and spycraft. After twenty-four years here in Antwerp, we have begun to teach a second generation, the sons of our oldest captains and agents."

When they came to the end of that block, he pointed out a separate smaller building. "That is our concert hall. We have occasional invited lectures, musical concerts, plays and performances." He winked at Beatriz. "Sometimes we New Christians gather for prayer and religious discussion."

"Ah ha, you are keeping the tradition alive. Just like Francisco."

"I will never be as learned as Francisco or as dedicated. But we do what we can, what we can get away with. Jews are only marginally safer here than they were in Spain and Portugal. We must be discreet at all times."

They turned the last corner, back out onto the Kipdorp, and passed his home, then turned into the gates, which were now open with guards standing at attention. They passed under the arch and through a second set of gates. Directly in front of them was a miniature park. The centerpiece was a life-size black marble Venus, fountains on four sides, surrounded by flower beds. The coachman guided the horses around the circle and came to a stop at the gate that led into a walled garden at the back of Diogo's home.

Beatriz found herself so overcome by Diogo's physical presence that she could barely take in the majesty of his home. Her hands and feet were sweating, she knew her face was flushed, and she could not deny the way her heart pounded in her chest. It had been months since she had felt physical desire, she'd almost forgotten the way it took over her being. And at the same moment she felt ashamed that she could have such feelings for her brother-in-law, and so soon after Francisco's death.

Diogo led them into the garden, which was filled with fruit trees and specimen rose bushes. Alcoves exhibiting marble busts of ancient Greek and Roman generals adorned the back wall of his mansion. Gods and goddesses, cupids and nymphs primped and posed atop massive dark oak carved doors and mullioned and stained windows.

As Diogo ushered Beatriz and Brianda into his home he said, "You can see why I insist you live here with me. I need some loved ones to make this a home. Marble versions of Seneca and Plato just don't fill the bill. What I've always needed here in Antwerp is family. Now I have one."

Beatriz spent the first full day in Antwerp organizing her home. The mansion was minimally furnished, Diogo readily admitted, "I know you have definite ideas about interior décor. Once you are rested, you need to come down to our warehouse. Whatever we don't have readily at hand, we will commission locally. We have marvelous artisans, silversmiths and furniture makers, ready to do your bidding. Whatever you want you will have."

"It's important, Beatriz, that your home, which will be one of our showcases, have the finest of everything, that's very important in the business we are in. Impressions, perception is everything!"

Diogo had assigned two of his oldest and most trusted retainers, New Christians themselves, Max and Anna Segovia originally from Lisbon, to be the head of her household staff. Their two sons were captains in his fleet, and their daughter was one of his accountants in his bank. Their loyalty to the House of Mendes was beyond question.

Nevertheless, Beatriz was determined to set down some rules which might seem overly restrictive. She brought the Segovias into the small parlor of her home on the first afternoon and instructed them. "When you serve me wine, you must bring the bottle, uncorked, to me. Open it in my presence, and leave the bottle in front of me. I will not drink wine unless I have seen it uncorked, and after it is opened, the bottle cannot be removed from my presence. You see, my parents, my husband, my brother and his wife were murdered from drinking wine in which some poisonous substance had been dissolved." Sympathetic, they nodded their heads in agreement.

"As to food, I insist that no prepared foods be brought into our kitchen. Everything must be prepared in our kitchen by employees who are beyond bribing, and I will hold you, Anna, responsible for all the servants we employ in the kitchen. In Lisbon, all the kitchen staff was murdered. Someone, a member of the household, had clearly been bribed and had informed the King that we were celebrating my father's birthday that evening. It was a perfect set up for him to send his henchmen in to do the dirty deed. We must always be on the alert for that kind of betrayal."

Anna promised, "My sister, Lidia, will be the head chef and all employees will be thoroughly known to her, I promise you that."

"Thank you. As to my daughter, Reyna, I will need a governess who will be with her twenty-four hours a day, as well as a tutor well-versed in classical studies. I want her to immediately begin to learn several languages."

"My oldest granddaughter, Alexandra, wants to be her governess, and I believe you will be very satisfied with her credentials. She is a lovely young woman...one of us."

"Good," Beatriz thought, "I want her to be surrounded by New Christians. There will be no gentiles inside this house. They may be gardeners and stable boys, but they will not be inside this house."

It had been a long day, and she was bone weary. Alexandra had proven to be everything her grandparents advertised, and now she slept in the same room with little Reyna, in a full size bed, ready to respond to any needs the child would have in the night. And that bedroom was right next to the bedroom Diogo had chosen for Beatriz. He had furnished it with a splendid Florentine bed. A deep brown mahogany four poster, canopied bed with wreaths, ribbons, flowers and all manner of mythological animals carved and embellished with gold leaf, the bed was enclosed by gold silk taffeta draperies embellished with gold silk tassels. It was truly something to behold, the focus of the room.

Wearily, Beatriz removed the black purse from the belt of her dress. She opened the purse and extracted a dagger. She placed the dagger on the table next to the bed. Then she removed her dress, her petticoats, and finally her corset. As she opened the corset in the front, she carefully removed two half-moon, cotton-filled, shaped pads from the brassiere and placed the two pads in the black purse. Then she placed the purse under the pillow of her bed. The pads contained more than a million ducats worth of diamonds; they only left her body when she slept, and then they resided under her head. Francisco had taught her well.

Chapter Thirteen

Diamonds, Temptation, and Sacrifice

Diogo and Beatriz sat in his morning room, overlooking the garden and the park, eating breakfast served on a small circular table inlaid with an Oriental pattern of vividly colored mosaic tiles.

"My first major affiliation when I arrived in Antwerp was with the established mercantile firm of Affaitati from Cremona in Italy," Diogo proudly told Beatriz.

"I've heard of that family." She nodded her head.

"Within twelve years, we controlled the pepper and spice trade. Working with King Manuel, we created a sales-syndicate that made us the sole importer of these goods. We purchased as much as twelve hundred thousand ducats worth of spice yearly. Because we had the monopoly, we could fix whatever price we chose to resell to foreign merchants." Even as he recited his successes, he marveled at Beatriz' stunning beauty.

She, in turn, could barely concentrate enough to absorb what he was telling her.

"The result," Diogo continued, his eyes glittering with enthusiasm, "is that because we purchase entire cargoes for ready cash from King Manuel, we made the Portuguese crown financially dependent on the House of Mendes. Some years we've provided a quarter of the crown's entire income."

Beatriz added, "I believe that's why we succeeded in holding off the Inquisition as long as we did. We had a great deal of leverage over the king of Portugal, King Manuel understood this, but somehow his son is too stupid to realize the damage we've done now that we've picked up stakes and moved out of Portugal."

"Don't worry, he'll soon realize it!" Diogo said bitterly.

"Diogo, I've never told anyone this before, but I feel terribly responsible for John's attitude toward the New Christians, and the Mendes family in particular. In fact, I wonder if it is my fault he murdered our family."

Diogo reached over and patted her hand, a shocked expression on his face. "Beatriz, that's ridiculous. How on earth could you possibly be at fault?"

"When I was very young and terribly much in love with Francisco, and he thought of me as a child, I deliberately tried to make Francisco jealous by flirting with John when we attended a ball at the palace. I knew there was no chance John would ever want to marry a New Christian, so I thought the flirtation was harmless. Well, it wasn't. After Francisco was murdered, the King sent for me, but I pled illness, and then we disappeared from Lisbon. You can't imagine how all this has weighed on my conscience these past months."

"Beatriz, you've got to stop thinking this way. King John is and always has been after our wealth. We'll get our revenge, that I promise you."

"I've been wanting to discuss that with you. Your ships pick up pepper and spice and raw diamonds in Asian waters. You can bring them directly to Antwerp and bypass Lisbon and payments to King John all together. Besides, I don't think our crews would be safe if the ships were docked in Lisbon."

Diogo sipped his coffee, then stood and paced back and forth in front of the window. "I've given a lot of thought to this too, believe me, Beatriz. I agree with you about the danger, and that's why more and more our ships travel in large convoys with the Fuggers and Affaitati. There's safety in numbers, and these ships are all well equipped with the most modern armaments. Our biggest fear is attack by pirates, but increasingly I'm worried about what King John might do. He wouldn't dare harm the Fuggers or Affaitati, he needs them to keep pouring money into his coffers. But I've already taken so much of the spice trade away from him, and if I will now take the diamonds away, well, I'm not sure what the consequences will be."

As they walked down the marble steps and out the front door where the carriage was waiting to take them to the diamond district on Pelikenstrasse, Diogo continued. "We will make John suffer for what he has done to us. I guarantee it! But we must watch our step and chart our plans cautiously. In Antwerp we are ruled by the same family, and the same religious fanaticism, which rules Iberia, southern Italy, and the Habsburg dominions of Europe."

Beatriz added, "And I suppose we have to show that our allegiance is to the Holy Roman Emperor, Charles V. You can assume that he has spies within your organization."

"Yes," Diogo said, "we've routed them out before. Charles is the ultimate power, and recently he has seen fit to throw his weight at the Vatican behind John of Portugal. So things are still not looking too good. We didn't get you out of Portugal one day too soon."

"Thank God!"

"But I have spies in the Vatican too. Money breeds money, and that's one thing the House of Mendes has plenty of. We've extended our operations and agents into France, Germany, all the Italian states, England, and believe it or not, even in the Americas."

When they disembarked in front of a three story brick building with the name Mendes carved into the stone frieze atop the massive oak doors,

Diogo began to discuss his thriving business in gemstones. "You are walking into the preeminent diamond cutting and polishing factory in the world. One of our men has devised a special polishing wheel impregnated with olive oil and diamond dust, a scaif, which has revolutionized the craft of diamond cutting. We can now cut and polish a diamond symmetrically, all the facets of a stone, so that it reflects a maximum amount of light."

"How marvelous! I can't wait to see some examples!"

They walked up a flight of stairs to a workroom where some thirty men sat at tables, various instruments at the ready. Diogo introduced Beatriz as his business partner and sister-in-law, and asked the director to demonstrate the scaif. She watched carefully as Lodewyk van Berken continued the cutting and polishing of a raw diamond into a multifaceted, glittering gem. When he was finished, he handed it to the director who in turn handed it to Diogo. "Shall we take it home as a gift to Brianda?" He asked Beatriz with a twinkle in his eye.

"She would be so thrilled, she adores beautiful jewelry."

"And now let's go back downstairs, and I'll show you some of our most priceless creations."

"Who are your customers?" Beatriz asked as they approached the back room, which opened, into a walk-in safe.

"Princes, dukes, kings, cardinals, the pope, and ordinary merchants who are now becoming a large group competing for luxury goods. For about the past fifty years, a diamond engagement ring has become essential for all merchant families as well as royalty."

"Everyone is in a race to outdo everyone else, even the clergy," he added. "Now, let me show you something really special." Diogo reached into a drawer and pulled out a navy blue velvet box. He opened it, polished the gem with his shirt sleeve and held it out to Beatriz.

"My God! I've never seen a diamond so large!"

"Exactly! One-hundred-thirty-seven carats, very fine quality. Purchased last week by Charles the Bold, Duke of Normandy. It's the largest one we've ever had pass through our hands. Quite a coup!"

Beatriz's eye caught sight of a magnificent gold chalice embellished with diamonds and rubies. "Who is that for?"

"That's a special commission for our current pope. What do you think?"

"Don't get me started on the papacy. I think the pope should be feeding the poor instead of spending his people's money on ostentatious goblets. It's nothing short of scandalous."

"I quite agree," Diogo chuckled, "but don't say that out loud. It wouldn't be good for business."

****

Beatriz stood quietly in the long corridor in front of the marble sheathed apse specifically designed for this bust of Homer. She reached out to touch the cool grey marble, her fingers running over the curling locks and down onto the smooth cheeks. In her left hand she held a candle to light her way down the long hall toward the pantry where she would find the makings of a cup of tea. Sleep eluded her this cool spring night, as it had so often since she'd found her family brutally murdered.

As she removed her fingers from Homer's marble face, she sensed the presence of someone in the corridor. Turning, she spied Diogo, also carrying a candle, walking toward her.

"Ah, so you can't sleep either?" he commented, taking her by the right elbow and leading her down the hall toward the pantry.

"I can't remember the last time I slept through the night," she responded, self-consciously closing the neckline of the blue velvet dressing gown she had quickly slipped on.

Diogo studied her in the pale glow of the candles. With her long dark hair cascading down her back and no make-up she might have passed for a school girl rather than a mature mother and businesswoman. Once again he felt the ache in his groin, which her presence in the same room caused him. He knew it wasn't right to feel this way about his brother's widow, but he couldn't stop his body from reacting to her. She was by far the most desirable woman he'd ever known. No wonder Francisco had written to him that his life began anew when he married her.

"I was going to make a cup of tea. Would that suit you?" she asked as they entered the pantry.

"No. I suggest we both have a glass of port, that is, if we want to get back to sleep tonight. Port will make us groggy, but tea will wake us up. That's what my friend and doctor, Amatus Lusitanus, advises me. He's coming to Antwerp for a few weeks next month. We'll entertain him at dinner. I think you'll find him most fascinating, a brilliant, well-traveled scholar as well as the finest medical man in all of Europe."

Beatriz smiled at Diogo, thinking once again how handsome he was with his dark hair and his broad chest and tremendous height. How could she bring up the subject which had been on her mind for weeks now, how could she fulfill her final responsibility to her parents? Without thinking it through, she blurted out, "Why have you never married, Diogo?"

Taken aback by the abruptness of her change of subject, Diogo gained time by sipping his port, then said, "Lots of reasons. I've never been overwhelmed with feelings for a particular woman, not to say there haven't been lots of them."

"Yes, I can imagine!" Beatriz laughed at his understatement.

"And I've always been aware that I might need to disappear rather fast. It wouldn't have been fair to subject a woman to the uncertainty and danger in my life. And, to be honest, I sort of like living dangerously. I also like beautiful women. Lots of them. I don't think I was ever cut out for marriage and fidelity."

"Since when has fidelity been required of a man? Especially an enormously rich man like yourself."

"Wise in the ways of the world, are you?"

"Don't forget, I attended Francisco's school. I learned all about the weaknesses of cardinals, kings, and wealthy patricians. I'm not the naïve, inexperienced, innocent widow I may appear to be."

"Are you perchance suggesting I follow the laws of the Old Testament and marry my brother's widow?" Diogo asked with a bright smile on his face, holding her attention with twinkling, laughing eyes.

Not surprisingly, Beatriz felt a surge of heat rush to her face. She was glad the dim candle light concealed her outward reaction to a deeply rooted passion she had attempted to hold in check since arriving in Antwerp. "No. Don't be ridiculous. I will never remarry."

"Then whom might you be suggesting?"

"My sister. She would make a splendid hostess for you, she's pretty and gracious, everything you could desire in a wife. It's time you had an heir, someone to carry on with the House of Mendes after you're gone."

Diogo felt his heart sink in his chest. Everything Beatriz said made sense. Yet it was Beatriz he wanted, not Brianda. It was not her immature sister, as beautiful as he thought her to be. Indeed, Beatriz was the heroine of his nightly dreams.

****

After several days of making the rounds of Diogo's enterprises, Beatriz was looking forward to Saturday and Sunday when she could devote herself entirely to little Reyna. Both she and Diogo were taken aback Friday evening when Brianda, with a teasing smile on her face, told Diogo that since he had spent the whole week exclusively with Beatriz, it was her turn, and she wanted him to show her around Antwerp on Saturday. He readily agreed, flattered that this beautiful young woman wanted the company of such an old man. He added the caveat that since it was the Sabbath they would walk. The horses and the stable boys had the day off, they would restrict their activities to art galleries and shops within walking distance of his home.

They set off on foot late Saturday morning, stopping first at a small art gallery where several of the most illustrious painters of the day exhibited their works. Diogo took great pleasure in introducing Brianda to the works of Ghirlandaio, Botticelli, Gentile Bellini, Carpaccio and one of his personal favorites, Albrecht Dürer.

Their next stop was at a jewelry store owned by Benjamin Panetta, a New Christian from Venice. Diogo explained that the House of Mendes supplied the fine gems and the Fuggers supplied the gold and silver that Panetta then turned into exquisite creations coveted by the crowned heads of Europe, as well as the Vatican. "He employs six of the finest master goldsmiths. Their designs are truly original, and based largely on the quality of the gems I supply."

Brianda quickly immersed herself in the complexity of the designs, and questioned Don Benjamin and his workmen for more than an hour. Diogo could see that his friend Benjamin was as entranced with Brianda as she was with the jewels. Their next stop was a small cafe where they ordered fruit filled crepes and coffee.

"I love to sketch gowns and jewels," Brianda confessed to Diogo. "Is there a shop nearby where we might buy a sketch book and some colored chalk?"

"Yes, three blocks north of here there is a store which sells art supplies, we'll make that our next stop."

When they left the café, Brianda took Diogo's arm, flashed an affectionate smile and said, "You can't imagine how wonderful it is to be with you, Diogo. I feel safe, protected, relaxed for the first time in many months. I'm having such fun today. Thank you for spending this day with me."

"It is truly my pleasure."

"I know you prefer Beatriz' company, she thinks like a man and is all business. I'm the opposite. Politics and business talk bore me to death, but I love beautiful art and clothes and jewels."

"That's a big assumption. What makes you think I don't enjoy you just as much as your sister? Your femininity, your candor, is very refreshing. I'm a sucker for flirtatious, charming, gorgeous women like you. And, I'm enjoying this day very much."

****

The next day Diogo gathered the whole family for a festive lunch in his garden. Brianda arrived last, dressed not in mourning clothes but in a bright yellow gingham cotton dress, which revealed all her feminine curves. Beatriz noticed, not for the first time, that she was an expert with cosmetics, having applied just enough to highlight her beautiful blue eyes.

Shortly after the herring salad was served, Diogo's butler presented him with a note from Don Benjamin Panetta, whose messenger was waiting at the front door for a reply. Beatriz and Brianda watched his face break into a broad smile as he read the note. He placed it down on the table and with twinkling eyes he said to Brianda, "My dear, it seems you have an admirer. Don Benjamin is asking my permission to court you!"

Without missing a beat, Brianda responded, "I don't want to be his wife, I want to be his apprentice."

"That's not appropriate for Brianda da Luna," Beatriz responded.

"He doesn't want you as an employee. You have enchanted him. He wants you as his wife." Diogo countered.

"What's a wife, Mommy?" little Reyna asked, all innocence.

Joseph and Samuel joined the adults in raucous laughter.

"I will design jewelry with Don Benjamin," Brianda announced to Diogo. "I will be your wife!"

Diogo and Beatriz looked at one another, momentarily speechless. Joseph and Samuel stared at their plates. Reyna asked again, "Mommy, what's a wife?"

Diogo turned back to his butler. "Please tell his messenger that I invite Don Benjamin to come here for a glass of wine and some conversation this afternoon at four." Diogo tucked the letter into his jacket pocket, and then turned to little Reyna. "Your mother tells me that you really enjoyed your new pony yesterday. Are you going to show us how well you can ride this afternoon?"

****

Beatriz was dressing for dinner when her maid brought a summons from Diogo. "Please meet me in my small parlor as soon as possible."

He greeted her with a kiss on the cheek, as was his habit. He'd already poured a glass of sherry for her, and as she took her first sip, he took a letter from one of the small drawers in his writing desk. She recognized her own handwriting.

"Some months ago, my dear, you sent me a letter in which you vowed you would never remarry. I've thought about this letter for months now, and our conversation a few days ago. I wonder if perhaps now that you are here in Antwerp and have seen my home and my businesses, if perhaps you've rethought that vow."

Beatriz took a deep breath. Things were moving too fast, much faster than she had anticipated. "Francisco and I talked about this, about the fact that he was so much older and in failing health. He told me that I should never remarry, that I should never let control of his estate fall into the hands of another man. He suggested that I should take a lover if I chose to, but never remarry. I promised him I would abide by his wishes."

"And now...how do you feel? I know you are keeping a year of strictest mourning, but do you think there is a chance you may change your mind at the end of the year?"

"No. I will keep my word."

"I must tell you, Gracia, you don't mind if I call you by your real name, do you? I must tell you that having you and your family here has made me so happy, so complete. I feel decades younger, I love the laughter, the fun of having the children here. I realize, belatedly, that I'd like to have children of my own. I see how much I've been missing." He paused to sip his wine. Then he stood and walked to the window and looked out on the Kipdorp. Finally, he turned and faced her.

"How would you feel if I asked Brianda to marry me?"

Her heart dropped to the pit of her stomach. Her hands began to sweat. It was what she had hoped, what she plotted, what she suggested to him, but the suddenness of his decision took her breath away. Now, she wasn't absolutely sure that this was the outcome she wanted; *he was so desirable, the sexiest man she had known...*

"I'd be so thrilled for both of you, oh Diogo, this is the answer to all my prayers."

He sat back down at his desk, took another drink of his wine. "Consider it done, then. We shall announce the betrothal soon and schedule the wedding for after the year of mourning is over. We'll make it a grandiose wedding at the Cathedral. But first, Brianda deserves to be courted, to be romanced before she settles into the duties of being the wife of Don Diogo Mendes." He set his glass down and stood, signaling that the meeting was over. "I trust you won't be too strict a chaperone, my dear." He kissed her on the cheek and ushered her out of the parlor.

****

On Monday morning Brianda was awakened by her maid with a note from Diogo. "Please join us for breakfast at eight o'clock." She was briefly annoyed, as it was her habit to sleep most of the morning, but as she dressed she decided this was a good omen. It meant he wanted her company, and he was not put off by her impetuous nature.

He stood and welcomed her with a big smile and kiss on the cheek when she joined them in the morning room. After she was seated, he said, "I have good news for you. Don Benjamin has agreed that you should join his staff and learn the business of designing fine jewelry. As to the other matter, I have informed him that you have an appropriate suitor and that he should not try to seduce you."

"Oh, thank you, thank you so much. When do I start?"

"Today would be a good time to start. He has a commission to design a suite of jewels for one of the most beautiful women in Europe. She has blue eyes like yours, and we believe that sapphires and diamonds would best suit her. Come with me today and we'll select the stones, then you can sketch out a necklace, ear rings, bracelet and ring. We want to have these pieces finished in about six months, so you need to get started today."

Beatriz could barely contain herself as she listened to Diogo, realizing that he was asking Brianda to design jewelry he would then present to her as a wedding gift. What a wonderfully thoughtful man he was, and then the next thought which flickered across her mind was *I hope Brianda never hurts this fine man.*

Chapter Fourteen

The Mendes Underground

The crowned heads of Europe, the Vatican, the Holy Roman Empire, even Henry VIII sent ambassadorial representatives to the splendid wedding of Brianda de Luna to the Spice King of Europe, Diogo Mendes. The ceremony was held in the Catholic Cathedral of Antwerp, presided over by Cardinal Sigismund, and it was followed by a gargantuan eight-course feast held in the ballroom of the Mendes mansion on the Kipdorp.

But as always happened following a gathering of those near and dear to Diogo, after the civil and church officials said their farewells, the members of the Portuguese "nation," the so-called Marranos, gathered in Diogo's grand library. In small intimate groups they exchanged news of Portugal, of King John, and of his now-operative Inquisition.

Beatriz, resplendent in a royal blue silk-velvet gown frosted with fine Bruges lace, moved from group to group exchanging warm greetings with relatives, close and distant. Again and again she was asked if she planned on moving her family to Ferrara or Turkey. Unsure herself, she responded, "We shall see; that decision hasn't been made yet."

Later, with a few dear friends who had recently made the trek from Iberia resulting in a loss of all their property and wealth, she cautiously discussed the initiative, which she and Diogo were putting into action. Using their position and wealth in Antwerp, as well as their vast transportation network of ships and overland carriages, ox-carts, horseback couriers and safe houses, they would assist their co-religionists in escaping the iron fist of the Inquisition. Under the cover of commercial activity of the House of Mendes, their agents would assist New Christians as they moved southwards, over the Alps and into Italian city-states or the Balkans, helping them transport their personal property, or changing it into bills of exchange which could be redeemed later by Mendes agents when they had safely arrived at their new home. Thus *converso* families were moved from one trusty Mendes representative to another, toward whatever haven of refuge seemed safe, either in Italy or Turkey. Mendes agents provided minute instructions: which roads should be taken, and whom to contact in case of an emergency.

The "Mendes underground" was the brainchild of Beatriz, and was put into place by Diogo's most trusted agents. Diogo then entrusted it back into Beatriz' hands to manage in every detail. He reasoned that if she'd been able to move her own family and much of her wealth in the dark of night from their home in Lisbon to the waiting *Doña Gracia* while the king's soldiers stood guard, no one was more suited to move the entire Portuguese colony of Jews through Christian Europe and on to safety.

"But it's not enough to move them to safety," Beatriz said to Diogo one afternoon. "We must help them relocate, help them learn a new language, adapt to a different culture, find employment. Yes, that is the most important of all. We must help them find a way to make a living."

Diogo had hired hundreds of the Portuguese Marranos to work for him in his transportation network, as couriers, and as banking agents. But even the far-flung House of Mendes could not absorb all the Portuguese refugees. Beatriz made plans on their behalf. "We must put them to work in the textile industry. Have your agents create contacts in Italy and throughout Flanders. It takes very little training to work in a textile plant, we'll set up some of our own if need be."

"If that's your plan," Diogo answered, "we should explore the possibilities in the Ottoman empire. That's a safe place for Jews; they can openly practice the religion. I'll look into it."

Beatriz added, "The other possibility is getting the more educated Jews involved in printing. There's a need for type-setting, for binding. Our people can make a real contribution."

"Hhmm..." Diogo mused "Perhaps I should contact Don Isaac Abrabanel in Ferrara. He has recently begun a large printing and binding operation."

****

True to his word, Diogo contacted Abrabanel who sent to Antwerp a young businessman, a partner in his printing company that had its headquarters in Ferrara, but also had an office in Venice. After several days of discussions, Diogo and Ben Zarella arrived at a decision to create a third branch, to be partially owned and financed by Diogo, to employ New Christians recently arrived from Portugal. Diogo would provide the training and the personnel; Abrabanel and Zarella would contract for the printing jobs, and subsequently distribute and market the books throughout Europe.

Brianda and Beatriz found Ben enormously entertaining, especially with his stories of the misbehavior of cardinals and popes at the Vatican, and with his description of the glamorous social whirlwind which was Venice. Repeatedly, they invited him to dine at Diogo's table. Often as not, when the evening was over, Ben would walk Beatriz through Diogo's garden and over to the garden which opened into her own home.

With the exception of her repressed erotic feelings for Diogo, Beatriz had felt no attraction for any particular man, though Diogo had spent much energy attempting to interest her in various merchants and scholars in Antwerp.

She was surprised when she felt mild stirrings of romantic interest in the handsome young businessman who read every history he could get his hands on in French, Spanish, Portuguese, Hebrew and Latin. Ben had been born of Spanish parents who had immigrated to Portugal in 1492. After the horrible uprising of 1506 his family had relocated to Antwerp where his father could build a new medical practice. Following in paternal footsteps, Ben had proven himself an amazing student of science, philosophy, and languages. After finishing his university studies, he was recruited by Don Isaac Abrabanel in Ferrara to join his company that was printing books by the thousands to satisfy the growing European market.

Tall and lanky as a young man, by the time Beatriz met Ben in 1537 he'd developed a well-muscled chest and arms due to his routine of daily exercise and a Spartan life-style. Ben had been enchanted by Greek and Roman history and purposefully chosen the ancient Spartans as an example to live by. He began each morning with one-hundred sit-ups, and then ran six miles no matter what the temperature or where he was living. His crisply waved dark brown hair was newly flecked with grey at the temples, and his blue-grey eyes, that could rage with fury when he discussed cupidity and lawlessness, were twinkling with mischievousness most of the time when he was in Beatriz' presence. She had heard him be brusque with men, but he was invariably gentle and tender in his relations with women and children. He became a deeply cherished friend and welcome dinner guest at the Mendes home. Little Reyna took to him, loved nothing better than to bounce on his lap or ride with him on his favorite stallion.

Ben was a fount of information and gossip of Rome and Venice, especially about the history of the church during the last fifty years. Many of his printing contracts were with the Vatican, and in his enthusiastic search of Vatican records, he stumbled on the hand-written diary of Johann Burchard, a papal master of ceremonies, who kept a diary of papal life.

During their last dinner, Ben reported an instance from the diary: "God has given us the papacy," Pius III wrote his brother. "Let us enjoy it."

Over and above his commanding physical presence, Beatriz was taken by his high regard for women. He spoke admiringly of England's queen, of Isabella d'Este, Caterina Sforza, and Benvenida Abrabanel of Italy, and of Catherine de Medici. Though he had scorn for many of the Borgias, he admitted he admired the willpower and mental competence of Lucrezia Borgia, "though her reputed morals leave something to be desired."

"Women are every bit as competent as men in handling business affairs, and it's to our credit as Jews that we see fit to educate them in worldly matters," he declared during the first dinner at the Mendes home. It was probably, at that moment, Beatriz later mused, that I fell in love with him.

Later that first evening, after brandy, when he was making his good-byes, she asked, "Ben, will you be joining us for lunch on Sunday?"

His eyes twinkled with glee. "If I know you'll be there, nothing will keep me away."

Beatriz had lain awake long into the night that evening, reliving the look in his eyes as he bent to kiss her hand. Thinking of Ben, of his ideas and his overwhelming intelligence that kept his raw physical power in check, she felt herself humbled and at the same time enchanted. He was not a man to be trifled with; he would not permit it. If she returned his flirtatious looks and words, she told herself, she must be prepared for whatever joy or pain fate had in store for them. It would not be a trivial relationship. "How often is it given to a human being," she thought to her self, "that even as it is happening, they feel the surround of history, the making of war or peace, of pestilence or well-being, of feast or famine? Of the possibilities of demanding and achieving freedom."

Perhaps, she thought that night, they should keep their distance, not allow their futures to coalesce. On the other hand, that look in his eyes was undeniable. She knew if he pressed her, she would succumb. She needed to think long and hard about whether she really wanted a relationship with this man. And if she did, she had to be prepared to stay for the long haul. He would require nothing less.

He came for the Sunday luncheon, but seemed distracted which left her vaguely disappointed. They met one another at social events in Antwerp half a dozen times during the next month, then he left for Venice, Ferrara, and Rome. Twice he sent her short notes from his travels, and when he returned to Antwerp the following fall, he hosted a dinner at his home to which he invited her and the newly-weds, Brianda and Diogo Mendes.

A splendid host, Ben seated her on his right, in the place of honor. As usual, after returning from a visit to the Vatican, he summarized the repeatable gossip including several delicious stories about the Borgias, then launched into a discussion with his guests about the rivalry between the ports of Venice and Constantinople. Suleiman the Magnificent was building the most glorious capital in the world, building ships at an unheard of pace, and clearly preparing to become the supreme power in the Adriatic. Both the Holy Roman Emperor and the Pope were alarmed: something must be done to keep the Sublime Porte under control. Piracy, meanwhile, was threatening all shipping, whether it was coming from the Christian or the Moslem world.

Beatriz listened carefully, learning what she didn't already know, storing away knowledge and strategy for the future, fascinated by this businessman whose knowledge of maritime affairs, of banking, of differing religious philosophies marked him as a valuable advisor to any crowned head, secular or religious.

At the final moment when the evening's festivities were over, and Ben was bidding farewell to his guests, he asked, "May I call on you this Sunday?"

"I'd be honored to have you come for dinner." She murmured as he kissed the back of her hand. Again, the twinkle in his eyes said it all.

Beatriz ordered a table for two placed by the window in the library that overlooked their private park. Gas lights glowed, setting off the dark statue of Venus, giving the water from the fountains a silver sheen. The pear and cherry trees were in flower, the moon shone brightly. The table was dressed in burgundy and silver taffeta, the china service was painted with tiny burgundy roses. A dozen candles lit the room, the crystal and silver sparkled under a candelabra holding another six candles.

Beatriz chose her gown carefully: a long-sleeved red sheer wool with a fitted bodice, slim skirt, and low-cut neckline that emphasized her small rounded bosom. With it she wore a dazzling three-strand pearl necklace from which a large diamond pendant was suspended. The necklace was designed by her talented sister, and she wore it with great pride.

She chose the menu with equal care: artichoke soup followed by snapper with pine nuts and raisins, followed by roast lamb with rosemary, garlic and lemon. For dessert she planned to serve almond filled pastries and a port wine. She took three bottles of French wines from Diogo's wine cellar, and two of his finest cigars for Ben for after dinner. It would be a splendid evening!

****

"...at one Vatican banquet," Ben told her, "the Holy Father watched with loud laughter and much pleasure from a balcony while his bastard son slew unarmed criminals, one by one, as they were driven into a small courtyard below."

"Recreational homicide," Beatriz sneered.

"Exactly. Also, we have Burchard's description of an orgy during Alexander VI's reign. 'After the banquet dishes had been cleared away, the city's fifty most beautiful whores danced with guests, first clothed, then naked. Guests stripped and ran out to the floor where they mounted the prostitutes or were mounted by them. Servants counted each man's orgasms, and the pope distributed prizes to the men who had the greatest virility!'"

"And these are Peter's heirs, the popes we must obey in all things at risk of being burned alive."

"Let's talk of happier things," Ben said, reaching over and taking her hand. "I find myself very attracted to you. I hope you don't mind my telling you."

She shook her head, waiting for him to go on.

"I've read much about your husband, and Diogo has told me more. I understand that you are devoted to his memory."

She nodded her head. "He was everything to me: tutor, best friend, mentor, the smartest businessman I've ever encountered. An enormously generous husband. And, of course, father to my daughter Reyna."

"I would never expect to replace him in your heart, but..."

"I understand," she interrupted, holding his hand with both of hers. "Perhaps we can try for a mutually agreeable relationship." She sipped her port, holding his eyes with her own. "Now, please tell me about Venice."

****

Beatriz was in the Mendes office she shared with Diogo, reviewing the journal that recorded shipping accounts for the past month, when she looked over at Diogo and realized he was staring at her. "What is it?" she asked.

Reluctantly, caught off guard, Diogo responded. "I'll never understand how you talked me into marrying your sister, and in such a rush..."

Beatriz felt a sharp pain in her abdomen, her whole body flushed with fearful anticipation. "What's happened?"

"Brianda is the most self-centered, superficial and vengeful person I've ever met. You must never trust her, Gracia, she will throw you to the lions if she can figure out how to..."

"Diogo! What a dreadful thing to say!" But even as her anger mounted, she remembered Francisco warning her about Brianda. "What has happened?"

"It's never been a secret that she is jealous of you, of your beauty, your cold-blooded business acumen, your language ability..."

Gracia interrupted, "She never wanted to go to Francisco's school, she always said business bored her. Her only interest has always been clothes and jewels, and at that she excels."

"I quite agree that is her outstanding talent. And I have indulged it every way I know how. I have denied her nothing. Nonetheless, she rails against you. She goes into hysterics if I dare to mention your name, to praise you in any way. She has tried on numerous occasions to forbid me to invite you into our home for our business dinners. She can't stand the fact that I spend every working day with you. She constantly tells me I love you more than I love her." He stopped suddenly, stood and walked over to Gracia. He pulled her to her feet.

"Of course, it's true. She's no dummy." Diogo pulled Gracia close, into a full embrace.

Gracia stiffened in his arms, pushed against his chest with the palm of her hand. "Diogo, no, we mustn't...we must not give in to that kind of temptation, hard as it is for both of us."

"I, I want you so." His strong arms pulled her closer, his lips sought hers in a soft kiss that deepened into a passionate heated embrace.

At first Gracia succumbed to his passion then coming to her senses, pulled away. "Diogo, I've not told you yet, but I've begun a relationship with Ben, a serious relationship."

He released her but continued to look deeply into her eyes. "I've thought as much and hoped it wasn't so at the same time I've hoped you and he would get together, I want you to be happy, Gracia. Surely, you know that." He brushed a tendril of her hair behind her ear and kissed her forehead softly. "I'll never stop wanting you, never in this lifetime. But I want you to be happy, not be alone."

"Diogo, ever since the moment I arrived in Antwerp I've been sorely tempted by my feelings for you. I've fought them every single day, just as I believe you have tried hard to be a faithful husband to Brianda. We must continue to do what is right, what is right for our family, what is right in the eyes of our God."

Gracia sat back down, smoothed her skirt, and looked up at Diogo. "Perhaps part of my motivation for becoming involved with Ben Zarella is to neutralize my feelings for you. Ben satisfies my sexual cravings so that you and I can continue to be successful, focused business partners. Besides, in spite of everything you tell me, I love my sister, and I would not betray her with her husband."

Chapter Fifteen

The Milan Commission
Spring, 1542

The repeated petitions of the New Christians to the civil and ecclesiastical authorities in Portugal came to naught in 1539 when the Holy Office authorized the Inquisition in response to the urging of King John, who was enraged by the House of Mendes. Thousands of New Christians, fearful that they would be thrown in a dungeon, tortured or burned at the stake, fled in a panic to Italy, France, England, Flanders and the Ottoman Empire. These refugees were supplied with money for travel, land and sea transportation, a route of safe houses and inns, all by agents of the Mendes underground. So many Portuguese flocked to Milan that the city fathers created a commission to investigate these Marranos, and in 1540 they began arresting dozens of Portuguese settling in Ancona and Salonica, charging them with Judaizing. When word of these arrests and torture reached Diogo and Beatriz, he called a conference at his home, inviting several of the leading merchants of Antwerp as well as his agents in London, Milan and Venice.

They gathered in the "war room" on the fourth floor of Diogo's house. Beatriz and her nephew Joseph, who was now a trusted agent-in-training for the company, greeted the local merchants as they were ushered upstairs by the butler. Meanwhile, Diogo was closeted with his trusted associate from London, Antonio de Ronha.

The "war room" was during the work-week the "map room", where a dozen master cartographers refined and copied the Mendes maps based on the latest information from returning sea captains. These maps were the most precious possession of the House of Mendes, kept under lock and key, and shared with only the Fuggers and the Affaitati, in spite of numerous requests from the Vatican and royal houses of Europe. These maps not only recorded the most preferable sea lanes, but also detailed safe routes over land throughout Europe and the Ottoman Empire.

Diogo, following a conversation with Beatriz, had created a few "faulty" maps which he supplied to agents he knew would give them away to his enemies, a bit of shrewdly placed disinformation.

This particular Sunday afternoon it was cold, wet and windy on the Kipdorp. The thirty candles in the massive chandelier, which hung over the conference table, the candle-lit sconces that lined the walls, and the flickering fires in the fireplaces at both ends of the massive room created a welcoming atmosphere. A small table was laid with fruit, pastries, wine and coffee.

When everyone had arrived and was settled at the table with their refreshments of choice, Diogo called the meeting to order. "Good afternoon gentlemen and Beatriz. We appreciate you giving up your Sunday afternoon, but we feel it is urgent that we exchange information and formulate a plan that we can agree on and present a united front to the newly created commission in Milan."

They had all seen one another, just hours earlier, at Mass at the great Cathedral of Our Lady. And they'd been certain to greet the Cardinal on leaving the Church; no one could claim that these New Christians, all of whom had been born either in Spain or Portugal, were not observant Catholics, thought Beatriz.

She reveled in the fact that she was included in this meeting; the leaders of the New Christian community had reluctantly come to accept the fact that she had great power, even though she was a woman, because of her equal partnership in the House of Mendes.

Diogo continued. "We all have different sources of information. Tell us what you've heard from your agents, whether you think it only rumor or fact." He turned to his right, gesturing for Manuel Lopes, a successful textile merchant, to begin.

Lopes was a short man, nearly bald, with piercing eyes and a gravely voice. "I'm told that the Inquisition has introduced something called the *Jungfer*. This contraption embraces a person with metal arms and crushes the condemned with spikes that create a hundred stab wounds and break every bone in the body. The contraption then opens and lets the body fall into a pit where the person dies slowly." Gasps of astonishment and anger filled the room. "Right now they are using this contraption in Germany, but rumor has it that they are building a second one in Lisbon."

An enraged Beatriz asked, "You mean burning someone alive at the stake isn't punishment enough? What kind of evil monsters has the Church spawned?"

Manuel Serano, who sold Oriental rugs from Turkey, spoke up from across the table. "I've heard the same thing. But in Milan, right now, they are using the *strapado,* which stretches one's body, and they force prisoners to walk across hot braziers with bare feet. People are tortured to the point where they confess whether they are guilty or not. We've got to find a way to get our people out of those Milan prisons."

Lope de Provincia, the manager of the Mendes emporium, which sold merchandise to the people of Antwerp, spoke up. "The rumor I'm hearing is that this is a scheme to make these New Christians pay a head tax for the right to settle in Ancona or Salonica, simply a scheme to put more money into the city treasury."

"How much do you think they want to charge per family?" Diogo asked. "We can probably live with that if it's reasonable."

Looking at each person at the table for agreement, Beatriz said, "It seems to me the first order of business is to find a way to supply food, medicine, and anything else we can to these prisoners. They need to know we are going to be supportive of them, and we've got to do this quickly."

Goncales Gomes, the Mendes agent stationed in Milan answered, "If we raise a relief fund here today, I'll start for Milan at first light tomorrow morning, I know some of the men on the Commission, and I'll be happy to take a message to them from all of you."

The discussion continued for several hours. By the time they had raised 2,000 ducats for Gomes to take with him back to Milan, Beatriz announced, "We've got to move our people out of the reach of the papacy, away from that filth. Convents are nothing more than brothels, altar boys are being sodomized by bishops and cardinals, and women are being molested in the confessional. Gluttony and intoxication are celebrated; pornography is nowhere more prized than at the Vatican. Banquets turn into sexual orgies. For the last hundred years the popes have had mistresses and spawned bastard children, then named these children cardinals in the church."

Beatriz paused and looked up and down the table at the male faces who were mesmerized by her passionate outburst. "Don't you want to move your wives and children to a place where they can openly proclaim their Judaism, where they will no longer have to pledge allegiance to this organized debauchery?"

After all their guests but one had left, the Mendes family sat down to supper with a distant cousin of Diogo, Gaspar Lopes, who worked for the company in London. He agreed that he too would travel to Milan and attempt to negotiate a settlement of these issues with the Commission.

Two weeks later Diogo arrived home with the news that Lopes had been arrested on "suspicion of Judaizing, and had been tortured on the *strapado*." Under such pressure, he snapped and turned informer. He'd given the officials the names of the participants in the Sunday meeting at Diogo's house, told them what was decided and who argued most strenuously, identified who the Mendes agents were in London, and supposedly had told them that the real purpose of the relief fund was to hire henchmen to murder the commissioners.

The news that Beatriz and Diogo were suspected of planning assassinations introduced a new level of fear into their lives, and Beatriz argued with Diogo that they had to move the family to safety.

The Emperor[1], hearing of Lopes' confession, ordered strictest surveillance of the Antwerp *Marranos*. Antwerp's city fathers, to their credit, countered with a detailed account of the contribution the New Christians made to the economy of Antwerp.

The proclamation of the city father's did not satisfy Diogo's need to protect his family. He ordered the household to pack essentials: clothes, food, medicines, the *Sifre Torah*, a complete set of maps, jewelry and other small items of great value. Shortly after the lamp lighter had made his rounds, Diogo, Beatriz, Brianda, Samuel, Joseph, Reyna and a few trusted servants slowly made their way through the underground tunnel which led from the mansion on the Kipdorp to a small dock on the northern end of the port. They boarded a caravel owned by the Fuggers, headed this evening for London, where they would wait to see what the Milan Commission decided next.

On the way to London, Beatriz again argued with Diogo that they had to start preparations to move the family to Turkey.

Finally, worn down by physical exertion and emotional exhaustion, Diogo agreed with Beatriz and Joseph, "You are right. We must move the family and the House of Mendes. The three of us will draw up plans, let's aim to leave Antwerp no later than twelve months from now, June of 1543. From their hiding place in London, Diogo organized the surreptitious removal of their most valuable household goods from their homes in Antwerp.

From that day forward, each ship headed for the Ottoman Empire from Antwerp carried crates of priceless leather bound books, Oriental rugs, statuary, art work, sets of maps, several Torahs, chandeliers, candelabra, china, crystal and silver. The Mendes agent in Constantinople made arrangements for safe storage of these priceless goods, awaiting the arrival of the Mendes family.

1 Charles I was the Holy Roman Emperor, King of the Netherlands and the Hapsburg lands, and reigned as Carlos V, King of Spain, which made him the head of the Spanish Inquisition.

After three weeks in England, the Mendes family returned to Antwerp, having "taken a short vacation to enjoy the sights and sounds of London." Diogo and Beatriz replaced their fine furnishing with lesser, relatively cheap furniture; they ceased their constant entertaining, pleading Diogo's failing health and Brianda's pregnancy. Only a handful of their closest associates guessed their real plans.

Chapter Sixteen

Diogo's Will

A hurried knock on her bedroom door, and Carmen Maria, Brianda's personal maid burst in, followed by Beatriz' butler Max. "Don Diogo is ill, Doña Brianda says you must come at once." Beatriz was seated at her small desk, writing thank you notes. She put the pen down, grabbed at her chest where a sharp pain resonated. *It's his heart, she thought, he's been so pasty looking lately, out of breath and coughing a lot.*

Max rushed to her closet and pulled out a heavy navy cloak to protect her against the cold damp weather during the short run through the courtyard to Diogo's home. Beatriz told him to summon Joseph and Samuel from their apartment across the courtyard. He nodded, and she flew downstairs and out the door with Carmen Maria. Max rushed across the cobblestone path to the young men's apartment.

Brianda, her butler and several maids, all of them weeping, were gathered in Diogo's vast bedroom. Beatriz' first glance confirmed her worst fear: he was dead. She walked slowly to his bedside, hoping against hope she was wrong. Tentatively, she reached up and touched the large vein in his thick neck. There was no pulse. His eyes were closed, and for all the world it seemed he was peacefully asleep. She turned her attention back to Brianda who, still in her dressing gown, was seated in a chair beside his bed, holding a white handkerchief to her face. "Bruno discovered him like this when he didn't come down for breakfast."

Beatriz turned to Bruno. "When did you last speak with Don Diogo?"

"Last evening, after he finished his cigar and brandy, I asked him if he needed anything else. He told me good night, and said he'd be going up to bed shortly." Bruno paused, then added, "He seemed very fatigued."

"Yes, I'd sent a letter to Amatus Lusitanus, his doctor, asking him to come to Antwerp, but he is in Rome attending the pope. Don Diogo has not been himself recently."

Just then, Joseph and Samuel followed by Max rushed into the bedroom. Joseph ran to the bed, picked up Diogo's hand and felt for a pulse. He sighed and then turned to Bruno, "Any sign of foul play?"

"No, sir, Don Joseph. He passed in his sleep, I found him like this when he didn't come down for breakfast."

Brianda stood and Beatriz wrapped her arms around her in a tight embrace. "Baby Beatriz will never remember her father."

"We'll tell her all about him, we'll keep his memory alive," soothed Beatriz, patting Brianda's back. She turned to Joseph, suddenly all business. "We must prepare his body for burial and notify his closest associates. The funeral will be tomorrow afternoon. Samuel, we'll ask you to deliver notes all over the city this afternoon, so be on standby. Max, I'll need you to work with Samuel on this. Bruno, please prepare to take a message to Cardinal Sigismund so he can notify the appropriate prelates and the choir. We will want a High Mass with all the special blessings. I will go to my office now and write a letter to the Cardinal."

"How can you be so...so cold and impersonal...at a time like this?" asked Brianda, tears streaming down her face.

"Because I have to be, I have to do what is best for the family, for all of us, for all those people all over the world who depend on the House of Mendes." She stopped, softened her voice. "My tears will come later."

And come they did, the next night after the funeral and burial, after several hundred of Diogo's business associates and friends paid their respects at the home of the now widowed Brianda de Luna Mendes. It was Beatriz' lover, Ben Zarella, who'd insisted on spending the night with her, who finally witnessed her grief.

"He's always been a part of my life. I think I had a crush on Diogo when I was ten, eleven years old, but my father considered Francisco the more serious, the more certain of success. And I loved Francisco dearly, with all my heart and soul. But Diogo...well, Diogo with his twinkling eyes was always more fun, a big tease, lots more fun than Francisco. After Francisco's death, I was determined to get Diogo to marry Brianda..."

"And you got your wish."

"Yes. And now we have baby Beatriz. And I've fulfilled my promise to my parents to take care of Brianda. She will share the wealth of the House of Mendes. Let's hope that she uses it wisely so it will last for generations to come. Yes, I fulfilled my promise, but oh my, how I will miss Diogo, every minute, every day of my life. It never stops hurting..."

Ben wrapped his arms around Beatriz and held her closely, then walked her to her bed and tucked her in before he joined her from the other side. "Sleep, my darling, you'll need every bit of your strength for tomorrow."

As was the tradition of the New Christians, they visited Brianda for the ten days following Diogo's funeral, consoling one another, and in the secrecy of her home offering traditional food and prayers and blessings.

Brianda and Beatriz dressed in full mourning, though Beatriz felt it essential to go to the office each day and supervise the business affairs of the House of Mendes.

On the eleventh day following the funeral, Diogo's solicitor gathered the family and a few trusted business associates in the library of the Mendes home for the reading of the will. As required by law, it would be published within thirty days of Mendes death. It was important for the heirs to understand its terms before it became public knowledge.

Don Duarte Soccino, the solicitor, read the pertinent parts aloud: "the sum of 1,600 Flemish pounds for the poor, out of the income of which one hundred pounds are to be distributed in charity each year in Portugal, or if this cannot be arranged, in Flanders. One-third shall go to needy prisoners, one-third shall go to clothe the naked, one-third shall go to orphans."

"In keeping with the business arrangements I have with my brother of blessed memory, Francisco Mendes, and his will, one-half of the capital of the House of Mendes belongs to his widow, Beatriz da Luna Nasi Mendes. Relying on Doña Beatriz' proven competence and integrity as a businesswoman, I nominate her to be head of the House of Mendes and make all business decisions for the House and all its affiliates for as long as she lives. She is to invest and distribute all funds resultant from the business of the House of Mendes on behalf of my wife's interest and my baby daughter's interest in the House of Mendes. I hereby direct that my wife, Brianda de Luna Mendes, immediately receive the 30,000 ducats, which were her dowry. I appoint my sister-in-law, Beatriz Mendes as the Administrator of this will. In the event that, for whatever reason, Beatriz Mendes is unable to comply with my wishes, I appoint her nephew Joseph Nasi and Agostino Enriques Benveniste as co-executors of this estate and of the House of Mendes."

Soccino placed the document on the table and looked at the startled faces surrounding him. "That document is a fake!" Brianda screamed. "Diogo could not have possibly wanted Beatriz to control my fortune. It's got to be a fake!"

Beatriz, as stunned by the contents of the will as Brianda was, felt her sister's pain at the same moment she felt pride in the faith Diogo had placed in her. And her next thought was the enormity of the responsibility. How could she possibly manage all his businesses, the shipping company, the diamond company, textiles, printing, Oriental rugs and household furnishings...it went on and on. And the biggest responsibility of all, the Underground, surreptitiously moving the family and other New Christians to Turkey, to safety and freedom. It was overwhelming.

Soccino was saying, "I assure you, Doña Brianda, it is exactly what your husband wanted, what he dictated. We spent many hours together working on this document, and it is exactly what he required. You may see his signature and speak to his witnesses if you doubt me."

"You tricked him into this, you and Beatriz working together, tricked him into writing and signing this. He never would have done it."

Beatriz rose from her seat across from Brianda and walked to where she was sitting. "Brianda, I'm sorry you feel so strongly about this. Believe me, it is a surprise to me too. I promised our parents I would always look out for your best interests, and I renew that vow this minute. I will see to it that you always have everything you need and want. I will be sure of the same for baby Beatriz. You have nothing to fear, you will always have every comfort it is humanly possible to provide. That is what Diogo wants, that is what I will always want." She finished this statement with her hand resting affectionately on Brianda's shoulder.

Brianda pushed her hand away, stood, spat at her and walked from the room, with hateful words flung back at her. "He always loved you more than he loved me. And this proves it!"

Everyone stood, astonished and embarrassed by Brianda's outburst and anxious to comfort Beatriz. Joseph was the first to approach her. "Don't worry, Aunt Gracia, Samuel and I will be with you every step of the way. We'll do this together, you can always count on us."

She turned to her tall, handsome nephew, the light of her life. "I know you will, Joseph. Diogo told me I could always count on you, and you see, he made it official with his will. We are very proud of the young man you have become." She wrapped her arms around him in a firm hug.

By order of the widow, Brianda Mendes, her home was closed to Beatriz with the exception of the map room on the fourth floor, which was accessible to Beatriz by walking over the arch that joined the two homes on the fourth floor. Due to her mourning, the widow Mendes planned no entertaining, no dinner parties, and very limited excursions outside her home. Bitterness and hatred of Beatriz became her obsession. She closed herself off, at the tender age of twenty-eight, to all social activities, except for going to Mass on Sunday.

Ben Zarella realized that Beatriz needed him more than ever for emotional strength and comfort, so he made arrangements to stay in Antwerp. He would manage the printing company during the days and spend evenings and weekends with Beatriz. "I believe it is what Diogo would have wanted," he told her, "at least for now."

Her plans to move the family to Constantinople were put on hold. There was so much to be settled, to be arranged before she could contemplate an escape. King Henry VIII of England had sent a message in which he asked to borrow 200,000 ducats; the Holy Roman Emperor had sent condolences and suggested that his nephew Maximilian, a friend and jousting partner of Joseph, be allowed to negotiate an additional loan to the Holy Roman Empire. And Joseph was badly needed in Lyon to settle some problems with the Mendes silk industry there.

"You should consider Venice or Ferrara," Ben coaxed her one Sunday morning after a delicious session of love-making. "Brianda would love the city, all the glamour, the balls and the Carnival celebrations. She loves gorgeous clothes and jewels, and there are so many opportunities in Venice to show off finery...Venetians worship wealth and beauty, and the two of you would be stars!"

"The Inquisition?"

"You'd find the Church is very lenient in Venice. They pretty much stay out of private affairs, as long as your public behavior is within bounds. As for Jews, they can openly practice their religion, but that applies only to those who live in the Ghetto, which is locked every evening. You don't want to proclaim your Jewishness in Venice. Better you should be a New Christian and enjoy all Venice has to offer.

"I'll think about it," she promised him, "and pray on it."

"You won't believe this document," Joseph exclaimed as he plopped down in a chair opposite Beatriz. He had just returned from Lyon, an international financial center, and meetings with representatives of Charles V, the Holy Roman Emperor. "It claims that Diogo Mendes was a heretic, plotting assassinations against various church officials and members of the Milan Commission. He was a secret Jew who spent his time, money and prestige fostering agnostic behavior and beliefs. This, in spite of all the money, all the bribes and loans to Charles and to the Church..." His face was red with anger, the veins in his neck bulging with each beat of his heart.

"Even though Diogo is dead and can do no more harm to the Church, the Emperor believes the imperial treasury is empowered to confiscate the capital, businesses, and property of the House of Mendes."

"What can we do?" Beatriz asked, tapping her quill on the desk in an effort to control her anger.

"We can request a hearing, but as always, it will be fixed in advance."

"We can do more," Beatriz declared. "We can inform all the merchants and bankers here in Antwerp, and elsewhere of the Emperor's intentions. There are lots of folks, including the cardinal, who will vouch for Diogo's unimpeachable Christian zeal. Remember, I gave the cardinal 10,000 ducats as a gift after Diogo's funeral. That's a pretty generous gift!"

Joseph nodded his agreement.

"Charles must have been salivating over the evidence he was being presented, and he was already mentally spending the money he would get from confiscating the Mendes' wealth. Diogo's death has cheated him out of that fantasy. These posthumous proceedings are a farce, and we've got to expose them for exactly that. A blatant effort to steal the wealth of the House of Mendes."

Beatriz stood and paced as she spoke. "We must make a list of outstanding merchants here and abroad, of church officials we've bribed in the past, of men like Amatus Lusitanus who has the ear of the pope. We must elicit letters and testimony from these outstanding Old Christians that Diogo was a true and faithful Catholic. And we must be prepared to grease the palms of officials here in Antwerp, make sure they attest to his outstanding contribution to the economic welfare of the community. Yes, and we must enlist the Fuggers and the Affaititi family also. Perhaps we could also get letters of recommendation from the Medicis and the Della Roverres. Get started on it."

"Right away."

"You have my authority to spare no expense. Do whatever you need to do to put this ridiculous matter to rest."

During the next few months, Joseph and Beatriz gathered letters, testimonials, and witnesses ready to testify in person. They bribed officials and gave jobs to numerous relatives of prominent persons who would testify; they created an overwhelming groundswell of support for the Mendes family among the merchants of Antwerp.

Two special hearings were held, during which church officials and businessmen testified in favor of the Mendes family. The only witnesses for the opposition were New Christians who had been tortured into confessions. Receiving word of these happenings, King Henry VIII intervened with the Holy Roman Emperor on behalf of his "good friend," Beatriz da Luna Mendes.

Shortly thereafter, an emissary of Charles arrived with a letter. The Emperor would withdraw charges and consider the matter closed if the House of Mendes would "loan" him the sum of 150,000 ducats at no interest for two years. Joseph responded, on behalf of Beatriz, that the House of Mendes was prepared to loan 100,000 ducats under the conditions specified by the Emperor. The deal was signed, sealed and the money delivered to Charles by Joseph Nasi in person. As it turned out, it was the first of many personal meetings between Joseph and the Holy Roman Emperor.

Beatriz hated making such a deal, but nonetheless considered it a victory. Giving up 100,000 ducats as a loan was a lot cheaper than permitting the entire Mendes fortune to be confiscated. And she believed it meant that Diogo Mendes' name was cleared forever as far as the Catholic Church was concerned.

Chapter Seventeen

“They Want Our Daughters!”

"We must seriously consider accepting this invitation," Joseph told his Aunt Beatriz, as they finished their breakfast coffee. He placed the heavy vellum letter from Queen Mary's secretary on the table.

Beatriz looked with great pride at her dynamic twenty-three year old nephew and protégé. "You must have made a very good impression on the Holy Roman Emperor, for him to insist that his sister invite us, two New Christians who have always lived under a cloud of suspicion of being Judaizers, to participate in a ball at her court in Brussels."

Joseph grinned, a bit sheepishly.

She sighed, "I must tell you, Joseph, I'm not enthusiastic about attending; it's a long trip, costly and perilous. I get exhausted just thinking about the preparations for such a grueling journey."

"Queen Mary has also invited Aunt Brianda. You can be sure, in spite of her mourning period, she's going to plan to go."

"Yes, she's always yearned to be part of the royal social circle. This is her big chance." Beatriz paused. "She may also be looking for a second husband. What better place to look!"

"I've an idea. Why don't I visit her and suggest that we all travel together to Brussels. If Ben Zarella is your official escort, after all, he's your business partner with the printing company, I'll be Aunt Brianda's official escort; no one can really make an issue of the fact that she's still in mourning. She's simply obeying a request of the Queen, who has been asked to include us in the royal circle by none other than Charles V, the Holy Roman Emperor, who happens to owe the House of Mendes 100,000 ducats. And you can be sure he wants to borrow more."

"It might be the perfect chance to mend my relationship with my sister. I'd like that. We'd be cooped up in that gilded coach for at least two days, lots of time to talk, to remember old times, you know, sentimental, emotional talk, talk about children. Yes, the expense and hardship of the trip would be worth it if Brianda and I could be loving sisters again. Do speak with her, Joseph. See if you can work it out."

Later that same day Beatriz received a note from Brianda: "Sister dear, I have spoken with Joseph and I quite agree that we should accept our Queen's invitation to the ball and subsequent festivities. Brussels should be quite beautiful in October. I designed a beautiful suite of emeralds and diamonds for Queen Mary, and I hear she is extraordinarily pleased with them. I very much want to meet her in person. I will make preparations to attend. I trust you will make funds available for the gowns and jewels I will design. Perhaps you would like me to create a new ball gown for you? Please have your secretary reply for all of us. Yours in Christ, Brianda"

Beatriz summoned Joseph. "What's this 'yours in Christ' all about? Has she gone mad?"

"It seems, based on gossip from her servants, that Brianda has become very Catholic. She attends mass and receives communion at least once a week in addition to Sunday, she receives the Cardinal at tea several times a month, and Bruno says she always gives him an envelope with money in it 'for the orphans'. You know that money goes directly into his own pocket."

Beatriz' disappointment showed in her grim expression. "She never has been much of a Jew, refused to study Hebrew, I wonder if we can trust her? What a sad state of affairs."

"We must consider her a traitor in our midst. Ben and I have spoken of this many times. We cannot trust Brianda. She hates you and spends emotional energy plotting revenge. However, she is acutely aware that she is completely dependent on you for her income. She's shrewd enough and manipulative enough that she'll not endanger her fortune and that of her daughter. You can count on that."

Beatriz hated hearing his words, but she knew they were true. "Watch her closely, Joseph, and keep me posted. In fact, make it a point to meet with her several times a week and gauge her emotional state. She can be unpredictable and impetuous, and she's also a great actress when she wants to be."

Six weeks later the widows' Mendes and their escorts were ensconced in a luxurious Brussels apartment made available to them by the court. They had traveled in a convoy of four coaches with two wagons to carry their luggage, and accompanied on the arduous journey by no less than twenty armed guards as well as their personal servants.

True to her promise, Brianda had designed for herself an exquisite white silk velvet gown with a sapphire velvet cloak lined in ermine. Gold braid gathered the velvet snuggly beneath her bosom and crisscrossed her rib cage, emphasizing her tiny waist; the slim skirt flowed over her hips with a fluid motion. Her deep décolletage was highlighted by a four-inch wide bowknot brooch of diamond and sapphire baguettes that showcased a sculptural three-dimensional design. With this newly-minted brooch, she wore matching sapphire and diamond ear rings and a two-inch wide bracelet. The brooch was quite simply the most beautiful jewelry creation Beatriz had ever seen. Her sister was indeed talented as a designer.

For Beatriz, Brianda had designed a ruby velvet gown with matching cloak trimmed in golden-brown sable that Joseph had imported from Russia. She chose to wear the three strand pearl necklace with the diamond brooch, which Brianda had designed several years earlier.

The four of them arrived at the court in the carved and gilded coach that Diogo had been so proud of, now cleaned and polished after the arduous trip. "They felt, and looked," Joseph commented, "as royal as the court!"

Queen Mary greeted them warmly, as if they were old cherished friends. Brianda's jewel caught her eye immediately, "My dear, you must make me one exactly like that; it is magnificent!" To Brianda's great delight, the queen was wearing the emeralds she had designed two years earlier. "I'm sorry it's taken us so long to get to know you," the queen said, as she patted her necklace. "We must have lunch later this week!"

Before long, knights of the court were whirling Brianda and Beatriz around the ball room, Joseph was off in a corner with the queen's nephew, Maximilian, and Ben Zarella was left alone at the table to contemplate the spectacle and talk to guests who were too old and infirm to dance.

It was nearly two in the morning when the foursome made their way back to their apartments, excited and weary and ready for a long night's sleep. They were awakened by a messenger from the court, telling Beatriz and Brianda that the queen wanted them to join her for tea at four in the afternoon.

Brianda was thrilled, certain that the queen would give her a new commission. Beatriz was wary, suspicious that the queen would ask for an additional loan, probably "without interest". Surprisingly, Joseph was not included in the invitation, but an hour later an invitation arrived for him to join Maximilian for a fencing match. Ben was on his own; he would visit the bookstores in the city.

"It's not a loan she wants, it's our daughters!" Beatriz announced angrily as they sat down to dinner late that evening. "Our daughters are to be auctioned off to the nobles of Europe. She wants to arrange marriage contracts for Reyna and baby Beatriz. Imagine! The arrogance of that woman! And she says the emperor himself suggested it; our daughters are to be 'a prize to be conferred on nobles'. Over my dead body!"

"They want the dowries. They are probably already promising some percent of the dowry will go into the Emperor's treasury," Ben added.

"And the Queen will get a portion for her treasury too!" Beatriz answered. "She had the nerve to ask me how big Reyna's dowry would be! When I told her that her father and I had not discussed it before his death, and I made no decisions yet, after all the child is only thirteen years old. She told me she thought the dowry should be at least one million ducats, as if she thinks she knows the extent of our wealth."

She sipped her wine, then continued. "I answered that it might be as much as 5,000 ducats; she didn't like that at all!"

"I'm surprised she'd not trying to find a husband for you, Beatriz," Ben added.

"Oh, that came up. She went on and on about my beauty, competence, and need for a husband. I told her that I would never remarry, never turn the fortune of the House of Mendes over to any man. For a moment, I thought I saw approval in her eyes, then she remembered who she was, what she was after, and strongly suggested again that I change my mind. She said she had several very fine gentlemen in mind, older men who would not expect much from me in bed."

Brianda, who had been quietly listening to Beatriz' raging, said, "What would be so awful about baby Beatriz marrying a duke or a knight? I think it would be wonderful for her to participate in the life of a royal court."

Ben and Joseph watched as Beatriz face became bright pink. "No Mendes woman will marry an old Christian. We will betroth our daughters to New Christians, or to no one. I would rather see Reyna and baby Beatriz dead than see them married to an old Christian."

"I am Beatriz's mother and I will decide who she marries."

"If you betroth her to an old Christian, she will not have a dowry from the Mendes estate. That is my final word on this issue." Beatriz rose from the table and imperiously made her way to her bedroom.

After a night's sleep, Beatriz realized that though she would like to pack up and leave for Antwerp immediately, she would have to remain in Brussels for at least two weeks to keep all the business appointments Joseph had made in advance of their arrival. They were slated to meet with numerous suppliers of the famous, much-coveted lace, which was hand made in Brussels. In addition to purchasing bed and table linens for their two homes, the Mendes women were buying fabric and lace for the wives of the merchants they dealt with back in Antwerp. They would also take back lace for the Mendes emporium managed by Lope de Provincia.

During breakfast, Brianda appeared, red-eyed and somber. "I'm sorry about last evening," she said in a trembling voice. "Of course, I don't want little Beatriz betrothed to an old man, regardless of what his religion is. We must protect both girls against the avarice of the crown."

Beatriz rose from her chair, clasp Brianda to her bosom, then wiped away a tear. She kissed her on both cheeks. "Brianda, dearest sister, I understand, I truly do. We must stick together in matters like this. You and I have a great deal to protect, and it's not going to be easy."

After several days of shopping and negotiating with the lace merchants, Brianda was thrilled to receive another invitation from Queen Mary. Would she come to the palace to discuss a jewelry commission? Beatriz urged her to go, taking only Joseph along to negotiate the finances. "I'm afraid, my dear, that if I am there she will again bring up the subject of marriage. I don't want to lose my temper; she needs to understand that I will never remarry, no matter what the pressure."

Two days later Brianda reported that the Queen had suggested that they move the girls to the Brussels court, that they be raised in the palace with tutors provided by the Queen, and that they would be betrothed to suitable nobles at the appropriate time.

"That's it!" Beatriz exclaimed, pacing back and forth before the parlor window, "We will leave as soon as we can get packed. I'll not meet with that woman again!"

Two days later the Mendes convoy left Brussels under cover of darkness.

Once back in Antwerp, Beatriz redoubled her efforts to prepare business affairs in such a way that she could remove her family to Turkey. Lengthy, not always amiable discussions were held with her numerous advisors. Some of them, Ben Zarella among them, insisted it would be better for the family businesses to move to Venice or Ferrara. Brianda favored this idea, as she had always wanted to visit Venice and partake of the extraordinary social life she'd heard about.

Beatriz, who suffered from severe rheumatism, dreaded the idea of spending many months on the muddy and rutted roads of France, then crossing the mountains and finally arriving in Venice. Joseph, and everyone else, insisted that it would be safer to go by land than try to go by sea. "Once they realize we are gone, they will stop all the shipping convoys in an attempt to find us. You can be sure, word would spread, and our movements would be interdicted. If you travel by land and stay only in the safe houses we've identified, I believe you could move the family to Venice where you would be very warmly received. If after living in Venice for a while, you still want to move to Constantinople, we can arrange it."

Pressure to arrange a marriage for Reyna became more intense in April when Charles V forwarded a letter from Don Francisco d'Aragon to the queen, who sent it on to Beatriz with a request that Beatriz meet with her in Brussels to discuss Don Francisco's proposal. "He is the son of Nuno Manuel of the Aragonese royal house," wrote Queen Mary, "and he had the honor of accompanying the Empress Isabella when she first went to Spain from Portugal. Recently he has been helping my brother as Commissary General. In that role, he investigated charges against the New Christians. He has become familiar with your family's recent history, and is anxious to become the husband and help-mate to your lovely orphaned daughter. The Emperor and I strongly recommend this liaison. It will be of great benefit to the future of your family to be strongly connected with this court by marriage."

"This is blackmail!" Beatriz raged. "The unwritten message is that if we don't let Reyna marry this elderly wastrel, they may again accuse us of Judaizing. If we agree to the marriage, they will look the other way when we practice our religion in secrecy. One way or another, they are determined to get their hands on our wealth!"

Beatriz immediately responded to the queen that her health was such that she could not embark on another grueling journey. The queen responded that she would be in Antwerp in July, and would look forward to meeting with Beatriz then.

Joseph, after a week of jousting and fencing with Maximilian, came home with the news that Don Francisco was proposing that "the mother should be disregarded and the arrangements concluded without consulting her."

"And if they try something like that,' Joseph stated, "I'll get all the merchants here to rise up as one, and we'll desert this country altogether. No way are we going to let the Court dictate our most intimate family matters or confiscate our estates. If we Jews take our families and businesses elsewhere, the economy of this country will become a shell of what it is now. That I can guarantee."

Beatriz responded, "I think Queen Mary is too shrewd to try such a thing. She's met me; she's heard about our family, and she knows our history. Let's see what happens when she's here in July."

Brianda and the talented goldsmith employed by Don Benjamin Panetta completed the queen's brooch in time for her July visit to Antwerp. The queen wrote Brianda a lovely note, accepting it, thanking her and inviting her to tea with several other ladies of the merchant class. Beatriz was not invited. She recognized it for what it was, a snub, and notice that the queen was displeased with her. She chose to ignore the slight.

Several weeks later the Queen sent word that she wanted to meet with Beatriz "privately to discuss a personal matter". A direct summons by the queen was something Beatriz could not realistically refuse. Insisting on the possibility of a trap, Joseph rode in the carriage with her, intending to wait with the coachman while she met with the queen. Beatriz had dressed in a coral linen shift, the coolest gown in her armoire. A matching coral linen bag, secured at her waist, held the dagger, which was always on her body. In her corset she had placed more than a million ducats worth of the finest quality diamonds. If this was a trap, she would fight or buy her way out of it.

The Queen greeted her in a small parlor off the ballroom. It was one of the hottest days of the summer and the queen's gown, a pale blue silk affair, stuck to her plump body. Perspiration glistened on her very pale face; she alternately mopped it with a handkerchief and fanned herself with an ivory fan. She was, Beatriz quickly realized, very anxious about the meeting. *Good! This gives me the upper hand.*

After pleasantries, the queen began to extol the character of Don Francisco. Beatriz listened patiently, not interrupting or asking questions. When the queen was unable to get a response from Beatriz, she began to talk about the history of the Mendes family. "We know, Charles has told me, that you have said many nasty things about the papacy. We believe that you and your late brother-in-law conspired to murder the members of the Milan Commission..."

"That is absolutely untrue, and whoever told you that knows that those slanderous statements were made by a New Christian when he was being tortured on the *strapado*. It is also a matter of fact, and your brother knows this, that testimony given under torture is not reliable. When someone is being tortured they will say whatever they think the person doing the torturing wants to hear. They will try to save their own lives by telling lies about others. You and your brother both know this."

The queen's face had turned bright red, her hands trembled as she lifted her tea cup.

Taking advantage of the queen's embarrassment, Beatriz continued, "You are correct. I have said that convents have become brothels. I have said that it is wrong for the Church to sell indulgences. I have said that Pope Alexander VI had an incestuous relationship with his daughter when she was seventeen; in fact, it is widely known that he fathered her child. The Catholic Church that you and I love so much has become a cesspool of debauchery, far removed from the teachings of Christ. In your heart of hearts you and I both know that. And your brother does too!"

Queen Mary's face had gone from bright red to ashen. She looked as if she were about to vomit. Beatriz continued, "I will not see my beautiful, innocent, well-educated daughter married to an elderly man who has for all his life participated in the debauchery of the Church. I would rather see my daughter dead than married to Don Francisco."

Beatriz stood, curtsied, and left the room. Queen Mary made no attempt to stop her.

Even as Beatriz savored the memory of the showdown with Queen Mary, she realized that the court would never cease its efforts to confiscate the Mendes fortune. Following the advice of Ben and Joseph, and others of her advisors, she made careful, secret plans to move her sister, niece and daughter out of harm's way. During the fall months, after the queen had returned to Brussels, Beatriz and her most trusted servants packed gems worth millions of ducats into various gowns, cloaks, pillows and heels of shoes. In a stroke of genius, Beatriz created a new hairstyle for herself and Brianda. Taking a length of black cloth the size of their head, they filled it with cotton batting and diamonds, sewing it up tightly. With their dark hair brushed down to its full length, they placed the roll around their head, bringing it together in front a few inches off their forehead. They brought their hair up over the roll, pinning their hair in such a way as to cover the roll completely. With their fingers they created a small coquettish pompadour, which dipped down over the right eye. It was a very attractive coiffure. "Queen Mary wears her crown of diamonds for everyone to see. We will wear crowns worth hundreds of times more, and no one will be the wiser."

Beatriz sent out word to their closest friends that she and Brianda were going to take the waters at Aix-la-Chapelle for her rheumatism. It was to be her first visit to France, and she and Brianda were excited, she said. Thus there were no problems when the two sisters with their daughters left Antwerp with two carriages and two wagons full of luggage and personal servants. Thirty armed men escorted the retinue, and three men advanced the party, making arrangements for overnight stays, for fresh horses, bedding and meals for the entire party. Ben Zarella had left a week earlier on horseback, with two armed guards. He would make preparations for their arrival, not at Aix-la-Chapelle, but in Venice. Joseph stayed behind in Antwerp to manage the family business and homes. And deal with the authorities.

Chapter Eighteen

The Holy Roman Emperor Demands His Share

Joseph Nasi shuffled some papers on his desk, took a deep breath, then stood and walked to the front parlor to meet his visitor, the Cardinal Sigismund, who had demanded an appointment, stating in his letter that he would be representing the Holy Roman Catholic Church as well as the Holy Roman Emperor, Carlos V.

How could one refuse such a visitor?

Once seated, Joseph offered liquid refreshment, the Cardinal declined.

"I'll waste no time, Nasi. We are disturbed that the de Luna sisters have vanished. Initially, we were informed they were taking the waters in Aix-la-Chapelle. Now we are informed by reliable sources they have decamped in Venice with every intention of making that their headquarters. We do not look kindly on this."

Joseph cleared his throat, tugged at the lace, which bordered his shirt sleeves. "I'm not certain that this is a matter within your jurisdiction. Both Brianda Mendes and Beatriz Mendes are Portuguese citizens. They have only lived here in Antwerp for a few years. If they have chosen to move on after the unfortunate death of their spouses, I don't see what business this is of the Church here in Antwerp. Or of the Holy Roman Emperor for that matter."

"We do have jurisdiction, as we suffer the loss of income from business conducted by the House of Mendes."

"Ah! But there is no reason to believe we are moving our business operations. Our large fleet of ships regularly stops here, our diamond business thrives, and we have recently established both a printing company and a textile importing company. We've ordered ten new ships, so great is the demand for sea transportation these days. I don't understand your concern."

"Well, young Nasi, I can tell you that based on what we know of the Mendes family, we believe that the time is not too far distant when you too will make your departure. The people I represent would be very upset if that were to happen."

"I see. My understanding of the legal situation is that merchants have every right to do business here, and then leave whenever it suits their business strategy. Together with all their personal property."

"That may be the case for most merchants. However, we have reason to believe that the de Luna sisters are secret Judaizers."

"That old charge! Whenever the Church or the local government wants to confiscate private property, that's the charge. A trumped up, dishonest, evil charge. I'm shocked that you, Cardinal, who has been so close to our family, especially Doña Brianda, are stooping to this level of hypocrisy. I challenge you to find anyone here in Antwerp who would make such a charge against either of these women."

His face beet red, the Cardinal continued angrily, "A charge of apostasy leveled by the Church will require the two women to appear before the Council of Brabant and defend themselves. I trust you will get in touch with them and encourage them to come back to Antwerp and to keep the House of Mendes here in Antwerp."

"So the Holy Roman Emperor can marry off little Reyna and Beatriz! Is that your plan? Is Charles V upset that he won't be getting a large portion of Reyna's dowry? He was depending on the 200,000 ducats, wasn't he? Face it, Sigismund, this isn't about apostasy, this is about the fact that Charles won't be getting the 200,000 he was depending on."

Cardinal Sigismund rose from his chair, his bloated face red. For a moment, Joseph thought he might have a stroke on the spot.

"I'll report this meeting to the authorities, you may be sure of it, Nasi!" he spat out as he left the room.

After the Cardinal left, Joseph walked back into the Mendes mansion. It was a depressing sight. All the precious household goods had been shipped to Constantinople where Beatriz eventually hoped to settle her family. The school was due to be closed within four weeks, the stables were empty except for one carriage, one wagon and half a dozen horses. Only a few servants remained to keep the two mansions in working order. Fortunately, only a very few persons knew the true state of the Mendes homes. When visitors came, they were limited to the front parlor where he had received the cardinal.

Joseph sat back down in the room he used for his office. Beatriz had communicated to him information concerning shipping, the size of fleets, piracy, and the on-coming struggle between Venice and Constantinople for control of the Adriatic Sea. According to her, it was imperative that the House of Mendes immediately contract for at least a dozen new ships, the largest possible, as there was a shortage of ships all over Europe.

"And who knows when we will need to use part of our fleet to defend our chosen country?"

Several weeks later, after charges of apostasy had been filed with the church authorities, Joseph took pen in hand and wrote a long treatise in defense of his aunts.

To the Council of Brabant:

I have in front of me your summons to the de Luna sisters to answer charges of apostasy. As you know, they are now living in Venice, having made the lengthy and arduous trip across the Alps last year. Unfortunately, the elderly Beatriz, now 38, suffers from severe heart problems as well as chronic rheumatism. She would probably not survive the journey back over the Alps. Her younger sister, Brianda, is among the most devout Catholics I have every known. She donates money to the Church nearly every week for orphans; she receives communion and attends mass several times a week. It is outrageous to accuse this deeply religious woman of apostasy.

On their behalf, I protest the fact that you have embargoed their personal property, including some forty chests containing clothing, books, jewelry, bed and table linens. These widows are not the extraordinarily wealthy women you seem to believe they are. Indeed, their entire fortune consists of 15,000 ducats each, left to them by their husbands. The remainder of the Mendes fortune was left to the daughters who are clearly too young to be prosecuted as apostates. Thus, it seems you should stop this foolishness, and let the House of Mendes continue to prosper in Antwerp. If you continue this harassment of the Mendes widows, I can promise you that the merchants of Antwerp will rise as one and the results for the economy of Antwerp will be disastrous.

However, I am not unreasonable. If the embargo on the Mendes property is removed and the apostasy proceedings quashed, I am prepared to make a loan to the Crown of 20,000-30,000 ducats on the usual terms.

Yours sincerely,
Joseph Nasi

The response of the emperor, Charles V, was not long in coming. Following conversations with his sister, Queen Mary of the Netherlands, he would be willing to recommend to church authorities that they cease ecclesiastical proceedings against the two sisters for a loan of 100,000 ducats, with no interest for two years.

Enraged, Joseph wrote back that 100,000 would be out of the question; it would be two-thirds of the entire Mendes fortune. "I would consider a loan of 50,000, but not a penny more."

More time was needed, Joseph decided, and he would drag out these negotiations for as long as possible, as every day he was able to ship additional crates of valuables to Constantinople on either the Mendes ships or the Fugger ships. Meanwhile, he knew that Beatriz and Brianda were safely ensconced in homes in Venice, protected there by Ben Zarella as well as other agents of the Mendes empire.

****

Beatriz was not one to surrender any of her possessions without a fight. When she realized that three of her treasure-filled coffers had been confiscated by German merchants, she immediately appealed to the Venetian authorities, and was permitted to seize property of those same German merchants which were in Venice, by way of compensation. The German merchants, realizing they'd been bested by Beatriz da Luna, quickly turned over the three coffers to the Mendes agent in Venice, Jerome Zoller.

She had won round one in Venice, and had established a reputation as a businesswoman who was both tough and shrewd, a woman to be treated with great deference.

Joseph, meanwhile, confident of his personal charm, magnetism and negotiating ability, asked for and received an audience with the Holy Roman Emperor, who was presently residing at Ratisbon. Such was his success, that Charles not only agreed to accept 30,000 crowns in settlement of all claims against the Mendes House, but he at the same time knighted Joseph, this being a much-sought after honor.

But the matter did not end there.

Queen Mary objected to the settlement and refused to release the sequestered property, claiming she would not be able to balance her accounts without the Mendes money. A three-way quarrel ensued, and ultimately Charles once again threatened persecution for heresy. Joseph offered another 200,000 *livres* for a year, interest free, in return for a final settlement. This did not satisfy the emperor. Letters passed back and forth between the emperor and Joseph, between the emperor and his sister, all to no avail.

Suddenly, the House of Mendes on Kipdorp Boulevard was closed and emptied of all valuables. The servants had all been dismissed; the school students and teachers were nowhere to be found. The printing company doors were closed and locked, the diamond factory empty. Ships belonging to the Mendes family never again docked in Antwerp, and descendants of the Mendes family never again lived under Spanish rule. The House of Mendes ceased to exist in the Netherlands.

Chapter Nineteen

Brianda's Promise
Venice—1545

Beatriz took the larger of the two homes that Ben Zarella had found for her family and turned the canal level into apartments for her gondolier and servants. On the *piano nobile*, or second floor, she set aside a small parlor as an office in which to meet with other merchants, and another small room as a showroom for the one-of-a-kind exquisite goods the House imported for sale locally. The grand drawing room and formal dining room on this floor each had French doors that opened onto porticos directly above the Grand Canal. The third floor of the *palazzetto* was devoted to bedrooms for the family: a huge bedroom for herself that also served as her private library and office, and smaller bedrooms for Reyna and her governess, and Samuel and Joseph. Rooms on the top floor were set aside as a map room, another room where six experienced diamond experts plied their craft, and several additional rooms for servants and special guests.

Determined as she was to only spend a few years in Venice, Beatriz accepted the condition of the house as it was, which was very good, it was only ninety years old, and made no plans for extensive refurbishing. She furnished the "public rooms," all of which had gorgeous Murano chandeliers and wall sconces, with sofas and upholstered chairs from local merchants, leaving the beautiful marble or parquet floors bare. The windows were clothed in the gorgeous silks and taffetas the Venetians were famous for, and on the walls she hung contemporary paintings by Titian, Tintoretto and Veronese.

The hardest part of getting used to Venice, she laughingly told Ben, was getting used to the smell of the Canal, especially on very hot days when the scent of spoiled fish and raw sewage predominated. She burned incense, candles, and had small dishes of perfume in every room in an attempt to offset the smell.

While Beatriz preferred to spend the evenings alone with Ben, a good book and a bottle of wine, Brianda reveled in the carnival atmosphere that seemed to permeate the city year round. She gathered around her several suitors, two New Christian men of whom Beatriz approved, and two devout Catholics, of whom Beatriz did not approve. So full was Brianda's social calendar, she kept two seamstresses busy full time making gowns.

When she wasn't designing gowns and jewels, she was shopping for her small *palazzetto*. She'd early on commissioned frescos for the drawing room and dining room; now they were furnished with ebonized pearl wood furniture with mother-of-pearl inlays. Tasseled silk pillows graced her sofa and chairs; fresh floral bouquets were on every table and chest. She set her tables with gold etched stem ware from Murano, silver flatware from Florence and fine china.

As had been directed by Diogo, Beatriz paid the bills for Brianda's extravagance. After more than a year of ever increasing bills, Beatriz asked Brianda to come over to her home for lunch, her purpose being to try to curb her expenditures without causing further resentment.

It was a lovely fall day, cool, and the air was unusually fresh. Beatriz set a table for two on the portico off the dining room, overlooking the canal. Brianda arrived carrying a small bouquet of mums she had arranged herself. "They are lovely, you have such an eye for color and design!" Beatriz exclaimed, marveling again at her sister's artistic eye.

When they were seated, and the butler had served the first course of artichoke soup, Beatriz asked, "Have you heard that Joseph was knighted by Charles? I'm simply astounded by this turn of events!"

Brianda smiled sweetly and answered, "Samuel told me yesterday when he stopped in for tea. I can't fathom what it means, except that a knight swears allegiance to the person who makes him a knight. I find it hard to believe that Joseph has sworn allegiance to the Holy Roman Emperor. Are they still arguing over money, or has Queen Mary given up?"

Beatriz frowned. "No, the Queen is still demanding money, Charles wants more than Joseph is willing to loan him. Nephew Maximilian argues on behalf of Charles when the two young men aren't dueling with one another. This whole thing is taking up entirely too much of Joseph's time, and I need him here in Venice. Several weeks ago I instructed him to wind up things in Antwerp and relocate here."

"You love being his boss, don't you," Brianda charged, her resentment overcoming her attempt at pleasantries. "He should be running things!"

You believe that with all your feminine charms, you could get him to do your bidding. He'd be easier to manipulate than I am. She looked squarely at her sister. "I never asked for so much responsibility, Brianda. Remember, you told us many times that business bored you. You never took any interest in the affairs of the House, other than designing jewelry and dresses, at which I am the first to admit you are very talented.

"On the other hand, I was tutored from childhood by Francisco, I went to his school and took all the most difficult courses, and after we were married, I worked with him twenty-four hours a day. When he died, I knew more about his plans and strategies than anyone in the House. When we joined Diogo in Antwerp, Diogo immediately took me in as an equal partner. It's obvious from his will that he trusted me to carry on and expand the House of Mendes for the benefit of both of us and our children, and our children's children for generations to come." She paused to sip her wine.

"I'm gratified to have Joseph as a deputy. He is superb, but I have no intention of relinquishing the responsibility which Diogo placed in me to Joseph, at least not yet."

"It's been suggested to me," Brianda said in a subdued voice, "that you intend to further strengthen your hold on your share of the family fortune by making Joseph your son-in-law."

Beatriz again sipped her wine, giving herself a moment to formulate an answer. "Announcing their engagement would probably stop all this crazy speculation about Reyna marrying an old Christian. For now, my focus is on getting the family to a safe place, and I've asked Reyna to bear with me, to be patient."

Brianda waved her hand; she wanted to change the subject. "I don't know why you are so anxious to leave Venice. I love it here, I'm planning to spend the rest of my life in Venice. We have everything, beautiful homes, a wonderful social life, stimulating, sophisticated friends..."

"And an inquisitional tribunal that can, without any justification, haul you before it and put you in prison for being a secret Judaizer! I don't feel safe here, not for a moment!" Beatriz spat out.

An angry Brianda interrupted. "Why can't you just be a Catholic? Why is that such a problem for you, Beatriz? You were baptized as a baby, you were married to Francisco in the cathedral, and you go to mass every Sunday. I don't understand why you have to make your life so difficult by insisting on being a Jew. You should follow my example and forget all this nonsense about being a Jew."

Beatriz took a deep breath and warned herself to control her temper.

She changed the subject. "One of the reasons I asked you to come to lunch today, dear sister, is to discuss your expenditures. Each month since we've been here, the amount of bills you have sent over for payment have doubled or tripled until what you are now spending on a monthly basis is truly obscene." Brianda attempted to interrupt, but Beatriz gestured with her hand, and said, "Wait, hear me out. I have no objection to your spending on clothes and jewels. They are portable. What troubles me is the amount you are spending on having frescos painted on four walls and the ceiling of all your rooms. You've employed three painters full time now for more than ten months. When we pack up to leave and move to Constantinople, you will not be able to take those frescoes with you. All that expense will be lost to you, mores the pity!"

"I told you, I have no intention of going with you to Constantinople!" Brianda's eyes blazed with fury.

"But you are only leasing your home, you haven't bought it and there's no assurances that the owner will sell it to you. Eventually, you may have to give it up and you will lose the money you've put into decorating it so lavishly. I understand from Joseph that you have ordered rosewood from Brazil for your dining room floor! I can't even begin to imagine what that will cost. There were no woods here in Europe good enough for your floor?"

Brianda stood and threw her napkin on her plate. "I'm leaving. I'll hear no more of this. You will pay my bills, no matter what they are, or I'll take you to court. I'll tell the authorities what kind of Catholic you are. I hate you, Beatriz, I promise you, I'll ruin you." She stomped out of the room.

Beatriz sat in her chair, immobilized. Her eyes filled with tears. She had no difficulty negotiating with merchants, with dukes, with church authorities. She could go toe to toe with any businessman, any banker. Coldly and without emotion.

What she could not handle with equanimity were disputes with her sister.

Chapter Twenty

Brianda's Revenge

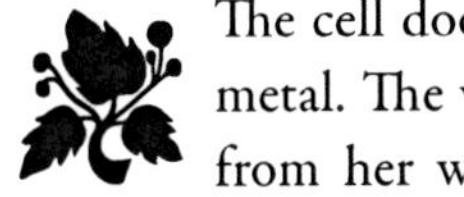

The cell door slammed shut, a piercing screech of metal against metal. The vicious-looking, putrid guard cut the hemp bindings from her wrists and freed her hands. He picked up leg irons attached to a bar at the far side of the cell and knelt down to fasten them to her ankles.

She watched, ashen-faced, detached, numb with disbelief that this could be happening. Not to her!

He lifted her long skirt and petticoats enough to snap the metal bracelets shut. Then with one last scathing glance at her face, then her entire body, he abruptly turned and opened the cell door. He slammed the door, turned the key, and locked her inside.

Suddenly Beatriz da Luna Mendes was alone. In a dungeon beneath the waterline of the Grand Canal in Venice, deep in the bowels of its commercial center.

Dazed by shock and fear, Beatriz slumped onto the crude wooden bench, the only piece of furniture in the cell. Her mind roiled with the terrifying events of the morning. She was snatched from her home by the police with only her servants as witnesses, not allowed to pack anything or to notify a family member. Roughly shoved into a carriage with drawn shades, she'd been bound and taken to the Inquisitional Tribunal courtroom, told that she'd been accused by her sister and, without permitting her to present evidence, found guilty of being a Judaizer.

By her sister! "Brianda da Luna Mendes, widow of Diogo Mendes of the House of Mendes."

Fury and seething rage broke through her shock. Beatriz stood to her full height and, dragging the leg irons and chain behind her, began pacing the hard dirt floor, *This is outrageous*! *How dare they imprison me, the head of the House of Mendes? Don't they know who my friends, my creditors are? The kings of England, of France, The Holy Roman Emperor Charles V, the pope himself! By God, I'll teach them all a thing or two! These arrogant Venetians, the Doge and his cronies!*

Even as Beatriz mentally rallied against her jailers, she recognized it as the predictable outcome of the double life her family lived. In addition to being a Nasi, she was also a Benveniste by virtue of her marriage to Francisco, who was privately known by his Hebrew name Semah Benveniste. The ancient Benveniste family boasted the physician Isaac, physician to the King of Aragon in the twelfth century, called "prince." In the fourteenth century Joseph Benveniste was counselor to Alfonso XI of Castile, and in the fifteenth century Abraham Benveniste had controlled the finances of Aragon as well as being the Crown Rabbi. But none of these ancestors had begun to realize the enormous worldwide financial and political power that the New Christian Francisco Mendes and his brother Diogo had brought to the House of Mendes. Their wealth and political clout was the equal of the Fuggers of Augsburg and the Affaitati of Cremona. This influence, this reputation, and prestige now resided in one woman: Gracia Nasi, publicly known as Beatriz da Luna Mendes.

After several minutes of pacing, her anger turned to grief and anguish, to a feeling of betrayal at the realization that it was her sister Brianda, her very own flesh and blood, a woman she had personally cared for, indeed, saved her life by getting her out of Portugal alive, who turned her into the ecclesiastical authorities. It was the worst of nightmares come true, but it was a prospect every New Christian family lived with.

She felt herself shivering in the cold dampness, felt her already arthritic spine ache. The pains in her chest were coming more frequently. Gradually, her eyes adjusted to the dim light of the cell. The place stank of urine and feces, of mildew and rotting fish. Nausea rose in her throat and she felt the need to vomit. She swallowed hard and forced herself to breath calmly. Pain flashed across her forehead and eyes, but she told herself it was the awful tension of the morning.

I must get a message to Joseph and to Ben, she thought as she adjusted the straps on her high heeled pumps. Her ankles were swollen from the long walk down into the dungeon. By now Samuel knows what has happened, she thought. Imagine me, the wealthiest woman in the world, being charged as a relapsed Catholic and thrown into this place! It's preposterous, it's unthinkable.

No, it is not!

Francisco, my beloved husband of blessed memory, always warned me it might come to this. He taught me how to manage his banking business, his fleet of ships, even how to escape from Lisbon. But we never talked about escaping from an ecclesiastical prison. He taught me, as well, how to bribe the church. Money. Surely money. Bribing church officials has always worked. Perhaps it will this time.

It's got to work this time! For Reyna, for Samuel, for Joseph. For me. I've got to think...think clearly. I must plan very carefully...

At that moment a plump, middle-aged woman opened the door to the cell and stepped inside, locking the door behind her. She stared at Beatriz. In a sarcastic voice, projecting an air of superiority, she declared, "So this is what a fine lady looks like. The famous Beatriz da Luna, the glamorous woman and confidante of kings!"

Beatriz remained seated but raised herself to a ramrod straight position, lifting her head proudly and looking directly into the woman's eyes. "And who might you be?"

"I am Matron Lucilla Giraldi. And I'm here to explain a few things to you. First, your family will have to bring a bed and some clothes for you, and you'll need to make arrangements to pay for your meals and lodging."

"That's preposterous! I should pay for this cell?"

"Those are the rules. And if you don't pay for your meals and lodging, well, we'll simply confiscate some of your fine jewelry or paintings from your home, sell them, and use that money to reimburse the Ecclesiastical Tribunal."

"This is outrageous! Wait until I speak with my solicitor..."

"Sorry, Madam. My orders are to treat you just like we treat all swine. What do you want to do about a bed?"

"If you'll give me a pen and some paper, I'll send a letter to my servants, and they'll supply everything. And I'll not pay for meals. I'll have my maid bring meals to me."

"That would be irregular, but I'll ask about it. Rules are that you are not to speak to anyone or send messages to anyone. I'll get you some paper and a quill, and once your servants have delivered clothes and a bed, you'll be allowed no more visits."

The matron left Beatriz but returned shortly with writing implements. "I've asked if you're to be allowed meals from home. Should get an answer before dinner time. Call me when you're ready to deliver the note, I'll see that it is delivered."

Beatriz felt that Lucilla had softened a bit. Perhaps she had been given some special instruction from her bosses. She seemed a bit less authoritarian. Beatriz sat down on the bench, put the paper and pen on the hard surface, and bent over to write.

My dearest Samuel,

In Joseph's absence I must rely on you. Please arrange for Manuel to bring me a bed and necessary bed linens, extra blankets because it's very cold in this dungeon. Also ask Helen Marie to pack several changes of simple clothes and warm undergarments. You must also arrange for the cook to prepare my meals, and for Manuel to bring them to me three times a day.

You know who my trusted friends are and I know you will prudently inform them of my situation, begging them in the names of Jesus and his Holy Mother Mary, to do everything they can to let the Tribunal know how faithful I have always been to the Holy Roman Catholic Church. I know I can depend on you.

Please give Reyna all the love and attention she needs and a big kiss and un caluroso abrazo from her mother.

With much love to my beloved daughter and niece,
Beatriz da Luna

She folded the letter. She then sat straight on the bench and waited for the matron to come get it. As she sat, she listened for the first time to the other voices in the corridor outside her cell. She heard a muffled woman's voice reciting the Mass in Latin, "Sanctus, Sanctus, Sanctus..." A few moments later the words changed to Hebrew and the voice began reciting the Kaddish. Further away, an agonized voice was reciting the rosary. Every few minutes she hear the metallic rattle of chains being dragged across the floor of the dungeon. And further away still, she heard the unmistakable sound of sobbing, sobbing filled with mental and physical anguish.

"Dear God, help me keep my wits about me..." Beatriz thought, concentrating once more on the reason she had been imprisoned. Brianda, her mean-spirited, selfish and irresponsible sister.

She remembered that rainy night in April fifteen years ago; it was the night Pope Clement VII had formally declared dead the despised Bull of December 17, 1531. The *converso* families had gathered secretly in the synagogue under the Lisbon home she shared with her rabbi-in-secret husband. The *conversos* had been thrilled to hear that the pope, after much bribery and negotiation, declared the Inquisition in Portugal terminated. It had seemed a night for rejoicing, for celebrating that they would not all be arrested and burned at the stake. Yes, but only for as long as they pretended to be Roman Catholics.

And yet her parents had somehow known, had prognosticated that very evening, not only that the Inquisition would be authorized again in Portugal, forcing families like the Nasis and Mendes to flee for their lives, but that the manipulative ways of the Church and State would rend the sisters' devoted love and make them the bitterest of enemies.

After the thanksgiving ceremony in the synagogue, her parents, Daniel and Rachel Nasi, sitting alone in her small parlor sipping sherry, had spoken solemnly to their beloved oldest daughter, then only twenty-three.

"You are the strong one of our daughters," her father had begun, his eyes misty and his voice husky with emotion.

Her mother, with a conspiratorial look in her eyes, added, "Your brother is so involved with the king, being his doctor..."

"What we're asking you, Beatriz," her father said, his voice quavering, "is that you will always look out for your sister. She's not as bright as you, hasn't the protection of someone like Francisco..."

"She's always been a bit flighty, you know..." Her mother's voice trailed off; she dabbed her eyes with her handkerchief.

Beatriz stared at her mother and father. "You two look healthy, Brianda has several suitors, surely there's nothing she needs from me."

"Not now. Not tonight. But there may come a time, is what your father is trying to say," Rachel answered, her eyes now full of tears.

"Promise me, dear Beatriz, that whatever should happen in the coming months, that you will take care of Brianda. You will have the money and the influence..."

"Of course," Beatriz responded, in her most consoling voice. How could her parents even doubt that she would not take care of Brianda? That they would even verbalize the request was painful.

"She's not the easiest person to get along with," her father added.

"I know that, Father. Sometimes she makes it impossible to even like her, but of course I'll always look out for her."

"We won't live forever..."

"Mother! What is this all about? Are one of you ill?"

"Your mother had a dream. You know how she believes her dreams prognosticate the future."

Rachel was now openly weeping, her eyes turned inward on some vision too awful to describe. Beatriz wrapped her arms around the sobbing woman, realizing once more how dreadful the threat was that hung over all their lives, how wearing and demoralizing it must be for these old people who had already fled once from their homeland.

"Of course I'll take care of Brianda. I'll always be sure she's well provided for and safe. I promise you, Mother. I promise both of you."

****

Later in the afternoon the matron returned to Beatriz cell, dragging a pallet. She pulled it inside the cell and positioned it at the far end of the cell. Unceremoniously, she dropped a dun-colored blanket on top of the pallet.

"Seems your family's negotiating with the Bishop. Won't do them no good. So while they're causing trouble, you'll sleep on straw like everyone else. I'll be back with a shift."

Beatriz eyed the pallet. The roughly woven coarse threads were stained and worn, punctured as if horses had been stomping on it. Dark straw sprouted out of tears and crevices. How can anyone lie down on that filth?

She was still staring at it when Lucilla returned with a ragged looking shift. "Here. You can sleep in this."

Lucilla watched Beatriz with a sneer on her face. "Not like the fancy French gowns you're used to, is it?"

When Beatriz didn't reach for it, Lucilla merely dropped it at her feet. "You'll change your mind in a few hours. There are limits to how long a lady can stay in those corsets without swelling up."

Lucilla had, of course, been wrong. When she could think of no other way to rest, Beatriz spread the stinking blanket out on top of the pallet and lowered her aching body to the floor, careful to move her shackled ankle which was now swelling, as little as possible.

She lay awake for a long time listening to the sounds from the passages outside her cell. The voice muttering in Latin and then in Hebrew had mercifully ceased, though the sobbing woman occasionally yelled an obscenity in Italian. Noises gradually subsided altogether, and Beatriz tired to calm her mind enough to drop off to sleep. Nothing more would happen till the morrow.

Yet, as she lay there, hunger spasms alternated with chills and cold sweats. The pain in her ankle diminished but the recurring pains in her chest continued. She thought again of Brianda, of her parents, their long trek across the Spanish plain in search of an elusive religious freedom, a freedom that lasted only five years to their dismay.

Toward morning Beatriz drifted off into a fitful sleep, peopled with gargoyles that had come to life and seemed to speak with the voices of her parents and Francisco. These strange spirits led her to a dark place where they too were imprisoned and tortured. She herself seemed fastened with hemp to a crucifix, stark naked, suspended from the cross for all the peasant folk to stone and curse.

And then, suddenly, she was wide awake and felt a rodent nibbling at her toes. She tried to jerk her foot but could not lift it because of the weight of the ankle irons. A horrifying inhuman noise she could not believe had come from her own throat brought her fully awake.

She screamed for the matron but got no answer. Only the snoring and wheezing from nearby cells.

Hours later, after more fitful dozing, hunger pains forced her to swallow a gruel like salty porridge that tasted of fish gone bad. That proved to be an error: diarrhea followed with cramps and spasms nearly as bad as she remembered childbirth to be. With great pain and loss of dignity and self-esteem, she managed to relieve herself over a hole in the ground at the far end of her cell, hating, for the first time in her life, the multiple skirts and petticoats she'd worn since a child.

There was nothing to do but lie back down on the pallet and wait. Wait for her nephew and her trusted agents to speed the information about her imprisonment to Joseph, to Ben, to the pope himself. Surely then, when the Holy See in Rome heard of her plight, she would be released and everything would return to normal. She was of more use to the church when she was alive and well and the House of Mendes was thriving. She would be of no value, none whatsoever, to either the doge or the pope if she were dead. Her millions were too dispersed around the world, her agents too wily, her businesses too diverse for any one king or cardinal to grasp from her.

Chapter Twenty-One

Checkmate

Shortly after noon, the matron announced to Beatriz that she was to have an important meeting with Bishop Guiliano Gonzaga. "Wash your face and comb your hair and prepare to come with me," she ordered as she detached the chains from the leg irons.

"The Bishop and I are well acquainted; he's been to my home many times. He shall see me as I am, degraded by these circumstances," Beatriz replied, standing and straightening her skirt and petticoats. She brushed a wisp of black hair back off her face, tidied her chignon with her fingers, and followed Lucilla down the hallway and up two flights of stairs, forcing herself to walk with an extra air of dignity in spite of the ankle cuffs.

When they arrived at an office on the second floor, Lucilla knocked, and then backed away, waiting for an answer. They heard a gruff, "Come in, come in."

"My child, my child, what has happened to you?" Bishop Gonzaga asked with a gasp and a feigned look of compassion, as he stared at her from a huge carved chair. He motioned to Lucilla to leave and close the door.

"Excellency, I'm sure you know exactly what has happened." Beatriz immediately took in the opulence of her surroundings, even here at the Inquisitional Tribunal offices. Lavish Oriental carpets, two large wall tapestries, three palatial oil paintings, handsomely carved oak furniture, and small bits of statuary. "This is no time for niceties or games. And I am not a child."

Bishop Gonzaga held out his hand for the expected ritual kiss. She refused, shaking her head. "Forgive me, Excellency, but my arthritis, made worse by a night in your dungeon, prohibits my kneeling or bending."

Genuinely surprised by Beatriz' nerve, the Bishop's pock-marked face reddened slightly, his smile changed to a severe seriousness Beatriz had never before seen. But she had only been in his presence during social events at her home or in other illustrious Venetian salons. He had been invariably charming, indeed flirtatious, with "the two beautiful and famously wealthy de Luna sisters." Barely controlling his annoyance, he rose from his throne-like chair, and paced to the window. His was a formidable stature: one of the tallest men in Venice, he was also of great girth, and well-known for his love of the finest foods, wines and women.

"Correct. This is not a time for social niceties. Your sister has made grave charges about your religious activities. The history of your family is well known to Church authorities. We believe Brianda's charges to be true."

Beatriz knew the Vatican's spy network was even better than that of the House of Mendes, but she wondered exactly how much they knew. "I was baptized a Catholic at birth, Excellency, and have never wavered from deep devotion to the Church. My piety and, I might add, my family's financial contributions to the Church in Lisbon, in Antwerp, and now in Venice, are legendary."

"Quite so!" Gonzaga turned and smiled at her, but the smile had a sneer to it. "Nevertheless, your husband, the late much-revered Francisco Mendes, was a secret rabbi to your people. After his untimely death and your secret departure from Lisbon, King John's men discovered a synagogue and hundreds of religious documents and books hidden in your home."

So they knew. Word had traveled from Lisbon to Rome to Venice. At least now I know what they know, she thought. "May I sit, Excellency? My back is hurting dreadfully. I'm not so young anymore."

"Indeed. Thirty-eight, if my information is correct. You've been a widow ten years now. Why haven't you remarried? Surely, a woman as beautiful as you has had many opportunities."

Beatriz sat down opposite the Bishop's chair, and he sat down also, took a sip of wine from a beautifully-etched goblet, then picked up a glass paperweight and turned it over and over in his pudgy hands.

"Being the head of the House of Mendes keeps me occupied full time," she answered, "I've no time for romance. And, besides, I've never met a man who could measure up to Francisco."

The bishop smiled, a sneer again, implying that he knew differently, he knew a great deal about her private life. "Perhaps the real reason is that if you were to remarry, your new husband would control your wealth. I rather think you like being the one in control, the big boss, so to speak. Yes, my dear Beatriz, you have many of the qualities of a man. Certainly the mind of a man."

"I take that as a compliment, my dear bishop. Now, if we can get down to business, since you realize that is my strong suit, tell me about your negotiations with my nephew. I trust he has made satisfactory arrangements for my release?"

"No. I've just come from a meeting of the tribunal, and based on additional evidence we've received, we believe your sister is also a secret Jew. We've placed her under house arrest, and having judged that she is not a suitable religious guardian for your daughter or her own, we've removed the girls to a convent where they will be given proper religious guidance and protection."

Beatriz' eyes blazed at the Bishop. "That's outrageous! You know as well as I that convents are rife with deviant behavior. Those two girls are virgins, and I'll not have some filthy monk or priest who pretends at celibacy molesting them."

The bishop raised both hands and gestured at her to calm down. "I guarantee Beatriz, on everything that's sacred, in the name of the Virgin, I pledge to you that those girls will be well-taken care of. Your sister, on the other hand, we are watching very carefully. She's developed some ties in France that we don't approve of."

"We long have had agents in France. As I'm sure you know, the House of Mendes has a very large outstanding loan to the King of France." The bishop nodded his head affirmatively. "And we also have large sums on loan to the King of England, to Charles V, and to the pope. Have you notified the pope of your charges against me?"

"Proper notification is on its way. Meanwhile, tell me of Brianda's friends in Lyon."

"I know nothing of her friends in Lyon. We do have agents there, as we conduct much business; we sell textiles, spices, jewelry, books, and fine oriental carpets in Lyon."

"And isn't it also true that your most trusted lieutenant, your late brother's son, Joseph is located at Lyon?"

His spies are good, Beatriz thought, as she made instant calculations. "That is correct. And my personal physician and dear family friend for ever so many years, Amatus Lusitanus, is currently in Rome attending the pope. You can be sure Samuel has already dispatched a messenger to him, just as he has to my highly-placed friends elsewhere in Europe." *My dear Bishop, surely you know that my information networks rival that of the Church.*

Again his face reddened, then for a moment anger shone in his eyes. "We are aware of your...shall we say, capabilities. Ever since you left Lisbon under cover of darkness ten years ago, we have understood your cunning and your nerves of iron. And we do not underestimate the power of your wealth. Perhaps a few months in our dungeon, as you call it, will bring some much needed humility to your soul. After all, that is my simple aim, to do God's work. And it seems to me, Señora that what you need most is a bit of bringing down."

Beatriz changed tactics and deliberately used her most charming, feminine, seductive voice. "I am certain that we can negotiate our differences,

Excellency. I have been told that I must pay for my room and board in your dungeon. I'm prepared to do that, but only if I'm moved to a decent room with decent furniture and privacy. I require food from my home, a serving girl, and some writing materials so that I can relay messages to my nephew. I'm quite sure that Charles V and the pope will find the House of Mendes of greater service to their causes if I am permitted to tend to business."

The bishop nodded his head in agreement. "I quite agree. We must move you to decent quarters. You will surely be required to stay with us for a while during which time we'll further investigate the charges of Judaizer. We will move you to a room on the fourth floor. I'll arrange for you to receive food from home, and I'll provide a serving girl. However, be on notice that every communication to and from your apartment will be delivered to me first for approval. Your special quarters will cost one hundred ducats a month, which I personally will receive, from your nephew. You may so inform him."

Beatriz could not prevent a look of purest hatred from passing over her face. "How dare you? That's twice what the finest university professor makes in a year! That's outrageous avarice on your part."

"We will use the money to feed the poor, my child. Now, you may go." It was an angry dismissal. He rang the bell that sat on the table next to him, and instantly Lucilla opened the door to retrieve her charge.

It was ever thus, Beatriz thought, as she walked slowly back to her cell on the basement floor. All the kings and church officials have ever wanted from the Jews is money. Money, money, and more money. They don't give a damn about our religious beliefs; they only worry about how to get their hands on our money. How many times did Francisco and Father tell me stories about King Manuel and the church in Lisbon? Even before I was born, they were extorting money from the Jews. *Will there ever come a time or will we ever find a place to live where we will be safe?*

After one more horrendous night spent tossing and turning on the straw pallet in the basement cell, Beatriz was finally moved to the fourth floor room promised by Bishop Gonzaga. She'd agreed to his terms of one hundred ducats and sent a message, via Lucilla, to Samuel to quickly pay the bishop off so she could get some surcease from the horrible chest and back pains she was experiencing.

I wonder now many thousand more ducats it will take to finally get me out of here and back home, she thought, as she settled into the sparsely furnished "Inquisitional apartment," as it was referred to by Lucilla. The matron took the opportunity to tell Beatriz that it was more luxurious by far than her own personal living quarters. Beatriz had a bed, three chairs, a screen behind which to dress, a small table to eat at, and a young peasant girl, Rosa, "selected by the Bishop himself," to be her servant girl. The first thing Beatriz ordered was a basin of hot water so that she might wash the filth and grime and stench of the prison from her body. Once clean and dressed in fresh clothing, she asked Rosa to assist her in combing her long black hair into a tidy chignon.

"Tell me about your family and home," she quietly asked the sweet, frightened young girl. "And how old are you?"

"My parents live in the country near Ravenna. They work in the vineyards, picking grapes."

"Ah...I see. And how many brothers and sisters do you have?" As she felt the girl's tender ministrations, she thought of her own eighteen-year old daughter, a beauty, pampered and well-educated, but not spoiled. Now imprisoned in a convent.

"Five sisters and eight brothers. I'm sixteen, the oldest."

"And do they live at home and help your parents with the grapes?"

"All but my two oldest brothers, they work here in Venice with the gondolas, as apprentices. They are very hard workers. They will make something of themselves."

"I see. And you," Beatriz murmured, thinking of how she might conscript this girl into her own cause, "do you want to continue to work here in the jail?"

"No ma'am, I'd like to work in a fine home. The pay would be better and..."

She'd been on the verge of saying something important, Beatriz thought, suddenly her hands had tightened and she'd actually pulled her hair. The poor child was frightened. "What is it, Rosa? What did you want to say? What scared you?"

"I don't like this job. The men..."

She didn't finish the sentence, but Beatriz instantly understood what she wanted to say. "Do the men, the guards, bother you? You are very fetching."

Shyly, her hands trembling, Rosa whispered. "Yes. They bother me and threaten me if I tell anyone..."

"In that case, you must stay here in this room with me as much as possible and I will protect you. And the next time one of the guards threatens you, be sure to tell me immediately. And Rosa..."

"Yes, ma'am?"

"When I'm released from this jail, I want you to come with me and work in my home. As my personal maid. For as long as you like."

"Oh, thank you, ma'am, I'll try hard to please you." She stopped brushing Beatriz long hair to wipe away tears, then said in a trembling voice, "But the matron says you'll never get out, she says they are going to kill you. She says they want all your money and your ships. To fight the Ottomans..."

Out of the mouths of babes...Beatriz suddenly realized that there was much more to this than her being a suspected Judaizer. Indeed, the House of Mendes was a pawn in an ongoing war between Venice and the Ottoman Empire for control of the Adriatic Sea. The pieces of the puzzle fell in place, and with that, her strategy became crystal clear. She felt as if she had just seen her way clear to checkmate, as she had once long ago when she had played chess with the king of Portugal.

Chapter Twenty-Two

“They’ll Be Watching You!”

"Do you have time for a game, David?" Beatriz asked the Venetian doge's representative on his third visit to her "Inquisitional apartment." One of the items she requested and received from her home was the ivory and black jade chess set which she and Francisco so enjoyed together. A duplicate of the set which Francisco long ago presented to King Manuel, it was the very same set she used during her game with the young King John on that fateful day when he had come to Francisco's school to court her. It symbolized many memories and she cherished it as a good luck charm.

David Torricelli first came to visit her on the third afternoon after her removal from the cell to the small room on the fourth floor. He was the same age as Joseph, on whom she placed so much trust. Shortly after introducing himself as a member of the doge's personal staff, David told her that he knew a great deal about her and her family as he went to the university with Joseph, and that the two young men remained in close contact.

Beatriz sized up the young man and his apparent knowledge of her family and business activities that afternoon, and decided that he was probably a secret agent who'd been recruited by Joseph. How perfectly placed in the doge's inner sanctum, how farsighted of Joseph. On his second visit she became sure of it when he confessed that his dark blond hair and blue eyes were due to his German blood, his mother's father, but that his knowledge of Judaism and its people were a gift from his mother whose family converted from Judaism to Catholicism in Spain two generations earlier. David's father was an Italian Catholic. But David was raised with a great reverence for Jewish people and all things Jewish.

Perfect, Beatriz thought. He couldn't be more perfectly placed.

At the end of his second visit, David told Beatriz that if she'd like to write a letter to her daughter, currently under the care of the Benedictine nuns, he'd be happy to deliver it to Reyna personally.

Immediately, Beatriz began the letter, taking great care lest she say anything that would later be used against her by the doge or by church authorities. As she wrote, feelings of deepest love and admiration for her daughter flooded over her. How difficult it was to conceive her, how terrible the birth pains, the great pity that Reyna had not known her father better before his death, how proud he would be of her if he could only see her now. How much in love with Joseph she was...ah, but that would have to wait.

Like her mother, Reyna became a brilliant student of science, physics, geography, and spoke seven languages fluently. Unlike her mother, she also displayed a great interest in things considered feminine: music, needlework, art and literature. She loved reading and cherished the splendid library her father had created and Beatriz had moved from Lisbon to London to Antwerp, and now to their future home in Constantinople.

Also, Beatriz thought, she attracted the unwanted attention of royalty. What a mistake that has turned out to be! Who knows how much we'll lose getting out of this awful mess!

"Your cousin Samuel is making every effort to satisfy the doge and the cardinal that our family is and always has been deeply committed to the Holy Roman Church," she wrote to Reyna, thinking at the same time of Joseph's deep love for Reyna. More than once the young people came to her, pleading with her for permission to marry. She turned them down, promising them that "at the appropriate time," she would consent.

Now Moses Hamon, the physician to the Ottoman Emperor, a fine Jewish doctor and eminent poet offered his son to be Reyna's husband. And Dr. Hamon, with his close connection to Suleiman the Great, was in a perfect position to assist the Nasi and Mendes families. The older she got, the more Beatriz realized that in her heart of hearts, that was her greatest dream, for herself and her family and for all her people. Ultimately, she wanted to take them to Constantinople.

****

David Torricelli wasted little time with pleasantries on the afternoon of the second Sunday after Beatriz was arrested. Immediately after sending Rosa out the door for an afternoon visit with her brothers, so he could talk with Beatriz without fear of being spied upon, he reached into his cape and pulled out a letter and handed it to Beatriz. "I received this by messenger this morning. I recognize the handwriting as Joseph's."

Without ceremony, Beatriz grabbed it from his hands, hungry for communication from her beloved nephew.

My dearest Aunt Beatriz,

I have only yesterday received word of the terrible events and your incarceration in Venice. Rest assured that dispatches are now on their way to Rome, Paris, Constantinople, Ferrara, London and elsewhere where the House of Mendes has friends.

While on the one hand we are reassuring the church of our allegiance, on the other hand we are beginning to close down factories and shops in the territories under the rule of Charles V. I've sent a messenger to him via his nephew Max, my good friend, putting him on notice.

The doge is aware that none of the ships of the House of Mendes will stop in Venice as long as you are incarcerated. Our ships are responsible for nearly a quarter of all goods delivered to the port of Venice, thus he is currently losing one-fourth of the customs duties he would normally receive. His treasury is becoming more diminished every day.

Our friends in France and Turkey remain steadfast, ready to come to our assistance when we give the word. If necessary, we will stop all commerce in Venice, if that's what it takes to resolve this ridiculousness. I will be in touch. My love to Reyna.

Joseph

After reading it twice, she handed the letter back to David. "I'm sure he intends for you to see this and relay this information to the doge as you see fit."

David read the letter carefully, sighed, and sat down opposite Beatriz. "He's making it clear that you're willing to risk outright warfare against them."

"Exactly." Beatriz smiled, thinking of how many times she and Joseph had talked about these possibilities. They had planned, over the months and years since Francisco's and Diogo's deaths, for every contingency.

"The House of Mendes will not be allowed to leave Venice," David said calmly, picking up the black jade king from the chess set.

"I don't really think the doge will risk a naval battle with Suleiman. With France and the ships of the House of Mendes aligned with the Turkish fleet, Venice will be defeated. I have no doubt of it. Surely, the doge realizes that."

"There's got to be a way short of warfare." David objected.

"The Mendes ships have rerouted their business, so that they do not stop in Venice. The doge is already losing thousands of ducats a week in customs duty. Those customs duties are what keep the doge and the church going, it's what makes Venice a hub of commerce."

Sarcastically, she continued, "And what will the Doge do for pepper and spices in his kitchen? Remember, we control the worldwide spice trade. We have the monopoly, thanks to the good advice of King Manuel."

Beatriz smiled sweetly at David, and moved her first pawn.

David sighed and moved his black pawn in response. "But Señora Mendes, you will have to leave Venice. After you get out of this situation, you'll want to be done with Venice. And they'll be watching you."

"We've been watched before," she responded with an air of victory, moving her white queen one space forward.

Chapter Twenty-Three

Victory

On the forty-second day of her imprisonment, Beatriz was rudely awakened by Lucilla before daybreak. "Samuel has brought this package, and says you are to dress for a meeting with the Tribunal at ten this morning. I've awakened Rosa, she'll bring you bath water and help you with your hair."

Beatriz felt her hands grow clammy, and her stomach churned, as she opened the package of clothing. Her family had sent one of her best day gowns, a dove-grey very light weight wool dress with white Venetian lace collar and cuffs, as well as fine stockings and her best black high-heeled shoes. They also enclosed two ornamental combs for her hair, encrusted with diamonds and pearls. "This must be a very important meeting," she said to Rosa, as she unpacked the items and prepared for her bath.

She had no appetite for breakfast. She agonized over what was about to happen, what were the possibilities? They could condemn her to torture on the *strapado*, or worse yet, they could burn her at the stake while her family and all the New Christians in Venice watched.

The Doge must be hurting very badly by now, she thought as she calculated his loss of revenue from Mendes ships.

I have the feeling that Joseph has done something, probably something ingenious, something that involved the Turks.

At 9:45 am Lucilla came to escort her to the Tribunal chambers. She held out her hands for the cuffs, but Lucilla shook her head. "No ma'am, they specifically said no cuffs and no leg-irons. Don't know why, either."

Lucilla escorted her to the small chamber adjacent to the courtroom and left her in the charge of the bailiff. During her previous visits to this court room, she'd been all alone, the court room empty except for the officials, but now, as she sat waiting to be taken before the Tribunal she heard the muffled voices of what sounded like a crowd. Perhaps they were planning to make an example of her to the *converso* community, a public condemnation.

As the bailiff escorted her into the courtroom, she was astounded to see a fully packed room. In the front row, immediately in front of the witness chair she was directed to sit in, sat Joseph, Samuel, and *God bless him*, her daughter Reyna and little Beatriz. Ben Zarella beamed at her from his seat next to Joseph. In the row behind her family she recognized many of the merchants the House of Mendes did business with, and in the far back row, she saw the bearded and yellow-hatted diamond cutters from the Ghetto. She recognized friends and acquaintances from all walks of life, the movers and shakers of Venetian society.

The bailiff told everyone to stand and the tribunal judges and the Doge entered the chamber and took their assigned seats. The crowd was deathly still. Joseph winked at Beatriz and Reyna mouthed the words, *I love you Mama.*

The door in the back of the chamber opened and four men dressed in the unmistakable uniform of the Turkish navy walked to the front of the room and sat next to Ben Zarella in the front row.

The doge nodded to his solicitor, and Jorge Badillo stood behind the rostrum and addressed the court and the crowd.

"We are here today to make a final judgment in the case of Beatriz da Luna Mendes accused of being a secret Judaizer by her sister Brianda. We have completed a thorough investigation during the past two months, and the court has concluded that this matter is a personal issue between two sisters, a domestic matter, over which the government and the church have no jurisdiction. We have concluded that Señora Beatriz da Luna, the head of the House of Mendes, was born and baptized as a Catholic in 1510 in Lisbon, that she has always been a faithful communicant and given generously to the church, to the poor and orphans. Indeed, she has led an exemplary life, and contributed much to this community.

"Her sister, Brianda, on the other hand, has out of spite and jealousy, brought unfounded charges against her, and has supplied the officials of this tribunal with false information. Such behavior cannot go unpunished. We will dispense with the matter of Brianda de Luna at another time.

"Today, we are releasing Beatriz da Luna from this facility, we beg her forgiveness for the inconvenience we have caused her and her family, and we are making restitution to the family in the amount of two thousand ducats.

"Señora, we wish you a long, happy and prosperous life here in Venice. That concludes my statement."

"Señora, you are free to join your family and go home."

He turned, nodded to the doge, and the officials stood as one and walked out of the chambers.

The minute the door closed behind them, the crowd broke into thunderous applause and cheers. Beatriz, with tears flowing down her cheeks, rushed to her family's arms and kissed them all.

Later that morning, after greeting all the Venetians who came to see her freed, Joseph directed their gondolier to take her to the port where the huge convoys of ships off-loaded their cargo. "What do you see, Beatriz?" he asked as they neared the lagoon.

"Why, there are no ships. No ship at all! Joseph, what have you done?"

"You have Suleiman to thank. He sent ten warships, and they have blockaded the port and kept all ships from entering Venice for three days now. He informed the doge that the blockade would continue until such time as you were released from prison, a public apology made to you, and restitution made to the Mendes family. The doge found himself losing more than forty percent of his daily revenue and, ultimately, control of the Adriatic Sea."

"Oh, Joseph, you are my hero. This is nothing less than a miracle."

"On the contrary, my dear aunt. You are the heroine. You stood toe-to-toe with the Catholic Church. You won."

Momentarily taken aback at this realization, Beatriz nodded, then added, "How did you ever get them to make that statement?"

A smile crept across Joseph's face. "It took us two days to draft that announcement, two days of tireless negotiating. You can't imagine how difficult it was to get them to apologize to our family and to pay us two thousand ducats. But Suleiman backed us up, and as you saw, he sent four of his highest-ranking officers to let the doge know he really means business.

"Of course," Joseph continued, "Suleiman has been looking for a chance to show the world his naval power, and we gave him that excuse. I don't think the doge is going to get in his way any time soon. Not after this week."

After they arrived back at their home on the Grand Canal, word spread about Doña Beatriz' release from prison, and New Christians and wealthy merchants began to spontaneously arrive, bringing flowers, wine, chocolates, pastries, and beverages. The Mendes home overflowed with Venetians from all walks of life, happy to celebrate the recovery of their leading businesswoman, delighted that the port of Venice would once again be open to commerce.

Late in the afternoon the four naval officers arrived carrying maps of Constantinople and the surrounding countryside, which had been sent by

Suleiman. Beatriz, Joseph and two of his young aides escorted the uniformed officers upstairs to the map room. When the maps were fastened to the wall so all could see, Joseph took a pointer and outlined the area called Galata, a rural area outside of Constantinople proper. "This is a beautiful area, twenty minutes from the Bosporus Sea, a snug little valley with trees, wonderful land for farming, and a major road that leads directly to the center of the city. It is here, Beatriz, that I propose we create the small city for our people."

"He turned to his two young aides, Abraham Scorcino and Jacob Padilla. "You need to spend some time in this area, plot out a complete city with every necessity."

Beatriz joined in. "I want a synagogue as grand as the cathedrals of Venice. We'll need several schools, a completely modern hospital, a business area with shops and cafes, several nice parks, but most of all, space for beautiful homes. We are not creating a ghetto. I want vegetation, trees, flowers, small houses and large homes and a few grand estates."

One of the officers asked, "How many of your people do you plan on settling here?"

Without hesitation, Beatriz answered, "At least ten-thousand. We must plan on a synagogue that will seat several thousand, schools for a couple thousand children, a hospital with at least three hundred beds."

Abe asked, "How much land do you wish to buy, Signora?"

Beatriz turned to Joseph for approval as she answered, "I think we should consider buying about thirty-thousand acres. You can never make a mistake when you buy land. We'll need land for textile factories, for a winery, perhaps even a ship building facility."

Joseph sat down and looked directly at Abraham and Jacob. "Go with these men tonight, you know what we are looking for, explore the valley and send me back maps and plans for the city. Identify builders we can contract with, find out what kind of permits we will need from the government. We want to get started on this immediately so that we might begin moving families into Galata within two years."

They talked for another two hours, brainstorming on all the details that would need to be in place before the House of Mendes could officially pull up stakes in Europe and move to the Ottoman Empire.

When Joseph was satisfied that they accomplished all they could that evening, he bade the officers and his aides "Godspeed!" and sent them on their way back to Constantinople, carrying a long letter of profound gratitude from Beatriz to Suleiman.

Finally, late in the evening, Joseph and Beatriz were alone in the small parlor on the *piano nobile* level. Joseph poured each of them a small glass of sherry, then sat down opposite Beatriz and pulled two letters out of his coat pocket. "This is a letter of invitation from the Duke of Ferrara, Dúke Ercole II of the House of Este."

My dear Señora Mendes,
We are hopeful that you will grace our beautiful city with your presence very soon. For many decades we have welcomed immigrants from Spain and Portugal, and we have a very substantial number of prosperous Jewish families of great distinction. The illustrious Doña Benvenida of the House of Abrabanel has spoken of you and your family on numerous occasions. She is hopeful that you will soon travel here with your family and allow her the privilege of being your hostess here in Ferrara.
Please know that we will welcome you with open arms and do everything in our power to make your stay in Ferrara a splendid interlude. You may be certain that you and your family will never be molested due to your religious beliefs, regardless of your previous affiliations. You will be free to practice Judaism and dress as you desire. If, after my death, my successor wishes to withdraw these letters patent, you are guaranteed at least eighteen months to settle your affairs and to leave, taking all your property with you, duty free.

The letter was signed by the duke, and the official seal of Ferrara was affixed. As Beatriz handed the papers back to Joseph, a tear slid down her cheek. "To live without fear...wouldn't it be wonderful?"

"Here is a letter to you from Doña Benvenida," Joseph said as he handed a second letter, this one on pale blue stationary with the crest of the House of Abrabanel at the top.

My dear Doña Gracia Nasi Mendes,
Your nephew Joseph has informed me of your desire to spend some time in our beloved Ferrara, and my family and I would be so pleased if you would let us entertain you. We have a large property

with several commodious guest houses, and we can make you and your family very comfortable. As we have long been associated with your family in the printing business, we feel that you are family to us and we are most anxious to be helpful to you during this time of difficulty with the Venetian authorities. We have conferred with the authorities here, namely Duke Ercole, and he has prepared the necessary safe-conduct papers and will be pleased to provide armed escort as soon as you cross the border into Ferrara. Please let me know by return messenger the approximate time of your arrival so I may have all in readiness.

"How soon can we leave?"

"In about three days, I would think. The servants have almost completed the packing. I'll need to send a man ahead of us to alert the duke to send the guards to escort us, but I do believe most of the arrangements are complete."

In a very quiet voice, barely audible, Beatriz looked at Joseph and asked, "Brianda?"

"Do you care?"

"Yes. She is my sister. That will never change."

"I've arranged for her to be released from prison in fourteen days. She'll be free to come back here to her home, or do whatever she pleases. Of course, she'll still be dependent on you for money."

"I'll arrange for a monthly allowance, perhaps one hundred ducats a month."

" That's more than generous."

"We must take little Beatriz with us, we can't leave her here without her mother."

"We will take her with us to Ferrara, and if her mother desires after she's out of prison, we'll have Samuel escort her back to Venice."

Beatriz nodded her approval, sipped her sherry, then stood. "I must go to bed, I'm exhausted." She reached for Joseph's hand, he stood up, and once again she hugged him. "When we're settled in Ferrara, I'll give you and Reyna my blessings for a betrothal ceremony. But we won't celebrate the wedding until we're settled in Constantinople. Now, go find your love and give her a kiss for me!"

Chapter Twenty-Four

Safe Haven
Ferrara – 1550

As promised, the Duke of Ferrara, Ercole II welcomed Doña Gracia Nasi, the Hebrew name she now preferred to be called, the widow of Don Semer Benveniste, previously known as Francisco Mendes, with all the pomp and circumstance reserved for a head of state. Ten days after her arrival, first giving her and her family a chance to unpack and settle into the sumptuous guesthouse on the Abrabanel estate, the Duke hosted a magnificent ball at his ducal palace. He gathered together the leading intellectuals and artists, businessmen, religious leaders, ambassadors from the Papal States, France and Germany, as well as the leading members of the Jewish community in Ferrara.

In his welcoming toast, he lauded Doña Gracia's extraordinary success in managing one of the largest banking houses in the world, her foresight in building one of the largest fleets of ocean-going ships, and her generosity and tireless efforts to rescue her fellow Jews from the iron fist of the Inquisition.

"I deplore what the officials of the Inquisition have been doing, spreading fear throughout Europe. Those of you in this room who have connections with the papacy should make it your business to stop this heinous behavior. Church officials must pay attention to the voices gaining strength in Germany and England. Our citizens are listening to the criticism of Erasmus, of Martin Luther. We here in Ferrara intend to continue our policy of welcoming people of all faiths. We are especially pleased tonight to welcome Doña Gracia Nasi, head of the House of Mendes."

Following the welcome by the civil authorities, Rabbi Yomtob, leader of the Spanish-Portuguese synagogue, invited Doña Gracia and her family to participate in a ceremony of reaffirmation of their Jewish roots during the Sabbath service. Gracia now felt it imperative that she, Reyna and Samuel educate themselves in the Torah. She sought the advice of Doña Benvenida.

"Reyna and Samuel have had very little exposure to the Torah, and I have forgotten much of what I learned years ago."

The two women were seated at a table in the gazebo in Benvenida's topiary garden. Red emperor tulips and brilliant yellow forsythia bloomed just outside of the gazebo; nearby, water trickled across rocks in a small rock garden. In the distance, a magnificent fountain sprayed water over statuary of animals and gargoyles.

"You've come to the right city." Doña Benvenida said. "We have two women, you met them at the synagogue last week, Pomona Modena and Bathsheba Modena, who are Talmudic scholars, as well versed and articulate as any man. Bathsheba is also an expert in the writings of Maimonides. I'll speak to them, and we'll set up a weekly Bible study session here at my home. We'll invite any member of the congregation who wants to join us to come. You can be sure, if only for the pleasure of being inside my home, our people will come by the dozens."

Benvenida had lost her husband, Samuel, three years earlier, but she, like Gracia, was determined to continue his work on behalf of his fellow Jews. "I have personally ransomed more than one thousand Jews and brought them here to Ferrara," she told Gracia that afternoon. "If a baptized Jew still harbors hope of a Messiah to come, if he keeps the dietary laws of the Mosaic code, if he observes Saturday as a day of worship and rest, or changes his linens that day, if he celebrates in any way any Jewish holy day, if he circumcises any of his sons or gives them a Hebrew name, he is guilty of heresy. And everyone is encouraged to inform against their neighbors, friends and relatives. The informants are promised full secrecy and protection. All of the Papal States are enforcing these restrictions."

Gracia sighed, and made a gesture of despair. "No matter how many you and I have ransomed and brought to safety, the Inquisition has burned and tortured more. We will probably never know the numbers for certain."

Doña Benvenida nodded her head and sipped her tea. "Samuel's information was that at least fifteen thousand persons of Spanish and Portuguese birth were burned at the stake, and another one-hundred-twenty-thousand have been tortured and imprisoned since 1492. You, my dear, are one of the ones imprisoned. And I can only guess at the mental torture you suffered during those days in the dungeon."

"You're correct," Gracia said. "Statistics cannot convey the terror we have lived with all the days and nights of our lives. Even now, safe here with you, I wake up with nightmares. Even in the secrecy of our family, in my relationship with my sister and my daughter, I must watch every word I utter. We've lived in terror that one of our servants would turn us in to the Inquisition office. I can't imagine a worse kind of mental oppression."

Benvenida responded, "One of the reasons my husband and I have been so fond of the Duke is that he takes a broad view of the world and history, even as it is being made. People have been taught to believe that the Church is the sole possessor of the truth. Any person or alternative religious organization that disagrees is the devil. We Jews do not accept Christ as the Messiah, thus we have become a despised minority, which must be destroyed, by whatever means it takes."

Benvenida continued, "The Duke disagrees with these teachings of the church, and is one of the most vocal voices attempting to reform the church. I pray he will succeed in tempering the powers that be, and we will have an end to the Inquisition in my lifetime."

****

It was at the second Bible study class that Gracia realized that one of the major problems confronting her people in Torah study was although it was translated into Spanish, the people did not have copies. "Most of our people are literate, they can read and write in Spanish. But they have never been exposed to Hebrew. We will be doing them a great service if we make it possible for every one to have their own copy of the Torah in Spanish."

She sent a message to Ben Zarella in Venice and asked him to come for a long visit as soon as he could arrange it.

"We must find half a dozen Spanish-speaking Hebrew scholars, hire them, and translate the traditional prayer book as quickly as possible," she told him at dinner during his first evening in the guesthouse. "I will pay their salaries, and we will find accommodations here in Ferrara. You can print the "Ferrara Bible" and the prayer books and distribute them wherever there are Spanish-speaking Jews."

One project led to another, and within a few weeks Gracia had convinced Ben that they would also translate vernacular Jewish literature, including the famous "Consolation for the Tribulations of Israel," by Samuel Usque and Abraham Usque. "This prose poem reviews the whole of Jewish history and attempts to provide arguments that will save agonized Jewry from despair," she told Ben.

Quite apart from their publication projects, Gracia and Ben enjoyed a month of relaxation and love on the Abrabanel estate. They rode horseback through the extensive woods and spent lazy afternoons in the shade of old oak trees by the pond. Ben reveled in lengthy intense discussions of politics and philosophy with Duke Ercole II who enjoyed spending an evening with Benvenida, Gracia, Samuel and Reyna.

"With each passing day," Gracia told Ben at breakfast one morning, "I feel less tense, more certain that we are safe here in Ferrara. It's a good feeling, and it's gradually seeping into my bones."

"How I wish I could convince you to make Ferrara your final destination," Ben said as he put down his coffee cup.

Gracia reached for his hand and held it. "Preparations have gone too far, I've pledged my word to Suleiman. He got me out of that prison, I can't forget that. I can't disappoint him now, and besides we've already moved hundreds of families to Galata, a lovely neighborhood outside the city. Joseph intends to make Constantinople the base of our operations."

"I'd hoped that you'd become so close to Benvenida and her friends you'd decide to stay here."

"She is my dearest friend, we share the same vision and goals. She's the first really close friend I've had, and I will hate to leave her when the time comes, but my obligation is to the House of Mendes, to the hundreds of families I've moved to Galata. I've got to be there and make sure they prosper in that new land."

Years later when Gracia remembered that idyllic month with Ben, what stood out in her mind was the serenity, a peacefulness that she had never before experienced and that she would not experience again. It was a blessed, almost sacred, month out of time.

****

Under Doña Gracia's direction, Joseph had created an underground operation in Portugal to identify and coordinate the travel plans of New Christians who desperately wanted to escape the Inquisition. He had emissaries throughout Europe, England, Antwerp, Brussels, France and Germany, who assisted the fugitives with money, safe houses, food, medical care and clothing. Whether by sea or by perilous land routes through the mountains, they were safeguarded by Mendes agents. Elaborate arrangements were made to move them from place to place, along with their money and minimal possessions. And when they finally arrived at either Constantinople or Ferrara, they were housed, fed and employed by the House of Mendes.

Messengers came and went on a daily basis from the guesthouse on the Abrabanel estate informing Gracia of the progress of the Portuguese families. Also, she received weekly reports on the progress of the settlement she was creating in Turkey.

One afternoon, nine months after her arrival in Ferrara, her nephew Samuel approached her at teatime, carrying a letter on thick vellum. "Cousin Gracia *la chica,"* the name by which they now called Brianda's daughter, "has asked me to intercede with you, Aunt Gracia, to ask if Aunt Brianda and little Gracia can rejoin the family here in Ferrara."

Gracia felt her heart plummet to her abdomen. Her mouth became dry, her throat scratchy. She suppressed the tears that began to form in her eyes. With moist palms, she wiped her forehead. "Oh, Samuel, I've prayed for such a moment as this. Yes, with all my heart, I want them, both of them, to join us here. We will ask the duke to send escorts. Please arrange it. As soon as possible." And then, as a tear fell down her cheek, she wiped it away.

"I will write a letter to Brianda, and you will see to it that it is delivered by the fastest possible messenger," she said as she rose from her chair and made her way to her writing table in her bedroom.

The next afternoon she explained her astonishing decision to Benvenida. "When I was in prison, I had a lot of time to ponder things, to think about family relationships. Though I don't condone them, I understood Brianda's actions. If Diogo had left control of Francisco's share of the company to Brianda, I would have resented it terribly. I'm sure I would have grown to hate her, just as she came to hate me.

"But she is my sister, her daughter is my namesake and goddaughter. I will see to it that they are always protected and have everything they need. Besides, we all know that Samuel is deeply in love with Gracia *la chica,* so we must provide for them all."

Two weeks later, on a blustery afternoon, Brianda, now called by her Hebrew name Reyna, arrived at the Abrabanel guesthouse. The first thing Gracia noticed was that she had gained considerable weight, and that she also seemed subdued, meek, almost depressed. Everyone was nervous, but Samuel broke the ice by taking Gracia *la chica*, in his arms and blurting out, "Now, now we will get married!" followed by a rousing kiss and embrace.

The sisters laughed at the young folks enthusiastic passion, then they hugged one another fiercely. Reyna whispered to Gracia, "I'm so sorry, please, please forgive me!"

"You are forgiven. Now, let us rejoice with our children."

Later, Reyna told Gracia heartbreaking stories of her months in Venice. "I was shunned by the New Christians for what I had done to you. I was shunned by the Cardinal for having given false information to the Tribunal. My seamstresses refused to work for me, all the servants left the house. And, worst of all, Benjamin Panetta refused to let me design jewelry for him. Everyone, everyone I depended on left me out in the cold."

"That's a problem I can fix," Gracia volunteered. "I've recruited a wonderful goldsmith here, his name is Abraham Saralvo, and I've already shown him some of the pieces you designed for me. He is anxious to meet you."

Chapter Twenty-Five

The Next Adventure
August-1552

"Take me through it one more time, Dr. Gomez," Gracia said as she plumped up the pillow and placed it behind her back. They were in her bedroom, she propped up in the bed and Dr. Duarte Gomez, one of her most trusted deputies, seated by her side. Gracia was recovering from a "summer cold" and wanted to be completely well when they left for the long trip to Constantinople the following week.

Gomez was a medical doctor-turned businessman who had been an agent for her company for more than four years. He was in his early fifties, a widower, an experienced businessman and diplomat, as well as possessing a wealth of information about medicine. His salt-and-pepper hair curled tightly around his skull, his eyes burned with excitement. She had put him in charge of the arrangements for the trip to Constantinople, bowing to his superior judgment as to routes and method of transport.

"We have removed the enameled coat of arms from the carriages, and painted the exterior a dull chestnut brown. The carriages will be very ordinary looking, shouldn't attract any special attention. We will fly small flags with the Duke of Ferrara's coat of arms in the front of each carriage until we arrive in Ragusa. We will replace them in Ragusa with flags bearing the coat of arms of the Ottoman Empire."

"What about armed guards?" she asked.

"The Duke will provide four armed guards, flying his flag. Two will precede your carriage, and two will be posted at the end of the caravan."

"What will be in our caravan?"

"We will need four carriages to transport the family, staff and servants. That's assuming four passengers in your carriage and six in the other three, for a total of twenty-two passengers. Following the carriages will be two large wagons, one for luggage and a second for provisions including two large tents, bedrolls, and some food. We will buy most of the food and feed for the horses in the villages and towns, especially the meats and fresh fish."

"We must take ample pure water."

"Yes, we will take three barrels just for water, and will refill them everywhere we stop."

"How many of our own guards are we taking?"

"Sixteen. That is the number that both Joseph and the Duke have recommended."

"Six vehicles, twenty-two passengers, twenty additional men as guards. And how many horses?"

"Forty horses in all."

"My God! What will it cost to feed these animals? What will this whole adventure end up costing? Do we have any idea?"

"No, Madam, we do not. Who knows how much we will pay out in bribes as we make our way? Who knows what we will pay for lodging and food? How much we will pay for information? In addition to what we have discussed, we will have four outriders, two advance parties who will leap-frog from place to place making sure we have ample lodging and food when we arrive, as well as making sure everything is safe for your arrival. We cannot take any chances."

"Oh, I agree. It's just so...so overwhelming. I'm not sure I would have agreed to it if I'd understood all it involved..."

He patted her hand. "Don't worry, I do believe we've thought of every contingency."

"Let's go over the route. We leave here next Wednesday morning at first light and make our way, hugging the coastline from Ferrara to Ancona. How long will that take us?"

"It's a well-worn pathway, and unless we run into bad weather it shouldn't take more than two weeks. We will travel on Wednesday and Thursday, rest on Friday and the Sabbath, then leave again at first light on Sunday, travel on Monday, rest on Tuesday. And that will be our pattern throughout the trip. We need to take it leisurely, make sure the horses and the guards have plenty of rest and are always alert when we are traveling. And I do believe that two days of travel in a carriage will be the maximum you can stand, given the pain you are suffering with your back and legs."

"Thank you for that " she responded. "Once we arrive in Ancona, what happens?"

"We will rest for a few days in a very nice inn, a real bed with clean linens and good food. You'll want to spend some time with the rabbis and the Jewish leadership there, leave them a few copies of your prayer book and Bible.

"Four ships of the Fugger fleet will be waiting for us at the wharf. You, your family, I and a few of the guards will travel in the flagship. Lady Reyna and her daughter and Samuel, with their servants and the rest of the guards will travel in the second ship. The third ship will carry the remaining luggage and two of the carriages and half of the horses. The fourth ship will carry two carriages, the wagons and the rest of the horses."

"What flag will the ships fly?"

"The entire convoy will hoist the Fugger flag as well as the flag of the Venetian Doge. We will be sailing in waters controlled by Venice until we are fifty miles from Ragusa. At that point, we enter waters controlled by the Ottoman Empire. When we alight from the ships in Ragusa, we will be under the protection of Suleiman and he is sending half a dozen armed guards who will escort us for the rest of the trip, all the way to Constantinople."

"I will be so relieved when we pick up the Ottoman guards. We can't get to Ragusa fast enough!"

"Ah, milady, that's when the hard part begins. Crossing the Balkans is one of the most arduous journeys a person can undertake. The old Roman road, *Via Egnatia*, is nothing more than rutted pathways up and down small and large mountains. In some places the path is very narrow, and the cliff drops several hundred feet down. If the horses become spooked, tragedy can result. And we will be dealing with some forty horses and frightened guards. It's a great shame that we aren't taking this entire trip by ship. It would be so much more comfortable for everyone."

"Part of me wishes that were the case, but Reyna and I and our daughters suffer terribly from sea sickness, and Joseph is adamant that we not risk being apprehended by pirates or the doge's men. He also worries about the weather at sea. Besides, it gives me a chance to meet with the leaders of our people in all these important ports. Knowing these people, the rabbis and the leaders of the congregations, may be very useful in the future."

"I realize all that. I only wish we didn't have to make that trek over the Balkans. You are going to suffer pain the whole way."

"In that case, we'll have to find a way to distract ourselves from the pain. Have you been able to arrange for a tutor to teach us Turkish?"

"Yes, we have a Spanish-speaking Turk joining us in Ragusa. You will have to pay him generously for having agreed to take this trip across the Balkans."

"Good. We will distract ourselves by study of Torah and Turkish! That is my plan. And it gives me a wonderful opportunity to spend many hours with my daughter. It's time she becomes a partner in all our projects."

****

All was in readiness; it was time for Gracia to thank all those persons in Ferrara who had been so welcoming to her and her family. It was time to say goodbye. She and her sister, Reyna, dressed in their best day gowns, began the day with a visit to Rabbi Yomtob who had invited Pomona and Bathsheba Modena to join them for coffee at the Rabbi's residence. The sisters brought gifts, small gold love knot earrings for the women, and a first-edition, leather bound volume of Plato's works translated to Spanish for the Rabbi.

"Our people," Rabbi Yomtob said, "will always be grateful to you for providing us with the Bibles and prayer books. We are the only congregation in Ferrara to have such riches. You will always be remembered for your generosity."

"My family is equally in your debt, Rabbi, for having sponsored our first visit to the *mikvah*, and introduced us to the study of Hebrew and the study of the Torah. I've even learned how to manage a kitchen according to the laws of Kashrut."

After a solemn blessing by the rabbi and a short prayer for their safe journey, the women took their leave. Their next stop was a lunch with the duke and Doña Benvenida Abrabanel at the ducal palace.

Gracia had asked Joseph to send a special gift for the duke, and he had selected the latest maps of the world, complete with the best sea-faring and overland routes for commerce. The maps were encased in a large ornately carved leather portfolio and fastened with a clasp of precious stones.

The duke's surprise and enthusiasm for the maps was palpable. He became so immersed in spotting the changes in what he believed to be the geography of the New World that he momentarily forgot his hosting duties. "Doña Gracia, I can't tell you how pleased I am to have these maps. I've always heard that no one had maps as good as the Mendes. Now I see for myself. Your people do good work!"

After a formal luncheon filled with gossip of Rome and the Venetian doge, Duke Ercole turned the conversation to Gracia's plans. "You will be spending some time in Salonica, I hope. I hear good things about trade with the merchants there. They're very big in textiles, especially wool. We'd like to import some of that wool."

"Dr. Gomez has arranged for us to spend about two weeks in Salonica. We have a large number of representatives there and this will be my first opportunity to get to know them."

"You must take lots of Bibles and prayer books with you," Benvenida said, "as there are more than twenty synagogues and over fifteen-thousand Jews."

"That is my intention. I wish we could organize our rabbis a bit better, have a way to communicate with all of them simultaneously. That's one thing I envy about the church, their organizational ability. The church seems to speak with one voice, that of the pope. We have no similar kind of universality. There are times when we Jews need to speak with one voice, a unified position."

"I see what you mean, Doña Gracia," Duke Ercole responded, "but in many ways you are better off without a tyrannical pope. Think of the damage the popes have done to the church in the past century. Alexander VI was more like Caligula than Jesus Christ. We don't need any more popes like that. And God only knows what the future holds for us. The College of Cardinals is full of rascals."

Gracia looked down at her hands, then lifted her head and spoke directly to the duke. "That's why we are moving the House of Mendes to Constantinople. After all these years of running from the Inquisition, I'm convinced there are no guarantees here in Christendom, not even here in Ferrara. I hate to leave you," she looked at Benvenida, her dearest friend, "but my first obligation is to protect all we've built over the years." Tears formed in her eyes. "I don't know how we'll adapt to this different Turkish Muslim culture. But we Jews have adapted over and over again through the centuries."

Nodding in agreement, the duke stood, signaling the luncheon was over.

He slowly walked the women to the front door of his palace, holding Doña Gracia gently by the elbow. He kissed her goodbye on both cheeks, then kissed Doña Reyna. He assisted the women into their carriage, and as they drove away, he waved to them until they were out of sight.

****

After a short nap, Gracia took pen in hand and wrote a letter to Ben Zarella in Venice:

My darling Ben,
Our trunks are packed, Reyna has completed our travel clothes, and we've made our farewell visits to the duke and the rabbi, and tomorrow morning at first light we will set off in a large caravan, to Ancona. My deepest wish is that you would be going with us. Oh, how happy, how complete that would make this move. I confess, I'm very anxious about so many things. How will the Muslims receive us? How

will we adapt to their ways, I've already admonished our women that they must wear some sort of head-covering, and long sleeves when they go to the market or anywhere in public. Reyna, bless her, has designed new "harem" pajamas for us, long pants gathered at the ankles with sleeveless tops in a wonderful silken fabric. She couldn't resist embellishing them with lace, you know Reyna!
My darling, I know you have a business to run, and a very successful one at that, but I hope you will plan on a long visit to Constantinople as soon as you can get away. I am so lonely for you, I need you. Do plan on coming soon.
Don't worry about us. I will send you a letter from Salonica; once we've crossed the Balkans the rest of the trip will be easy.

Love from your Gracia

****

The carriages and wagons were loaded, the guards stood at attention. Dr. Gomez came into the guesthouse to escort the four women to their carriages. He took Gracia *la chica,* Samuel and Doña Reyna to the second carriage, then came back for Doña Gracia and Reyna *la chica.* Once they were all safely in place, he joined Doña Gracia and the procession began. As they passed Doña Benvenida's home, Gracia was surprised to see the woman standing in front of her door, waving farewell with her handkerchief. Gracia asked the coachmen to stop, she alighted from the coach, ran up the steps to Benvenida and kissed and hugged her one last time.

Tears streamed down both their faces as they said farewell. "I will write to you from Salonica," Gracia said then hurried back to her carriage.

As they rode through the city of Ferrara, they were astonished to see the streets lined with Jewish families. They threw flowers at the carriages as they passed. Several of the women were weeping.

"And I thought we could keep our leaving a secret!" Gracia said to Duarte.

"There is a huge font of gratitude to you, Gracia. These people will not forget you."

****

The trip to Ancona was uneventful, the weather cooperated, and after several days of meeting with Mendes agents and Jewish leaders, Gracia was anxious to board the ship and get on the way to Ragusa. She was apprehensive because they would be traveling through Venetian-controlled waters, and she was well aware that the doge would do anything he could to prevent the House of Mendes from joining forces with the Ottoman Empire.

As she had so many times in the past, she forced herself to sublimate her anxiety and concentrate on the future. As she sat in the cabin with her daughter, she began to unveil her plans for the Jewish settlement in Galata. "I'm going to make you my chief deputy for community development," she told her. "Dr. Duarte Gomez will be my chief deputy for running the businesses, along with Joseph."

Reyna, eager to become a businesswoman like her mother, responded with enthusiasm.

"I've designed our home with a large kitchen and dining room on the ground floor. We will welcome Jewish families for a dairy breakfast, a mid-day meal with meat, and a dairy supper. The dining room will be furnished with large tables and benches, nothing fancy. There will be no charge for these meals, as these people will not have money when they first arrive in Galata. However, we will have a box where they can drop coins if they so desire.

"On the same floor, I want you to set up an employment office. Everyone will register with this office, and we will be a central clearing house for jobs. You must match the skills of the people with the need for workers, and if we do not have jobs for them in our companies, we will try to help them find jobs elsewhere in the community.

"Everyone must affiliate with one of the synagogues. The Turks expect us to govern our own communities, and we can best do that through the synagogues.

"The children must go to our schools, up to the age of sixteen. When they are sixteen, they will be free to go to work, and we will help them find the right job. If they possess the right intelligence and drive, we will see to it that they get further education. And all the children will be taught the Turkish language. It is imperative that as many of our people as possible learn the language of our new homeland.

"I want you, Reyna, to take the lead in establishing the schools. Follow the pattern of the schools in Antwerp, the one Diogo set up. That was a model curriculum and the one I want to offer to our young people.

"And we must also build a hospital and staff it with the best doctors and personnel we can recruit."

Day after day Gracia, Duarte and Reyna discussed their plans and divided up the responsibility. The time flew by, and four days later they entered waters controlled by the Ottoman Empire. During supper that evening, Gracia took a deep breath and announced to her table mates that she felt safe, "safe, at last!"

****

She smelled him before she saw him. A putrid animal smell, like garbage. Her hand crept under her pillow and she grasped her dagger. He had somehow gotten past the guards and opened the door to her cabin. She opened her eyes just enough to see that he was focused on Reyna. In his right hand he held a huge dagger. A bandanna covered his face, another covered his head.

With her dagger hidden in the folds of her new harem pajamas, she jumped out of bed and in the same instant threw open the lid of the trunk that sat between her bed and Reyna's. "Don't bother with that woman," she burst out, "you can sell what's in this trunk for more than one-hundred-thousand ducats. This is what you want!"

As he reached down into the trunk, she jumped onto his back, wrapping her legs around his waist, and thrust the dagger into the back of his neck, then slowly twisted it.

He crashed to the floor, nearly beheading himself on the trunk.

"Mother!" Reyna was beside her on the floor.

Gracia felt his neck for a pulse. There was none.

"He is dead."

"My God! Oh my God!" Reyna wrapped her arms around her mother and tried to raise her to her feet.

The door burst open and three of the guards rushed in, along with the captain. They helped Reyna lift Gracia to her feet, then helped her sit on the side of the bed.

"Get him out of here!" she ordered the captain. "And clean this mess up."

The guards dragged the body out the cabin door, the captain took Gracia by the elbow and led her out to the deck, and from there to the galley where he poured the two women some brandy.

Shortly, Dr. Duarte Gomez joined them.

"They killed three of our guards," Captain Saunders reported. "We killed seven of them. Before we killed the last one, we interrogated them, and you can rest assured that they were acting alone and are not attacking the other ships. Your sister and her daughter will be safe."

Gracia nodded. "Thank you, sir."

"Tell us what happened," Dr. Gomez asked.

After she described in great detail what had happened, he said, "I'm astonished that you had the presence of mind to divert his attention like that."

"At a time like that, you don't think carefully. You react, a sort of body memory takes over. Remember, I was Francisco's star pupil in his martial arts classes some twenty years ago. My body has never forgotten that training. Besides, I regularly fence with Samuel and Joseph. Francisco always stressed to me the importance of keeping physically fit in order to protect myself. I've never forgotten that." She looked down at her legs, and smiled at the harem pants. "I can't wait to tell Reyna how wonderful her new pajamas are. I could never have grabbed him around the waist with my legs if I'd had a long skirt on!"

Reyna *la chica* was still trembling, in spite of the brandy. "Mother, I can't help thinking...if you weren't such a light sleeper...who knows..."

Gracia moved closer to her daughter, put her arm around her. "Remember, darling, the most important of God's commandments is 'Choose Life!' That is our guiding principle."

Chapter Twenty-Six

My People Live In Squalor!
Salonica-1552

Dr. Duarte Gomez' advance team had arranged to lease a suitable house in a largely Muslim neighborhood on a hillside overlooking the city, They had chosen this neighborhood rather than the Jewish quarter below on the Gulf of Salonica because drainage and ventilation were better, the odors in the Jewish quarter were known to be worse than the canals in Venice. From the hillside, the view of the city and the water were lovely, and added benefits of being removed from the central business district were less noise and more spaciousness. Gracia was pleased with the accommodations, and made plans to stay through the Jewish holidays of Rosh Hashanah and Yom Kippur.

After two days rest from the journey over the Balkans, Gracia was prepared to meet with the Managing Director of the Mendes Brothers Textiles company. Dr. Gomez escorted Nathan Solomon into the library and introduced him to Gracia and Reyna *la chica* . Solomon was very tall, and wore a well-trimmed short salt-and-pepper beard that covered his chin and the lower part of his cheeks. He was dressed in a floor-length robe of finest navy wool over a long pastel-blue linen garment, which was belted with a gold braided rope. His head was covered, in Ottoman style, with a beige linen turban.

Presenting a stark contrast, Dr. Gomez and the Nasi women were dressed in the European styles of Venice. After coffee was served, Gracia opened the formal meeting; it was her first meeting with this president of one of their most lucrative companies.

"We are so pleased to have arrived safely, and have the pleasure of meeting you, Señor Solomon. Joseph has told me much about this company and your fine leadership of it, and we are anxious to learn much more."

"Doña Gracia, we too are pleased to have you visit with us. We are planning many festivities in your honor. Our wives are especially anxious to meet you. There are so few women active in business, and you are quite a sensation!"

Gracia accepted his comments modestly, then added, "My daughter, Reyna, is joining the management team of the House of Mendes, and I'd like to ask you to recount for her benefit the history of the company, how it got started and the progress made in recent years."

Solomon cleared his throat, taking time to organize his presentation. "Early in the century, I believe it was in 1515, Diogo Mendes negotiated an exclusive concession for the House of Mendes with the sultan to manufacture all the uniforms for the janissary infantry corps. What started out as a small operation has grown over nearly forty years. We can now boast that we are one of the principal producers and exporters of cloth in the entire Mediterranean.

"We begin by harvesting the wool. We send agents out into the countryside to recruit sheep farmers. If need be, we subsidize their initial purchase of the animals or enlarge their flocks. We arrange for the transport of the raw wool to our factory here in Salonica. After the wool arrives in our warehouses, it is dyed, brushed, and woven into cloth ready for the tailor. We have nearly a thousand men employed turning raw wool into cloth, nearly all of them Jewish refugees from Spain and Portugal.

"The next step is to cut the uniform in all the various sizes needed by the infantry corps. We have more than thirty tailors who do nothing but cut the uniforms according to patterns provided by the Sultan's people.

"Finally, the fabric is sewn into uniforms by several hundred well-trained tailors."

Gracia smiled at Solomon, thanking him for the carefully described presentation. Reyna asked, "But don't you also export cloth for regular clothing?"

"Ah, yes, indeed. Initially the Sultan insisted that we only manufacture uniforms, but after many years of proving to the court that we could meet their demands, no matter how great, they agreed to let us sell fabric to our citizens here in Salonica. The next step was to get them to agree that we could export bolts of cloth. We now export to Jewish merchants in Buda, Ragusa and Ancona. The Mendes ships take large shipments of cloth and sell them as far away as London."

"Do you have difficulty hiring enough weavers to meet the demand?" asked Dr. Gomez.

"We rely on Joseph Nasi's underground to supply us with workers. We hire unskilled men, train them for about three months, and then put them to work. We watch the quality of their individual output, and reward the best weavers handsomely. We've had good luck over the years keeping our skilled weavers."

"How secure is the relationship with the court? Do you see any danger of our losing this concession?" asked Gracia.

"Señora, I have been Managing Director for twelve years now, and I consider a major part of my job keeping up excellent relations with the janissary infantry corps. We fill every order within six weeks of receiving it. In fact, we keep a pretty large inventory on hand so if there is a sudden military emergency, we can cope with it. No, I don't see any danger of our losing the concession, and Sultan Suleiman seems very pleased with our relationship. I don't anticipate any competition."

"Do you feel a need to expand your factory?" Reyna asked.

"Our people are working in terribly crowded conditions, as you will see when you visit tomorrow." He turned to Gracia, "After your visit, we may want to talk about the options for expansion, if that is your desire, Señora,"

"I look forward to a tour of the Jewish quarter and a visit to the factory. I've been very curious to understand the entire process of cloth-making, as I see it as a far preferable occupation for our people than tax-farming."

Solomon nodded his agreement, then added, "The next project the Sultan wants the House of Mendes to take on is supplying his infantry corps with ammunition, gun powder and cannons. They have asked me to bring this up with you and see if you are interested in selling weaponry to the Ottomans."

Gracia looked intensely at Duarte. "I wish Joseph were here for that discussion."

"Agreed!"

Gracia was both pleased and displeased with what she saw in the Jewish quarter and at the Mendes factory. The narrow, claustrophobic lanes of the residential district suffered from overcrowding, bad ventilation, raw sewage, and stagnant pools of refuse. Modest wooden houses behind walls with gates housed the workman, fishermen, peddlers as well as the wealthy merchants and managers. Houses grew up, with new stories added on top of existing homes as families expanded and new refugees arrived. The modest unpretentious synagogues were on rutted back streets. Noxious smells of vats of urine filled the air. The odors from tanneries and slaughterhouses added to the mix. It was nearly impossible to breathe!

My people are living in squalor, Gracia realized, even before she stepped foot into the factory.

The four-floor factory occupied a city block, and every section was severely overcrowded. But, Gracia was heartened by the positive spirit of the working people. With tears in their eyes, they greeted her, thanking her for their jobs, for saving their lives, for honoring them with this visit.

Afterward, on the ride back up the hillside, they discussed what they had seen.

"I don't understand," Reyna said, "if they are well paid and secure in their jobs, why don't they move away from the central district, why don't they move up into these hills?"

"Several reasons," Gracia patiently responded. "Most of them do not have a horse for transportation, they must walk to work, so they need to live near their workplace. Also, since they cannot ride on the Sabbath, they must live in walking distance of a synagogue. And, finally, they choose to live with their co-religionists, rather than live in the Christian or Muslim neighborhoods. They feel safer."

"If you talk to the people the way I have the last few days," Gomez added, "you will see that they consider this a "little Jerusalem." They are safe for the first time in their lives, they have jobs, they have time for Torah study, and they have good schools for their children. In spite of the horrid living conditions, these Jews are happier than they have ever been, and they bless the name Mendes every day of their lives."

Gracia shook her head. "No, Duarte. It's not good enough. It's not what I want for our people. We will think and pray on it. We will find a way to improve these living conditions. It is my priority."

Several days later Gracia invited the Managing Director of the House of Mendes bank in Salonica to brief her on the operations of this branch of the bank. As usual, she asked Reyna and Duarte to join her for the meeting. Abraham Soncino was a young man from Antwerp who had been trained by Diogo, and specifically chosen for this position. His special training was in accounting and diplomacy. He had also mastered the Turkish language and studied Islam.

"The Sultan's people are very pleased with the way the Jewish rabbis collect taxes from the Jews. It's turned out to be a very good system, and gives us all the autonomy we need," Abraham said, beginning to explain the unique Turkish system to Gracia and Reyna.

"Every Jew must affiliate with the synagogue of his choice. There are more than twenty here in Salonica: German, Italian, several Spanish and Portuguese. People who used to live in Lisbon have formed a synagogue.

People who used to live in Aragon have their own synagogue, and so forth. The rabbis collect the taxes from the congregants, and deliver them to the House of Mendes. We take our percentage, and send the rest on to the Sultan's treasury. If some of the congregants are too poor to pay the head tax, the wealthier members make up the difference; it makes no difference to the Sultan."

"But how do you collect from the peasants, those farmers who barely subsist on what they grow?" Reyna asked, displaying the kind of compassion her mother hoped to see in the daughter who would eventually inherit the company.

Soncino explained, "We have agents, very well trained by our people, who go out into the countryside. They can tell from seeing first-hand, how rich or poor the family is. If it is truly a poor family, a family with no cash, we take some hay, or a few dozen eggs, or garden vegetables. We keep very careful records of what we take. Then we sell it at local markets or here in Salonica, and we use that money to pay the treasurer. We convert the produce into cash."

Gracia went on, "When people don't have enough to eat and keep warm, and they see the wives of the tax farmers in the market place wearing gold bracelets six inches up their arms and diamonds the size of peas on their ears, and they know those women are married to the men who visit them four times a year and clean out their larders, they hate the Jews. And with reason." Gracia sighed. "I truly wish we could get out of the business of farming the taxes."

Duarte Gomez looked intently at Soncino. "How lucrative is this business here in Salonica?"

"We keep ten percent of what we collect. Truth is, we don't collect all that much from the peasants. The bulk of the taxes comes from the labor force here in Salonica, and more than 70 percent of the taxes from this city come from the Jewish population even though we are a little more than 50 percent of the population. The fact of the matter is that the sultan trusts our accounting systems, and I think it would be a major mistake to give up this concession."

Gracia stood, signaling the meeting was over. "Señor Soncino, you are doing a fine job. Just see to it that your agents treat the peasants with compassion. We don't want to create anti-Semitism here in Turkey."

****

Still concerned with the squalid living conditions in the Jewish quarter, with no solution in sight, Gracia agreed to spend a day meeting with the families the Mendes underground had brought to Salonica. She was prepared for a joyous party, a sort of "indoor picnic" in the large cafeteria on the ground floor of the factory. She was not prepared for the emotional impact of the festivities.

Nathan Solomon and Abraham Soncino had collaborated with Duarte and Reyna on the arrangements: Gracia, who suffered from severe back and leg pains, could not stand for a long period of time. They brought in a comfortable overstuffed armchair, and surrounded it with six folding chairs. With Reyna by her side, Gracia welcomed the first family.

Fathers and mothers carrying babies and holding toddlers, some trailed by teenagers in their best synagogue clothes, introduced themselves, one family at a time. They carried small bouquets of flowers, boxes of homemade candy, small offerings of perfume, pottery, and local metal and leather work.

"I was one of the first students in Francisco's school, he sent me and my family here to Salonica in 1517. It's been a good life, one I could never have had without his training," one of the elderly master weavers said, tears in his eyes, holding tightly to his wife who was bejeweled with gold bracelets, diamond and sapphire earrings.

Behind them in the line of families were three adult children with their spouses and small babies. "You saved our lives, you saved the lives of every one in this room," the weaver's eldest son said as he bowed to Gracia.

They had come on Mendes ships at no cost, been fed and clothed by Mendes agents, and brought to the Mendes factory and bank for employment. It is one thing, Gracia thought as she listened to their stories of fear, hunger, darkness and disease back "in the old country", to tell myself, "I've saved one thousand families from the Inquisition." It is quite another to meet the families, hold their hands, receive their kisses and thanks, and see and hear the results of what we have accomplished.

As she ended the conversation with each family, she presented them with a copy of the Spanish version of the Ferrara Torah. "Now you can study Torah at home."

Later that day, as she and Reyna were being driven back to their temporary home on the hillside, with great emotion, she said to Reyna, "I feel as if I am the one who should thank them, they have given me a great gift today. They have given me a sense of towering accomplishment, greater than any I ever imagined. If I were to die tonight, I would know my life has been worthwhile."

****

Rosh Hashanah evening was a revelation to Gracia. As the four Nasi women made their way upstairs to the women's section of the small synagogue, a sort of hush fell over the other women. They nodded their greetings, all the while scrutinizing the clothing of their guests. Several women seated in the front row immediately gave up their seats and motioned for the four women to be seated in the best seats. The congregants continued to stare unabashedly at the Nasi women in their European gowns.

Gracia and Reyna took an equal interest in the "best dress" of the congregants, which consisted of long skirts of dark blue, brown, black or charcoal, with white long sleeved high-neck blouses, and a bolero-type jacket with lapels matching the white blouse. Long, dark scarves covered their hair.

It was the jewelry on several of the women that caught Gracia's eye: diamonds the size of small almonds, row after row of pearls, cabochon sapphires and rubies the size of grapes, diamond rings of the finest quality adorned their fingers. Jewelry the equivalent of what you would see at court in Venice or Antwerp!

Surely this display of wealth is an affront to the poor Christians and Muslims, the populace!

And sure enough, when Gracia met with all the rabbis of Salonica several days later, it was one of the first issues they brought up. "Our women have a penchant for external display," Moises Almosnino, the leader of the Jewish people, told Gracia. "In spite of sermons admonishing them to wear their fine jewels only in the privacy of their homes, we can't seem to cure them of this desire to be ostentatious."

"Our wealthiest families," he continued, "have African slaves for servants, wear silk and gold-laced costumes, display gold bracelets, pearl chokers, diamonds, and give huge, obscenely expensive weddings and parties. Our concern as rabbis is that we will incite envy, which will result in riots, and sumptuary laws such as exist in Europe. We've got to find a way to curb these excesses before they destroy the very freedoms we cherish."

"Perhaps you rabbis should consider passing a rabbinical ordinance forbidding public wearing of jewelry, under pain of excommunication,"

Gracia advised. "I know that sounds harsh, but having just escaped from the Inquisition, I strongly feel that we have to govern our own people in order to prevent a recurrence of what is going on in Europe here in the Ottoman Empire." Then she added, "Of course, I'm speaking against my own interests, as the Mendes family has always been a major purveyor of precious stones to the courts and the Vatican."

****

Several evenings later, Gracia was surprised by a visit from her sister Reyna accompanied by the goldsmith Abraham Saralvo. She knew they had become lovers, and afforded them complete privacy by arranging for different housing for them. They kept to themselves while in Salonica, touring the city and its outskirts at their leisure.

"We've come to tell you that we've decided to stay here in Salonica," Reyna began tentatively. "We like the climate and the people. It feels like we're back in Lisbon, everyone speaks Castilian, we don't have to bother learning Turkish. And we feel we can establish a jewelry design company and do very well here."

"I see." Gracia was not completely surprised with this turn of events, and as she quickly absorbed the information, she realized it might be a very good idea. Yet, when it came to Reyna, she always harbored a nagging suspicion that she was up to something, something not good. "What about Samuel and Gracia *la chica?* What are their intentions?" she asked Reyna.

"Oh, they will continue to Constantinople with you. Samuel is determined, and now that they are married, of course Gracia will agree to whatever Samuel wants to do."

"Well," Gracia considered, "perhaps this will work. If, after you are here a while, you change your mind, you can come to Constantinople. I am building a wonderful home for you on the family estate..."

"You can let Joseph live in that house, or perhaps you can let Samuel and Gracia have it."

"I'm building a home for them too, so I guess I'll have Joseph use it until he builds his own home."

Abraham, who had listened nervously to the exchange but not said a word, effusively kissed Gracia's hand and thanked her. Gracia realized they expected her to object, but as the idea sunk in she thought it would remove a burr from her everyday happiness to have Reyna so far away. It is probably in everyone's best interest, she thought, especially for Samuel and Gracia. It will give them a chance for marital happiness without a burdensome mother-in-law watching over them on a daily basis.

****

The Jewish holidays were over, Gracia completed her business in Salonica; it was time to resume the journey to Constantinople. Gracia did not look forward to the weeks ahead, riding in the carriage over rutted roads, stopping in small inns for a days rest, then resuming the arduous journey.

And she hated leaving Salonica with no definite plan to improve the living conditions of her people. Finally, two days before departure, she summoned Duarte, Samuel, Reyna and Nathan Solomon back to her library.

"Nathan, I have given a lot of thought to conditions here in the Jewish quarter. I want you to organize an investigative team to find a large segment of property on which you can build a new, greatly expanded factory with the most modern equipment you can find. Near the factory, walking distance, I want you to build modest homes, townhouses, gardens, parks, schools, a hospital and two or three synagogues. You've got to think through garbage collection, sewage disposal, as well as disposal for the refuse from the factory. Plan this very carefully. I'll want to see the plans on paper before I'll invest a single ducat."

Refusing to hear any objection, Gracia continued, "We will build the homes and sell them or rent them to our factory workers. We will educate our children according to the standards established by Diogo in Antwerp. Ultimately, some day soon I hope, we will get out of the business of tax farming and focus on textiles, and yes, on supplying the Sultan with the ammunition, cannons and gunpowder he wants. So, as you make your plans, think in terms of a second factory not far removed from the residential district, so we can begin manufacturing the ammunition the Sultan desires."

Gracia turned to Samuel. "Samuel, I want you to be the one who communicates with Nathan on a regular basis to make sure this project proceeds quickly. I'm putting you in charge of our end of it."

Samuel nodded his acceptance of this responsibility, and Dr. Gomez smiled in approval.

"Now," Gracia added as she stood, "I can leave for Constantinople with a clear conscience."

Chapter Twenty-Seven

Home, At Last!
Constantinople-1553

To her surprise and delight, the Mendes caravan was greeted at the entrance to the city with a small *mehter* marching band and eight janissaries flying the flag of Suleiman the Magnificent. The infantry corps sported uniforms that she recognized from drawings she'd seen in the Mendes factory in Salonica: burgundy velvet turbans, jackets of the same fine stuff trimmed with gold braid, and black breeches of finest merino wool.

The caravan stopped a few miles outside the city the day before to refurbish the carriages and prepare for their grand entrance. Gracia and Reyna rode in the lead carriage, which was freshly painted in the original gold paint. The large enameled House of Mendes medallion was replaced on the sides of the carriage, the velvet upholstery and draperies brushed clean of traveling dust. The white steeds were washed and brushed, and dressed with silver-encrusted reins. The coachmen wore House of Mendes blue and gold livery, and the flag of the House fluttered at the front of the carriage.

Gracia sat very upright and dignified, dressed in a royal blue silk-taffeta cloak and skirt with a blouse of finest Bruges white lace. A matching lace mantilla flowed from a small pearl coronet atop her black hair; pearl earrings were her only jewelry in addition to her gold wedding band.

Reyna had chosen a pale apricot-colored silk brocade, spiced with dark burgundy tulips. The lining of her burgundy cloak matched the brocade of her dress; her jewelry was simple gold love-knot earrings. Apricot-colored lace graced her silken hair, which flowed around her shoulders.

The two women sat straight-backed, avidly returning the waves of the hundreds of Jewish families who lined the street on the way to the entrance of the Topkapi Palace grounds. The crowd cheered and threw small bouquets of flowers at the carriage. Their cheers kept time with the large kettledrums of the marching band, and soon the crowd was chanting "Welcome, Señora. Welcome, Gracia."

When they arrived at the gates of the Topkapi Palace, Dr. Gomez, Samuel and Gracia *la chica,* joined Gracia in her carriage. The rest of the procession would continue on to Gracia's new home. Led by the janissaries and the band, the golden carriage came to a stop at the entrance of the Palace. As protocol demanded, Dr. Gomez and Samuel Nasi went into the palace to present their papers to the officials. Shortly, the men returned to the carriage, all smiles.

"That was easy," Samuel exclaimed. "His Excellency, The Supreme Sultan of the Ottoman Empire will receive Doña Gracia Nasi and her family next Wednesday at lunch, and we were told as if it is a great state secret that it is possible Roxalana, the Sultan's favorite wife, will join us for the lunch in your honor." He grinned mischievously.

"Normally, these state affairs are limited to men only," Duarte explained. "I suspect the women in the Sultan's harem are dying to get a look at you. Roxalana has convinced him her presence is appropriate. All very intriguing..."

"And we must be very careful. We must not make a false step!" Gracia cautioned.

The procession continued over the Galata Bridge, past the Galata tower, and up into the vine-planted hills outside Galata. They passed several huge mansions with large gardens, and as they passed the wrought iron gates, Gracia saw that these were foreign embassies.

And then suddenly they were home.

The janissaries signaled a stop. Two uniformed guards opened the wrought iron gates from inside, came out, spoke briefly with the coachmen, and then invited the caravan inside the high walls of the House of Mendes estate. They drove up a cobblestone driveway lined with tall Bosnian pines. They came to a clearing, and there it was: a classic Grecian-styled mansion of grandiose proportions. Limestone walls, mullioned windows, a slate roof, columns, and terraces all welcomed the weary travelers. The driveway circled a fountain, which sprayed silver water, catching the reflection of the late afternoon sun. Large stone urns guarded the doorway, filled with an array of early spring flowers.

Anna and Max Segovia, who had traveled from Antwerp with Gracia all those years ago, greeted them at the double front door. "Welcome home, Señora!"

****

Gracia chose her dress for the luncheon with the Sultan with great care. She anticipated that the women would wear their most valuable jewelry and elaborate day gowns. While she wanted to measure up to them, she did not want to inspire envy. She chose a sheer navy wool tunic with a bateau neck and long trumpet sleeves, over a matching floor-length slim skirt. The wool had been dyed and woven at the Mendes factory in Salonica. A bolt of it was shipped to Ferrara, and her seamstress made it up according to a drawing Gracia had presented to her. She chose a three strand oval collar of faceted Murano milk glass, mounted with six large pearls, silver bicones and midnight-blue faceted goldstone glass. While this was a most impressive creation, the stones were not precious, but rather man-made. Though the collar was dramatically beautiful, it was not fabulously expensive. She cautioned Reyna and Gracia *la chica* to dress in an equally understated manner.

The group rode in two carriages to the Topkapi Palace grounds. They were greeted at the entrance by two janissaries, who escorted them into the Palace. They were escorted through the Gate of Felicity and into the Throne Room. Immediately, the Turkish tutor who had accompanied Gracia from Ragusa, joined her. "The Sultan has asked me to translate his words for you."

Suleiman was seated on a throne fashioned of red and green enamel on gold leaf, encrusted with 25,000 pearls and precious stones. Members of his cabinet were seated on a lower semi-circle. The escort led them to two rows of chairs on the ground level, immediately opposite the Sultan.

"Señora, we are so pleased to have the honor of welcoming you to our Court and our Empire. We hope you will have a long and happy life among our people."

"Your Excellency, we are equally pleased to have arrived safely, and we are very pleased with what we saw in Salonica and here in Constantinople. We look forward to working closely with you and your Cabinet to insure that the Sublime Porte will remain the greatest empire in the history of the world."

Suleiman smiled graciously, acknowledging that Gracia had spoken the entire speech in Turkish without notes.

"I see our tutor has done his work well."

"Yes, Excellency, and we are thankful to you for providing him, as well as the guards from your janissary corps. Those men gave us a feeling of safety, for which we are indebted to you."

The initial formalities over, the Sultan introduced the members of his cabinet, as well as the three women who were present. "Roxalana is my first wife, Giulana is the mother of two of my daughters, and Calista is the mother of my youngest son." Gracia noted with pleasure that while Roxalana was about her age, the two younger wives were approximately the age of Reyna and Gracia *la chica*. He had given this luncheon a lot of thought.

Introductions over, they moved to a dining area, which consisted of a long, low table, covered with a woven damask cloth, and pillows on the floor. After everyone was seated, Gracia realized that the Sultan was on a slightly higher platform than the rest of the diners. The first course was a preparation of fresh tuna and tomatoes, followed by a spicy chicken with apricots, raisins and almonds served with rice.

"This is wonderful!" Gracia exclaimed to Roxalana who was seated opposite her.

"It's one of my favorites, and we make it with spices from your booth in the Grand Bazaar. Have you been there yet?"

"No, I'm planning a trip to the bazaar next week, and I also want to see the magnificent Hagia Sophia."

"If you would permit me, I will arrange for a private tour. There are always so many people there, and it's much more interesting if we have one of the *imams* take us through."

"I would like that very much, and I'm sure Samuel, Reyna and Gracia would like to accompany us."

"Good. We will arrange it for next Thursday."

This is going well, it can't hurt to become friends with the Sultan's favorite wife!

After a dessert of dates stuffed with almond paste and stuffed butter cookies, the group adjourned back to the Throne Room. Roxalana invited the two young women to visit the harem with her and see their famous Turkish bath. Dr. Gomez told Gracia that the Sultan wished to "discuss business" with her and Samuel in the library.

Gracia, Duarte and Samuel spent a week rehearsing for this meeting; they knew exactly what they would request.

After a lengthy discourse on why the Empire needed to develop armaments both to insure peacetime shipping and a potential sea battle, the Sultan said, "We are ready to enter into negotiations with the House of Mendes to develop and manufacture weapons, cannons, guns, and the ammunition for those weapons."

All eyes were on Gracia, waiting for her response. "Your Excellency, you are extremely far-sighted in making these preparations now. We have discussed this possibility, and have some preliminary ideas about how we might accomplish what you request.

"First, we will need you to designate a large parcel of land outside the city, but as close as possible to the city. It must be located on a waterway, as the armaments will be shipped to their ultimate destination. You must build a large factory for as many as a thousand workers. You will need a separate warehouse to store the armaments and ammunition until they are needed."

"I am grateful you have given this detailed thought," the sultan said.

"You must also be prepared to provide comfortable housing for the workers and their families within walking distance of the factory. Assuming you build this in the countryside, you should plan ample open spaces for parks, gardens, schools and shops. And, most important, you must plan in advance for sanitary living and working conditions, for the removal of garbage and sewage, so that our people will not be plagued with lung disease or The Plague."

Gracia noticed that while she was talking one of the ministers was making notes, obviously calculating the cost of what she was proposing. He stood, walked over to the sultan and whispered in his ear. They conferred for another minute, then the sultan responded.

"What you suggest is a major undertaking, the creation of a small city unto itself. It will be costly, but that is not a problem. We will raise the money. But, tell me, do you Jews have the manpower to invent and manufacture these weapons? Where will the workers come from?"

"Excellency, just as we have recruited and trained workers in the textile company in Salonica, my nephews Joseph and Samuel will recruit and train the men who will invent these new weapons and ammunition, and we will also recruit and train the workers who will manufacture according to design. We've had no difficulty finding workers for the textile plant, and if I send a message to Joseph, I'm sure he will recruit all the workers for this munitions factory and they will be here as soon as you can build the plant and the housing."

A big smile broke out on the Sultan's face; he nodded to his assembled cabinet, as if to say, "I told you so!"

"Señora, this has been a most productive discussion. I will immediately begin a search for the property and we will commission the drawing up of plans for this new city. We will begin building in a few weeks, I promise you!"

****

"There was no discussion of profit for the House of Mendes," Samuel said, as they rode across the bridge into Galata.

"That will come. The sultan will bear the initial cost of construction of a factory, a warehouse, and housing. That was my main concern that we not have to provide capital for that piece of it. We shall think of a formula, which makes sense for us, for the sultan, and for the workers. Suleiman trusts us, that was clear today. We will become full partners, never adversaries. We must notify Joseph to begin recruiting inventors and chemists and metal workers. This is an exciting new venture!"

****

Dearest Benvenida,

So much has happened since I last wrote you from Salonica. We have now safely arrived in Galata, and almost everything is as I expected it to be. The trip was long and arduous, and I don't ever want to travel across country again! But aside from the usual aches and pains in my legs and back, I am fine and the young people are fine.

The house is everything I dreamed it would be, and it's so wonderful to walk on the gorgeous blue and cream Persian carpets that Francisco and I chose when I was a young bride, to enjoy the beautiful Murano chandeliers and sconces in every room. He loved them so. And his books! What a joy to walk into the library and see the rows and rows of books he treasured. It probably sounds silly, but when I pick up one of his favorite books, I feel that he is in the room with me. I miss him so, as I know you miss your beloved Samuel.

And I miss you. I never had a close woman friend, someone I could really pour my heart out to the way I did with you. So many afternoons, around four, I find myself wishing I could walk across the lawn and join you in the gazebo for a cup of tea or a glass of sherry.

Reyna and I have become very close, but there are some things you don't discuss with a daughter.

Poor girl! How she pines for Joseph! We're hoping he will settle all his affairs in Lyon and come here by spring of next year. We have a new project, manufacturing armaments and munitions, for the sultan, and I think that will pique his interest sufficiently that he will hurry here. It's a tough decision, though, because once he comes here, is circumcised and welcomed into the Tribe of Abraham, he can never return to Europe. And he dearly loves court life.

I must tell you about the Grand Bazaar. Suleiman's wife took me there last week, and it was quite an experience. Great buildings with vaulted arches over many blocks contain individual merchant's stalls. Everything you can imagine is for sale: precious stones and gold and silver jewelry, dressmakers, tailors, furniture, decorations, food, rug merchants, books, cafes and tearooms. And yes, the House of Mendes is well represented especially with spices and in another building, textiles. The textiles are the most exciting I've ever seen: woolens, silk brocades, silk velvets, embroidered organdy, and the most magnificent laces ever. Brianda would go crazy there!

Not everything is what I expected. I told you how horrified I was with the living conditions of our people in Salonica. I'm hoping to change that, but it will take several years to accomplish it.

Here, I had expected to feed our poorest people in a large room on the ground floor of the house, but that won't work because we live outside the city walls, up on a hillside with beautiful vineyards. It is too far for the poor people to walk, so we have bought a large building not far from the Galata tower and turned it into our business headquarters.

The ground floor is a large dining area where three meals a day are served to whoever comes. We register them, help them fill out the paperwork to join a synagogue of their choice, and Reyna, bless her heart, has perfected a system of finding them jobs according to their talents, education and wishes. She has had great luck placing more than seventy men and a few women since we arrived. She helps them find housing as well, and we are adding several families every week to our little Jerusalem here in the East.

The second and third floors house our offices. The fourth floor has two small apartments for Reyna and me to use if we choose to rest during the day or stay overnight. The top floor is Duarte's private apartment. We believe this arrangement will work very well for all of us.

Words cannot describe what it means to me to actually meet these families, to hear their stories, to watch them gradually relax and feel safe. Before, when we lived in Antwerp and began this refugee underground, I heard numbers every week. Now the numbers have become living, breathing, suffering human beings.

And we are able to change their lives! I cannot express how much that means to me.

So, dearest Benvenida, though I miss you dreadfully, I'm so glad we made this move. I feel enormously fulfilled, each day more so.

God love you and keep you well and safe,
Your dear friend, Gracia Nasi

****

Cheerful bird song woke her up. She attempted to change positions, but the pains shot through her back and down her legs. *I'm alive,* she told herself, remembering the words of Rabbi Yomtob. "When you awaken to stiff joints, pains in your legs and feet, thank God because you know you're alive. That's better than the alternative!"

It was beginning to be spring, the forsythia was blooming and soon the tulips would flaunt their joyous colors. *Joseph is coming, he's almost here!*

It was nearly four years since she'd seen him, not since he'd obtained her release from the prison in Venice. He had spent most of his time in France, some of it in Antwerp, under a fictitious passport, and some time in London. Now, he was on his way from Salonica to Constantinople via one of the Mendes ships. With him were hundreds of his fellow New Christians, as well as equipment and chemicals for the munitions factory. She expected him to arrive within two or three days.

She rose from bed, dressed and went downstairs for her breakfast, the whole time feeling that something was wrong, a "feeling in my bones" she told her housekeeper, Anna Segovia, as she accepted a plate of fruit and cheese.

"Don't worry, Señora. Young Joseph will be here soon, and safe. We have a suite of rooms prepared for him upstairs, and all his favorite food in store."

"I hope our wines will be to his liking. He's become quite a connoisseur while in France."

"Max spent all afternoon at the Bazaar choosing fine wines for Joseph. I know he'll be pleased."

Just then Max entered the breakfast room. "Señora, Don Samuel is here. He needs to meet with you urgently."

"Please ask him to join me for some coffee. Thank you, Max."

Samuel seemed unusually pale and tense as he kissed her cheek and took a seat on her right at the table. Max immediately served coffee, Samuel declined fruit. As soon as Max had closed the door to the kitchen, Gracia asked, "What is it? What has gone wrong?"

Samuel flushed bright red, stuttered for a moment, then said, "It's Aunt Brianda. She's filed a lawsuit against the House of Mendes claiming that one-half of the profits from the company must come to her and her daughter each year. She claims that you have cheated her and Gracia *la chica* out of her inheritance from Diogo."

Gracia slammed her coffee cup down on the saucer. "I knew she was up to no good over there in Salonica! Is this the first you've heard of this?"

"No," he stammered. "She's been writing Gracia *la chica* for months now, demanding that her daughter join her in this law suit. I've argued against it, sent her several letters myself asking her not to do this. My wife wants no part of it, she's totally opposed to it, but she's helpless to influence her mother."

Gracia's mind was spinning, attempting to plot out the best way to proceed. She had so hoped this business was over with after Brianda rejoined the family in Ferrara and begged to be forgiven.

She sipped her coffee again. "Samuel, I expect you to back me totally in this matter. If you feel, out of loyalty to your wife, that you cannot, then you cannot continue to work for the House of Mendes."

"I understand, Aunt Gracia. My loyalties are completely with you and I only wish I'd been able to persuade Aunt Brianda to drop this foolishness. You are so generous with her and with me and Gracia. We have no complaints at all. My darling wife is terribly embarrassed by this, and begs you to understand. I'm concerned that she's so upset it may cause problems with her pregnancy."

"You tell her not to worry about me. I do not blame her in the slightest for her mother's perfidy. And she's six months along now, this shouldn't upset her pregnancy. She's the picture of health."

Gracia stood and walked to the window and looked out at her garden. It was exquisite, everything she had dreamt of. *And now this craziness*! She turned back to Samuel. "You must make some inquiries, and get us the best possible solicitor. I'd like to meet with him no later than tomorrow morning. I'd like to get this under control before Joseph arrives."

"I understand." He stood, preparing to depart. "I'll have someone identified this afternoon, and I'll stop by later today with whatever additional information I can come up with."

****

Gracia gave herself a few hours to vent her anger at Brianda and think through her options. She realized that the rabbinical ordinance that had recently been promulgated in Salonica forbidding Jewish women from wearing silver or gold rings, chains or gems in public ruined Brianda's jewelry business. The rabbis were justly afraid of exciting envy. *They are right to urge restraint*, Gracia thought, as she paced up and down the floor of her library.

Finally, she sat down at her writing desk and took quill in hand:

Sister,

Samuel notified me that you have filed a lawsuit against me and the House of Mendes here in Constantinople. You need to understand that the Jews in Turkey have complete autonomy from the civil government, and this lawsuit will not be prosecuted in the civil courts but rather in the rabbinical courts.

I deeply regret that you have chosen to besmirch the reputation of the House of Mendes and myself in this matter. It is an unforgivable act on your part, for which I will never pardon you.

I have been exceedingly generous with you since Diogo passed away, giving you twice as much money each month as I allow myself. That monthly payment will now cease. You will have to make do as best you can, with no further income from the House of Mendes, as you have refused to abide by the terms of Diogo's will.

Gracia Nasi Mendes

Late that afternoon, Samuel arrived with the information that he had retained the services of Sol Levi, a famous New Christian solicitor from Rome who immigrated to Constantinople more than ten years earlier. He was totally familiar with the Turkish justice system, and highly thought of in rabbinical circles. He would come to Galata for a meeting with Gracia the next morning.

Gracia spent more than two hours filling Levi in on the background and history of the dispute over the ownership of the House of Mendes. She gave him copies of the wills of Francisco and of Diogo.

"I will speak with the Chief Rabbi immediately, and we will begin hearings on this matter. It is essential to keep it in the rabbinical court system rather than let it expand into the civil courts. That is our first priority," he said after listening to Gracia's explanations.

"I am confident," he continued, "we will prevail with a tribunal of rabbis. But just as important, I believe, is that we establish for future generations that the capital of the House of Mendes is under your sole control for the duration of your lifetime. I also advise, Doña Gracia, that you immediately draw up a will which divides up the estate between your daughter and Diogo's daughter. We don't want this fighting over money to destroy family relationships."

After Sol Levi left, Gracia thought long and hard about the future of the House of Mendes and a possible division of ownership. As she walked in her topiary garden, a plan slowly materialized. She would think and pray on it, and eventually discuss it with Joseph. He was the one person she trusted to guide the House long after her death.

Chapter Twenty-Eight

Joseph And Reyna

Joseph's arrival at the city gates of Constantinople resembled the entrance of a powerful foreign potentate. His golden carriage, decorated with medallions proclaiming the House of Mendes, was preceded by janissaries sent by Selim, and followed by a long caravan of carriages and wagons carrying his senior staff, liveried servants, and five hundred New Christians who had come to work in the munitions factory. In addition, mule-driven wagons carried chemicals, weapons, forging ovens, and metal working equipment. Additional wagons carried goods from all over Europe destined for stalls at the Great Bazaar.

After a quick stop at the Topkapi Palace to present papers, Joseph parted from his caravan and directed his coachman over the Galata Bridge, through Galata, and up the hills to Doña Gracia's mansion. She had been alerted that he was on his way, and she and Reyna greeted him on the front steps of the mansion.

He had matured and become even more handsome over the last four years; he was tall, with a carefully trimmed black beard, and his powerful build radiated both physical and mental strength. His European dress was sumptuous, of the finest fabrics and latest style. Her inclination was to run to him, but protocol demanded that he come to her. He mounted the steps, his eyes darting back and forth from his beloved aunt to his gorgeous fiancé, Reyna.

He embraced Gracia and Reyna in one big hug saying, "What a day. You can't know how I've longed for this moment to be with you, my aunt, my sweet cousin, my dearest friends..."

Gracia looked into his eyes, tears brimming from her own. "We have waited so long for this moment. You are finally here to stay."

"Yes, I'm finally home." He broke from Gracia but held Reyna in his arms. "My bride, I love you with all my heart. You are even more beautiful than I remember. And, so grown up!" He laughed and turned her face up so he could kiss her lips. "Perhaps now, your mother will let you marry me!"

"Ah, but first," Reyna teased him, "you must agree to my dowry. Perhaps it won't be enough!"

"My darling, if there were no dowry at all, I would still claim you to be my wife."

****

Joseph settled into his guest suite and bathed. Refreshed, he joined the family in the library for a glass of wine before a magnificent banquet. Throughout the evening he regaled them with stories of the French court and his experiences in Lyon and Paris. Gracia and Reyna told him of their recent experiences with the Sultan and his "favorite wife" Roxalana who had chosen, for reasons of her own, to become a confidante of Gracia.

"There is a lot of intrigue going on. Roxalana wants her son to succeed Suleiman, but his first wife wants Prince Mustapha to become sultan. The two women have become archenemies and the members of the harem are being forced to take sides. It's not pretty."

After the banquet, they retired to the library. After bidding good night to Samuel and Gracia *la chica,* they talked till the wee hours of the morning. When Gracia could stay awake no longer, they parted with Gracia's final words: "Tomorrow morning we are going to have a serious discussion. Be prepared."

Years later, in his old age, Joseph remembered how Gracia had tried her best to be stern with him. The two of them had finished breakfast and moved into the library for a discussion of "Reyna's dowry." Gracia had preceded it with a sermon she'd obviously rehearsed for days. "Joseph, I have tried not to focus on the many love affairs I'm certain you've enjoyed over the last fifteen years. Yes, word has trickled back to me...but I understand a young man must experiment. And you certainly had a role model in Diogo.

"But I will not allow you to hurt my Reyna. If you want her for your wife, you must promise me on all that is sacred to you, that you will be a faithful husband to her. We are not like the Christians, adultery is not considered acceptable in our tradition. I want you to promise me that you will be a faithful husband.

"If you will promise me this, I will make you one of the wealthiest men in all the world."

Joseph did not miss a beat. "I can't even conceive of being unfaithful. Reyna is so compelling, brilliant and sensuous. I love her more than life itself, you can depend on my love and loyalty."

"Thank you for that assurance." She wiped her eyes with her handkerchief, then tucked it back inside her sleeve.

"This is my plan. Her dowry will be ninety thousand ducats."

A broad smile broke out on Joseph's face. He'd been hoping for fifty thousand ducats.

"And a large quantity of diamonds and precious stones. In addition, working with our solicitor Sol Levi, I have made up a will as well as drafted a new business plan, which will be in force from now on.

"The profits from the businesses started by Francisco and Diogo shall be divided evenly each quarter. One-half of the profits will go to Diogo's daughter, Gracia *la chica,* and her husband Samuel, who is your deputy, and will help you manage those monies. If they choose to support her mother, that is their business. I have cut off all allowances to Brianda.

"The other half of the profits from these same businesses will come to me. I will continue to manage them in my lifetime. After my death, you will take over the management of those monies on behalf of Reyna and her heirs.

"Henceforth, all new business opportunities you and I develop will belong to the House of Nasi. For example, this munitions factory, the profits from that project will belong to you and me. We will be equal partners in the House of Nasi. We will invest our funds equally in new business opportunities. If Samuel wishes to invest in the House of Nasi, we will include him and grant him an interest in proportion to his contribution.

"Now, tell me how does this sound to you?"

A broad smile lit his face. "It sounds perfect, I was about to propose something similar but you have beaten me to it. Will this help you to settle the lawsuit with Brianda?"

"I don't know what her reaction will be. But Levi believes if we propose this to the rabbinical tribunal, they will quickly respond in our favor. And, quite frankly, I'd like to get that mess behind us, I'm sick to death of all the wasted emotion. I want it over with."

****

Ten weeks later Gracia *la chica* gave birth to a healthy baby girl whom they named Deborah after Samuel's great grandmother. The mother's first choice had been to name the baby after Gracia, but she had demurred saying it was already too confusing to have two Gracias and two Reynas in the family. Deborah was a better idea!

****

"The wedding of a King and Queen could not have been more lavish!" For more than a hundred years after the event, people spoke in hushed, awe-filled tones about The Wedding.

Gracia threw all her rules about ostentation out the window as she listened to Joseph rail about the courts of Europe and his determination to exact revenge for what they had done to him, his family, and his people. "I can guarantee you, Aunt Gracia," he protested one Sunday morning, "the morning after the wedding a dozen letters will go to the crowned heads, to the Vatican, and to Charles V. I want those bastards to know that the House of Mendes and the House of Nasi have merged into the wealthiest bank in the world. I want them to know we are full partners with the Ottoman Empire. I want them to hear that we are building canons and stockpiling munitions and that when they attack the Turks, the ships of the Mendes fleet will be armed and will join the Turkish armada. I tell you, the only thing these monsters respect is wealth. Wealth and military might!"

As weeks went on, she realized The Wedding was going to be more a political affair than a social or religious event. She had watched with amazement and great satisfaction as Joseph insinuated himself into the court. It had begun with a visit "to pay his respects" to the Grand Vizier to express his thanks for the kindness and protection afforded his family. What should have been a fifteen minute meeting turned into a three-hour discussion of the personalities who ruled the courts in the countries Joseph had visited during the past few years: Naples, Rome, Florence, Ferrara, Venice, London, Paris, Lyons, Antwerp, and Ancona.

The following morning, Joseph was summoned back to Topkapi Palace to brief Selim first-hand. After the initial briefing, Selim demanded that Joseph stay and discuss with his brother the issues of dispute with the Venetian Doge, Charles V, and the Vatican.

After that, Joseph spent more time at the palace than in his office. Nearly every day he met with one or the other of the brothers, or the Grand Vizier or another member of the Divan. They became dependent on him for advice on any matter that had to do with foreign policy. Meanwhile, the munitions factory was complete and the development work had begun. It was time for the House of Nasi to conclude a contract with Sultan Suleiman outlining the financial terms of their relationship.

Gracia, Reyna and Joseph began the sensitive task of putting together a guest list. First they listed the fifty most influential and wealthiest Jewish families, followed by key employees of their company. They added five rabbis and their wives. Joseph, who had paid calls on the Ambassadors of England and France, said they would both welcome an invitation. He would not even consider inviting agents or ambassadors from the Papal States or any of the countries that had expelled the Jews. Nor would he invite representatives of the Vatican or the Holy Roman Empire.

As the sultan was absent on a military campaign in Persia, he spoke with Selim, gently feeling him out about who might represent the sultan.

"You can't imagine how the women in the harem are jockeying to be the lucky few I agree to bring to the wedding," Selim said.

Delighted to hear this, Joseph asked, "How many seats shall we save for your people?"

"Let me speak to my mother, and I will let you know tomorrow."

The next day Selim reported that Roxalana would be pleased to include three of the women from the harem, her two sons and their wives, and she would also like to see a number of the cabinet officers and their wives included. "She has also asked if you would let the Palace provide the entertainment at the wedding."

"We would be honored to host whatever entertainment you have in mind."

That night, in conference with Gracia and Reyna, it was decided they would plan a regal banquet for no less than two hundred guests.

****

Two days later a ship arrived from Venice carrying a package for Joseph. He walked into Gracia's office and told her that he would need to have a private meeting with her and Reyna that evening.

After their usual formal dinner, Joseph asked Max to serve them champagne in the library. As soon as the wine had been served, he produced a small velvet box for Gracia. The diamond ring inside was unlike anything she had ever seen: a blue not quite the color of a robin's egg, though crystal clear. "It is extraordinarily rare. It was mined in Brazil, and weighs fourteen karats."

Gracia put it on the ring finger of her right hand, and held it up to admire it. "It's lovely, the most beautiful gem I've ever seen, and you know how I love anything blue! Thank you, my darling Joseph." She kissed him and hugged him with an overwhelming affection.

"And now for the princess!" He handed a large velvet box to Reyna. She opened it and nearly fainted at the sight: a necklace of canary yellow diamonds, diminishing in depth of color as they circled to the front of the throat, with an almond-sized white diamond drop. Accompanying the necklace was a bracelet of seventeen perfectly matched similar stones, each weighing more than two karats. The earrings were a cluster of three two karat stones, one deep yellow, one pale yellow, and one white. And finally, the engagement ring was a huge deep-yellow square-cut diamond with a triangular baguette on each side.

As the women admired the jewels, Joseph said, "It took Lodewyk nearly ten years to accumulate those yellow diamonds and cut them to match exactly. I've been watching his work, a bit nervously I might say, for that long, hoping for the perfect gift for my bride." He picked up the ring and holding her closely, put it on her ring finger on her left hand.

Gracia, ever the practical mother, said, "I'm so glad these jewels arrived today, they will make a difference in the design of her gown. I must immediately contact our people in Murano and order the right beads for the bodice."

****

The parties began in June. The Ambassadors of France and England each invited several dozen of their closest associates to banquets honoring the young couple. The wealthiest Jewish families competed with one another to host the most splendid dinners. Roxalana and the harem invited Reyna, Gracia and Gracia *la chica* to a luncheon in the harem and showered Reyna with perfumes, ointments, bath oils, cosmetics, exotic lingerie, and much advice about "pleasing your husband" and "getting pregnant!" The highlight for all three women was the massage following a luxurious, gossip-filled Turkish bath. Inevitably, the men-only dinner, which Selim hosted for Joseph, ended with a special demonstration of belly dancing!

August 24 finally arrived; Gracia had managed every minute detail, and even the weather cooperated with sunny skies and a light breeze.

Guests began arriving by carriage shortly after five. After they alighted from the carriage in the front of the mansion, the carriages and coachmen were directed to the far western wall where they would wait for their employers during the evening's festivities.

Liveried servants directed guests to the topiary garden where magnificent flower beds and a dozen fountains claimed center stage. A few minutes before the ceremony was to begin, they were seated under a large white marquee filled with large urns of late summer flowers: roses, delphiniums, larkspur, and lilies. A long white carpet was rolled down the aisle. Selim and his entourage entered and made their way to the front rows. A harpist played soaring music, accompanied by a flautist.

The chuppah had been draped in palest blue satin, tied back with golden braided ropes. Yellow roses mixed with small delphinium branches peaked out of the ropes. Yellow rose petals floated over the floor of the carpeted gazebo. Five rabbis and the Chief Rabbi stood at attention, waiting to receive the wedding party. Joseph and Samuel, dressed in pale blue velvet jackets, white satin breeches, white hose and black boots entered from the side and stood at attention.

The harp music increased in intensity. Gracia *la chica* made her way down the aisle in a pale lavender confection with a full sweeping skirt, a bodice, which accentuated her tiny waist, a broad portrait collared neckline and billowing sleeves. When she reached the chuppah, Samuel stepped forward and took her elbow, and they turned to face the guests.

Reyna and her mother walked down the aisle slowly, smiling to guests and holding tightly to one another. Gracia wore a striking violet-navy embossed-silk organza dress with the same portrait, collared neckline and billowing sleeves, but with a floor length sheath skirt topped with an over skirt, which came to her knees in front and curved down gracefully to become a long train in back. She wore the blue diamond ring, a gift from Joseph, and sapphire and diamond jewelry that had been a gift from Francisco.

The bride's dress had been designed to go with the priceless canary diamond jewelry. The white silk organza bodice had been encrusted in a delicate floral design with tiny yellow and silver glass beads from Murano and seed pearls from France. The design continued down the long skirt and ended in the lengthy train. Reyna's Brussels lace mantilla had been similarly decorated with the tiny beads; it covered her face and hair and flowed down her back, almost to the floor.

When the two women reached the chuppah, Reyna stopped at Joseph's side, and Gracia *la chica* stepped forward to arrange the train.

The harp music ended. The Chief Rabbi stepped forward and began the ages-old ceremony.

Gracia, deep in the moment, thought, *It's all been worthwhile, to reach this day!*

****

The ceremony concluded and the guests were directed to another large white tent where they were served wine or fruit drinks. Small tables and chairs were available for those who wished to sit, but most of the guests gathered around an enormous *hors d'oeuvre* display: three kinds of pastry turnovers filled with beef, lamb or chicken; chafing dishes with meatballs in savory sauces; marinated olives; zucchini cups with tuna; skewered white fish in a curry sauce; and marinated salmon on tiny breads with a sweet and sour sauce. Courtesy of the sultan, a small musical group from the janissary corps played popular music in the background.

After more than an hour of socializing, uniformed waiters passed through the tent asking the guests to enter the mansion for the dinner. They walked up the steps and into a black and white marble foyer, then up the double-wide marble staircase to the ballroom.

More than a thousand candles blazed from Murano wall sconces and the twenty tables arranged around the perimeter of the room. Embroidered organdy table clothes with gold brocade runners from Spain dressed the round tables. Gold chairs with blue velvet pillows awaited the guests. Centered on each table was a five-foot crystal centerpiece filled with yellow roses, yellow lilies, blue delphinium and larkspur, with variegated ivy trailing down the side. Below the centerpiece, a dozen hand-blown candle sticks of various heights held cream-colored candles. Each place was set with fine china with a blue and gold band and three gold-embossed crystal wine glasses. The silver flatware had been imported from Florence. Cream vellum place cards with the names of guests in gold calligraphy completed the table setting.

After everyone was seated, with the bride and groom's table at the far end of the room, and Selim's table next to theirs, the Chief Rabbi stood and made a blessing over the white burgundy Joseph had imported from France. The waiters served a first course of *Albondigas de Pescado*, a light vegetable soup with fish dumplings.

As the waiters cleared the first course, the famous Tumbling Acrobats of the janissary corps filled the center of the room and entertained the guests. Dressed in red, white and green-stripped pantaloons with a white and gold top, their clown-like antics added color and laughter to the festivities.

The second course was *Pescado con Ruibarbo*, halibut with rhubarb sauce, a specialty of Turkish chefs, followed by a performance of Anatolian folk songs by an ethereal Greek woman dressed in flowing chiffon robes.

The main course was a Turkish favorite, roasted leg of lamb with Mendes spices and an eggplant salad, accompanied by a fine French cabernet sauvignon. Joseph then took to the floor to tell the guests that they were about to be entertained by "maskers" who had written a satire especially for the evening. "Do not be concerned," he warned, "the Palace has approved the script and you may laugh right along with them!"

As the dessert was about to be served, Gracia felt herself relax. Everything had gone perfectly so far. The waiters and the cooks had outdone themselves. It was no mean feat to prepare a banquet for this number of people, making sure everything was in accordance with the laws of Kashrut.

Crystal bowls with five different species of melon balls macerated in blood orange juice and sprinkled with mint, along with fresh coconut macaroons dipped in chocolate were passed by waiters. When this service was complete, the waiters returned to each table and passed out four copies of an announcement on creamy vellum paper.

> *In accordance with the custom of our Jewish community who celebrate weddings by giving to the poor, I have founded an orphanage for one hundred children here in Constantinople. All children, regardless of their religious faiths or background will be welcomed. They will receive loving nurturing, and the best health care and education available. Reyna Mendes Nasi will serve as the chair of the management committee for as long as she shall live. The orphanage will be named The Reyna Mendes Nasi Orphanage in honor of this occasion. My will endows the orphanage for one hundred years after my death. Thank you all for participating in this most happy event. May God bless and keep all of you safe.*
>
> *Gracia Nasi Mendes, House of Mendes*
> *August 24, 1554*

The final entertainment, the ultimate entertainment in Turkey, was a very special presentation by the finest belly dancers of the court accompanied by music provided by the janissary corps.

The evening had been a huge success, Gracia thought as she stood in the foyer bidding her guests good night.

The sultan's party departed first, then the carriages lined up according to the order in which they had arrived. Several times she glanced at Joseph, watching him charm guest after guest. He was in his element; he'd make a great ambassador, she thought as she watched her beloved Reyna catch his eye. They were so in love, had been for so long!

Francisco, if you can see this from where you are, I hope you are as happy as I am at this moment!

Chapter Twenty-Nine

Pope Paul IV - A Reign Of Madness

The Monday after the grand wedding Gracia received dozens of thank you notes raving about the marvelous wedding. Four of them, including one from Roxalana, asked Gracia to assist them in buying table linens, china, crystal and silverware like those Gracia used for the wedding. Gracia pondered the requests, realizing that this was a real opportunity for the House of Nasi. Perhaps Gracia *la chica,* who expressed an interest in making a contribution to the family business, could open a shop in the Great Bazaar and sell these fine household items. And perhaps the women of the synagogue would work with her and some of the profits could go to the synagogue.

Gracia summoned her niece for breakfast the following morning, and explained her idea. "It will take about six months for you to accumulate enough merchandise to open a shop. I will give you the information about the merchants in France, Flanders, and Venice. You can order half-a-dozen different patterns of each item as samples, and when the women come in to make a purchase, you let them choose which patterns to order."

Gracia *la chica* was thrilled with the opportunity, and immediately began to organize her life to start "Gracia Nasi's Table Settings" shop in the Bazaar. The women of the Jewish community couldn't wait for six months, they began to come to her home and place orders sight unseen, wanting everything to be "exactly like *La Señora's* table setting at the wedding."

Meanwhile, Gracia arranged to have delivered to Roxalana a complete china, crystal, silver and candlestick service for twelve, as well as a table and twelve gold chairs "for use in the harem."

"I insist that this be a gift to you, Roxalana, in honor of our friendship. We were thrilled with the entertainment you provided for the wedding, and equally important, for the shipment of ice. The melon balls and the champagne were much improved because we could chill them. Please express my appreciation to the sultan."

In September, Joseph reported that the sultan, soon after returning from Persia, signed the contract with the House of Nasi for the management of the munitions factory. "We will receive a management fee of twenty percent of the cost of the munitions, a very lucrative contract! It will continue indefinitely!"

Gracia beamed at Joseph, proud and happy for him. "You seem to spend most of every day at the Palace."

"Yes, and much of that time I would appear to be doing nothing of substance. But the reality is, Selim and Bajazet require separate briefings on all issues. They can spend hours questioning me about every court in Europe, and each decision that's been made in the last few years. And the Grand Vizier wants equal time. I go from office to office, offering information and reassurance that the Ottomans are pursuing the right path."

"Someday soon you may be required to make a choice between Selim and Bajazet," Gracia opined. "What a terrible way to run a country, pitting brother against brother!"

"Yes, but it's been their way since they organized themselves a hundred years ago. I don't look forward to making a choice, and I hope that day is a long way off. I'm very pleased with our relationship with Suleiman. And you've been doing a great job with Roxalana. We cannot underestimate the incredible power she has with Suleiman. He's actually given up all his other wives and the harem; the gossip is that he only sleeps with Roxalana. Very unusual for a sultan!"

A month later Gracia had very good news herself. The Talmudic Tribunal of Joseph ibn Leb, Joshua Soncino, Samuel de Medina, Moses di Trani and Joseph Caro ruled that Francisco and Diogo's wills would be honored by the religious court. Doña Graci Nasi Mendes would continue to control the financial empire of the House of Mendes.

Once she had a copy of the Tribunal's decision, she called a meeting with her daughter, her niece and her two nephews. They met in the library in her home. When everyone was settled with a glass of sherry, she held up the document and said, "The ruling of the Talmudic Tribunal has been handed down, and this is a copy which each of you should read. It settles the matter of control of the wealth of the House of Mendes for all time. As long as I live, I will honor the commitment I made to Francisco before his murder. I will retain control. When I pass away, control will revert to Joseph as Diogo intended.

"Joseph and Samuel, you have the responsibility of managing your wives' estates in accordance with both rabbinic decisions and civil law here in Constantinople. I expect you to write wills and make arrangements for the wealth of the Mendes family to be passed down to my heirs, your children and grandchildren.

"Samuel and Gracia, I expect you to make provisions for your mother. I will not have any further relationship with her. My information is that she intends to remain in Salonica, and that's fine. I'll not let her break my heart one more time. That's my final word on Brianda."

The serious part of the evening was over. The family adjourned to the dining room for a celebratory feast of lamb with Mendes spices and a special wine Joseph received from France. As he made the first toast of the evening, Joseph surprised the family: "To Aunt Gracia, congratulations on your victory with the tribunal, and also, congratulations on the fact that you will soon be a grandmother!"

Everyone turned to Reyna who blushed bright pink. "Yes, we are expecting a little one in about six months!"

"That's the best news ever!" Gracia enthused, as she touched her crystal glass to Reyna's and took a sip of wine.

****

The relative happiness and serenity of the Nasi-Mendes families was shattered in May of 1555 when Pope Julius III died and Cardinal Giovanni Pietro Caraffa was elected to the papacy, and took the name Paul IV.

"The man has been head of the Holy Office of the Inquisition for the past few years. He hates the Jews more than any man in Rome," Joseph reported to Gracia. "He is a fanatic, famous for his perpetual anti-Jewish agitation."

"Benvenida writes that he's the prelate most responsible for the public burning of Hebrew literature, those prayer books and Bibles and books of Samuel Usque we worked so hard and spent so much money to produce!"

Week after week Joseph and Samuel gathered information from newly arrived New Christians about what was actually happening in the Papal States. Each night during dinner, Joseph reported to Gracia and Reyna the latest news.

"The pope seems to believe that Jews are like an infectious disease. If Christians are exposed to the company of Jews, they will become contaminated with the disease of Judaism. The Jews must be quarantined in ghettos, behind high walls, locked in at night like cattle. And these ghettos are always in the least healthy parts of town, where garbage infects the water and obnoxious smells strangle one's breath."

"We must pass the word," Gracia interjected, "through your underground, that these Jews are welcome and will be protected here in

Ottoman lands. We can provide jobs for them in Constantinople and Salonica. We must bring as many of them as possible here as quickly as possible."

Gracia received word of the newly issued papal bull from Benvenida:

The pope has rescinded all previous privileges to the Jews. They can no longer live wherever they please, nor can they have any social or business relationship with any Christian. They are strictly limited in what they can wear outside the home. The only profession allowed to Jews is selling second-hand clothes, rags. No longer can doctors practice medicine or lawyers practice law. Goldsmiths cannot make jewelry, scribes cannot translate or prepare manuscripts for printing. They cannot work in the textile industry. There is literally nothing left for Jews to do to make a living.

We cannot own land, I shudder to think of what will become of my properties if the pope has his way in Ferrara! We cannot own homes. We must live in a ghetto of their designation, in crowded squalor. We must wear the hated Jewish badge of shame or a yellow hat.

This reign of terror will continue, I've no doubt, as long as Paul IV lives. In truth, it is a reign of madness. Nothing good will come of it, and all of Europe who falls under the sway of this pope will suffer economically with the removal of the Jews.

I envy you, Gracia. You escaped with your family and your wealth in time. You have reached a place of peace and great prosperity and a great future. How I wish I'd had the good sense to go with you. But I am too old now, nearly sixty, too old and decrepit to consider pulling up stakes and trekking over the Balkans.

I miss you, I love you and I pray for you each day. Please do the same for me.

As always, your admiring friend,
Benvenida de Abrabanel

Chapter Thirty

Roxalana's Death

Bad news followed bad news. A week later Gracia received a messenger from the Palace with an urgent request from Roxalana that Gracia visit her as she was near death.

Gracia immediately made her way to the Palace. She was ushered into Roxalana's presence.

The sultan's favorite wife was deathly pale, burning with fever, and appeared to have lost much weight in a few days. Three eunuchs stood by her bed, fanning her while her maid urged her to drink cold water. She had been stricken suddenly, first with a violent headache, then aches and pains throughout her body. Her fever had risen within hours to the point where she suffered intermittent bouts of delirium. Then she began a tight cough and had increasing difficulty breathing.

Gracia stood by her bed, holding her feverish hand. "How can I help you, Roxalana? Please tell me."

"Your Joseph, he must continue with Selim...Selim will need him...Selim is the better choice...better personality for ruling...you will see to it?"

"You mustn't worry about the succession now, Roxalana, just concentrate on getting well. That's what we are all praying for."

"No, no...I cannot recover...my lungs...they are drowning...help my Suleiman. He needs your wisdom..." She pulled her hand away from Gracia to stifle a rumbling cough. "You have been my dear friend...thank you." She closed her eyes and seemed to fall asleep.

Gracia left Roxalana's side, puzzling over her choice of Selim. She is the mother of both men, and yet on her deathbed she feels strong enough to choose between them, for the good of her country. An amazing woman. I would not have that responsibility, I could not choose between sons!

Several weeks later, after the country had been plunged into mourning for the Sultan's wife, the first few refugees from Paul IV's Europe began to arrive in Constantinople. Joseph and Samuel tried to meet with each new arrival, questioning them about the repercussions of Paul's ascendancy to the papacy.

Joseph, in turn, kept the sultan and his sons informed of what was happening in Europe. "Those people are stupid! Don't they realize they are forcing their best minds and all that wealth out of their countries?" Suleiman responded. "What can we do to help?"

"Excellency, you are already doing everything I can think of by making our people welcome, by protecting them on the seas on their way here, and by making it possible for me to offer them a way to sustain themselves once they arrive. We are grateful to you for this, and you can count on us to be loyal citizens."

Two days later, the quiet office decorum was temporarily shattered when Gracia burst forth with cries of joy after reading a letter from Ben Zarella. "He is coming here, he is coming to stay," she exclaimed to Reyna, tears filling her eyes. "I can't wait! Oh, I'm so sorry he's forced to do this, but I'm so glad. I've missed him so much!"

She handed the letter to Reyna:

February 12, 1556
My dearest love,

This afternoon I was visited by a representative of the Apostolic Commissioner of Venice in my shop. This is the third time he has come to see me since Paul IV took office. I have refused to move into the ghetto here in Venice and they are threatening me with imprisonment. They have given me seven days. Already, three of my employees have been forced to move their families into the ghetto. Living conditions there are disgraceful, filthy and crowded, fit only for rats. And there are plenty of those.

I hadn't planned on retiring this early, but it now seems the best course. I hope you are still willing to welcome me into your home, as you have offered so many times in the past. Knowing I had the possibility of coming to you has been the hope that has sustained me during the past few months.

I have watched my best typesetters and binders leave and try to find work as rag dealers, it is a tragic development, the way we Jews are being degraded and debased.

Homes have been confiscated; we cannot be seen carrying on conversation with a Christian. Our every move, every word is watched and recorded by their spies.

I can't tell you exactly when you can plan on my arriving at your doorstep, as it will have to be a stealthy removal if I am to succeed in bringing anything with me. I have Joseph's agents' names and contact points, and I will rely on his good services to bring me safely to you.

With my undying love and devotion,
Benjamin Zarella

Reyna passed the letter back to her mother. "You really love him, don't you Mother?"

"Yes, I do. Oh, Reyna, he will never replace your father in my heart, don't worry about that, but I miss his companionship, his soft voice, his good counsel. And yes, I miss him in bed too. Once you've enjoyed that kind of relationship, you always miss it when you don't have it. Yes, I love him and I don't care who knows it. I can't wait for him to get here. My happiness will be complete!"

Chapter Thirty-One

Ancona

Upon hearing the news that the Apostolic Commissioner in Ancona, Giovanni Vincenzo Fallongonio, had imprisoned one hundred Jews and New Christians, the entire Portuguese community in Ancona, on charges of heresy and apostasy, Gracia immediately asked Joseph to arrange for an audience with Sultan Suleiman.

Though he was still in mourning for Roxalana, he agreed immediately to meet with Doña Gracia.

Joseph and Gracia were escorted into the Throne Room by the sultan's son, Selim. Sultan Suleiman was seated on his bejeweled throne with his Grand Vizier Ahmed Pasha, on his right.

"Excellency," Joseph began, "we have confirmed that approximately one-hundred of our people, including four employees of the House of Mendes, are imprisoned in Ancona by the Apostolic Commissioner in Ancona. They are charged with heresy or apostasy. The Church confiscated their homes, their belongings and all their money. We understand they are being tortured on the *strapado*. They are at risk of being burned at the stake."

"Excellency," Gracia continued, "yours is the greatest military power in the world today. Just as you helped me escape from the Inquisition in Venice, you can do something to gain freedom for these people, and help them regain their homes and belongings."

The Sultan turned to his grand vizier for his advice.

Ahmed Pasha answered, "You say four of these prisoners are employees of your company, a company which has its headquarters here in Turkey. Thus, we have a vested interest in protecting our commercial interests and those of our citizens. Property belonging to Jews who are Turkish subjects has been confiscated. Excellency, we have an obligation to intervene."

"Agreed!" Suleiman enthused. "We will issue strong letters to the pope, to the officials at Ancona, and to the Apostolic Commissioner. I will send Selim to Ancona to meet with the officials there and demand the release of all those prisoners who are Turkish-protected citizens, and we will threaten appropriate reprisals if this request is not complied with forthwith. I will sleep on it tonight, Joseph, and meet with you and Selim tomorrow morning to see if we have additional ideas about how to deal with this."

Gracia effusively thanked Suleiman and Pasha, and then entered her carriage for the ride back to Galata with Joseph. When they were outside the Palace gates, Joseph turned to her and quietly said, "This is only the beginning of what Suleiman will do, this is the part for public consumption, for the history books. Whatever else we do, I cannot discuss with you. Suleiman doesn't believe women have the stomach for real revenge, for military measures. It's for the best that you won't know what we are doing for the next few weeks. Just trust me."

"I trust you totally, Joseph, but I implore you not to take unnecessary risks. Hundreds of people are dependent on you. You must take care of yourself."

He kissed her cheek. "You can be sure, beloved Aunt, I will not endanger the life of my bride's husband!"

Planning for a covert operation began the next morning. "You will take two hundred janissary troops, three canons, guns and ammunition. Take these troops and equipment as far as Ragusa. Joseph, you stay in Ragusa. I don't want you in Ancona; they would like nothing better than to burn you at the stake!" Suleiman said, seated at the head of the table in his ornate library.

"Selim will cross over to Ancona and spend several days in negotiations with the papal and civil authorities."

"Meanwhile," Joseph added, "I will take an elite team of twenty of my brightest, strongest and most agile young men, men who are fluent in Italian, Ladino, Castilian Spanish and Turkish, and can pretend to be deckhands and stevedores, on one of my fastest galleys with at least ten small row boats."

The detailed planning went on all day and into the wee hours of the night. Joseph returned home to pack a few clothes, write a quick note to Gracia, and kiss his bride goodbye with the information that he was off on a trip to Salonica to work on a special project for Suleiman. Reyna, understanding that she could ask no questions, held him closely and promised to take care of "Mother."

By late afternoon of the following day, Joseph culled seventeen men from his workers at the munitions factory, gave them a minimal briefing, and told them to be ready to leave at first light the next morning.

The caravan set off from outside the Palace gates: Selim and Joseph in the lead carriage, followed by eight wagons carrying munitions and provisions. The seventeen select men rode in the wagons. Two hundred uniformed janissaries followed on horseback.

As they traveled eastward, Joseph and Selim refined their plans. "We will need to recruit three "serving-girls" from the prostitute community in Ragusa; one to serve the Apostolic Commissioner, and two to serve the guards in the jail. We will pay them well when the job is complete."

"I know just the place to find them, a special 'coffee house' in Ragusa, near the port. The sailors frequent the place, and it's known for its beautiful women. They give great massages!" Selim laughed, as he remembered his evenings in that establishment.

They stopped in Salonica long enough for Joseph to recruit an additional three men for his special team. He had in mind a certain young genius, David Hamon, to be the leader of the team. David was the third generation to work for the Mendes; his grandfather had crossed Spain into Portugal in 1492 with Francisco, and then joined him as a ship's captain. His father was captain of the entire Mendes fleet. Now David, twenty-one years old, showed promise of being one of the most astute military strategists Diogo's schools had trained. He was a natural leader of men and he was strong, agile, and multi-lingual. Exactly the right man for the job.

After a long trip overland, the caravan arrived safely in Ragusa. The troops set up camp outside the city while Selim and Joseph, using aliases, secured lodging in a small inn a few blocks from the port. They no longer looked like court officials, but rather more like stevedores or ship captains. Their hair and beards had grown long and were unkempt, their clothes were deliberately dirty and of the kind worn by stevedores.

For several days the twenty men of the special team hung out in coffee shops and cafes near the docks, picking up what information they could about conditions in Ancona. When the time was right, Joseph brought the twenty men together into his bedroom, and finally told them the details of their mission. He deliberately excluded Selim, telling him "The less you know, the safer you will be."

Selim cleaned himself up, dressed in the clothes of a diplomat, and set sail in one of the Sultan's warships outfitted with the new canons, bound for Ancona. He would keep the civic and church officials busy with complex negotiations and demands while Joseph managed the covert operation.

Joseph, meanwhile, took over a small galley with ten rowboats. A small crew and the twenty special troops and ample ammunition were loaded onto the ship. When they arrived a few miles off the coast of Ancona, they dropped anchor and idled south of the port, far enough away that the ship could not be seen with the naked eye.

Under cover of darkness, the twenty men were lowered down into the rowboats and headed toward the shore. They rowed toward a patch of deep woods, hid their boats, and stealthily made their way into the outskirts of the city. They pretended to be "deckhands" and "stevedores" and "liked to have a good time."

Orders from Joseph were to nose around and find out as much as they could about what was going on inside the jail, how many prisoners were there, how many guards, what kind of daily routine, were the prisoners being tortured? Two nights later, as planned, they returned to the ship with the information Joseph needed.

"The guards make their last round at eight o'clock. Then they drink their ale, play dominoes, sleep, and mess around with the serving girls. They pretty much ignore the prisoners after that."

"Many of the prisoners have been badly crippled and otherwise injured by the torture and the *strapado,*" David informed him. "Those who can't walk are kept in a separate part of the jail. I don't see how we'll be able to bring them through the woods to the boat."

"Two of the men badly injured are your people: Jacob Mosso and Ben Zarella. If we succeed in getting to them, we will have to be prepared to carry them through the woods, a very treacherous affair."

"Fallongonio, the cardinal, is a drunken sot. He begins drinking about four in the afternoon and by seven-thirty he's asleep in his chair. Nothing could rouse him. And he has a huge safe in his bedroom, we actually watched him counting stacks of ducats. He's an easy target!"

The men drew a diagram of the jail for Joseph, showing him how they would enter, overtake the guards, release the prisoners, and make their way back through the city and into the woods. They would pick up the stashed rowboats, and bring the prisoners to the ship, which would be decked out with flags indicating it was a pirate ship, and then set sail back to Ragusa.

Joseph and David discussed their options for hours. It would be difficult enough to free the healthy, able-bodied prisoners and get them safely to the ship. It would be nearly impossible to free the sick and injured. In addition, there was the problem of getting to those who were sick and injured as they were in a separate, very secure and heavily guarded area of the jail.

Joseph settled for a "dress rehearsal" of the escape plan. The team would go back ashore and attempt to free three to five prisoners. Depending on what problems they encountered, they would make a decision about the remaining prisoners.

During that first night they freed four prisoners, and strangely, they did not seem to be missed the next day. The next night they freed seven more, and took all eleven back to the waiting ship.

Joseph interviewed each of them, learning additional details about the remaining prisoners and the conditions of the jail. Some of them had been imprisoned for more than nine months; their health was at severe risk as the cells were filthy with human excrement and urine, rats, vomit, and blood. Open sores were left to fester. Dozens of persons had been broken on the *strapado*; many of them could no longer walk or use their arms. Many of them had lost the power of reason. Some of them prayed for death.

Though it pained him to make the decision, Joseph told the team they must focus on bringing out the healthiest first, and if all went well, they could make a second try for those who were infirm.

"But I want Fallongonio!" Joseph demanded. "I want him here on this ship, and I want him alive!"

The ship left its mooring place each morning for a four-hour trip in the Adriatic Sea, then returned to the same spot every evening at dusk. On the seventh day, when they assumed the guards would be relaxed again after the earlier prison escape, the team of twenty men left the ship and made their way through the woods to the jail. They alerted the "serving girls" that they would be making a major move the following evening, and needed as many of the guards as possible to be asleep.

Wine or ale with sleeping powders should do the trick!

Twelve of the young men took control of the prison. Only two guards were conscious, and when discovered, quickly murdered. The prisoners, alerted to the escape the previous week, were expecting such a plot, and eagerly helped one another dress and gather their few belongings. They followed orders exactly, reaching the woods outside the city within minutes of leaving the jail.

Meanwhile, David and seven of his most trusted men, entered the sleeping Fallongonio's home. They bound his arms and legs, gagged him, and lay him on a litter. David opened the safe in his bedroom and extracted a large bag full of ducats. This money would be returned to the Jews!

Joseph sat on the deck of the ship in the moonlight, working worry beads through his right hand in the Turkish fashion. He alternated between being freezing cold and feverish sweating.

It was so hard to wait.

He wanted so badly to be there at the jail, at Fallongonio's home. But reason demanded that he stay away from the scene of battle, that he be able to escape back to Constantinople and his responsibilities there. He would not let himself participate in the excitement; he was forced to discipline himself.

It was after midnight when he began to see shadows in the water, hear muffled sounds of oars slapping the water. He looked through his binoculars, and yes, they were coming.

Boats full of men, one after another.

His whoop of joy alerted the crew, and they hastened to his side to assist the passengers as they climbed up the rope ladder and came onto the deck. One by one the freed prisoners greeted Joseph, fearful that he really was a pirate, as the ship was flying the skull and bones.

"Have no fear. You are on a ship of the House of Mendes. I am Joseph Nasi, and we are here under the protection of the sultan of the Ottoman Empire. You are safe, we will take you to your new home."

When all the prisoners, some fifty-two in all, had come safely aboard, and the "serving girls" had joined them, the ship set sail for Ragusa. It was important to get out into international waters before daybreak.

Fallongonio was taken on the litter to Joseph's cabin. Joseph had him moved to another cabin and put a special team of guards on the man. That accomplished, Joseph and David tried to get a couple hours of sleep, but sleep was hard to come by after such an exhilarating experience.

As they neared the halfway point between Ancona and Ragusa, Joseph called all the former prisoners to the deck. He sent the three women to his cabin, there to gossip among themselves and not be witness to what was about to happen on the deck. He told the guards to bring Fallongonio to the deck where he was stripped naked and tied to a post, his arms bound behind him and his legs in irons.

Joseph addressed the assembled passengers and the team of young men, saying, "This man you see before you is a Catholic priest. He is supposed to be a man of God. He has imprisoned you, tortured you, confiscated your homes, your belongings and your money. He has forced you to endure filth, fed you salty gruel, threatened to break your bodies on the *strapado* and then burn you at the stake.

"Though I am normally a compassionate man, I have not an ounce of compassion for this man. We are going to do to him what he would do to us. We are going to kill him with a thousand knives, and then we are going to feed him to the sharks. I will throw the first knife."

Joseph threw his dagger, hitting Fallongonio in the throat. He then stood back and watched as man after man sent sharp knives into the Apostolic Commissioner. When the last man had wreaked his vengeance, two stevedores tossed the dead man overboard. A great roar of celebration filled the air.

Once again, Joseph called the crowd to attention. He asked the passengers to line up, give their names and date of birth to the recording secretary, and he then gave each passenger three-thousand ducats with which to begin their new lives in Salonica, Ragusa, or Constantinople.

"Do not despair," he counseled. "We will send a ship next week to pick up your wives and children and all other relatives. Our efforts will not cease until we have you safely in new homes surrounded by your families and with jobs."

Joseph reunited with Selim in Ragusa, and learned, much to his dismay, that the pope was so furious over the prison outbreak that he had sent a new Apostolic Commissioner, Cesare della Nave, to represent the Vatican in Ancona. This man was reputed to be as fanatical as the pope in his hatred of Jews, and was absolutely incorruptible. "No chance we'll be able to bribe him," Selim reported to Joseph.

"By the way, the pope believes that Fallongonio absconded with the 300,000 ducats and himself freed the prisoners!"

"The bad news," he continued, "is that the remaining prisoners are now shackled to one another, and the living conditions have become even more wretched."

Two days later informers told Joseph that Cesare had moved the *strapado* to the public square and was now torturing prisoners on a daily basis in public, for all the citizens to watch.

Joseph and Selim received a message from Suleiman. He'd heard of their successful mission and wanted them back home in Constantinople, in spite of the fact that there were still nearly fifty prisoners in Ancona. The caravan loaded up and proceeded westward, back to Constantinople, receiving very little news on its way back.

Suleiman, however, had news for them when they arrived, terrible news. While they had been traveling, on April 13, in an *auto da fé* on the *Campo della Mostra*, a jeering crowd attended the strangling and burning of Doña Maiora, Simeon ben Menahem, Samuel Guascon, Abraham Falcon and Joseph Oheb.

Two days later Isaac Nahmias and Solomon Aguades were burned at the stake.

On April 16th, six more men were murdered, including Ben Zarella and Jacob Mosso.

Thirty-eight of the prisoners were "reconciled" with the Church and exiled to the island of Malta. Eleven prisoners remained in the jail at Ancona.

****

With a heavy heart, Joseph rode up the hills of Galata toward his home. He gathered Reyna in his arms, held her tightly, and whispered in her ear the dreadful news. Ben was burned at the stake. I don't know how I will ever tell Gracia...I can't face it. She will want to know the details..."

"Joseph...don't...she expects this news...she's been preparing herself. The sooner you tell her...it will be a mercy..."

He bathed, put on clean clothes, drank a glass of wine with Reyna, then they both walked across the yard to Gracia's home. She seemed to be expecting them. Perhaps Max had spotted his horse.

"Come in, come in...it's so good to see you are safe...I've been praying..."

"Mother..." Reyna couldn't speak. The words wouldn't come.

"It's fine. I know the truth. I felt it in my bones. We lost him, didn't we?"

Joseph wrapped her in his arms. She was so thin, so frail, so suddenly... old. Old and vulnerable.

They sat for a few minutes in her small parlor, she quietly weeping into her handkerchief. Reyna offered to stay the night, but Gracia protested, "You must be home with your husband and child. I won't hear of it!"

For two days she grieved in her bedroom, in her topiary garden. People dared not approach her, she shooed them away with a gesture. She ate little, and drank only tea. She seemed to be shedding pounds, her eyes red and swollen, her face was pale and wan.

Chapter Thirty-Two

The Boycott Of Ancona

Gracia asked Max to summon Joseph and Reyna and Samuel and Gracia *la chica* to the house for a breakfast meeting. She announced to Max that she wanted him and Anna to participate in the meeting. Once they were seated with full plates in front of them, Gracia began to speak. She was still pale and had swollen eyes, but her demeanor had changed noticeably from the previous day. She was once again a woman in command.

"We are going to take action against the civil authorities of Ancona. We cannot take on the Vatican; it's too powerful. It's the civilian authorities, and the jeering citizens, who carry out the wishes of the Vatican and conduct these horrific *autos da fé.* We can take on the civil authorities of that small port. We can do to them what the Sultan and the House of Mendes did to Venice when I was imprisoned there. We will organize a boycott of the port. We will ask our fellow Jewish merchants to refuse to import or export to Ancona. We will attempt to get our Turkish friends here to join with us. We will appeal to the Jewish community in Ragusa, Salonica, Ferrara, and what's left of it in the Papal States to refuse to ship to Ancona.

"We will starve the populace of goods including wheat, and we will bring the economy of that town down. The rest of the world will take notice, and if they don't want the same kind of boycott, they will stop this horrible reign of terror against the Jews."

"That's a brilliant idea, Aunt Gracia," Samuel enthused, and the two women joined in the praise.

"If you are going to do this, Aunt Gracia," Joseph intoned solemnly, "you need to put one-hundred percent of your resources behind it so it will succeed. You are inviting the wrath of the Vatican and the Emperor as well as the Doge."

"I intend to put every ounce of my energy and all our wealth behind this effort. We must stand up and make a difference; we must let the world know they cannot continue to abuse our people in this fashion. We must demonstrate the kind of chaos we can bring to world trade if the Vatican persists in the Inquisition.

"Samuel, you arrange for messengers to take a letter to all the rabbis this morning. I want them all here this afternoon at four for an organizational meeting. We have given vast sums to every one of them and asked nothing in return. Today, I am summoning them here for this meeting, and I consider their attendance and cooperation obligatory if they expect to receive another ducat from the Nasi-Mendes families."

"Understood!"

"Joseph, I want you to take a walk down at the bazaar and invite the fifty biggest merchants to a buffet dinner tomorrow evening here at the house at five o'clock." She turned her attention to Max and Anna. "Please prepare a buffet dinner for about seventy people. We'll serve them here on the first floor, let them wander around and look at the furnishings and art, then take them upstairs to the ballroom. I want the ballroom set up with chairs theater-style so everyone can be comfortable during what I believe will be a contentious and lengthy meeting."

Joseph, Max and Anna all nodded their approval.

"Gracia and Reyna, I'll need you to work with me today on dozens of letters which I want to get out quickly. Gracia, please see if you can recruit at least twenty women from the synagogue who have good handwriting and are proficient in Castilian Spanish. Most of our correspondence will be in Spanish. We will pay them for working with us, and it's likely to last for months. We'll need constant communication and reinforcement of our message."

Gracia and Reyna both nodded enthusiastically.

The young folks were pleased to see that Gracia was once again her old self, no longer mired in grief, but focused on clear goals and working through the details.

This, thought Joseph, is what has made her the extraordinarily successful businesswoman that she is, this ability to set aside grief, come up with a plan of action, and put it into play. She is a genius at this kind of thing.

"One last thing," Gracia said looking directly at Joseph, "please brief the sultan and the grand vizier on our plans. I want to be sure they are fully supportive of everything we are about to do."

"I have no doubt they will applaud your actions. Suleiman likes nothing better than planning a military operation, and planning a boycott isn't that different from planning a blockade. The fact is, we may need to ask him to blockade Ancona if your boycott doesn't work."

"It will work! We Jews have no choice!"

****

Later that day, after a visit with the sultan and his advisors, the grand vizier prepared a letter to the consul designate of Ancona demanding the release of the eleven remaining prisoners and return the property of Doña Gracia Nasi of the House of Mendes that was impounded by the civil authorities. "If this request is not honored immediately, steps will be taken to make her losses good out of the property of the Ancona merchants trading in the Levant."

To put teeth into the threat, Suleiman issued orders to impound all vessels in Turkish waters that belonged to Ancona citizens.

Similar letters were sent to the Florentine consul designate as well as representatives of other Papal States.

Joseph dictated a special missive to the French Ambassador, Michel de Codignac, asking the French king to use his good offices to put an end to the Inquisition "before there are further serious international repercussions." This letter was signed by the grand vizier.

The sultan then asked Joseph to draft a letter to go out under his name to the pope. This was to be an ultimatum from the Ottoman ruler. The final draft would take its place in history books:

> *...you must know that certain persons of the race of the Jews have informed my Elevated and Sublime Porte that...their goods and property have been seized on your instructions. This is in particular to the prejudice of Our Treasury, to the amount of 400,000 ducats, over and above the damage done to Our subjects...you will be pleased to liberate our above mentioned...subjects, with all the property which they had and owned, in order that they may be able to satisfy their debts...By so doing you will give Us occasion to treat in friendly fashion your subjects and the other Christians who traffic in these parts...*

****

David Hamon, now a full time member of Joseph's staff, asked to see him urgently, before Gracia's meeting with the rabbis. Joseph asked him to join him to ride up the hill from the office to the house. They could talk with no fear of being overheard.

"I've been thinking about the thirty-eight prisoners who were 'reconciled' and are exiled to Malta to be galley slaves. We can't have our people be slaves to the church, it is a crime against humanity!"

"Agreed. What do you have in mind?"

"If I could take the same men, arm a fast, small ship with canons and muskets, and head out to Malta, we might be able to intercept them and free them at sea, or if they are already incarcerated, we'll devise another jail break. What do you think?"

Joseph's face lit up with understanding. "You're willing to risk your life? What about your men? Have you discussed it with them?"

"Only a couple of them. They're ready. If you give the word."

"Draw up some very careful plans. Let me know what you need in the way of provisions, cash, arms, and let's chart it out on a map. Meet me at my house, tomorrow morning at seven." They dismounted in front of Gracia's home. "I like your spirit, David, I think you're right on target. See you tomorrow morning."

To Joseph's surprise Gracia invited a special guest to speak to the rabbis: one Judah Faraj, a fugitive from Ancona who had managed to escape with his life. In graphic words, he described the conditions of the prison in Ancona and the horrendous cries of those tortured on the *strapado*. "Let no man trade with the city of blood, not even to the extent of a single copper; let no merchant visit the place, no cargo be consigned to it, no ship be directed thither." He pleaded with the attending rabbis that they enjoin their congregants to support a full and complete boycott of Ancona.

"If you do this," he admonished, "the city of Ancona will lie desolate and ruined, a monument to the criminal folly of Pope Paul IV and his barbaric action."

The audience of the most distinguished rabbinical and lay leaders of the Turkish Empire sat mesmerized by Faraj. Tears streamed down their faces as they visualized their fellow Jews strangled and burned at the stake.

As Faraj completed his plea for a boycott, there was a stir in the back of the room when the sultan's son Selim walked in and asked for an emergency audience with Joseph. Joseph hurried to the back of the ballroom and conferred with Selim, then walked to the front of the room and said to Gracia, who was chairing the meeting, "Selim has news he wants to convey to this group. It is not good news!"

Gracia felt her hands grow clammy, her stomach turned over. She nodded at Selim, and asked him to address the audience.

"It is with great sadness and sympathy that I come to you with the latest news of Ancona. One of our ships has just returned from that city, and the captain personally witnessed the last of the eleven prisoners being burned at the stake. We regret to tell you that he was in the employ of your hostess, La Señora Gracia and a subject of the Ottoman Empire.

"This is an affront to the Sublime Porte, and we take this insult seriously. There is no longer any point in preventing further death, as all those accused of heresy and apostasy have been murdered or have escaped from the prison.

"However, it is not too late for revenge. The Sultan has asked me to tell you that he will support all your efforts to boycott Ancona. We are prepared to help in all the ways that seem feasible. Joseph Nasi will be our advisor in all these matters."

Gracia thanked Selim, her eyes wet with tears. Joseph escorted him out of the ballroom. When the room was again quiet, Gracia stood in front of the assembled guests. "I recommend," she began, "that the rabbis here assembled proclaim a boycott of the port of Ancona to last for eight months, until the next Passover. At that time we will meet again to decide whether or not to continue the boycott.

"We must bypass the port of Ancona and dispatch all merchandise destined for that port to Pesaro instead, which will enable the goods to reach central Italy. We must have solidarity, and you as rabbis are the ones who can enforce this boycott with your congregants.

"Effective today, all Mendes ships will boycott Ancona. I will communicate with the rabbis in Salonica and elsewhere and we will further communicate with our friends in Ferrara and Germany."

After heated discussion, the motion for the boycott was finally passed by the rabbis. The consequences would soon be felt in Ancona.

****

Two days later, while Joseph was preparing a letter for his agent in Ferrara, his secretary, somewhat agitated, told him that a strange man who looked like a stevedore insisted on seeing him in person to deliver a package "from Ben in Ancona."

Joseph felt for his dagger, securely fastened to his belt, then, rising from his desk he said, "Show him in."

The man was tall, heavily muscled, swarthy of complexion, possibly Anatolian. He was dressed in the dark pants of a dockworker and a billowing white shirt. He looked clean enough, though he could use a good barber, Joseph thought as he gestured for him to take a seat.

The man sat and placed a large package wrapped in brown paper and twine on the table in front of him. "Name is Nicodemus. Those who know me call me Nicco."

"And what brings you to this office?"

"Met this fellow, Ben, in Ancona. He told me you would reward me generously if I brought this package to you. But I could only give it to you, no one else. It's for a woman called Gracia. Some relative of yours I think."

"How did you happen to know Ben?"

Nicco allowed himself a slight smile. "We was roommates, you might say."

In jail together! Joseph told himself. "I see."

The two men looked intently at one another, as if sizing up an opponent.

"What would you consider an appropriate reward for bringing this package to me?"

"Look, *padrón*, I came all the way from Ancona to Constantinople. That's a long trip. And now I gotta go back."

"How did you get here? Overland or by ship?"

"Came in my own ship, I did. I'm captain of *The Zaviera.*"

"I see. What kind of merchandise do you handle?"

"This and that. Everything. Cloth, jewelry, food."

"And what ports do you call on?"

"Everywhere in the Adriatic Sea. That's our home base. I got me three ships, we usually travel together. But I made this run here to Constantinople alone. Always wanted to come here, this was my first chance."

Joseph stood. "Nicco, I do want to reward you and I don't have the necessary funds here in the office. I'd like to get to know you better. Perhaps we'll have some business for you, make this trip worth your while. I'd like to show you around the city, take you to the bazaar, and have a few glasses of ale with you. How does that sound?"

A big smile lit Nicco's face. "That's fine, *padrón*!"

Joseph took the large package, unopened, and placed it in a cabinet, which he then locked, pocketing the key. He told his secretary that he would be gone for the day.

The two men rode horseback to Joseph's home where he changed from his gentleman's finery to coarse workman's clothes and boots. He grabbed a wool cap for his head and a red and white bandanna for his throat. In such a get up, he would not be recognized as they made their rounds of the coffee shops and pubs down on the dock.

They rode back down the hills to Galata, then across the bridge into the city. After spending several hours in the bazaar, they went to the docks and found a small pub filled with deck hands and stevedores. After they'd ordered their meal and had two ales each, Joseph asked Nicco about Ben. "Was he tortured before they killed him?"

"*Padrón*, it was awful, pitiful. Five times on the *strapado*. Musta' broke every bone in the man's body. He begged me to end his misery...I couldn't. I had to get outta there myself."

Joseph nodded, too emotional to speak.

"I stayed long enough to see him burned, though. Promised him I'd deliver the package. He was delirious most of the time toward the end..."

"If you ever meet her...I don't think you will...but you must never tell Gracia about the torture."

Nicco nodded his agreement.

"Tell me more about your ships. How large is your crew?"

"Eight men on each ship, more if we need 'em."

"Armed?"

"Just this," he said, opening his shirt enough so Joseph could see his dagger.

"Would you like to have canons and muskets?"

"Hell, yes! But who can afford that, and even if we could afford it where would we be able to buy the guns and ammunition?"

"Do you recognize the flags of the House of Mendes? Of the Fuggers?"

"Course! I make it my business to know the other fleets, who owns them and what they usually carry and where they do their business."

"Then you know who I am?"

"Sure, *padrón*. You're the boss of the House of Mendes. Everyone knows that's who Joseph Nasi is. You think I don't know who I 'm dealing with?"

"This is becoming a business negotiation, Nicco. A private, confidential discussion. You and I will put nothing in writing. And if you ever tell anyone you know me, I'll call you a liar. If you see me walking down the street, you don't know me. Understand?"

"Sure, *padrón*. We'll be secret partners. No one will ever know."

"Correct. Now let's get down to specifics. The House of Mendes has many friends doing business on the Adriatic. The Fuggers. The fleet of the Ottoman Empire. Ships belonging to the Abrabanel family. These are our allies, you don't touch them."

"Understood."

"Two days ago our associates, merchants here in Turkey, agreed to boycott Ancona because of what they have done to the Jews there, those three *autos da fé*. Our friends in Salonica, Brusa, Ferrara, and Adrianople will join in the boycott."

Nicco nodded his understanding, his eyes gleaming with anticipation.

"It's possible you and your men could aid our effort. You know... discourage ships from docking in Ancona. Perhaps some scare tactics..."

"Right up our alley, *padrón*, exactly what we do best!"

"Any merchandise you recover, bring it here and I'll take it off your hands at a good price. We'll make it worth your while."

"Say no more, *padrón*. I know exactly what you want me to do!" He drank heartily from his mug.

"You'll need muskets and cannons and ammunition. We've got a warehouse in Ragusa where we store ammunition. I'll send word to Adrian to give you whatever you need. He'll charge it to my account."

"But the cannons and muskets."

"Tomorrow morning. My men will deliver a couple dozen large crates to your ship early in the morning. You need to set sail immediately after the delivery. I'll meet you at your ship at nine sharp. And I'll have your reward with me."

Before first light Joseph arrived at the munitions warehouse. He instructed the men to load six cannons, forty muskets and another dozen crates of ammunition onto two mule-driven wagons. He signed the inventory clerk's log, then grabbed the document and told him, "I'll take this to the office myself."

He rode horseback alongside the loaded wagons down to the docks. Captain Nicco greeted him with a broad smile and large cup of coffee. Joseph boarded the ship and followed Nicco to his private quarters. After some basic instructions concerning the canons and muskets, Joseph produced a fat envelop from his jacket pocket.

"This is my first installment, Nicco. Ten thousand ducats."

"*Padrón*, that's great! Ben was right!"

"Remember, you've never met Joseph Nasi. When you come back to Constantinople with merchandise you want to sell, send a deckhand to my office with a note. I'll make arrangements to meet you."

Joseph bid Nicco farewell and Godspeed. He rode his horse back to his office in Galata, and only then did he carry the unopened package into Gracia's office and present it to her.

Tears filled her eyes as she cut the twine and unwrapped the package. Inside was a single large, ornately carved, thick book with a clasp set with colorful stones. Both Joseph and Gracia marveled at the thickness of the leather binding. It was at least three-quarters of an inch thick on each side. The words 'Book of Jewels' was inscribed in gold leaf across the front.

Gracia reached into the small pouch she wore at her waist and pulled out a ring of keys. She unlocked the clasp with one quick turn and opened the thick leather cover. Immediately, she saw it was a book of poetry written by one of her favorite poets, Samuel Usque. She flipped through the pages, looking for something unusual, but nothing caught her attention. *Why was it so important for Ben to get this book to her?*

And then she knew.

She reached back into the pouch and extracted her dagger and quickly began to separate the leather binding from the cardboard cover to the book. Joseph watched in fascination as she extracted large cotton balls from the hollow interior of the binding. When she had recovered all the cotton from the inside of the front cover, she began to peel the cotton off the fine large stones: diamonds, rubies, sapphires, emeralds and pearls. Dozens and dozens of them. She slit the leather binding from the back cover and discovered more priceless gems.

"Amazing! They succeeded in killing him, but they didn't get his wealth! I hope you paid his messenger well, Joseph."

"Yes, I daresay he was thrilled with his reward."

****

By August, numerous bankruptcies were filed; bolts of cloth were piled high on the wharves and in the warehouses in Ancona. Imports from Turkey were stopped. The New Christians in Pesaro were so thrilled with the traffic into their port that they sent a special message to Doña Gracia congratulating her on the success of the boycott. "You have broken the arms of the wicked who live in the City of Blood, in whose skirts is the blood of our martyrs. Please continue with your efforts."

Gracia sent out letters to her contacts throughout Europe and the Levant asking them to cease all trade in Ancona. She told them that vessels sailing for the House of Mendes were using the port of Pesaro instead of Ancona for shipments into Europe.

Later that month, the family celebrated quietly when word arrived that the thirty-eight New Christians who had been exiled to become galley slaves in Malta had "miraculously" overtaken and killed their captors and were on their way to safety in Constantinople.

"While it's true that twenty-five Jews have been burned at the stake in Ancona, our efforts have saved the lives of ninety of our people. You can be sure the pope has put a price on our heads!" Joseph warned the family, even as they sipped champagne in celebration.

Chapter Thirty-Three

Disappointment

Eight months after the boycott of Ancona began, Gracia and Joseph were alarmed by the growing determination of the rabbis in Constantinople, who were originally from Italy, to end the boycott.

"It will only be successful if we Jews exhibit solidarity, and if we continue the boycott until the economy of Ancona is ruined," Gracia argued.

The counter argument, voiced by the rabbis from the Italian and German synagogues, was that if Ancona were ruined by the Jews of Turkey, Pope Paul IV would avenge himself on the Jews still living in the Papal States. Rabbi Joshua Soncino was particularly persuasive with a lengthy legal brief in which he argued that, according to Talmudic law, a man must not protect himself at the expense of others.

Gracia convened a conference of all the foremost Talmudic scholars and rabbis at the principal *Talmud Torah.* The conference began with eyewitness accounts of the persecution of the New Christians in Ancona, including presentations by some of those who had been rescued on their way to Malta. Once again Judah Faraj spoke emotionally about the importance of trade to the merchants of Pesaro, and the danger that would exist for those Jews if the boycott were suddenly lifted in Ancona. Yet, in spite of all the speeches and Talmudic arguments, the conference was inconclusive. The rabbis would not agree to speak with one voice to the Jewish merchants of Turkey.

As a final effort, in desperation, Gracia invited the leading members of the opposition to the continuation of the boycott to her home for "dinner and discussion."

After a superb three-course banquet and much wine, she directed them to her living room for a debate.

She sat in a large upholstered chair in front of the fireplace and faced her guests. Joseph, Samuel, and David Harmon stood at the back of the room, the better to watch the interaction of the guests.

She began by introducing three Spanish and Portuguese rabbis who had signed on as supporters of the continued boycott: Rabbi Joseph ibn Leb, Rabbi Solomon Bilia and Rabbi Solomon Saba. After each of them had given a spirited endorsement of their success at Ancona, she invited Moses di Sigura, the President of the Italian synagogue, *Sinagoga Mayor*, to present the arguments of his congregation.

"While we revere Doña Gracia and all that she has done for our Jewish community, we cannot support this boycott. First, this boycott has harmed those few Jews left in Ancona. Second, the boycott has infuriated Pope Paul and he is taking his wrath out on the Jews in Italy. Finally, we have already avenged the death of the twenty-five, in a limited way to be sure, but we have punished the merchants and citizens of Ancona. It is not necessary to continue this punishment indefinitely. We must consider the plight of the Jews who remain in lands controlled by the pope."

Gracia countered with quotes from Talmudic scholars in Salonica, Joseph Caro and Moses ben Jacob di Trani.

Solomon de Toledo, one of the lay leaders of *Sinagoga Mayor*, stood to be recognized. He addressed Gracia directly. "We have heard that your family has already avenged these deaths. Rumor has it that you are responsible for the prisoners escaping from the jail in Ancona, and that you are also behind the rescue of the Jews bound for Malta. Surely that is victory enough for you!"

Joseph, angrily striding to the front of the room, rudely interrupted Toledo. "Sir, you do our cause great damage when you give credibility to rumors such as that. We can all be sure that the Vatican has spies, and paid assassins, here in Constantinople. There is already a price on our heads. Your attempt to confirm those rumors will only serve to increase the price on our heads. There is absolutely no proof, none whatsoever, that any person in this room had anything to do with those escapes.

"We should be proud of our fellow Jews who had the brilliance and courage to escape from prison and from that ship taking them to Malta. We must applaud their actions. We, the Jewish community in Turkey, have done our part by welcoming these refugees into our homes and businesses. We are helping them get settled into their new lives, and no one can fault us for that."

Toledo was back on his feet, demanding the floor. "Nasi, you've become intoxicated with all your wealth and power, your influence at Topkapi Palace. You seem to think you can single-handedly dictate Jewish policy for all of us. And I might as well say it, there is also a rumor that certain pirates who are wreaking havoc on ships attempting to dock at Ancona are in your pay!"

Gracia shot to her feet. "That statement is an outrage! Everyone knows that pirates are the bane of the shipping industry. How dare you suggest such a thing!"

"How do you explain the fact that Mendes' ships are not attacked by pirates?"

Joseph signaled Gracia to let him answer. In a very calm, well-modulated voice he answered: "There are several reasons why our ships are seldom attacked successfully by pirates. First, our ships usually travel in large convoys. Second, our ships have been armed with the latest in firepower for the past thirty years, and finally, our crews are trained in hand-to-hand combat and their reputation for winning is well known.

"There is a network amongst pirates. They make it their business to know which fleets are armed, which ports they dock at, and what kind of goods they carry. Fortunately, we have not been attacked in the Adriatic Sea for several years. We are not so lucky elsewhere in the world."

Gracia again took the floor. "It seems like we cannot reach agreement on continuance of the boycott. With all due respect to the learned scholars in this room, I believe we Jews need to respond to these outrages, this reign of terror instituted by Pope Paul, with political and economic action. Prayer and fasting and paying bribes haven't worked in the past, and they won't work in the future. We must use the leverage we have which is economic. We must become politicians, we must learn to put aside our petty differences and speak with one voice. While we revere Talmudic law, we base our decisions on a thorough understanding of the politicians in the Vatican and elsewhere in Europe.

Gracia continued, "I can only speak for myself and my family. Our ships will never again dock in Ancona, Venice, or Antwerp. And our money will support only those Jewish institutions which have joined us in this boycott."

****

Gradually, over the next few years the port of Ancona revived, business in Pesaro dropped off. In Gracia's eyes, the citizens of Ancona were not adequately punished, and the pope had continued his persecution of the Jews in the Papal States.

In June of 1558, the pope inaugurated the Inquisition in Ferrara, leading to the burning of many of the books Gracia arranged to have printed. One way or another, it seemed, the pope would avenge himself against the Nasi-Mendes family.

A year later, however, Paul IV died. Throughout Europe and even in the Levant, Christians, Jews and Muslims danced in the streets to celebrate the end of his reign of terror.

Chapter Thirty-Four

Dreamers Of A Great Dream

For more than six months after the pope's death, Gracia fretted and argued and cajoled her fellow Jews, trying to talk sense to them about the necessity for speaking with one voice, and for becoming "political" in their relations with the outside world, especially with the Vatican. Reyna and Joseph tried to console her. She had to face the fact that the boycott was a limited success, and that she had done all she could possibly do to make it a success.

Early in 1560 she received a letter from Benvenida Abrabanel, written in the spidery, unsteady scrawl of an old and infirm woman.

My dearest friend Gracia,

That man, you know who I mean, died in the nick of time, before they could take my home away from me. We said many prayers of thanksgiving. I have the satisfaction of knowing I outlived him, though I fear not for much longer.

The new pope seems less harsh, time will tell.

Your efforts with the boycott are famous here, and much applauded. You are a true heroine of our people. May God bless you and keep you always.

Benvenida Abrabanel
Ferrara, December 10, 1559

It was the last communication Gracia would receive from Benvenida. A few weeks later she received word of her passing. One more reason to mourn!

****

Joseph found reason to jolt Gracia out of her depression a few days later with a proposal from Sultan Suleiman himself. "Would you like to lease the city of Tiberias and the seven surrounding villages in the Holy Land as a permanent home land for your people?" he had asked Joseph at lunch that afternoon.

"That was always Francisco's dream that we would move our family back to the Holy Land. It would be our greatest dream come true!"

"It would be an enormous undertaking, something you could really sink your teeth into, Mother," Reyna enthused, knowing her mother needed a new cause to throw her energies into.

"We would begin by rebuilding the ancient city of Tiberias. I understand there's not much there now," Joseph continued.

"We wouldn't want to do it if the lease does not give the land to Our People permanently," Gracia added, reasonably. "Couldn't we just buy the land from the Ottoman Empire?

"He's not going to agree to that. He wants to lease it to us at a very reasonable price, one thousand ducats a year. Then, when we have created some successful industries there, he will tax us accordingly. That's always been his *modus operandi*, acquire the territory, then tax the people, but let them have their own local government and customs. He suggested that we could create a refuge for persecuted Jews. Our People would have complete religious and economic freedom."

"Who lives there now?"

"Nomadic Arabs have made a temporary home there, but Suleiman is willing to place them elsewhere so this land and all the industry would be for Jews."

Gracia, always quick to make a decision, instructed Joseph: "Tell the sultan we'd like to enter into negotiations with him immediately. This is an opportunity we cannot pass up. His sons and grandsons must sign the lease also. And when I die, the lease must revert to you, Joseph. We must reclaim the Holy Land as a Homeland for the Jews, a sacred place where we will always be safe."

In less than a year the final contract was drawn up according to Gracia's terms. It was signed by the present Sultan Suleiman, the future Sultan Selim, and his son Murad.

Joseph sent his brother Samuel with letters of introduction to the local rulers. He sent a team of architects and engineers to draw up plans for the reconstruction of the city.

Meanwhile, Gracia requested and received audiences with the congregations of all the synagogues in Constantinople. She thrilled them with her vision for a homeland for the Jews, describing in great detail the plans she and Joseph had for the city. "We will build a grand synagogue and hospital and schools. We will build small homes on plots of land large enough so every family can have their own garden.

"Joseph has already ordered mulberry trees to be planted for silk worms so that we might begin producing fine silks in a new textile factory

"We will start a flock of the finest Merino sheep to be raised for their wool. Our people have always prospered in the textile industry, and this time they will be working for themselves.

"You must write to your friends and relatives back in the Papal States and tell them of this opportunity. We need skilled craftsmen and women, merchants, scholars, doctors and lawyers. Joseph and I will provide their transportation in our ships and we will have fine new homes waiting for them."

Joseph's team returned with news: Tiberias was currently occupied by Portuguese fishermen and Arabs who worked the farms for absent Jewish landlords. There were lush fields of date palms and orange groves and Jewish beekeepers. There were also Hot Springs, which had become a famous tourist attraction, attracting nearly two thousand visitors annually. This could be a source of significant income for the Nasi-Mendes family if the baths were rebuilt more in tune with the Turkish baths of Constantinople.

Of primary importance, the men reported, is the rebuilding of the city walls for security.

Upon hearing the report of the team, Gracia began drawing up floor plans for a palace near the lakeshore that she would occupy, "my final home." She also asked Rabbi Joseph ibn Leb to draw up plans for a yeshiva, and to plan on becoming the director of that yeshiva himself.

****

"Mother, we have news for you," Reyna announced, as she ushered Joseph and two of his staff, very young men by name of David Hamon and Aaron Zangarelli into her small parlor.

Gracia, who'd had only a few minutes warning that she was having guests, summoned Max with a small silver bell. "Max, please bring these men brandy or wine, whatever they'd like, and bring me some of that wonderful cream sherry from Spain. And some mince pies as a special treat."

After everyone had been served and was relaxed on the sofas facing her, Gracia said, "What is this news you are absolutely bursting to tell me? I can tell from your eyes that it is welcome news." She looked directly at Joseph, expecting him to be the one to lead off.

"Aunt Gracia, we remember well your distress over the outcome of the Boycott of Ancona, your disappointment that it did not last longer, that it did not send a loud message to the rest of the world. Your despair that we did not really punish the Anconians who cheered while our people burned at the stake."

Gracia nodded her head affirmatively.

"This young man," he said, gesturing toward David Hamon, "came to me with a very complicated plan a few weeks later. We discussed it thoroughly, and after refining it we took it to your dear friend, Sultan Suleiman. He approved in principle, and told me to put it into action. It has taken us nearly ten years to realize the result."

"My goodness, you really have my attention!"

David took over the story. "My idea was that if we could precisely identify the most prominent Catholics in Ancona, where they live, what their work habits are, we could do what I call a "selective plunder and kidnapping." We sent Aaron Zangarelli, a New Christian without any family, over to Ancona with lots of money. He moved there in 1557, started the first coffee shop in Ancona, went to Mass every Sunday, and listened and learned for nine years. By the end of eight years he'd identified the leading Catholics, their place of work and where they lived. He drew us a detailed map of the town, showing their homes in relation to the town square where the *auto da fé* was held. The map also showed the cathedral and the house where the Bishop lives. These maps and all correspondence were carried back and forth by Joseph's friend, Nicco.

"Three weeks ago Suleiman left with his army and a squadron of Turkish war ships for the Mediterranean. I took twenty of my best men and went with him, map in hand."

David stopped, took a deep breath, a sip of his wine, then continued. "We arrived in Ancona during siesta. The city was asleep, the streets empty, the shops locked and shuttered. Suleiman dedicated 8,000 of his troops to this side mission. First, we took control of the city square, and three of our troops built a pyre with a strong stake in the middle. Meanwhile, working in teams of four men each, we rounded up the thirty most influential Catholic men. My orders to the troops were firm: there was to be no raping, no beating of women and children. They could take jewelry and other goods as they wished from the homes of these men, but the women and children were not to be harmed.

"We marched these men to the city square. Meanwhile, another team, which I headed, went to the Bishop's home, roused him from his drunken nap, and marched him out to the city square. The Bishop's home and the cathedral were set on fire, just as the homes of the thirty men had been set on fire.

Gracia and Reyna turned ashen with anxiety.

"We told the Bishop, the captured men, and all the townspeople that we were paying them back for laughing and cheering while our people were murdered by the Inquisition in 1556. There was no doubt in anyone's mind that this was our revenge, and that it was backed by the Ottoman Empire.

"We strapped the Bishop, who was pleading for his life, to the stake and set him on fire.

"Then we marched the thirty men to the harbor and loaded them onto a warship. Those men will spend the rest of their lives as galley slaves. They will have a long time to think about what they did to our people."

David sipped his drink, and there was a loud sound of relief as everyone who had been holding their breath resumed breathing again.

Slowly, a slight smile, a warm look of approval spread over Gracia's face.

"Suleiman told me he was doing this for *La Señora*, a special gift to *La Señora*," Joseph added.

During the next five years, progress in rebuilding Tiberias was spotty, largely because Joseph was preoccupied with intrigues in the court of Suleiman where his attendance was required on a daily basis.

The walls were completed in 1564, only after a prolonged strike by the Arab workers who resented the fact that only Jews were to be allowed to have homes in Tiberias.

Gracia planned her move to Tiberias for the summer of 1566, but that move was postponed when Sultan Suleiman died during a prolonged war with Hungary. Selim II won the battle for supremacy over his brother with the help of Joseph. Joseph's instant reward was being named the Duke of Naxos; the first time in a thousand years a Jew had received such an honor.

Now, all Joseph and Reyna's attention had to be focused on taking control of the islands of Naxos. The further development of Tiberias became less important as Joseph struggled to consolidate his position in the new court as well as in the duchy of Naxos.

Gracia, meanwhile, in her late fifties, had aged rapidly. Her back and legs rebelled against long carriage rides. The pains were so bad she could barely sleep at night. Only long sessions in the warm waters of her private Turkish bath gave her any surcease from pain. At the same time, the chest pains she had suffered intermittently for years became more severe and troubled her on a daily basis. She could no longer climb the steps in her mansion, but had to be carried by her servants.

By the summer of 1567 she admitted to herself that she could never make the long trip to Tiberias, and that, in truth, it made no sense for her to leave her family in Galata. With Joseph's accession to the position of Duke of Naxos, and with Selim's constant reliance on him for guidance in foreign policy, it would be impossible for him to consider moving his family to Tiberias.

She could never leave Reyna and her granddaughter, Judith, now blossoming into a beautiful young woman. Instead, she would continue her support of Tiberias as a homeland for the Jews from a distance.

Her money continued to support the development of the city and her ships continued to carry refugees from Europe to new homes and new careers. And though she had mellowed in old age, she continued to invite Talmudic scholars to her home in the hills of Galata. "You must," she told them again and again, "encourage our people to become politically active, like Joseph is. He is an example for all of us. History books will someday record the fact that he has saved the lives of countless Jews because of his close relationship with the sultans."

Chapter Thirty-Five

"Gone Is The Glitter"

The years 1565 to 1570 were terrible years for the Nasi family. In the winter of 1565 fourteen-year old Judith Nasi, daughter of Joseph and Reyna, died. She was the light of their lives, a sort of tiny Gracia. Like her grandmother, she radiated energy, enthusiasm, brilliance and natural charm. She had her grandmother's dark hair and flashing brown eyes, and her mother's gorgeous porcelain complexion. She had Joseph's aptitude for language, and spoke most European languages fluently.

Reyna and Joseph had big plans for her. They'd hired the best tutors in every subject imaginable, but Judith expressed a preference for science and told them she intended to be a doctor when she grew up. They knew of no female doctors, but that didn't stop them from encouraging her to follow her dream.

But then the unexpected happened, she became ill with influenza, developed a high fever and nasty cough, and within four days God took her from them. Reyna was devastated; her whole world revolved around that little girl, and she'd given up on ever getting pregnant again.

Gracia realized she lost her only chance of leaving descendants, something she greatly desired. After Judith's passing, Gracia took to her bed and complained of chest pains, back and leg pains, and refused to eat much of anything for several weeks. Joseph had never seen her so morose, so listless. She even lost interest in her dreams for a Jewish state in Tiberias.

****

Then in 1566, Suleiman the Magnificent, the greatest of the Ottoman sultans, died in a royal tent during his thirteenth military campaign, far away in Hungary. He was a friend to Jews and had welcomed thousands of them to settle in his lands and even challenged the Vatican and European rulers when they persecuted Jews.

He was the close ally and friend of the Nasi/Mendes family. During the eleven years they had lived in Turkey, Joseph and the sultan had become very close political allies, a relationship that continued with his successor Selim. Suleiman never ceased expressing his admiration for Gracia. Every time he got a new tree or new flower, he sent her a cutting for her garden. Between them, they possessed the finest gardens in all Turkey.

****

Then came the greatest blow. Doña Gracia Nasi died in her sleep on a beautiful spring morning in 1569. She had been ailing for months, experiencing more and more difficulty walking. Joseph and Reyna had dined with her the evening before, and they had found her frailty shocking.

What was totally unexpected though, was Samuel's death a few months later from a slow wasting disease. He was ill for more than two months, and passed away in August, 1569.

Within a matter of months, the Nasi family lost its matriarch and its future. Almost before the survivors could grasp what had happened, the Jewish cemetery in Galata held three family members: Judith, Samuel and Gracia.

Memorial services for Doña Gracia sprang up almost simultaneously all over the Levant and in parts of Europe. Saadiah Lungo, the famous Salonican poet, celebrated her passing with an elegy:

Of all we treasured most we stand bereft
Throughout the lands of thy dispersal, Ariel;
And every mother-town in Israel
Weeps for the fate of those in anguish left.
Gone is the glitter;
My mourning is bitter,
And broken my heart.

Author's Note

The schools, orphanages, hospitals, yeshivas and synagogues that Doña Gracia Nasi had built continued to flourish well into the twentieth century. In July of 1943, most of the 45,000 descendants of the Spanish and Portuguese families in Salonica that the Mendes Underground had rescued from the fires of the Inquisition, were shipped to Auschwitz. According to German records, within a few hours of arriving most of them had been killed in the gas chambers.

Historical Characters

(In order of appearance)

Francisco Mendes, Founder of the House of Mendes
Dr. Benjamin Mendes, physician to King Manuel of Portugal, father of Francisco
Deborah Mendes, wife of Dr. Benjamin Mendes, mother of Francisco and Diogo
Dr. Daniel Nasi, assistant physician to King Manuel
Diogo Mendes, younger brother of Francisco
King Manuel of Portugal
Rachel Levi, bride of Daniel Nasi, mother of Brianda, Beatriz and Samuel
Gracia Nasi, also known as Beatriz da Luna, daughter of Daniel and Rachel Nasi
King John II of Portugal, son of Manuel
Joseph Nasi, son of Samuel and Judith Nasi, grandson of Daniel and Rachel Nasi
Samuel Nasi, younger brother of Joseph, son of Samuel and Judith Nasi
Brianda Nasi, also known as Reyna, daughter of Daniel and Rachel Nasi
Duarte da Paz, spy and secret agent in the Vatican
Reyna Mendes, daughter of Francisco and Gracia
Bishop of Sinigaglia, a Catholic bishop in Lisbon
Henry VIII, King of England
Pope Paul, Pope who began the Inquisition in Portugal
Charles Brandon, Duke of Suffolk
Katherine Brandon, Duchess of Suffolk, 4th wife of Charles Brandon
Mary Tudor Brandon, sister of Henry VIII, 3rd wife of Charles Brandon
Jose Diaz, House of Mendes agent in London
Jane Seymour, new wife of Henry VIII
Queen Mary, Regent of Belgium, mother of Maximilian
Baby Beatrice, also known as Gracia la chica
Suleiman the Magnificent, sultan of the Ottoman Empire
Dr. Moses Harmon, physician to Suleiman
Duke Ercole II, Duke of Ferrara
Doña Benvenida Abrabanel, prominent Jewish personage in Ferrara
Selim the Sot, son of Sultan Suleiman who becomes Sultan in 1566
Edward Seymour, Earl of Hertford, brother of Queen Jane Seymour
Thomas Seymour, younger brother of Queen Jane Seymour

John Dudley, member of the Council of the Regency
Katherine Parr, Queen and widow of Henry VIII
Dr. Duarte Gomez, principal agent for the House of Mendes
Roxalana, favorite wife of Suleiman the Magnificent
Pope Paul IV, pope from 1555 to 1559, arch-enemy of the Jewish people
Joseph ibn Leb, member of The Talmudic Tribunal of the Ottoman Empire
Joshua Soncino, member of The Talmudic Tribunal
Samuel de Medina, member of The Talmudic Tribunal
Moses di Trani, member of The Talmudic Tribunal
Joseph Caro, member of The Talmudic Tribunal
Giovanni Vincenzo Fallongonio, Apostolic Commissioner in Ancona
Doña Maiora, burned at the stake in Ancona
Simeon ben Menahem, burned at the stake in Ancona
Abraham Falcon, burned at the stake in Ancona
Joseph Oheb, burned at the stake in Ancona
Jacob Mosso, burned at the stake in Ancona
Judah Faraj, a refugee from Ancona who escaped alive
Rabbi Solomon Bilia, Rabbi in Constantinople
Rabbi Solomon Saba, Rabbi in Constantinople
Rabbi Solomon de Toledo, Rabbi in Constantinople
Judith Nasi, daughter of Joseph and Reyna Mendes Nasi
Joseph ven Ardut, Joseph's representative in Tiberias
David Oliverias, wool merchant in Tiberias
Dr. Francisco Coronel, Lieutenant Governor of Naxos
Chaabon Reis, notorious pirate of the Agean Sea
Piale Pasha, Admiral of the Turkish Fleet
Lala Mustafa, Commander of Turkish forces at Nicosia and Famagusta
Ochiali, a pirate in the Aegean Sea
Kara Hodja, a pirate in the Aegean Sea
Marcantonio Bragadino, a Venetian Senator who ruled Cyprus
Don John of Austria, Commander of the Holy League forces at Cyprus

Bibliography

Beeching, Jack. *The Galleys at Lepanto.* New York: Charles Scribner's Sons, 1982.

Birnbaum, Marianna D. *The Long Journey of Gracia Mendes.* Budapest: Central European University Press. 2004.

Brooks, Andrée Aelion. *The Woman Who Defied Kings: The Life and Times of Doña Gracia Nasi.* New York: Paragon House Publishers. 2003.

Durant, Will. *The Renaissance.* New York: Simon and Schuster, 1953.

Durant, Will. *The Reformation.* New York: Simon and Schuster, 1957.

Gerber, Jane S. *The Jews of Spain: A History of the Sephardic Experience.* New York: The Free Press, 1992.

Goldstein, Joyce. *Sephardic Flavors: Jewish Cooking of the Mediterranean.* San Francisco: Chronicle Books, 2000.

Jardine, Lisa. *Worldly Goods: A New History of the Renaissance.* New York: Doubleday, 1996.

Kamen, Henry. *Empire: How Spain Became A World Power, 1492-1763.* New York: Perennial, 2004.

Kinross, Lord. *The Ottoman Empire.* London: The Folio Society, 2003.

Manchester, William. *A World Lit Only By Fire: The Medieval Mind and the Renaissance, Portrait of an Age.* Boston: Little Brown and Company, 1992.

Kertzer, David I. *The Popes Against The Jews: The Vatican's Role in the Rise of Modern Anti-Semitism.* New York: Alfred A. Knopf, 2001.

Mazower, Mark. *Salonica: City of Ghosts, Christians, Muslims and Jews, 1430-1950.* New York: Vintage Books, 2004.

Nassi, Gad and Rebecca Toueg. *Doña Gracia Nasi: A Legend in her Lifetime.* Tel Aviv. Women's International Zionist Organization. 1991.

Netanyahu, B. *The Origins of the Inquisition in Fifteenth Century Spain.* New York: Random House, 1995.

Roth, Cecil. *Doña Gracia of the House of Nasi.* Philadelphia: The Jewish Publication Society of America, 1948.

Roth, Cecil. *The Duke of Naxos of the House of Nasi.* Philadelphia: The Jewish Publication Society of America, 1948.

Roth, Cecil. *The Spanish Inquisition.* New York: W. W. Norton & Company, 1964.

Sachar, Howard M. *Farewell España: The World of the Sephardim Remembered.* New York: Alfred A. Knopf, 1994.
Sloan, Dolores. *The Sephardic Jews of Spain and Portugal: Survival of an Imperiled Culture in the Fifteenth and Sixteenth Centuries.* Jefferson, North Carolina: McFarland. 2009.
Vitoux, Frederic. *Venice: The Art of Living.* New York: Stewart, Tabori & Chang, 1991.

Gaon Books
Sephardic Traditions
Isabelle Medina Sandoval, Editor

1. Paloma, Vanessa. 2007. *Mystic Siren: Woman's Voice in the Balance of Creation.* ISBN: 978-0-9777514-5-7 (Paper).

2. Hamui Sutton, Silvia. 2008. *Cantos judeo-españoles: simbología poética y visión del mundo.* (Judeo-Spanish Songs: Poetic Symbolism and World View). ISBN: 978-0-9820657-0-9 (Cloth); 978-0-9820657-1-6 (Paper).

3. Martinez, Mario. 2009. *Converso.* ISBN: 978-0-9820657-7-8.

4. Medina Sandoval, Isabelle. 2009. *Guardians of Hidden Traditions.* ISBN: 978-0-9820657-8-5.

5. Toro, Sandra. 2010. *By Fire Possessed: Doña Gracia Nasi.* ISBN: 978-1-935604-06-8.

6. Paloma, Vanessa. 2010. *The Mountain, the Desert, the Pomegranate: Stories from Morocco and Beyond.* ISBN: 978-1-935604-03-7.

7. Medina Sandoval, Isabelle. 2010. *Grandmother's Secrets.* ISBN: 978-1-935604-05-1.

Forthcoming

8. Toro, Sandra. 2011. *Princes, Popes and Pirates.* ISBN: 978-1-935604-11-2.

9. Jalfón de Bentolila, Estrella. 2011. *Haketía: Judeo-Spanish Language and Culture of Morocco.* ISBN: 978-1-935604-09-9.

10. Weich-Shahak, Susana. 2011. *Sephardic Romances from Morocco.* ISBN: 978-1-935604-10-5.

11. Raphael David Elmaleh and George Ricketts. 2011. *Jews under Moroccan Skies: Two Thousand Years of Jewish Life.* ISBN: 978-1-935604-19-8.

CPSIA information can be obtained at www.ICGtesting.com
Printed in the USA
BVOW021358250712

296130BV00002B/437/P